**Also available from Rachel Reid
and Carina Press**

The Game Changers Series

Game Changer
Tough Guy
Common Goal
Role Model
The Long Game

HEATED RIVALRY

RACHEL REID

carina
press

carina
press®

Recycling programs
for this product may
not exist in your area.

ISBN-13: 978-1-335-46843-7

Heated Rivalry

First published in 2019. This edition published in 2023 with
revised text

For questions and comments about the quality of this book,
please contact us at CustomerService@Harlequin.com.

Carina Press
22 Adelaide St. West, 41st Floor
Toronto, Ontario M5H 4E3, Canada
www.CarinaPress.com

Printed in U.S.A.

CONTENTS

This book is dedicated to Matt,
the Frog to my Toad.

HEATED RIVALRY

Prologue

October 2016—Montreal

Shane Hollander was as close to losing it as he ever allowed himself to get.

He'd endured two periods and twelve minutes of one of the most frustrating hockey games he'd ever played. It should have been a glorious win at home for his Montreal Voyageurs against their archrivals, the Boston Bears. Instead it had been a grueling humiliation, and the score stood at 4–1 for Boston, with less than eight minutes left on the clock. Shane had had no less than five beautiful scoring chances. He'd taken shots that should never have missed. But they had. And the Bears had capitalized on the Voyageurs' mistakes.

One man had capitalized more than anyone. The most hated man in Montreal: Ilya Rozanov. The near century-old rivalry between the Montreal and Boston NHL teams had, over the past six seasons, become personified by Hollander and Rozanov. Their intense animosity was clear even to the fans in the farthest, cheapest seats.

Hollander bent at the face-off circle now, facing Rozanov as the referee prepared to drop the puck after the Russian's second goal of the game.

"Having a good night?" Rozanov asked cheerfully. His hazel eyes sparkled the way they always did when he was talking shit.

"Fuck you," Hollander growled.

"Still time for a hat trick, I think," Rozanov mused, his English barely comprehensible between his thick accent and his mouth guard. "Should I do it now, or wait until last minute? More exciting that way, yes?"

Hollander gritted his teeth around his own mouth guard and didn't answer.

"Shut up, Rozanov," the referee said. "Last warning."

Rozanov stopped talking, but he managed to find an even more effective way of getting under Hollander's skin: he *winked*.

And then he won the face-off.

"Fuck!" Jean-Jacques Boiziau, the Voyageurs' giant Haitian-Canadian defenseman, hurled his stick at the wall of their dressing room.

"That's enough, J.J.," Shane said, but there was no real threat behind it. To make it clear that he was in no mood to fight, or even argue, with anyone, he slumped into his dressing room stall.

Shane's left wing line mate, Hayden Pike, sat on the bench next to him, as always. "You all right?" Hayden asked quietly.

"Sure," Shane said flatly. He tipped his head back until it met the cool wall behind him and closed his eyes.

Using the word "passionate" to describe Montreal hockey fans would be an understatement. Montreal loved the Voyageurs to the point of absurdity. Their arena was one of the toughest places for visiting teams to play, because they faced not only one of the best teams in the league, but the loudest fans in the league as well. The fans also had no problem letting their own beloved team know exactly how disappointed they were with them.

But when Montreal fans were really devastated, like they had been tonight, they were almost silent. And that was Shane Hollander's least favorite sound.

"You know what would be sweet?" Hayden asked. "You know that movie, *The Purge*? Where you get to, like, break whatever laws for one night with no consequences?"

"Sort of," Shane said.

"Man, if that was real, I would murder the fuck out of Rozanov."

Shane laughed. He couldn't disagree that bludgeoning that smug Russian face would be at least a little satisfying.

Their coach entered the room and voiced his disappointment with remarkable calm. It was early in the season—this had been their first regular season matchup against Boston—and they had been playing well most games. This was a glitch. They would move on.

Then it was time to face the press. At that moment, Shane would have preferred to see a pack of starving wolves enter the room, but he knew there was no avoiding the reporters. They always wanted to talk to him, specifically, after every game, and especially after games where he faced Rozanov.

He pulled his sweat-soaked jersey off over his head so the CCM-branded athletic undershirt would be seen on camera. Part of his endorsement contract.

A semicircle of cameras, lights, and microphones formed around him.

"Hey, guys," Shane said tiredly.

They asked their boring questions, and Shane gave them boring answers. What could he even say? They'd lost. It was a hockey game, and one team lost, and that team was his team.

"Do you want to know what Rozanov just said about you?" one of the reporters asked gleefully.

"Something nice, I assume."

"He said he wished you'd been playing tonight."

The crowd of reporters was silent. Waiting.

Shane snorted and shook his head. "Well, we play in Boston in three weeks. You can let him know that I will *definitely* be at that game."

The reporters laughed, delighted that they had gotten their Hollander vs. Rozanov sound bite for the night.

An hour later—showered, changed and finally alone—Shane drove himself home. Not to his Westmount penthouse, but to the one nobody knew about.

Shane only spent a few nights a year at the small condominium in the Plateau. It was where he went when he wanted to be sure of total privacy.

He parked in the tiny lot behind the three-story building, let himself in the back door, and quickly climbed the stairs to the top floor. He knew the other two floors were unoccupied because he owned those too. The bottom floor was rented to a high-end kitchenware boutique, which had closed for the night hours ago.

The condo on the third floor looked like what it was: a demo condo that had been decorated by a professional house stager. Technically, this was the condo that would be used to sell this one and the one below it. If Shane was ever interested in selling. Which, he told himself, he definitely would be doing. Soon.

He had been telling himself this for over three years.

He went to the stainless-steel fridge and took out one of the five bottles of beer—the only things in the pristine refrigerator. He twisted the cap off and sat himself on the black leather sofa in the living area.

He sat in silence and tried to ignore the way his stomach churned on nights like this one. He drank his beer quickly, hoping the alcohol would help at least numb the disappointment he felt in himself. The disgust at his own weakness. He needed to dull it because he knew he sure wouldn't be doing anything to fix this mess. He'd been trying for over six years.

The knock at the door came almost forty minutes later. It had been enough time that Shane had almost convinced himself to leave. To put an end to this foolishness. But, of course, he hadn't. And if the knock had come hours later, even, Shane would still have been on that sofa, waiting for it.

He opened the door. "What the fuck took you so long?" he asked, annoyed.

"We were celebrating. Big win tonight, you know?"

Shane stepped back to let the tall, smirking Russian man into the apartment.

"I got away as soon as I could," Rozanov said, his tone less teasing. "Didn't want to draw attention, right?"

"Sure."

And that was the last word Shane got out before Rozanov's mouth crashed into his.

Shane gripped his leather jacket with both hands and pulled him closer as he kissed Rozanov breathless. "How long do you have?" Shane asked quickly, when they had broken apart for air.

"Two hours, maybe?"

"Fuck." He kissed Rozanov again, rough and needy. God, he needed this. This horrible, fucked-up thing.

"You taste like beer," Rozanov said.

"You taste like that horrible gum you chew."

"Is so I don't smoke!"

"Shut up."

They grappled and maneuvered each other until they reached the bedroom, where Shane shoved Rozanov roughly against a wall and continued kissing him. He felt the familiar slide of his rival's tongue in his mouth, and slid his own tongue over teeth that had been fixed and replaced god knew how many times.

He wanted a lot tonight, but they didn't have time for a lot. Rozanov grabbed him and pushed him down on the bed; Shane watched the other man drop his jacket on the floor and pull his T-shirt off over his head. A gold chain hung crookedly around Rozanov's neck, the shiny crucifix resting on his left clavicle just above the famous (ridiculous) tattoo of a snarling grizzly bear ("For Russia! I had it before playing for Bears!") on his chest. Shane would make fun of it later. Right now all he could do was watch Rozanov strip his clothes off, and belatedly realize that he should be doing the same.

They both took off everything, and Rozanov fell on top of Shane, kissing him and moving a hand down to grasp his already embarrassingly rigid cock. Shane arched up into his touch, making stupid, desperate noises.

"Don't worry, Hollander," Rozanov said, his lips brushing Shane's ear, "I am going to fuck you like you want, yes?"

"Yes," Shane exhaled, a mixture of relief and humiliation sweeping through him.

Rozanov slid down his body, kissing, sucking, licking, until he reached Shane's cock. He didn't tease any further. He took him into his mouth, and Shane was grateful that they were alone in the building because his moan echoed throughout the sparsely decorated room.

He propped himself up on his elbows so he could watch. Part of him wanted to lie back and close his eyes and let himself believe that it was *anyone* other than Ilya Rozanov making him feel so good. But most of him wanted to see *exactly* who it was.

Rozanov was a stunning man. Light brown curls that were always a mess fell into his playful hazel eyes and over his dark, thick eyebrows. His strong jaw and cleft chin were covered in stubble. His smile was lopsided and lazy, and his teeth were unnaturally white due to most of them not being real.

His nose was crooked, having been broken more than a few times, but the fucking thing only made him look more rugged. And for a Russian living in Boston, his skin was a lot more golden than it had any right to be.

Shane fucking hated him. But Rozanov was really good at sucking cock, and he was, for whatever reason, willing.

Shane hated *this*, but he had taken great pains to protect it, and he would continue doing so as long as Rozanov was willing. Their lives being what they were, this was not an easy thing to get. Maybe, when they had started seven years ago, they hadn't expected their lives, their famous rivalry, to get to the point it was at now. Maybe they should have stopped by now. But, despite the wrongness of it, this was comfortable. This was familiar. And it was as close to safe as either of them were going to get.

That's all it was.

Rozanov worked his talented mouth on Shane's cock, and Shane tossed the lube down the bed from the well-stocked nightstand. Rozanov took it without pausing what he was doing, and poured some on his fingers so he could get to work opening Shane up.

This was never Shane's favorite part because he felt so fucking vulnerable. He felt weak and ridiculous every time they were together like this, but he always felt it most acutely when Rozanov had his fingers inside him. As a result, the preparation usually took a while.

Rozanov, on the other hand, always seemed completely at ease. He was good at this, and he knew it. He slid his mouth off of Shane's cock with a parting lick to the head that sent a jolt straight through Shane's body, and said, "Relax, yeah? Is not much time, but enough."

Shane took a deep breath and let it out slowly. He hated that voice so much on the ice, and in the interviews he saw on television where Rozanov mocked him in an obnoxious, teasing tone. But here, in this bed, Rozanov's tone was patient and gentle, his voice soft and his accent wrapping elegantly around boxy English words.

Shane relaxed as Rozanov opened him with strong fingers and pressed openmouthed kisses on the insides of his thighs. When he was ready, Shane wordlessly handed Rozanov a condom before rolling over and getting on his hands and knees. He couldn't look at Rozanov. Not tonight. Not after that humiliating loss.

Rozanov seemed to understand. He entered him carefully, not taking him roughly like he had many times in the past. This was slow and considerate. Shane felt big hands on his hips and waist, holding him steady as

Rozanov pushed inside. He even felt Rozanov's thumbs brush gently over his lower back.

"There. This is what you wanted, yes?"

"Yes." Because it was. It was what he always wanted.

Rozanov started to move and Shane cried out. It never took long for him to just give in and start moaning and gasping and asking for more.

"Fuck, Hollander. You love it."

Shane responded by turning, he was sure, beet red. But he couldn't deny it.

If Shane hadn't known the building was empty besides the two of them, he would have been worried about how loud he was being as Rozanov fucked him. But he felt safe here, so he let himself go. He cried out with every thrust and maybe said Rozanov's name a bunch of times.

Shane *really* hoped no one could hear them.

When Rozanov reached around to take Shane's cock in his slick hand, Shane became desperate for release and started bucking back against him. This was the point where he was always reminded why he couldn't give this up. It was too good.

"You gonna come for me, Hollander?"

Hollander *was* going to. And he did. He punched the mattress and swore loudly and coated Rozanov's fist with his release.

Rozanov picked up speed behind him, sending aftershocks rocketing through Shane's body with each thrust. Just as it was becoming too much for Shane, Rozanov stilled and cried out and pulsed inside him.

Afterward, they lay on their backs next to each other, and Shane felt the familiar aftermath of guilt and shame creep in.

"Well, you won at *something* tonight," Rozanov mused.

"God. Fuck off." Shane lifted his arm to flip him off, but Rozanov grabbed his wrist and pulled him over so Shane was on top of his chest, looking down at him. Rozanov's playful smirk faded as he held Shane's gaze, and Shane felt suddenly breathless.

"Still have that stupid tattoo, I see," Shane said quickly, to distract himself from whatever the fuck was happening.

"Aw," Rozanov said, the obnoxious little grin returning to his face. "He missed you."

Shane snorted.

"He *did*," Rozanov insisted. "Give him a kiss."

Shane rolled his eyes, but he did dip his head to Rozanov's chest. Instead of pressing his lips to the tattoo, though, he trapped Rozanov's nipple lightly between his teeth and tugged.

"Fuck," Rozanov said, sucking air between his teeth.

As an apology, and also because Shane knew it would work him up even more, he brushed his tongue over the sensitive nipple. Rozanov put a hand in Shane's hair and guided their mouths back together. After a long, oddly tender kiss, Shane lifted his head and saw that Rozanov was, again, looking at him very seriously. He swallowed, but didn't say anything as Rozanov brushed fingers through his hair. He hoped the fear he felt wasn't showing on his face.

"You are very beautiful," Rozanov said suddenly. It was said very matter-of-factly.

Shane wasn't sure how to react. They didn't really *say things* to each other. Not like that.

"Hottest Man in the NHL, according to *Cosmopol-*

itan," Shane joked. It was the only way he knew how to talk to Rozanov, besides yelling obscenities at him.

"They are idiots," Rozanov said, the spell broken. "They put me at number five. Five!"

"It does seem generous."

Rozanov rolled over, pinning Shane to the mattress. Shane looked up at him, laughing.

"I have to go," Rozanov said, and he sounded like he truly regretted it. "Shower first, but then I have to get back to the hotel."

"I know."

They showered together, and Shane dropped to his knees because he couldn't let Rozanov go without tasting him. Rozanov murmured his approval as he loomed over Shane in the spacious rainfall shower. His strong hands cradled Shane's head and long fingers curled in his wet hair. Shane turned his eyes up and found Rozanov gazing down at him with that damn crooked smile. Shane immediately closed his eyes and felt his cheeks flush and, to his embarrassment, his own cock get harder.

It was bad enough that he loved being fucked so much, that he loved having a dick in his mouth. But for it to have to be *this* son of a bitch, to the point that on the extremely rare occasion when it wasn't, Shane was left wanting...

So maybe it wasn't *just* that this was convenient. But that was something Shane didn't want to think about.

He brought Rozanov right to the brink and then pulled off, catching the man's release on his chin and lips and probably on his neck. The evidence was quickly washed away, down the drain, and Shane fell back to a sitting position against the shower wall. He scrubbed his hands over his face and pulled his knees in. He heard Rozanov panting in Russian.

"Shit," Rozanov said, still standing with his head leaning back against the tile opposite where Shane was sitting. "You been practicing that, Hollander?"

"No," Shane grumbled.

"No? You been saving it for me?"

Shane didn't reply, which was as good as confirmation.

Rozanov laughed. "You need to get laid, Hollander. Waiting for a quick fuck every couple of months is not healthy."

"I'm *not* waiting," Shane said. It wasn't quite a lie. He obviously wasn't one hundred percent straight, but having sex with women didn't *repulse* him. It just didn't do it for him like men did.

One man in particular.

But women were safe and easy and *everywhere*. And maybe if he kept trying he might find one he'd like to spend more than a single night with. Someone who could finally put an end to...whatever *this* was.

Rozanov turned off the water and reached a hand out. Shane huffed, then took it, letting Rozanov pull him to his feet. They stood, chest to chest, and Shane watched the water that dripped from Rozanov's hair onto his shoulder and down toward his navel.

Rozanov rested a hand on Shane's face and tipped his head up. He looked at him fondly, with a little smile on his lips, and then he kissed him.

"I have ruined you," Rozanov said when they broke apart. "No one else will do."

"Fuck off."

"Such a mouth on you."

"Don't say it."

"I preferred it when it was on me."

"Dammit, Rozanov." Shane pushed the other man back against the shower wall and kissed him aggressively. It was always like this. Shoving and cursing each other and battling for control until one or both of them gave in and allowed themselves the release they both craved.

"I do have to go," Rozanov said, but even as he said it he was scraping his teeth along Shane's jaw.

"I know."

"I'm sorry."

"Why? I don't care. I think we're done here anyway, aren't we?"

Rozanov stopped kissing him and looked at him, considering. "I suppose we are."

They left the shower and got dressed quickly. Shane stripped the comforter from the bed and loaded it into the washing machine. He would make sure the place was left as spotless as he had found it.

"Three weeks, then," Rozanov said as he stood at the door, ready to leave.

"Yup."

Rozanov nodded, and Shane thought that was going to be it, but then the other man grinned and said, "Was it me tonight?"

"Was what you?"

"Distracting you. On the ice tonight."

It took Shane a moment to realize what he was suggesting.

"Fuck. You."

Rozanov's smile spread. "Couldn't play at all, thinking about my dick, right?"

"Good night, Rozanov."

Rozanov blew him a kiss on his way out the door, leaving Shane furious and strangely relieved. It was good to be reminded of the fact that they didn't actually like each other.

Shane pulled another beer out of the fridge and sat on the sofa to wait for the comforter to be clean. It was late and he was exhausted, but he wouldn't sleep here. He should really talk to a Realtor about selling this building.

He would sell the building, and he would stay in his goddamn hotel room when they played in Boston and not slip out into the night to Rozanov's penthouse. He would end this, and he would move on.

He realized, as he was making this plan, that he was brushing his fingertips over his lips. They still tingled from the memory of the other man's mouth pressed against them.

He knew making plans to end this was pointless. As long as this was being offered, Shane would never be able to say no.

Part One

Chapter One

December 2008—Regina

Ilya Rozanov trudged through the bitter cold of the hotel parking lot to the team bus. Like most of his teammates, it was his first time in North America. He had expected to feel more overwhelmed by that, but Saskatchewan was hardly New York City. Here, there was nothing to focus on but cold and hockey, and those were two things that Russians were very familiar with.

It was two days before Christmas, but for the world's best teenage hockey players, Christmas meant the World Junior Hockey Championships. For Ilya, it meant the chance to finally get a firsthand look at Shane Hollander.

There had been much made of the seventeen-year-old Canadian phenom. Ilya was sick of hearing the name, which had caused such a stir in the hockey world that even Moscow wasn't far enough to escape the hype. Both Ilya and Hollander were eligible for the NHL entry draft that coming June, and they were already expected to be the number one and two overall picks. The expected order of those two picks depended on who you asked.

Ilya knew *his* answer.

He had never met Shane Hollander. Never played against him. But he was already determined to destroy him.

He would start by leading Russia to a gold medal victory, here in Hollander's own country. Then he would lead his team back in Moscow to their championship. And then, surely, he would be chosen first in the draft. This was the year of Ilya Rozanov. Since he was twelve years old, 2009 had always been the year he was expected to burst onto the world stage. No Canadian pretender would change that.

The Russian team arrived at the rink for their scheduled practice at the tail end of the Canadian team's. Ilya paused with some of his teammates to watch the Canadians run drills. The practice jerseys didn't have names on them, so he couldn't pick out Hollander before he was told by his assistant coach to get his ass into the dressing room. The schedule at the practice rink was very tight.

They took to the ice as soon as it had been cleared by the Zamboni. The rink was small, and kind of dumpy. The actual games would be in the large arena downtown. There were a few people sitting in the stands, watching the Russian team practice. Some scouts, no doubt, and the few family members who had actually made the trip from Russia, as well as several local hardcore hockey fans.

Halfway through the practice, Ilya noticed a young man sitting a few rows above the penalty box, wearing a Team Canada ball cap and jacket. He was flanked by a man and a woman, who were probably his parents. It was hard to tell from the ice, but Ilya thought it might be Hollander. His mother was Japanese or something, right? He was sure he had read that somewhere...

"Care to join us, Rozanov?" his coach bellowed in Russian across the ice. Ilya turned, embarrassed to find the rest of his teammates huddled around the coach.

He didn't like that Hollander—if that *was* Hollander—was here watching them. Or maybe he did. Maybe Hollander was nervous about facing him later in the tournament. Maybe he felt threatened.

He should.

After the practice, Ilya showered and dressed quickly. He headed back out into the rink to stand behind the glass and look at the stands. Hollander and his parents were gone. The Slovakian team had taken to the ice for their practice.

Ilya shrugged and made his way to a vending machine. He bought himself a bottle of Coke and wondered if he could slip outside for a quick smoke before getting back on the bus.

He zipped his Team Russia parka up to his chin and slipped out a side door. It was cold as fuck outside. He pressed himself against the wall of the brick building, stuffed his Coke into his coat pocket, and pulled out a cigarette and a lighter.

"You're supposed to smoke over there," someone said. It took Ilya a moment to translate all of the words.

He turned to see the person that he now definitely recognized as Shane Hollander. He had a very distinct look. Some of his features were clearly from his mother—jet-black hair and very dark eyes—but his father was of some bland, Anglo-European heritage. His skin, however, was flawless. Distractingly so. Smooth and tan with—and this was his most striking feature—a smattering of dark freckles across his nose and cheek-bones.

"What?" Ilya said. Even the single word sounded stupid with his accent.

"The smoking area is over there." Hollander pointed to a far corner of the parking lot, next to a large snowbank. It looked very windy there.

Ilya settled back against the wall and lit his cigarette. *This fucking country.* Bad enough he couldn't smoke indoors anywhere—he needed to go sit in the fucking snow while he did it?

"I'm surprised you smoke," Hollander said.

"Okay," Ilya said, exhaling a long stream of smoke between his lips. There was an uncomfortable silence, and then Hollander made another attempt at conversation.

"I wanted to meet you," he said, extending his hand. "Shane Hollander."

Ilya stared at him, and then felt his lips twitch a bit.

"Yes," he said. He pinched the cigarette between his lips and shook Hollander's hand.

"You're an awesome player to watch," Hollander said.

"I know." If Hollander was expecting Ilya to return the compliment, he was going to be waiting a long damn time.

When Ilya didn't say anything else, Hollander changed the subject. "Are your parents here with you?"

"No."

"Oh. That must be rough. With Christmas and everything."

Ilya struggled a bit to translate so many words, then said, "Is fine."

Hollander shoved his hands in his jacket pockets. "It's cold, huh?"

"Yes."

They leaned against the wall together, side-by-side. Ilya rolled his head against the brick to look down at Hollander, who stood a good four inches shorter than him. He was very interesting to look at. His cheeks were rosy from the cold, and his breath was emerging in white clouds from between his pink lips.

"Next year these are gonna be in Ottawa. My hometown," Hollander said.

Ilya finished his cigarette and dropped the butt on the ground. He decided to make an effort, since this guy seemed so determined to talk to him. "Is Ottawa more exciting?"

Hollander laughed. "Than here? I don't know. A little. It's just as cold."

"Your parents are here."

"For this? Yeah. They're here. They always try to come see me play wherever I go."

"Nice for you."

"Yeah. I know. They're great."

Ilya didn't have anything to add to that, so he stayed silent.

"I should probably go. They're waiting for me," Hollander said. He moved away from the wall and turned to face Ilya. Ilya's eyes went right to those damn freckles. Hollander stuck out his hand again.

"Good luck in the tournament," he said.

Ilya accepted the handshake and grinned. "You will not be so friendly when we beat you."

"That's not happening."

Ilya knew that Hollander truly believed that. That he

would get the gold medal and be the NHL's number one draft pick because he was the fucking prince of hockey.

Maybe Hollander expected Ilya to wish him luck as well, but Ilya just dropped his hand and turned to go back inside the rink.

In the car, Shane told his parents that he had been talking to Ilya Rozanov.

"What's he like?" his mother asked.

"Kind of a dick," Shane said.

When the final game of the tournament was over, the Canadian team had to suffer one more humiliation. The Russians stopped celebrating long enough to line up so the teams could shake each other's hands—a show of sportsmanship that, at that moment, Shane did not feel in his heart.

For one thing, the Russian team had been *dirty*. He had hated playing against them.

For another thing, Ilya Rozanov was really fucking good. Infuriatingly good. And over the course of the tournament, the media had put a lot of effort into building up their rivalry. Shane tried to ignore the press, but it was possible that they were stoking the flames of his hatred.

When he reached Rozanov in the handshake lineup, he could see camera flashes all around them. He made sure he looked Rozanov right in the eye when he tersely said, "Congratulations."

Rozanov smirked and said, "See you at the draft."

They hung a silver medal around Shane's neck that may as well have been a dead rat, for all he wanted it. He respectfully endured the playing of the Russian national anthem, blinking back frustrated tears that he refused to let fall, and then he was finally allowed to leave the ice.

It wasn't supposed to have gone like this. He was supposed to have led his country to gold *in* his country. It was what the nation had expected. Canada's hopes had been heaped onto his seventeen-year-old shoulders and he had let them all down.

Every face-off he had taken against Rozanov, the Russian had looked him dead in the eye and smirked. Shane was not easily shaken by anyone, but that goddamn smirk threw him off balance every time.

Maybe it was just that, after a life of playing at a level above everyone else, Shane had finally met his match.

He was sure that was all it was.

Chapter Two

June 2009—Los Angeles

"Shane, could you move a little closer to Ilya, please?"

Shane felt Ilya Rozanov's arm brush against his as he stepped closer to him for the photographer.

"That's perfect. All right, smile, boys."

Shane's eyes were bombarded with camera flashes. He stood pressed against Rozanov, who seemed to have grown another couple of inches since January. To Rozanov's right was a giant American defenseman named Sullivan, who had been drafted third overall by Phoenix.

Rozanov had been drafted first.

Shane had spent the past six months since the World Juniors being a little bit…obsessed…with Ilya Rozanov. They had quite a bit in common, career-wise. They were both the captains of their respective teams, and had both led their teams to the championship this season. Both men had been named league and playoff MVPs, and both had been the scoring leaders of their respective leagues. The only difference between them was that Shane had a silver medal at home, and Rozanov had gold.

And now Shane had come in second place again. After a life of always coming first in hockey.

This fucking guy.

It wasn't all bad. Shane had been drafted by the Montreal Voyageurs, who, besides being the most legendary franchise in the league, were also only a two hour drive from his hometown of Ottawa. It was a good fit for Shane, who was fluent in both French and English, and who had always had a lot of respect for the Voyageurs, despite having grown up an Ottawa fan. But still. Being picked second stung.

Adding to the drama of the day was the fact that Rozanov had been drafted by Montreal's archrivals, the Boston Bears. Shane knew his career was now going to be inescapably linked to Rozanov's. If one of them had been drafted by a team in the Western Conference, maybe the rivalry would never have gotten off the ground. But this was going to be intense.

Which didn't mean that Shane couldn't be polite to Rozanov now.

"Congratulations," he said, turning to shake Rozanov's hand when the photographers were done.

There was a definite smugness in Rozanov's smile when he said, "Thank you."

Rozanov didn't congratulate Shane. Instead, he patted Shane's fucking shoulder, like he was consoling a child who had struck out at Little League. Shane jerked away from his touch, and was about to say something that was decidedly less polite than "congratulations," but they were both immediately pulled away in opposite directions for interviews.

Shane didn't see Rozanov again until he was back at the hotel. The lobby was packed with athletic young men in suits, but even in that crowd Rozanov stood out. He was one of the taller men there, and cleaned up— with his dark navy suit hugging his body—he looked like a *GQ* model.

Shane felt short. He had turned eighteen last month, but he felt like a kid.

Rozanov had turned eighteen too. Just last week. Which Shane knew because he was obsessed with him.

That night, in his private hotel room (his proud parents were across the hall), Shane couldn't sleep.

It had been an exhausting day, and, yes, he had been drafted by the NHL. He had achieved the thing he had worked his whole life toward. And being chosen second overall was nothing to sulk about.

He wasn't sulking. Not really. He was just…bothered. By something.

He sighed and rolled out of bed. He threw on some sweats and his sneakers and headed down to the hotel gym. Maybe he could shut his mind off with some exercise.

The gym was mercifully empty. Shane stepped onto one of the two treadmills and started running at a gentle pace. He didn't wear headphones; he just lost himself in the noise of the machine.

He didn't notice when someone else entered the gym. He only realized he wasn't alone when the other man stepped onto the treadmill next to him.

Ilya Rozanov gave him a quick nod and turned to face the white wall at the front of the room as he started running alongside Shane.

Shane tried to ignore Rozanov's presence. There was nothing weird about it; he must have been having trouble sleeping too. Or maybe he always hit the gym after midnight. Or maybe the time zone was messing with him. Or maybe...

Rozanov increased the speed on his machine. He didn't glance at Shane at all. Because Shane was petty and competitive, he increased the speed on his own machine... just a little faster than Rozanov's.

Within a minute, Rozanov did the same thing, raising the bar and silently waiting for Shane to match him. Shane glanced over and saw a slight smirk on Rozanov's lips. Shane shook his head and fought his own smile. He cranked up the speed.

They kept on this way, caught in a silent battle, until they were both testing the limits of their machines. They were running at a sprint pace for far longer than was comfortable, and Shane's entire body was burning in protest. But he didn't want to stop, or even slow down, until Rozanov did. Rozanov *smoked*, for fuck's sake. Shane could beat him.

But Rozanov showed no signs of quitting.

They kept up that pace for another minute or two, and Shane finally slammed his hand on the emergency stop button and stumbled off. He leaned against the back wall, gasping for breath, before sliding down to sit on the floor. Rozanov stopped his own machine, and was holding on to the console for support.

"Fuck," Shane wheezed. Rozanov laughed and joined him on the floor, wedging himself into the corner and sitting perpendicular to Shane. Rozanov's gray, sleeveless shirt was soaked through with sweat. They both sat with their legs sprawled out in front of them; Rozanov's sneakers were almost touching Shane's ankle.

Rozanov ran a hand through his damp hair in a move that was more interesting to Shane than it should have been. Rozanov was so...*masculine*. Shane was baby-faced and short, and couldn't grow proper facial hair, and barely had any chest hair. Rozanov was almost exactly the same age as him, but he looked like he had crossed over a magical line to adulthood.

Shane quickly turned his gaze to the floor, and hoped the flush from the exercise covered his blushing.

"What a fucking day, huh?" Rozanov said.

"Yeah. Totally."

"Everything you dreamed of?"

Shane looked him dead in the eye. "Almost."

Rozanov grinned back. "Sorry I ruined your big day."

"Fuck off."

"Montreal is nice, yes?"

"Yes."

"Is Boston nice?"

"Sure. Yeah. I've only been there a couple of times, but it's a good town."

Rozanov nodded.

They were silent a moment, and then Rozanov tapped Shane's ankle with the bottom of his sneaker. "Hey. We will see a lot of each other."

It took Shane a minute. "Oh. Yeah. Montreal and Boston play against each other a lot."

"Should be interesting."

Rozanov took a long haul from his water bottle. Shane pretended he was only looking longingly at the way his throat worked because he had forgotten to bring a bottle for himself. It wasn't until Rozanov's Adam's apple stopped bobbing and his lips were dark and glistening that Shane realized he was staring. The lips quirked up a bit, and Rozanov extended his arm, offering Shane his bottle.

"Oh. I'm all right. Thanks."

Rozanov shook the bottle at him, and Shane took it. He needed water. It would be dumb to refuse.

The tips of their fingers touched briefly together. Shane held the bottle away from his lips and quickly squirted water into his mouth. Rozanov watched him.

It was the first time that Shane felt it. It was like the air in the room had thickened. Everything inside him was buzzing and on edge, like he was about to jump out of a plane.

He didn't know if Rozanov felt anything. But in that moment, Shane wanted…*something.* He couldn't even name it.

He passed the water bottle back, and this time he could swear Rozanov let his fingers brush Shane's wrist on purpose. It was a moment that seemed to last forever, but was probably less than a second.

Shane wanted Rozanov to touch him again.

Shane wanted to touch him back.

Maybe Shane wanted to *kiss* him.

Shane scrambled to his feet. "I'm going to bed. I guess I'll…see you around, right?"

Rozanov looked up at him from the floor. "You will be seeing plenty of me."

Shane nodded and left the room as fast as he could. He waited until he was back in his room before he let himself freak out.

What the fuck was that?

He had never… Jesus Christ, he had a *girlfriend.* He wasn't…

A girlfriend you are hoping will break up with you. She didn't even come on this trip to see you get drafted.

Well, that was true. But she had just started a new summer job...

And you haven't thought about her all day until right now. You haven't even called her yet.

Yeah, all right. Maybe it wasn't really working out with her, but it wasn't like she was the only girl he'd ever...done stuff with.

You're half hard right now. From sitting on the gym floor with another man.

Okay, that one he couldn't explain.

But he *could* get in the shower and jerk off and try like hell to think about his girlfriend, or *any* girl. Anything other than those red, wet lips and that dark stubble and those hazel eyes...

For the rest of his life, Shane Hollander would have to live with the fact that he had ended his NHL draft day by getting himself off to thoughts of Ilya Rozanov.

Chapter Three

December 2009—Ottawa

Ilya watched the red glowing numbers on his hotel room's alarm clock flick from 11:56 to 11:57.

The room was completely dark. His roommate was down the hall, along with half the team, watching the American New Year's Eve celebrations on television.

Ilya had been in that room too. He had watched the Black Eyed Peas perform and had eaten chips and made jokes with his teammates.

And then he just wanted to be alone.

11:58.

There was no mistaking that Ottawa was Shane Hollander's hometown. It was Shane Hollander fucking mania here. His face and his freckles were everywhere: newspapers, television, buses, banners, the sides of buildings.

Of course Hollander was from Canada's capital city. Of course the city was as inoffensive and bland as he was.

Their teams hadn't played each other yet, and they likely wouldn't before the gold medal game. It would

be a shocking upset if it didn't end up being Canada
and Russia in the finals.

11:59.

Ilya would be moving to Boston this summer. To
America. He had never been out of Russia for more
than a couple of weeks at a time. He would begin his
NHL career. He would be rich and famous. He would
be his own man, away from his family.

Midnight.

"Happy New Year," he muttered to himself.

He sat up on the bed and grabbed the package of
nicotine gum off his nightstand. He popped a piece in
his mouth and frowned as he chewed it. He could hear
fireworks outside, and his teammates cheering in the
rooms around him.

He wanted a real cigarette. He wanted to fuck someone.

He wanted to go down to the hotel gym and find
Shane Hollander on a treadmill.

But Shane Hollander wasn't staying at this hotel.
Shane Hollander was probably ringing in the New Year
with friends and family in his perfect hometown that
loved him so very, very much.

That night in the hotel gym in Los Angeles, six months
ago now, Ilya had very nearly embarrassed himself. He
probably could have covered it up with his usual cocky
charm, but he had been damn close to flirting with Hollander. Or possibly just pressing him against a wall and
taking his mouth.

The thing was, he wasn't so sure that Hollander
would have hated it.

Unless Ilya was very bad at reading people—and

he definitely wasn't—Hollander probably would have kissed him right back.

And, Jesus, that thought had consumed Ilya since draft day.

Ilya had probably fucked, in his rough estimate, dozens of women since then. He certainly had no reason to obsess over his fucking archrival. Or his archrival's freckles. Or his dark eyes. Or the way his cheeks glowed red when he exerted himself.

Fuck. *Anyway.* Russia was undefeated in the tournament so far. Canada was also undefeated. Only one team would stay that way until the end. Ilya had more important things to think about than freckles and polite Canadian boys.

Shane couldn't have been happier that his second, and last, World Junior Championship was being held in his hometown. He had spent Christmas with his family, and New Year's Eve with his teammates at the hotel. His parents had been at every game, as usual, and he had been able to visit with lots of friends.

He'd been in a great mood for the entire tournament, and he'd been playing outstanding hockey.

And now it was the night before the gold medal game, and Canada would be facing Russia for the second year in a row.

And Shane would be facing Ilya Rozanov.

He hadn't seen Rozanov at all for this entire tournament. The Canadian and Russian teams had been practicing at different rinks and staying in separate hotels. This game would be their first match.

But Shane had watched every game Russia had

played. And he'd been studying video footage of Rozanov. And this time he was going to beat his ass.

He had mostly forgotten the way it had felt when Rozanov had brushed his fingers against his hand when
he'd handed him the water bottle in that hotel gym
six months ago. He had barely thought at all about his
flushed skin, or the way the damp curls of his hair had
fallen into his hazel eyes.

It had been…adrenaline. The afterglow of the thrill
of competition, when they had been sprawled out on the
floor after pushing their bodies as hard as they could
on the treadmills. It had been a glitch in his brain,
which had been overstuffed with emotions from a roller
coaster of a draft day. He had been tired and confused
and his brain had just turned all of that into something
ridiculous.

So Shane had gone back to life as usual after that
night. Well, he'd broken up with his girlfriend, but that
had been overdue anyway.

There was one other thing that had changed: Shane
had found himself *noticing* men. Not his teammates or
his friends or anyone like that. Just…like a guy at the
airport Starbucks. Or the guy who'd been in the cereal
aisle of the grocery store in Kingston a few weeks ago.

Or the guy who was on *Friday Night Lights*.

But it's not like he wasn't into girls. Girls were *very*
into him, and they were throwing themselves at him
now that he was about to become a millionaire superstar. So, yeah, he'd been hooking up with girls. Plenty
of girls.

Like, at least two girls. Since breaking up with his
girlfriend.

Not, like, all-the-way sex. But sex stuff.

He had definitely been blown by two different girls since July. And he had enjoyed it. With his head tilted back. And his eyes closed.

And he hadn't thought about Ilya Rozanov's dark, wet lips or his crooked smile at all.

"Are you getting tired of second place?" Rozanov smirked.

"I'm winning this game," Shane growled.

"There is not an 'I' in team, right?"

"There's an 'I' in 'suck my dick.'"

Rozanov raised an eyebrow as they bent for the face-off.

"There is also an 'I' in 'silver,'" he said.

Shane made sure he won the face-off. And he made sure he was exactly where he needed to be to score a goal forty seconds later.

And he made sure they won that game.

For all his cockiness and teasing, Ilya took hockey very seriously. And he hated to lose.

But this time he had lost. And he would be going back to Russia with a silver medal. He wasn't proud of it.

He didn't want to return to Russia at all. He wanted to stay in North America and start the next phase of his life. He didn't want to hear his father—who likely hadn't even watched any of the games—shame him for not bringing home a gold medal. He didn't want to live with his father, or depend on anyone anymore. He wanted to be rich and famous and loved and have a huge garage full of sports cars. He wanted expensive clothes and gorgeous women and hot nightclubs. He wanted the weight of his family, and his country, lifted. He wanted to be himself.

On the ice, in the lineup to shake hands at the end of the game, Hollander had looked into Ilya's eyes. It had only been for a second, but it had felt like everything around them had frozen and fallen silent. Hollander's damp, sweaty hand had wrapped itself around Ilya's damp, sweaty hand and, when their eyes had locked, he'd squeezed Ilya's fingers, just a little.

That look, and that squeeze, had said so many things to Ilya.

I know.

We were supposed to stand alone at the top, but we will always be there together. We will keep climbing until no one else can reach us, but it will always be together.

There had been nothing apologetic in Hollander's eyes, but there had been no gloating either. And by the time Ilya had shaken the last Canadian hand in the lineup, he was smirking to himself. Because soon the real battle between himself and Shane Hollander would begin.

And he couldn't fucking wait.

Chapter Four

Shane had signed a lucrative endorsement deal with CCM, one of the biggest hockey equipment companies. He hadn't played a single game in the NHL yet, so he was pretty stoked about it.

Then he found out that CCM had also signed Rozanov.

And *then* he found out that they wanted to launch an ad campaign with both of them. Together.

So Shane found himself in a dark, mostly empty rink in the suburbs of Toronto on a Wednesday in July. He would be reporting to training camp in just over a month. He hadn't seen Rozanov since the World Juniors back at the beginning of January.

Spotlights had been set up around the ice, creating some very dramatic lighting. There were going to be two parts to the day: first, they would do a photo shoot, both separately and together, and then they would skate around and do some fancy stickhandling for the television ads.

Shane was getting used to photo shoots, and to having cameras on him in general. This seemed like a bigger production than he was used to. This felt like he was starring in a movie.

Costarring.

He took a couple of laps around the ice while he waited for the crew to finish setting up. He was wearing head-to-toe CCM gear, of course, including a custom black jersey with a big CCM logo on the chest where a team logo would normally go. His name and number, 24, were on the back.

Shane was wearing makeup, and it felt weird. He wasn't supposed to sweat at all before they did the photo shoot. He decided he'd better stop skating and sit on the bench while he was waiting. He watched the crew fiddle with the lighting.

After a few minutes, he felt the unmistakable presence of Rozanov at the end of the bench. He turned and saw him standing there, huge and handsome, and also wearing makeup.

"Very pretty," Rozanov teased him. "Like a doll."

"You're painted up too."

Rozanov leaned on the top of the boards and grinned. "Yes, but I'm not pretty."

Shane rolled his eyes. He had been called "pretty boy" a few times before, usually during games, and he hated it. He *wished* he hated it this time.

In his makeup, with his carefully styled hair, and in this dramatic lighting, Rozanov did not look pretty. He looked *stunning*. Once again, Shane was astounded and irritated by how *manly* Rozanov was. The sharp edge of his jaw framed cheeks that didn't have any of the baby fat that lingered on Shane's own. And his eyes were like sparkling…somethings. Shane couldn't think of a gem that had that many shades of gold and green.

The photo shoot took a lot longer than Shane had been expecting. It was mostly just standing on the ice, holding CCM hockey sticks in various positions. They did a few photos standing together, but most of them were separate. They finished with a posed photo of the two of them hunched over in the face-off position. They held the pose for what felt like an eternity, with their faces inches apart, staring into each other's eyes.

"Try not to laugh, fellas," the director said. "I know it'll be challenging."

Laughing was not what Shane was worried about. He needed to relax his eyes so Rozanov's features blurred, just to keep himself from staring at the man's lips.

"A little more intensity in your eyes, if you could, Shane."

Shane blinked and tried his best to stare Rozanov down, like it was a real game. But a real game would only require him to hold this position for a few seconds. This was awkward.

He saw Rozanov's lip twitch, and then the big Russian snorted and started laughing. Shane cracked too, and started giggling.

"Just a few more seconds, guys. Please."

"Sorry," Shane said, trying to school his features back into a fierce glare. It was no use. As soon as he looked at Rozanov, both men started laughing again.

"All right, we've probably got enough anyway. Let's take a break and then we'll do the film footage."

"That was your fault," Shane said as they skated over to the bench.

Rozanov shook his head. "Your face's fault. Made me laugh."

Shane bumped him with his shoulder.

The filming was much easier. They both donned CCM helmets and visors and skated around showing off for an hour or so—probably a bit more competitively than necessary. Shane was looking forward to seeing the final commercial. With some music and some voiceover, it would probably look pretty badass.

The director thanked them both, and the two hockey players were left to get showered and changed in the dingy dressing room.

Shane undressed quickly and went into the shower, which was, like most rinks, communal style with a row of showerheads facing each other on both sides of a corridor. If he hurried, maybe he could be out of the shower before Rozanov came in.

No such luck.

Shane had just gotten his hair wet when Rozanov entered the showers and stood under one *almost directly across from him*. Shane's eyes landed on the large bear tattoo on Rozanov's left pec. It was absolutely ridiculous. He also noticed the gold crucifix that he guessed the guy never took off. The chain caressed the base of Rozanov's long neck, the cross resting comfortably on his muscular chest.

Shane quickly turned his eyes to the floor. He had showered with hundreds of guys in his life, in rooms just like this one. It was just part of the game. He had never *looked* at any of his fellow players before. It was just…unthinkable.

He glanced up again, and saw that Rozanov had turned his back to him. Shane was left to stare helplessly at the display of naked, rippling muscle. His eyes trailed over Rozanov's broad shoulders and down the muscles of his back down to his tapered waist and his…

Shane blushed hard. He couldn't…why would he want to check out another guy's ass? That was just weird.

But it was a *really* impressive ass. Not that he was comparing it to others. It was just…perfect. And as Rozanov scrubbed water over his face, the muscles in his ass flexed and Shane was transfixed.

And aroused. *Visibly* aroused. In a shower. With Rozanov.

He only had time to look down at his thickening cock with horror before he noticed that Rozanov had turned back around.

Rozanov glanced down at Shane's crotch and raised an eyebrow.

"Fuck off," Shane grumbled. "It's nothing."

"Like what you see, Hollander?"

"No. It's not… I was thinking about something else." Shane wanted to die. He knew he didn't sound at all convincing.

"Something else?"

Shane should have just left the showers then. He was clean enough. This was torture.

But Rozanov was grinning at him in a way that was *not* helping Shane's…situation. And Shane didn't seem to have the ability to move. Rozanov was teasing him, but he wasn't punching him in the face.

And *he* wasn't leaving either.

Shane wished he could at least make himself look away from Rozanov, but he was spellbound. Rozanov just seemed to be considering him curiously, and maybe enjoying the effect he *knew* he was having on him.

Just another goddamn thing for you to hold over me, Shane thought.

He was so busy being mortified that he didn't immediately notice that Rozanov's own dick was starting to swell.

The grin had faded from Rozanov's face. His eyes were full of an intensity that was much more heated than what Shane had been facing during their photo shoot.

Shane needed to get out of here. This was too bizarre. He absolutely could not do...whatever this was.

But Rozanov let a hand trail down his stomach and wrapped it around his own dick to give it a slow, firm stroke.

Shane gasped. Loud enough that the running water couldn't mask it.

"What were you thinking about?" Rozanov asked, his voice low.

Shane swallowed. His throat was bone dry.

"You," he said quietly.

Rozanov heard him, and smirked. He gave himself another stroke. "You want to touch me, Hollander?"

Shane actually just wanted to watch Rozanov jerk himself off. But...

"Not here," Shane stammered. "Someone could come in."

Rozanov nodded and released himself. He turned and shut off the water. Shane waited, heart racing, until Rozanov had left the showers before he turned off his own water. What the hell was happening? Rozanov couldn't possibly be suggesting that he and Shane...that they...

Holy shit. Shane had to get out of here. He wondered if he could possibly smash through the tile wall of the shower room and escape that way. Anything would be preferable to facing Rozanov again.

He took a few deep breaths to settle himself. He

could do this. He could talk reasonably to Rozanov and end this thing. Determined, he wrapped his towel tightly around his waist before returning to the dressing room.

Rozanov was already half dressed and sitting, shirtless, on one of the benches.

"Look," Shane said to the floor, "that was…we can just pretend that never happened, okay?"

"Is that what you want?"

Shane's answer should have been a lot faster. "Yeah. I mean…yeah. Of course."

Rozanov stood and crossed the floor until he stood right in front of Shane. "You are a bad liar."

Shane scowled at him.

"What is your room number?" Rozanov asked.

"Fourteen ten," Shane said, far too quickly.

Rozanov's mouth twitched up. "If I knock on door of room 1410 tonight…maybe around nine?"

Shane fought to keep his voice even. "I might open the door."

Rozanov smiled. "I might knock."

Shane spent the evening freaking the fuck out in his hotel room.

He considered his options. He could leave. Just go out for a few hours so he wouldn't be there when Rozanov knocked. That would be the sensible thing to do.

He could stay and just ignore Rozanov's knock. There could be something satisfying in that. Give him a little bit of power over him.

He could open the door when he knocked, invite him in, and they could talk about this whole ridiculous… misunderstanding. Then they could go their separate ways forever.

Or…he could open the door and he could spend the evening exploring Rozanov's body with his mouth.

Shane blushed just thinking about it. He couldn't really *want* that, could he?

He had more or less decided on the second option: he would talk to Rozanov. They would put this behind them as quickly as possible so things wouldn't be weird when the season started. He tidied up the room, even though it was already perfectly tidy. He changed his shirt to a nicer one for no reason at all. He brushed his teeth, flossed, and rinsed with mouthwash. Because if he was going to be talking to Rozanov, it would be rude to have bad breath.

He fixed his hair a bit. He switched his phone to silent mode.

He decided to turn on the television, just so it wouldn't look like he'd just been sitting there staring at the door.

He flipped to a baseball game and turned the sound down low. He shut off the overhead light and turned on all of the lamps. He checked himself in the mirror. Again.

The knock came at seven minutes after nine o'clock. Shane checked the peephole just to make sure Rozanov wasn't pranking him or anything.

It was just Rozanov. Alone.

Shane turned off the television, because having it on suddenly seemed dumb. He opened the door and let Rozanov in.

Rozanov looked like he may have put a little effort into his appearance too. He was wearing a black button-up shirt, his gold chain winking at Shane from the wide-open collar. His hair, which was usually a mess of curls, had been tamed a bit, though one lock had already escaped and was tumbling adorably onto Rozanov's forehead.

"Thought you might have chickened out," Rozanov said in his infuriatingly blunt manner.

"No," Shane said. "I mean, I just want to talk. About… you know."

"I do know. Yes."

"Uh, do you want to…sit? Maybe?"

Rozanov took a step toward him. "Not really."

He was so close that Shane could feel the heat of his body. Or maybe he was imagining it.

"I don't think this is a good idea," Shane said weakly.

"What?" Rozanov said, tucking a knuckle under Shane's chin and tilting it up. "This?"

He brought his mouth down on Shane's, and Shane flooded with panic. He was stiff against Rozanov, lips pressed together, eyes open. But Rozanov persisted. Shane felt the tip of Rozanov's tongue trace the outline of his lips, seeking entry. Long fingers threaded into his hair, and Shane surrendered. He parted his lips and closed his eyes, and Rozanov deepened the kiss, pushing between his lips and pressing his tongue to Shane's.

Shane had never kissed a man, and somewhere in the back of his splintering brain he wondered if Rozanov ever had either. He certainly seemed to know what he was doing.

Shane felt like he was made of alarm bells. Like his panic was going to somehow wake up the entire hotel. If it was just that he was kissing a man, he might be able to get a grip. But kissing *this* man in particular was so absurd and wrong wrong wrong…

But his dick didn't seem to think so, especially not when Rozanov wedged a knee between his legs and rubbed a thigh against Shane's arousal. Shane whimpered and Rozanov tipped his head back farther, using his height and coming down hard on Shane's open mouth.

Shane wasn't sure what to do. He hesitantly slid his palms up Rozanov's chest. He heard Rozanov give a soft moan when Shane's fingers moved over his nipples, and that one little sound made Shane lose any remaining self-control.

He kissed Rozanov back, hard and frantic and wanting more but not knowing exactly what to ask for. Rozanov crowded him back against a wall and started unbuttoning Shane's shirt. When he got the last button open, he grabbed Shane's hand and pressed it against his crotch. And, oh, Shane had his hand on Ilya Rozanov's dick. Shane could feel the solid length straining against Rozanov's jeans, and he felt his own cock grow harder even as he struggled against freaking out.

He gripped Rozanov through the denim, and one clear idea of what he wanted popped into his head. He wanted the denim barrier to be gone. He wanted to see Rozanov's cock and hold it and feel it pressed against him, which was *weird*. He shouldn't want that. He shouldn't want *any* of this.

And yet…

With a goal in mind, Shane unfastened Rozanov's fly and worked his hand inside. When Shane had his hand wrapped around the thick, smooth length, Rozanov inhaled sharply and stopped kissing him. Both men looked down to watch Shane's hand move under the cotton of Rozanov's briefs. Shane could see the tip of Rozanov's cock poking out of the waistband, and he had the sudden, wild urge to kiss it. To press his tongue to the slit and taste him.

Fuck. This was really gay.

Rozanov didn't seem troubled, though. Instead, he was pulling his own shirt-off and reaching to cradle Shane's face with his hand. Shane turned his eyes up and Rozanov was looking down at him with dark eyes, his mouth slack and lips swollen. His face was pure desire.

Shane stood, frozen, as Rozanov dragged his thumb over Shane's lips and then gently pushed it inside. Shane closed his eyes and sucked it into his mouth, letting his tongue wrap around it. He was shocked at how naturally he did this; by how much he loved the sensation. He heard Rozanov's breath catch, and Shane felt lightheaded. He wasn't sure how much longer he could stay standing. He wondered if Rozanov would let him…if he wanted him to…

Shane released Rozanov's thumb and slowly sank to his knees.

"Fuck," he heard Rozanov murmur. Shane knew there would be no going back from this, but they'd probably already crossed that line anyway; may as well take what he wanted. With shaking hands, he pulled Rozanov's jeans and briefs down and lined up his mouth with his thick, rigid cock. He took a breath and, very carefully, pressed his tongue to the head.

"Yes, Hollander…" Rozanov hissed.

It tasted like…skin. Shane slowly moved his tongue around the head, completely unsure of what to do. He liked to be excellent at everything. His only experience with this sort of thing had been at the receiving end, so he tried to mimic what some of those girls had done.

He took Rozanov deeper into his mouth, and it felt so *weird*. He just sort of stayed like that for a moment, his tongue flattened by the weight of Rozanov's cock. He knew he must look ridiculous.

Rozanov's expression didn't suggest that he was watching something ridiculous. He held Shane's face with one big hand and gazed down at him with hooded eyes. He murmured something in Russian and then said, "Look at you."

Shane's face flushed. An image flashed through his mind of their roles being reversed. What would Rozanov look like on his knees, taking Shane in his mouth? Would Shane ever find out?

Shane moaned involuntarily, which made Rozanov shudder. His thumb brushed Shane's cheekbone, and Shane closed his eyes and began to move his mouth. He sucked and licked, letting himself get used to the sensation of having a dick in his mouth. His mind was racing, worrying about technique and about what exactly this all meant. But then Rozanov's fingers were tangled in Shane's hair, and Shane was reminded that this was fucking *hot*. That he'd fantasized about exactly this, alone in his bedroom, even if he had been embarrassed afterward.

He sighed around Rozanov's cock and bobbed his head slightly, losing himself in the slide of rigid flesh against his tongue. He was sure he was doing a terrible job, and his fears were confirmed when Rozanov suddenly yelped, "Stop! Stop. Stop."

Shane pulled off quickly and stared up at Rozanov, who was grimacing with his eyes squeezed shut.

"Sorry," Shane said. "I'm not... I've never..."

Rozanov laughed. "Is okay. Was..." He waved a hand

around, as if trying to physically grab the English word he was looking for. "It was…too much."

"Oh." *Really?* Shane felt that he had barely done anything.

"Just…ah…very, um…"

Overwhelming? Intense? Wrong? Shane could think of a few words, but he didn't want to guess at what Rozanov was feeling.

"A lot," Rozanov finished. Then he made a frustrated sound. "No. I cannot think of word."

Shane rose off his knees because he felt foolish staying on them if he wasn't going to be doing anything down there. When he was standing, he looked curiously at Rozanov. "Have you been…thinking about this?"

Rozanov gave a crooked grin and shrugged. "I like trouble."

Shane laughed. "Well, I think we've found it."

"You have not done this," Rozanov said plainly. "With a man."

"No. Have you?"

Rozanov looked at him, and Shane knew he was deciding whether or not he could trust him, and then must have realized it was too late anyway if he didn't. He nodded. "In Russia. My coach's son."

Shane sputtered. "Holy fuck. You *do* like trouble! Was he on the team?"

"No. Not a hockey player."

"Did anyone…find out?"

Rozanov shook his head. "He would never tell. I would never tell. It was safe."

"Safe," Shane repeated. It didn't sound at all safe.

"Just fooling around. Not serious. Was…what is it?"

"Curious?"

Rozanov smiled. "Yes. Curious. And *you* make me curious."

"Oh."

He leaned in and breathed against Shane's ear in his heavily accented English, "Do I make *you* curious?"

Rozanov made Shane a lot of things: confused, infuriated, terrified, aroused, and, yes, curious.

"Obviously," Shane said, a little irritably.

"Did you like sucking my dick?"

"Oh, *those* English words you know?"

Rozanov licked under Shane's ear, and Shane gasped.

"Did you like it?" Rozanov asked again.

Shane swallowed his saliva and his pride. "Yes."

"Would you like me to lie on the bed and let you do it some more?"

"*Let* me?"

Rozanov chuckled against Shane's neck. "I'm a nice guy."

Shane shoved him and Rozanov stumbled back, pants around his knees. He laughed as he tumbled backward onto the bed.

Now that there was some distance between them, Shane could take in the full splendor of Rozanov's mostly naked body. Rozanov seemed to enjoy the attention, and stretched his muscular arms up over his head, grinning and arching his long torso. He had dark brown hair on his chest and trailing down from his belly button to his bobbing erection, which was still slick with Shane's spit.

Rozanov sat up and pulled his pants all the way off, along with his shoes and socks. Shane's eyes fell on the way his stomach muscles flexed as he curled forward, and on his thick, muscular thighs.

Once again, Shane felt very young. Very boyish. He

realized that he was still mostly dressed, and he wasn't sure if he should change that or not.

Rozanov made the decision for him. "This is a bit… not fair." He moved a hand through the air, back and forth between them.

"You want me to…"

"*Da.* Yes. Let me see you."

"You've already seen me. In the shower."

"I want a better look."

Shane removed his clothes quickly. Being naked in the presence of other guys was not foreign to him, but there was nothing familiar about this scenario. He stood in his underwear for a moment, then tried not to blush as he removed them.

Shane stood with his arms out. *Well?*

Rozanov grinned and waved a hand over his own chest. "So smooth."

"Look…"

"Like a swimmer."

"I don't…it's natural, all right?"

"Yes. Come here." Rozanov patted the bed next to him.

Shane blew out a breath and moved onto the bed. He lay flat on his back next to Rozanov, unsure of what to do next.

"What do you want?" Rozanov asked.

"I don't know."

"No?" Rozanov asked, and he leaned over him and kissed him. "Nothing?"

"I…"

"What about…" Rozanov pressed a palm against Shane's erection and curled gentle fingers around it. "Okay?"

Shane nodded. It was shockingly okay for Ilya Rozanov—a guy, a hockey player, his *rival*—to have his hand wrapped around Shane's dick.

"Relax," Rozanov said, and kissed him again. His hand stroked Shane carefully, without lube, and Shane was spellbound. Rozanov's soft, accented words and his gentle hands and his confident kisses were all working together to ensnare him.

Dizzy with sensation and lust, Shane lightly pushed on Rozanov's shoulder until he was flat on his back. Then, before he could talk himself out of it, Shane slid down his body and took his cock into his mouth again. He wasn't any surer of his abilities, but he knew what he wanted. He wanted to get Rozanov off. He wanted to take him apart.

He let his jaw slacken and took Rozanov as deep as he could. He was nervous about biting him by accident, so he kept his mouth open wider than was probably necessary and used a lot of tongue. It was sloppy and very wet, but he could hear the encouraging sounds Rozanov was making. When Shane turned his eyes up, he could see Rozanov had propped himself up on his elbows and was watching him give his first blow job with great interest.

Shane wrapped a hand around the base of Rozanov's cock and stroked up to meet his mouth. When Rozanov arched and moaned, Shane repeated it, stroking him hard and fast.

"Hollander...fuck." Rozanov switched to Russian, and Shane didn't know what he was saying, but he figured he should probably get out of the way because he wasn't sure he was ready to take a load in his mouth.

He pulled off just in time. Rozanov put his own hand

on his dick to replace Shane's mouth and stroked himself roughly until his release fell all over his own stomach.

Shane stared, dumbfounded. It was the hottest thing he had ever seen.

Rozanov flopped back on the bed, breathing hard. "Not bad, Hollander," he said.

Shane was still staring at the mess on Rozanov's stomach. His own cock was like iron. He thought about stroking himself until he came on Rozanov. He thought about Rozanov putting his mouth on him...

"Okay. Well. Good night," Rozanov said, and moved to get up.

Shane's mouth dropped open, and he was about to be furious when he noticed the playful, crooked grin.

"Fuck you," Shane said.

"Did you need something?" Rozanov asked innocently.

Shane glared at him. Rozanov chuckled and grabbed some tissues from the nightstand so he could wipe his stomach off a bit.

"Lie down," Rozanov instructed.

Shane did. Rozanov crawled on top of him and kissed him.

"You think I'm an asshole," Rozanov said.

"You *are* an asshole."

"I would not leave you like that."

"No?"

He kissed him again. "No."

As they kissed, Rozanov reached a hand down and gripped Shane's cock. Shane gasped into his mouth.

"Let me show you," Rozanov murmured, "how to do this."

He kissed his way down Shane's body, which felt so

good that Shane forgot to be insulted. When he reached
Shane's cock, Rozanov greeted it with a long, slow lick
with the entire surface of his tongue, like it was a fucking ice-cream cone or something.

"Jesus." Shane shuddered.

Rozanov licked and sucked the head, tonguing the
slit and pushing Shane dangerously close to the edge
already. He gripped the hotel bed comforter and tried
to hold on. Rozanov was shockingly good at this. How
many fucking times had he met up with his coach's son?
Shane felt like he should be paying attention—maybe
taking notes—but his brain had left the room.

Shane reached down to run his fingers through the
golden-brown curls of Rozanov's hair. He dragged his
fingers down over the stubble on his cheek, the sharp
line of his jaw. Shane had enjoyed watching some truly
hot girls sucking him off in the past, but this was beyond
anything he had ever experienced before. Watching this
big, beautiful man, who knew exactly what to do with
his tongue and lips and—god, his *teeth*—work him like
there would be a medal awarded for performance…

"Ah, god. Rozanov! I'm gonna…"

He expected Rozanov to get the hell out of the way,
but instead he sucked him harder and Shane emptied
himself into his mouth.

A stream of nonsense fell out of Shane's mouth.
"Holy shit. I'm sorry. Oh my god. I'm so sorry. Fuck.
Wow. God."

Rozanov pulled off, not at all hurried, and wiped his
mouth with the back of his hand. He laughed at Shane's
babbling. "Sorry? Why sorry?"

Shane choked out a hysterical laugh. "I don't know!
I just… I wasn't expecting you to…"

Rozanov shrugged as if Shane was thanking him for bringing in the mail. "I don't mind it."

Shane felt stupid that he hadn't even tried to…properly finish the job on Rozanov. This guy was determined to one-up him at every turn.

Rozanov sat on the edge of the bed with his back to Shane. He rolled his neck and idly rubbed his jaw. Shane sat up and swung his legs over the opposite side of the bed. He gripped the mattress with both hands and looked at the floor. He felt panic surge up in him again.

He heard Rozanov blow out a breath, which made Shane laugh for some reason. The absurdity of the situation was hitting him.

"You're laughing."

"Yeah, well…this whole thing is a little nuts."

"I want a cigarette," Rozanov said.

"You're not allowed to smoke in the hotel."

"I know. Stupid country." Rozanov sighed. "Doesn't matter. Bears told me to quit. I am trying not to smoke."

"Oh. That's good. Smoking is bad for you."

"Is it?" Shane could *hear* Rozanov's eyes rolling.

"So, um…" Shane said, still keeping his back to Rozanov. "This won't leave this room, okay?"

"You think I will tell people?"

Shane sincerely doubted it. "No."

"No."

He felt the bed shift as Rozanov stood up.

Shane had the stupid urge to ask him to stay. He imagined falling asleep in his arms and *what the fuck?* This thing they'd just done was, above all things, a huge mistake. As far as hookups went, Shane really could not have chosen a less appropriate person. And even forgetting that, there was no reason to pretend this was anything more than a quick, no-strings fuck. And why would Shane even *want* to pretend that?

He didn't. He wanted Rozanov out of his hotel room. He wanted to forget that this ever happened. He did *not* want to reach for him. To pull him back on the bed. To do everything they just did two or three more times.

When Rozanov was fully dressed, he gave Shane one of his playful, crooked smiles. Shane had managed to put his underwear back on, but other than that, was still naked.

"My flight is early tomorrow," Rozanov said. There was maybe a note of apology in it. Or maybe Shane was imagining things.

"All right."

Rozanov nodded. "I'll see you around."

"Yeah," Shane said awkwardly. "I'll see you on the ice, I guess."

"Yes."

Shane wanted to kiss him one more time, because he was sure he would never get the chance again. But Rozanov was already opening the door.

"Goodbye, Hollander."

"Bye," Shane said to the closed door.

Chapter Five

September 2010—Montreal

Shane was a man of routine.

He woke every morning at six o'clock, and immediately went for a ten-kilometer run. He would then return to his (new) apartment to do sets of pull-ups, push-ups, and crunches. Then he would stretch before he would make himself a smoothie and a bagel, which he would eat while watching *SportsCenter*. Then he would shower.

The rest of his day would be dictated by whatever was scheduled for him. He very rarely had a day with nothing planned.

He had completed his first NHL training camp, and he had secured himself a spot on the Montreal Voyageurs' roster for the 2010–2011 season. That was no surprise, but he was still damn proud of himself. He was starting the preseason games the next day. The city of Montreal had already warmly embraced him. He was excited.

On the television, the *SportsCenter* anchors were talking about Ilya Rozanov.

Shane hadn't seen, or spoken to, Rozanov since their…encounter…in the Toronto hotel room over two months ago. He would like to be able to say that he hadn't thought of him either, but that would be far from the truth.

Suddenly, Rozanov's face filled the screen. Shane felt his own face flush a bit, which was ridiculous because he was alone and not actually in the presence of those sparkling hazel eyes or that playful, lopsided smile.

He was watching the television, entranced, but not listening to a word of the interview. He didn't snap out of it until he heard Rozanov say, without a trace of irony, "The Bears will be happy with me this season. I will score fifty goals."

"Fifty goals?" the stunned interviewer asked.

"Are you fucking kidding me?" Shane asked at home.

"Yes. By end of February," Rozanov said.

Shane snorted. He was stunned by the audacity of this guy. He was announcing before the season had even started, before he had any idea how much ice time he'd even be getting with the Bears, that he would be scoring fifty goals this season? As a nineteen-year-old rookie?

Shane had every intention of scoring at least as many goals himself, but he certainly wasn't going to *announce* it. Jesus Christ, what would his new teammates think of him? They'd think he was a cocky little asshole, that's what. And if Shane didn't perform, he'd look like a fucking idiot.

But there was Rozanov, bold as brass, calmly announcing his intention to do what maybe four or five rookies had been able to do? Ever? In history?

Ridiculous. Infuriating.

"Do you feel pressure to outperform Shane Hollander this first season?" the interviewer asked.

"Who?"

Fuck. You. Rozanov.

Rozanov looked directly at the camera, and Shane froze. *He can't see you, dummy.*

He watched Rozanov wink at the camera and Shane's eyes narrowed. He was going to shut this fucker up when their teams finally met.

The opportunity came a month later.

The hype leading up to the first meeting between Hollander and Rozanov seemed, to Shane, to be a bit much. They were both only nineteen, and their NHL careers were only weeks old. He wasn't sure what anyone was expecting to happen.

Montreal was hosting Boston. Shane met his parents for lunch the day of the game. They came to every home game, but this day they came up from Ottawa a little early because they knew how nervous he was.

"The league is always looking for a marketing angle, Shane," his father said. "It's just a game like any other."

"I know." He poked at his pasta. He couldn't imagine what his parents would say if they knew the real reason he was nervous about facing Rozanov. Pressure he could handle. He lived for hockey, and he was extremely good at it. Normally he'd be looking forward to the chance to prove himself against a rival.

You had to go and make it weird, didn't you, Hollander?

"Is Drapeau going to be starting tonight?" Shane's mother asked. "He was weak on his left side last game. Is he hurt?"

"He's fine," Shane said with a small smile. In a nation of rabid, knowledgeable hockey fans, Yuna Hollander ranked near the top. Her parents had emigrated from Japan, but Yuna had been born and raised in Montreal.

She couldn't have been happier that her son had been drafted by her beloved Voyageurs.

Shane was the only child of Yuna and David Hollander, and they had given him all the support in the world. Shane loved them, and he knew how lucky he was. He definitely wouldn't be where he was without them.

Shane knew most guys in the league didn't have their parents coming to almost every home game, but he wasn't ashamed to admit that he was grateful his folks lived so close. He'd played his junior hockey in Kingston, which was close enough to Ottawa that he'd seen his parents at most games there too. He'd never really felt that need to distance himself from them. Maybe it was because he was an only child, or maybe it was because he knew how much his parents had given of their time and money and energy to get him to where he was now.

Plus, he liked them.

"You need a lamp beside your couch in that apartment," Mom said, completely out of nowhere.

"What?"

"Your living room. It's too dark. Do you want the one from the den at home? We don't need it."

"That's okay, Mom. You keep that. I'll get one."

"Yuna! He doesn't need our old furniture! He's a millionaire!"

"It's a nice lamp!" she argued. "They don't make nice things anymore."

"If you have the money, they'll make anything," Dad said.

"Next time you guys drive up we can go lamp shopping, Mom."

That seemed to please her. "Have you had any friends over yet?" she asked.

"One guy. Hayden. You know…"

"Hayden Pike. The rookie. Left wing. Played in the Quebec league for Drummondville," Mom recited. "Yes."

"Yeah. He came over to check the place out one night before we went out with some of the other guys."

"He seems like a nice boy," Mom said. "I saw him interviewed."

"He's cool. Everyone has been great so far, really."

Dad laughed. "Of course they have been! They're damn lucky to have you."

"I'm just another guy on the team."

His parents looked at each other, but didn't say anything. Shane let it go. He knew how proud they were of him.

"Anyway," Dad said, "what were we talking about? Rozanov? We're not worried about Rozanov, right?"

"He's a dirty player," Mom growled.

"He's a *good* player is what he is." Shane sighed.

"Not as good as you. Not in any category," Mom said firmly.

"He's bigger than me."

"You're faster than him."

"Maybe."

"And you're a leader. A nice young man. Rozanov is a jerk."

Shane laughed. "Yeah. I know."

He's better at blow jobs than me. The thought crashed to the front of Shane's brain, and he quickly grabbed for his water glass, nearly knocking it over.

His mother narrowed her eyes. "What's wrong with you, Shane? You aren't usually this nervous."

"Nothing! I just want to win tonight. That's all."

It seemed to be the right thing to say, because she smiled. "You will. Screw Ilya Rozanov, right? That can be your mantra tonight."

Or not.

Shane forced a smile. "Sure. Screw him."

"All right, fuck it," Coach LeClaire said. "Rozanov, get out there and take the face-off against Hollander. Let's give 'em what they want."

Rozanov vaulted over the boards and headed for the face-off circle. He was on the ice with Hollander for the first time in an NHL game.

"Shane Hollander," he said casually when he reached his opponent.

"Rozanov."

Ilya let his lips curl up a bit into a little smile. Hollander's face hardened and he shook his head slightly.

The crowd was so fucking loud. This city was nuts.

"Will you disappoint them, Hollander?"

"Nope."

They bent for the face-off.

Ilya wished he didn't have the mouth guard in because he would have loved to do something distracting and sexy with his tongue.

He probably should have been focusing more on the puck and less on bothering Hollander, because he lost their first face-off. And that was something he'd never get back.

Ilya scowled at the ceiling of his Montreal hotel room. He was furious with himself—not at his team, at *himself*—for losing this first match against Hollander.

He didn't know what to do with his anger. It was not the best moment for his phone to ring.

It was his goddamned brother, Andrei.

"What is it?" Ilya said, forgoing niceties. It wasn't like Andrei was calling just to chat.

"Did you play tonight?"

"Yes," Ilya said tightly. He had teammates from the Czech Republic whose families back home watched every game online.

"Oh. Did you win?"

"What do you want?"

Andrei was quiet. Ilya's heart sank. "Is Dad...?"

"Fine. Why wouldn't he be?"

Ilya's jaw clenched. His brother could pretend all he wanted that there was nothing wrong with their father, but it was increasingly obvious that it wasn't the case. He decided to ignore Andrei's lies for the moment.

"Do you need money, then?" Ilya asked. It was the only other possible reason for Andrei's call.

"Just...not much. Like...twenty thousand?"

"Twenty thousand! *Dollars?*"

His brother laughed. "Not rubles. Of course dollars."

"What the fuck for?"

"Life," his brother said vaguely. "You know what it's like here."

He knew what his *brother* was like. He was either making a bad investment, or had already made a bad investment. Or was gambling. Or something else that a police officer really shouldn't be doing.

"I gave you ten thousand like two months ago. Where the fuck is that?"

"Life, Ilya. Like I said."

"Life. Right."

"It's not like you can't afford it. I know what your signing bonus was."

"I'm sure you do." It was probably the only part of Ilya's career that Andrei had bothered to follow.

"I wouldn't ask if it wasn't important, Ilya."

Ilya rolled his eyes at the phone. He could say no. He *should* say no. He didn't owe his asshole brother a goddamned thing.

But if he said no, then his father would call next to give him the speech about family and being a good son. And as much as Ilya hated Andrei, he was still his brother. But this was the last fucking time.

"I'll send you the money. But don't ask again."

"Could you send it now? What time is it there?"

"What? No! Fuck you, I'll send it tomorrow. I'm going to bed."

"Fine. Good night, then."

"You're welcome."

Andrei ended the call. Ilya threw his phone down on the bed.

He turned on the television, and there was Shane fucking Hollander's face, filling the screen. All sweaty and flushed and happy. Answering questions in perfect goddamned French. Ilya couldn't even say a basic English sentence without sounding like a cartoon villain. He hated his stupid accent. He hated his asshole family.

Shane Hollander was speaking French and he was breathless and smiling and drenched in sweat with his hair sticking up in all directions. His cheeks were pink and his lips were dark and wet. He looked so fucking proud of himself.

Ilya told himself the twisted feeling in his stomach was just jealousy, but he was terrified that it was something much, much worse.

Chapter Six

Ilya swiped his key card for the third time and his hotel room door finally unlocked. Once inside, he fell back on the king-size bed with his arms outstretched, pleasantly buzzed from the drinks he'd consumed at his All-Star team's dinner.

He had expected to be on a team with Hollander, since they played in the same conference, but the league had decided to change it up this year and have North American players form one team, and European players form the other. No secret as to why. The league couldn't get enough of the Rozanov/Hollander rivalry.

Ilya was close to making good on his promise to score fifty goals by the end of February. He had already scored thirty-eight.

Hollander had scored forty-one.

Fucking Hollander.

Ilya'd spotted him in the lobby earlier that evening, but that was it. No words had been exchanged. He hadn't even gotten a nod of acknowledgment from him.

Ilya wondered what Hollander was doing right now.

He wondered if there were any cute girls at the hotel bar.

Was Hollander in his own room, lying on his bed? Was he wondering what Ilya was doing?

Why was Shane Hollander so fucking hard to shake? They'd hooked up *once*. Months ago. It had been a mistake, obviously. A giant, ridiculous mistake. Or, at the very least, something that should be forgotten about. Not a big deal.

On the ice it was easy enough to focus on the game. Ilya actually *loved* playing against Hollander. He would never actually *tell* him, but Hollander was really fucking good. He challenged Ilya in ways that Ilya wasn't used to. He loved taking the puck from Hollander. He loved slamming him into the boards. He loved skating around him. He loved shit-talking him because his eyes would get all squashed up in anger and his pink lips would curl into an adorable little attempt at a snarl. Like an angry kitten.

Okay. It wasn't entirely easy to focus on the game.

And after the games…and all the days between their games…when Ilya had to watch Hollander being interviewed with his lovely fucking manners and his adorable, boyish smile. When Ilya watched him play against other teams, and watched how he moved with flawless, calculated grace. When Ilya heard him switch effortlessly between perfect English and perfect French at press conferences. When Ilya thought about how eager his mouth had been back in that hotel room in Toronto…

He didn't even have Hollander's phone number.

He'd see him tomorrow night.

Shane should have been expecting the press conference.

Saturday morning, the day of the All-Star Skills Competition, he had received a phone call from someone from the NHL's PR office telling him there was a short press conference scheduled for that afternoon. Two o'clock. It would just be him…and Ilya Rozanov.

"Why?" Shane had asked.

"It's your first All-Star Game! You're both having legendary rookie seasons! And besides, the press love the idea of getting you two together."

Shane had flushed a little.

So now he found himself sitting behind a raised table, staring at a room full of reporters and cameras. That part was very familiar, and didn't cause Shane any stress. The large Russian man next to him—who was sitting so close their forearms were almost touching where they rested on top of the table—was the one responsible for Shane's dry mouth and (probably) noticeable stammering.

"Ilya," one reporter said, "you announced at the beginning of the season that you would score fifty goals by the end of February. You've scored thirty-eight so far. Do you think you'll keep your promise?"

Rozanov took a moment to reply. Shane wondered if he was working through all the English words.

"Yes," Rozanov finally answered. There was scattered laughter when it became clear that he wasn't going to elaborate.

"Shane, you've scored forty-one goals this year already. Do you think you'll beat Rozanov to fifty?"

"I don't really think about stuff like that," Shane said carefully. "This is a team sport, and I'm happy when my team is doing well. I just try to contribute."

Rozanov was wearing a ball cap and had his head down so the reporters couldn't see his reaction, but Shane could *feel* him rolling his eyes beside him.

"Ilya, how's it feel to play with a team of Europeans for this All-Star Game?"

"Good. Perfect. Locker room makes more sense than usual."

More laughter.

Shane watched the way Rozanov was slowly rubbing the knuckle of his forefinger with his thumb. He probably didn't even realize he was doing it. Rozanov had nice hands…

The questions kept coming, and they were all exactly what Shane had been expecting. He did his best to answer them, and even chanced a glance over at Rozanov's profile next to him. His curls poked out from under his All-Star Game ball cap, and his jawline was covered in stubble. He was wearing a V-neck T-shirt, and Shane could see the glint of his gold chain where it disappeared beneath the fabric.

Shane turned his head abruptly back to the reporters.

He took a sip of his water and sat back in his chair. Except now he had an even better view of Rozanov, and the way he was hunched forward over the table. Shane could see the muscles in his back and shoulders straining against the thin material of the T-shirt.

"Shane?"

"Sorry?" Shane snapped his eyes forward.

"Just a quick one from the *Toronto Star*: Would you like to play on an All-Star team *with* Ilya in the future?"

"Oh. Sure. Yeah. I mean…" He took a breath. "Ilya's a great player."

"Ilya? Same question?"

"If Hollander does not mind me being starting center. Yes."

Shane made a show of rolling his eyes as the room

laughed. He clasped his hands together and rested them on the table in front of him, leaning over his microphone as he awaited the next question. Rozanov's elbows were resting on the table too. His left elbow was almost brushing Shane's right. Shane could swear there was an electric current in the narrow space between them. He felt like the hair on his arm was standing up.

"Both Montreal and Boston have been out of the playoffs for three seasons now. Do you guys feel the pressure to restore your team's legacies, even this early in your careers?"

Shane rubbed his arm and furrowed his brow. He turned his head and saw that Ilya was looking at him, and his face showed that he was hoping Shane would field this one. Rozanov probably only understood about half the words. Shane thought it was a pretty stupid question, honestly.

"Um," he said. "I can't speak for Rozanov, or what it's like in Boston, but I know the fans in Montreal love their team and definitely are expecting us to turn things around and get back in the playoffs and win some cups. And, you know, I feel the exact same way. So… I guess my answer is that I don't really feel any pressure that I'm not already putting on myself."

He hoped that satisfied him. Unfortunately, the reporter didn't pick up on the fact that Rozanov was clearly struggling with understanding the question, and said, "Ilya?"

"Ah," Rozanov said. "What Hollander said. Yes."

He gave the room one of his playful smiles, and everyone laughed again. Shane looked at him, and Rozanov caught his eye and winked. Shane pursed his lips to stifle a grin.

Under the table, he felt Rozanov's foot tap against his own. It was the chastest contact in the world, but it still made Shane's heart stop.

The press conference ended. Both men stood as the room erupted into the chaos of dozens of people packing up recording equipment. Shane offered Rozanov his hand, and Rozanov shook it. When Shane released their handshake, Rozanov slowly slid his fingers along Shane's palm.

"I'll see you later, Hollander," he said in a tone that was far more suggestive than it should have been.

Shane swallowed. "Yeah. Later."

Shane allowed himself a moment, on the ice, to take everything in. The NHL's All-Star Skills Competition was held the night before the All-Star Game, and was a chance for the stars to show off and try to prove themselves the fastest skater, or the hardest shooter. It was just a laid-back, fun night, and no one took it very seriously, but he was *here*, dammit. He was a rookie and he was an NHL All-Star. He could be a little proud of himself.

All of the players from both teams were on the ice now, clustered in front of their respective benches. Some of the players kneeled as they waited for their events to be called. Others stood and chatted with their just-for-this-weekend teammates. The league had been less than subtle about their desire to see Shane and Rozanov go head-to-head in one of the competition events. That event ended up being the shot accuracy competition.

Rozanov went first. The net had four foam bull's-eye targets—one in each corner—fastened to the goalposts. When the timer started, the object was to break all four targets with shots from the blue line as fast as possible. The league record was about seven seconds.

When the whistle blew, Rozanov wasted no time. He broke the top two targets with the first two shots, then missed the next one, then cleanly broke the bottom two targets with his fourth and fifth shots.

Eight seconds.

Shane shook his head and watched Rozanov play to the crowd. Rozanov skated around the ice holding his stick like a rifle, celebrating his skills by pretending to shoot at the rafters.

Shane skated up to replace Rozanov on the blue line, and Rozanov came to a stop right in front of him. "Sorry about that, Hollander."

"You think I can't beat that?"

Rozanov just winked and nudged Shane a little as he passed him. Shane heard the crowd's delighted reaction.

Fuck it. Fuck *him*. Shane could do this. He could do this with his fucking eyes closed.

The whistle blew and Shane just locked on to those targets. He watched each one burst apart with four perfect shots.

Six. Point. Seven. Seconds.

The crowd went wild. Shane threw his arms over his head and celebrated more than was probably necessary or sportsmanlike, but fuck, it felt *good*.

He smirked at Rozanov as he skated back to his teammates. Rozanov wasn't smiling now, but the look in his eyes was...

Shane flushed and turned his attention to his teammates.

His contribution to the competition completed, Shane could now just relax and enjoy himself as he watched the others battle each other. He would like to say his gradual movement down the line in front of the bench to where the two teams met was not deliberate, but that would be a lie. And it seemed he wasn't the only one making that journey.

Shane leaned casually against the boards at the end of the bench, pretending to focus on the players competing for hardest shot, instead of on the man who was standing a couple of feet from him.

"Nice job, Hollander," Rozanov drawled.

"Thanks."

"Have fun last night?"

"Last night?"

"With your teammates. Dinner somewhere? Get drunk?"

Shane looked down at the ice. "Oh. Yeah. It was fun. Um…how about you guys?"

"Lots of fun. No fucking Canadians or Americans. Was perfect."

"Ah."

He turned his gaze to Rozanov's face. No one wore helmets for the skills competition, since there was no actual body contact, and Shane could admire the profile of his chiseled jaw, and the soft curls of his hair.

"Going to bed early tonight. I think," Rozanov said suddenly.

Shane's mouth went a little dry. "Oh?"

"Yes."

They stood in silence, watching the action on the ice. Loud music blared and the crowd cheered as another record was broken.

Rozanov leaned down. His breath ghosted over Shane's ear when he said, in a low voice, "Twelve twenty-one."

A shiver ran through Shane's body, and before it had even left him, Rozanov was gone. Shane watched him skate down the ice to talk to a fellow Russian player.

Shane hoped he wasn't blushing.

"The fuck did Rozanov want?" asked Liam Casey, a defenseman for Pittsburgh.

"Nothing," Shane said quickly. "Just shit-talking, you know?"

"Guy's a fucking asshole."

"Yeah," he said.

Ilya wasn't surprised at all when the knock came.

It was late. After midnight. He had been back in his room for almost two hours.

Hollander pushed into the room as soon as Ilya opened the door. He turned and flipped the bar latch as if someone was going to burst in any moment.

He looked terrified.

"Is there a ghost out there?" Ilya asked, amused.

"No. Fuck you. This is fucking dangerous and you know it."

"Is it? We are not doing anything."

Hollander looked at him hard. His dark eyes were a mixture of anger and lust. Ilya decided to drop the act.

"You came anyway," he said.

"Yeah," Hollander said, his voice tight and full of forced courage. "I guess I did."

Ilya nodded, and then Hollander swore under his breath and lunged forward to kiss him. He grabbed Ilya's T-shirt in a tight fist and pulled him closer.

Ilya moaned at the hot slide of Hollander's tongue against his. He tugged roughly on the hair at the back of Hollander's head, tipping his head back so he could deepen the kiss.

They broke apart and Hollander looked at him, eyes wild and dark hair a mess, silently begging for instruction.

"On your knees," Ilya said softly, just to see what he would do.

Expecting Hollander to tell him to fuck off, Ilya's breath caught in his throat as he watched him sink fluidly to the floor. His gaze stayed on Ilya. Those eyes that were always so sharp were now hazy with desire as he leaned forward to nuzzle and mouth at the bulge in Ilya's sweatpants.

"Christ, Hollander," Ilya breathed, gently pulling at Hollander's hair as he pressed hot, openmouthed kisses to the fabric that pulled tight over Ilya's erection. He felt dizzy and less in control than he wanted to be as Hollander tucked fingers into Ilya's waistband and pulled down until Ilya's cock was freed.

Hollander didn't hesitate. He dragged his tongue up the length before wrapping his lips around the head and sinking down. Ilya couldn't even make a smart remark. He just gasped and let his head fall back, completely overwhelmed by Hollander's need for this. He certainly didn't have the ability to conjure English words right now.

Hollander reached a hand up and slid it, fingers splayed, under the hem of Ilya's T-shirt. He pushed the shirt up until Ilya took the hint and pulled it off over his head. He carefully stepped out of his sweatpants, Hollander's mouth never leaving him, and planted a hand on the back of Hollander's head. He was careful not to hold him too firmly in place. This wasn't control—Ilya just wanted to touch him. To let the silky strands of his hair slip through his fingers as Hollander gave in to what he had clearly been craving.

Hollander's hands wandered as he sucked him. His touch was light and curious, his fingertips almost tickling Ilya as he explored his thighs and hips and around to his ass. Ilya wondered how far Hollander was willing to go with him. He wondered if he'd done anything with another man since their last time. The desperate, unskilled motion of his mouth and the slight tremble in his hands suggested that he hadn't.

The idea that Ilya was probably the only one who ever saw him like this—that he was the only person in the entire fucking world who knew what it felt like to have those pretty pink lips wrapped around his cock…

Ilya swore in Russian and pulled away. He grabbed Hollander by the front of his shirt and hauled him up, kissing him roughly before throwing him on the bed. He wanted to know how much he would give him tonight.

Hollander stared up at him, lips dark and wet and parted. His hair was everywhere. Ilya just stood there and watched him toe off his sneakers, never breaking eye contact. Hollander was breathing heavily, as if he wasn't one of the most physically fit people on the planet.

Ilya bit his lip and watched him pull his shirt off. In seconds Ilya was covering him on the bed with his body, and kissing him hungrily.

Ilya had always been this way. He loved sex, and he loved it more when it was dangerous—when it was with someone he *knew* he shouldn't be with. Whether that was his coach's son, or his brother's girlfriend, or his teammate's sister, Ilya couldn't resist a bad idea.

And Shane Hollander was a *bad* fucking idea. The *worst* idea. Wrong in every way imaginable. Two men. Two NHL players, poised to be the two biggest stars in the league soon enough. Two bitter rivals on opposing teams that had hated each other for almost a hundred years.

Plus, Ilya hated this guy. He hated his pretty boy face and his perfect goddamned English and his perfect goddamned French and his loving parents and his polite little manners and his million-dollar smile. He hated how serious he was. How *earnest*. He was everything the league wanted from their stars.

Ilya kissed his dumb mouth and swallowed his stupid little sighs and felt his annoying fingers in his hair. He pulled back so he could look at his horrible face with its ridiculous freckles.

Fuck.

Ilya kissed him again so he wouldn't have to think about him. He wanted to fuck him. God, would Hollander let him fuck him?

They kissed each other frantically, rolling and taking turns straddling each other and pulling off what was left of Hollander's clothes in the process. Ilya kissed his way down his body and took him into his mouth. Hollander's hips jerked off the bed, nearly forcing Ilya off him, but Ilya held on. He sucked him and enjoyed the desperate noises he pulled out of him.

He let his fingers trail down below Hollander's balls. He tapped one finger against his puckered opening and waited for a reaction. Hollander's body stilled on the bed, so Ilya drew light circles around his hole, just a casual suggestion.

He could feel Hollander tense up. He was completely

silent now. Ilya pulled his mouth off him and looked up at his face.

"Have you ever?" Ilya asked.

Hollander shook his head.

"Would you like to?"

"I don't know."

"You are scared."

"No! No, I'm not *scared*."

"Is okay to be."

Hollander exhaled loudly. "I'm *not* scared," he said again.

"Have you ever touched yourself," Ilya asked, circling his finger again, "here?"

Hollander's face flushed bright red, and Ilya grinned.

"Jesus Christ," Hollander muttered.

"You are embarrassed."

"Well!"

"You don't play with your ass? It makes you gay?"

"Oh my fucking god…"

"You know what makes you gayer?"

"Rozanov…shut the fuck—"

"Sucking my dick. You were doing that a minute ago."

Hollander sat up. "I've played with it, all right? I've—I've got a…thing."

"A thing?"

"A dildo! Okay?"

Ilya grinned so hard it hurt. "What color?"

"Fuck you!"

"Is it big?"

"I'm leaving."

Hollander moved to get off the bed. Ilya quickly covered him and pinned him back down. He held him down

by the wrists, and Hollander made a halfhearted attempt
to fight him off, but stopped when Ilya kissed him.

"I want to fuck you, Hollander," Ilya said against
his ear.

Hollander shuddered, and Ilya was sure he was going
to say yes, but instead, "I...no. I can't. Not here."

Ilya considered his answer, and nodded. Not here.
Not in a hotel surrounded by their fellow NHL players. By the media. By fans. Not now, when they would
both have to be as close to silent as possible when Ilya
entered him for the first time...

"Okay," Ilya said, nipping at his throat. "Next time,
then."

Hollander snorted, but he was smiling hopefully.
"Next time?"

Ilya shrugged one shoulder. "We play in Montreal
in two weeks."

"That doesn't mean we can... I mean, how *would*
we? *Where* would we?"

"Are you homeless?"

"No."

"Well then..."

"So, what? You're just gonna sneak out of your hotel?
What will you tell your teammates?"

"The fucking truth! I'm going to get laid! Like every
city we play in!"

Hollander's brow furrowed. "Oh."

"Yeah. Oh."

"So...after the game you just want me to wait at
home for you?" Hollander's voice was tight, like he was
angry about something.

Ilya rolled his eyes. He had no idea why they were

wasting time talking right now anyway. "Yes! Wait for me. I will come to your house and fuck you."

Hollander looked embarrassed again. "It's an apartment," he mumbled.

"Jesus! Fine! I will fuck you in your apartment. Can we get back to things now?"

"Yes." Hollander frowned. "But…"

"But?"

"In the shower. The water will drown out…anything."

Rozanov huffed, but it *was* actually a good idea.

"Yes," he said, springing off the bed and onto his feet, "but hurry the fuck up."

Hollander shoved him as he walked by, leading the way to the bathroom. He turned the water on, and as they waited for it to get hot, Ilya kissed him against the closed door until Hollander shoved him away so he could pull Ilya into the shower. He slammed Ilya against the tile and wrapped a hand around his cock as he kissed him. Ilya grinned against his mouth. This was the Shane Hollander he wanted: competitive, aggressive.

"Your hands are so soft," Ilya said. "Like a girl's."

"Fuck you."

Ilya laughed. Hollander jerked him harder, as if trying to prove how strong and masculine his hands were.

Ilya bit his own lip and gave up teasing his rival. For now. He reached for Hollander and they brought each other off frantically and roughly in the shower, letting the rush of water muffle their English and Russian profanity.

Hollander got dressed quickly when they were done. Ilya stood with a towel wrapped around his waist, waiting to hear what Hollander would say.

"Um…"

Ilya didn't say anything back. He waited.

"I know we said…about Montreal…but…"

Ilya crossed his arms and leaned against a wall.

"We probably shouldn't," Hollander finished.

"No?"

"No. I mean…obviously, right?"

Ilya watched Hollander run a nervous hand through his damp hair.

"It's stupid," Hollander said, more to himself than to Ilya. "This is stupid. I don't know why we did this. Again."

Ilya walked slowly toward him. When he reached him, he put a hand on the side of his face and tilted his head until he could look directly in his eyes. "Give me your phone."

"My phone?" Hollander asked weakly.

"Yes."

Hollander fumbled the phone out of his pocket and handed it to Ilya. Ilya took it and entered his number into Hollander's contacts, under the name Lily. Hollander snorted when he saw it.

"Who should I be?" he asked as he picked up Ilya's phone from the dresser. "Shannon?"

"Jane," Ilya said.

"Jesus Christ," Hollander muttered as he typed.

"No. Just Jane."

Hollander glared at him as he handed his phone back. "This isn't a yes, just so you know," he said.

"It will be."

Hollander shook his head, but Ilya could tell he was fighting a smile.

"Good luck tomorrow," Hollander said.

"Sure."

Hollander turned to open the door, but stopped. "Hey, um…you wanna take a look out there and see if the coast is clear?"

Ilya couldn't quite translate his words. "Sorry?"

"Just…take a look and see if the hall is empty. I don't want anyone to see me coming out of your room!"

Ilya opened the door enough to stick his head out. "Empty."

Hollander blew out a breath. "Okay. Well…bye."

"Good night."

Hollander nodded. And left.

Chapter Seven

February 2011—Montreal

Fifty minutes on the treadmill and Shane still couldn't get his brain to quiet down.

He had a very nice gym in his apartment, which was close to the Voyageurs' practice rink in Brossard. Some younger players shared apartments or houses with other young teammates, but Shane preferred to live alone. He had been under intense focus since he was sixteen, and it had made him cling to whatever private moments he could steal. Also, he walked a dangerous line with his teammates as it was; his…status…in the hockey world had a tendency to make his teammates understandably jealous. He was sure any tension would only be made worse if he lived with any of them.

Shane was supposed to be focusing on the game that night against Toronto as he pushed his body on the treadmill. Instead, he kept thinking back to a certain Russian's promise to come to Shane's *home* and…

There were too many things to process. Ilya Rozanov had gotten him off in a hotel room. *Again.* Ilya Rozanov wanted to sneak out of his team's hotel the next time they were in Montreal (next week!) and meet Shane at his *apartment* so he could *fuck* him.

Ilya Rozanov wanted to *fuck him*.

Shane was both terrified and undeniably aroused by the idea. Undeniably *extremely* aroused by the idea.

But that didn't change the fact that it was a really, *really* bad idea.

Shane had accepted the fact that he was more than okay with having sexual encounters with a man. Fine. He had suspected that about himself for a while now, and maybe Rozanov was just the first man to see that in him, to offer him the chance to experiment a little. So maybe what Shane actually needed to do was find *another* man to fool around with.

But who the fuck was *that* going to be?

This was *Montreal*. He was *Shane Hollander*. If his career went the way he was planning, that situation was only going to get more impossible. He definitely didn't want any rumors of his sexuality—whatever it was—getting out there. The NHL liked to pretend it was inclusive now, but Shane knew what it was like on the ice, and in the dressing room. There had never been an openly queer NHL player, and homophobic slurs were thrown around enough that Shane couldn't imagine that happening. Whoever came out first was going to have to be brave as hell. It sure as shit wasn't going to be Shane.

One thing he was certain of about Rozanov: he wasn't going to tell anyone. He had as much to lose as Shane did.

As far as Shane could figure, he had three choices: Forget about fucking men entirely and just stick to women; Risk finding men, or even just *a* man, who could be discreet and…patient; Let whatever the fuck was happening with Rozanov keep happening and try not to think too much about it.

Obviously the first option was the most sensible. Certainly the safest.

Also the most unappealing.

Fuck.

Shane slowed the treadmill to a cool-down speed and grabbed his water bottle.

Yeah. No. Okay. He definitely had to end this nonsense with Rozanov. He'd made it to the NHL and was at the beginning of what he hoped would be a very impressive career. A giant fucking scandal probably wasn't the best way to kick things off. And Shane couldn't see a way that they could possibly keep this thing quiet if it continued.

Why was he even *thinking* about that? A long-term secret relationship with Ilya Rozanov? Was that what some part of his dumb brain was hoping for?

No. Definitely putting a stop to this. This was just Shane being…nineteen. He was nineteen and horny and oddly lonely, for a star athlete. Just because Rozanov was making himself *available* didn't mean Shane had to accept.

Pleased with his decision, he stepped off the treadmill and headed to the chin-up bar. There would be nothing to it. Rozanov would text him to ask for his address, and Shane would write back *no*.

Next week—Montreal

Lily: I need your address.

Shane: No.

Shane smirked at his phone, very pleased with his prompt and clear reply to Rozanov's text.

Lily: Fuck off. What is it?

Shane: None of your business.

Lily: Fine. Your loss.

Shane stopped smirking. He sat down hard on his couch and turned on his brand-new lamp. The Bears would roll into town the day after tomorrow. They would play later that evening, and then...

Shane chewed his lip, thinking. It's not that he didn't want to...*see* Rozanov. If he was being honest, he'd been obsessively thinking about it since the All-Star weekend. He just didn't want his archrival coming to his home. That seemed like too big of a line to cross.

He wrote back. Could we meet somewhere else?

He felt a flush of embarrassment as he hit send. God, why couldn't he just have left it where it was? He'd successfully rejected Rozanov. Why give the power right back to him?

Lily: Like where?

Shane: I don't know!

Lily: Figure it out. Let me know.

Shane hated how relaxed Rozanov was about all of this. It wasn't fucking fair. He almost wrote back *For-*

get it, but instead just stood and slipped his phone into his pocket.

He would figure it out.

Shane: 1822.

Lily: ?

Shane: Room number.

Lily: OK…where is the room?

Shane: Same hotel you're in.

Lily: See you soon.

Shane sat on the end of his king-size hotel bed. Then he stood up. Then he sat back down again.

This was so fucking dumb. Why was he doing this? Booking a room in the same hotel as the entire Boston team (several floors above theirs, but still) so he could hook up with a man he *didn't even like*? If they were caught it could be devastating to both of their careers.

At the very least, it would be *very* embarrassing.

Shane stood and went to the mirror. He checked his teeth and nudged a stray lock of hair back into place.

There was a sharp rap on his door. He spun around, startled by how loud it sounded, and quickly crossed the room to open it. "Jesus. You trying to get *everyone's* attention?"

Rozanov slid into the room. His ball cap was pulled low over his eyes. Shane closed and latched the door quickly behind him.

"You are nervous," Rozanov said. It wasn't a question.

"No," Shane lied.

"Is just sex, Hollander," Rozanov said.

"I know."

Rozanov pulled the ball cap off and brown curls tumbled out, falling messily around his grinning face. He was wearing a charcoal-gray T-shirt with a small Nike logo on the chest and black track pants. Shane was wearing dark blue pants and a striped cashmere sweater and felt ridiculous.

"You look nice," Rozanov said. His tone was flat like he was just stating a fact rather than offering a compliment. *You look nice. It's cold outside. This hotel is big.*

"Thanks," Shane said, because he had to say *something.* "I feel overdressed."

"Yes. We both are," Rozanov said, and he pulled his T-shirt off over his head before bending to remove his high-top sneakers.

Shane's eyes fixed on the way Rozanov's gold cross dangled in the space between his knees and his chest; the thin chain glinted against the back of his neck.

When Rozanov stood again, Shane couldn't remember why exactly this was a bad idea.

"Come here," Rozanov said.

"No. *You* come *here.*"

Rozanov grinned and shook his head, and stepped toward Shane.

Shane must have taken a step forward himself because they kind of crashed into each other. A second later, he was against the wall, and Rozanov was attacking his mouth. Shane shoved back against him, and was reminded that Montreal had won the game that night. Rozanov had to be at least a little pissed off about that, and Shane felt he might be taking it out on him. Shane had no problem with that. He sank his fingers into Rozanov's biceps and hauled him closer. He wrapped his foot around Rozanov's ankle, and Rozanov growled and, without warning, grabbed Shane's thighs and hoisted him up the wall so that Shane had no choice but to wrap his legs around the taller man's waist.

Which Shane should have been angry about, but instead he gasped and kissed Rozanov even more wildly.

"Could fuck you just like this," Rozanov growled. "Against the fucking wall. You would like that, yes?"

Would Shane like that? Probably.

"Not tonight," Rozanov continued, moving his mouth close to Shane's ear. "Tonight I will go easy on you."

Shane wanted to tell him to fuck off, but Rozanov was kissing his throat, scraping his teeth over the sensitive skin, so instead he threw his head back against the wall like the eager slut he apparently was.

He felt Rozanov chuckle against his throat, and then Shane felt himself being pulled away from the wall and carried—*carried!*—to the bed like a fucking child!

"Put me down, asshole!"

"Shhhh."

"I can walk!"

Rozanov's big hands gripped his ass as they crossed the room. Shane pushed back off Rozanov's shoulders, and he could see that crooked smile and those playful eyes.

"Put me down."

Rozanov turned and dropped Shane on the bed. Shane glared up at him. He was about to tell him off, but he got distracted by the tall, bare-chested, muscular form looming over him. Shane suddenly felt very small on the bed, which was ridiculous—he was five feet, ten inches and built of solid muscle himself. But Rozanov was gazing down at Shane, who was still fully clothed, like he was trying to decide where to take his first bite, and Shane felt...vulnerable.

And he was kind of *into it*.

Rozanov slid his track pants down and off and stood at the end of the bed wearing only his black boxer briefs, his gold chain, and his stupid fucking bear tattoo. Shane's eyes went right to the briefs, and the hard length that was trapped beneath. He also noted the way Rozanov's enormous thighs burst out of the legs of the shorts, hard muscles jutting out from the straining fabric.

Rozanov leaned down and planted a knee firmly on the bed between Shane's sprawled legs, dangerously close to his crotch. Shane looked up, wide-eyed, as Rozanov descended on him and captured his mouth again. Two big hands landed on Shane's chest, stroking him over his sweater.

"This is soft," Rozanov murmured.

"It's cashmere," Shane said stupidly.

"Yes. Take it off."

He did. Rozanov pulled up and watched as Shane stripped down to his own briefs.

Shane lay there, waiting for Rozanov to cover him again, to press his weight down on him, but instead Rozanov lightly dragged his fingertips up one of Shane's legs, tickling his skin and making every hair stand up. He drew a path up to where Shane's skin disappeared into the leg of his briefs, and then paused. Shane felt like there was an electric current running through him. He could see his own cock twitching in his shorts, begging for attention. He bit his lip and waited.

Rozanov dipped his head and kissed Shane's stomach. He did it over and over again, his lips almost as gentle and teasing as his fingertips had been. Shane inhaled sharply. How was Rozanov so good at this?

Rozanov's mouth found one of Shane's nipples and bit it gently before licking it. Shane squirmed and Rozanov wrapped a hand most of the way around Shane's thigh to hold him down. Shane once again marveled at how big his hands were.

When Rozanov returned his mouth to Shane's, he *finally* moved his hand to palm Shane's erection through his briefs. Shane made an embarrassing noise into Rozanov's mouth.

"Did you bring everything?" Rozanov asked.

"Yes," Shane said. He was pretty sure he had everything. Lube and condoms, right?

"Good boy."

"Fuck you."

"Yes."

His hand slid inside Shane's shorts and pulled his erection out. Shane slipped a hand in between their bodies so he could rub his hand over the front of Rozanov's shorts.

Rozanov kissed him hard and ground his crotch against Shane's, holding himself up with one hand planted next to Shane's head.

Shane moaned at the feel of Rozanov's hips and pelvis rolling against him.

He's going to fuck me.

His whole body tensed up. Rozanov noticed.

"Relax," he breathed against Shane's ear. "You will like this."

"Yeah," Shane said, his voice strained. "Just…"

Rozanov pushed off him for a moment so he could quickly rid himself of his briefs. Shane did the same. When he returned his eyes to Rozanov, he was struck by how big his cock was. He'd seen it before, of course, and he knew it was a decent size, but looking at it now, with the idea that it was supposed to somehow fit *inside* of him…

He must have been wearing his anxiety all over his face. Rozanov laughed. "It will fit."

Shane blushed furiously, which made Rozanov laugh more.

"Trust me. Where is the stuff?"

Shane, grateful for something to do other than stare at Rozanov's cock in horror, reached over and opened the nightstand drawer. "I've got, um, lube. I ordered it online. It's supposed to be the best for…this."

"Ass fucking?"

Shane rolled his eyes. "You sweet talk all your sex partners like this?"

"I'm very charming." He took the bottle from Shane and inspected it.

"I have condoms too," Shane said. He pulled a strip of them out of the drawer.

Rozanov raised an eyebrow. "Are you sure that will be enough?"

"All right, look…"

Rozanov grinned that sexy goddamned lopsided grin and Shane laughed too. He watched as Rozanov poured a good amount of lube on his fingers, then wrapped those fingers around Shane's cock.

"Oof," Shane huffed. "It's cold! You coulda warmed it up a bit!"

"Shhh. Relax."

Shane had something smart to say back to him, but it dissolved on his tongue as Rozanov rubbed his thumb over Shane's slit.

They both watched as Rozanov teased the slit until

he drew out a bead of liquid. He smeared it over the head of Shane's cock, and Shane's fingers grabbed at the bedding.

With his other hand, Rozanov gently rolled and tugged at Shane's balls. He was so confident, but so careful. The combination was making Shane throb with need.

"Please," he whispered.

"Please what?" Rozanov asked with a raised eyebrow.

"I don't know," Shane answered honestly.

"Please touch you…here?" Rozanov asked, his fingers trailing below Shane's balls and over the smooth skin that led to…

"Yes," Shane said. He closed his eyes and let his head fall back on the pillow.

"Do you know how this works, Hollander?"

Not really. "Yeah. Sure." He opened one eye. "You've done this before?"

"Yes."

"With…the coach's son?"

Rozanov shrugged. "Sure. He was one."

"Oh."

"Girls too, Hollander. You have not done this with a girl?"

Shane had never really wanted to do anything with a girl that was complicated. Or that would…make things take longer.

"No," he said.

Rozanov stilled both of his hands. "You have had sex before, yes?" he asked.

"Yes! God!"

"Okay." Rozanov went back to stroking Shane's cock and dancing his fingers closer to Shane's opening.

"You really think I haven't?" Shane was outraged.

Rozanov shrugged.

"I've had plenty of sex, Rozanov. Lots."

"Fine."

Shane didn't like how amused Rozanov looked.

But he *did* like it when Rozanov poured more lube over his fingers and began to stroke them over Shane's hole. He sucked in a breath and his whole body shuddered.

"Just relax, Mr. Lots-of-Sex," Rozanov said. "I will make sure you are ready for me."

Shane wanted to scowl at him, but in truth he was sort of charmed by the level of care Rozanov was showing. Still, Shane was at least thirty-five percent terrified.

Rozanov kept gently brushing his fingers over Shane's hole, while at the same time lazily stroking Shane's cock. Together, it all felt wonderful. Shane felt his body release a lot of the tension he had been holding, and he floated a bit on the good feelings that were coursing through him. It was so good, he could almost forget to be embarrassed about where Rozanov was touching him.

"Good?" Rozanov asked.

"Mmm…" Shane sighed.

And then he felt the tip of Rozanov's finger enter him, and he clenched in response.

"Sorry." Shane winced, then took a breath.

He *did* know how this worked. He *had* done a little… experimenting. On himself. With the aforementioned dildo. But those times had been him alone. In private. This was…

"Is okay," Rozanov said in a low, soothing rumble. "We will go slow, yes?"

"Thank you," Shane mumbled.

The other thing about the private dildo sessions was that Shane had been kind of…bad at it. At least, he had been pretty sure he had been doing something wrong. It hadn't felt *bad*, necessarily. But it hadn't been mind-blowing either.

Rozanov dipped his head and took Shane's cock into his mouth. Shane felt himself relax; each stroke of Rozanov's tongue making him forget to be nervous. He took slow, even breaths as Rozanov worked his finger in a little deeper and then…

Oh.

Shane arched and gasped. "Holy shit!"

Rozanov pulled his mouth off him and smirked. "Good, yes?"

He rubbed his fingertip again over what had to be Shane's prostate. Shane had kind of nudged it himself before, when he had been alone, but Rozanov seemed to know exactly where it was and what to do with it.

Shane squeezed his eyes shut and bit his lip. If he didn't, he was going to do something embarrassing, like whimper. The combination of Rozanov's mouth on his cock and his finger inside of him was like nothing he had ever felt before. And there was no way he was going to last long enough for Rozanov to fuck him if this continued.

"You gotta…fuck. Just…wait a minute," Shane rasped out.

Rozanov stopped immediately. "Okay?" he asked.

"Yeah. Yeah…very okay. *Too* okay."

"Ah."

Rozanov used the break time as an opportunity to give his own erection a few lazy strokes. Shane watched him, and noticed again how absurdly large Rozanov's dick looked.

"We do not have to," Rozanov said, noticing Shane's face.

"I want to," Shane said quickly. Too quickly.

Rozanov nodded, and reached for the lube and the condoms. He got himself ready, and then returned his attention to Shane. Shane felt two fingers press against his opening before they slipped inside. There was less burning this time.

"Stroke yourself," Rozanov instructed.

Shane nodded and obeyed.

Rozanov let out a low noise that sounded like a growl. "Turn over," he said.

Shane got on his hands and knees, because that's how this worked, right? He was pretty sure. He had watched about forty seconds of gay porn, once, before he'd gotten embarrassed and closed his laptop. Now he wished he had endured a little longer, if only for re-search purposes.

He felt Rozanov's hands grab his thighs, and he was hauled back until his knees were at the end of the bed. Rozanov put one foot on the mattress, next to Shane's knee, and placed a hand firmly on Shane's hip.

And then Shane could feel it; the much-too-large blunt head of Rozanov's cock bumping against his hole. He clenched his eyes shut, and braced himself for pain.

When Rozanov pressed in, it was slow and careful, but Shane's whole body trembled anyway. The pain was there, but not as sharp as Shane had been expecting. The pressure was the most overwhelming sensation. He felt impossibly full, and couldn't imagine how Ro-zanov was supposed to move once he was all the way in. Shane was struck with the sudden, horrific thought that Rozanov would become *stuck* inside him. Oh Jesus, they would have to call 911 or something!

Shane forced himself to take a breath and pushed images of doctors trying to separate them while all of Rozanov's teammates watched out of his mind.

"Okay?" Rozanov asked again. He ran a hand over Shane's back, slow and soothing.

"Yeah," Shane said. His voice sounded strained.

Rozanov pulled out a little then pushed back in, even deeper this time.

"Fuck," Shane gasped. "Wow."

Encouraged, Rozanov repeated the motion. And again.

Then Rozanov adjusted his hips a little and, on the next thrust, hit Shane's prostate, sending a jolt of pleasure through him.

"God. Yes! Fuck. Keep doing that."

"I will. Don't fucking worry."

Shane wasn't feeling any pain now, and he wasn't scared. He started to push back against Rozanov when he thrust into him, which Rozanov seemed to take as an invitation to go harder. His thrusts became faster, causing the bed to shake and Shane's arms to tremble as he struggled to hold himself up. It was more than Shane had thought he'd be able to take, but he wanted it. He loved it.

Rozanov's fingers were digging hard enough into Shane's hips to leave marks. He was hauling Shane back against him as he pounded into him. Shane lifted a hand up to his own mouth so he could bite his knuckles to keep from screaming out.

This, he realized, was why people were so wild about sex. He had never, ever felt like this with anyone before.

And of course Ilya Rozanov, all of nineteen years old, fucked with the confidence and skill of, like, a sex god.

Shane chanced taking his hand out of his mouth so he could wrap it around his dick. He wished he had put a towel down or something—he was going to come all over this hotel bedding. He knew he was going to feel bad about that, but not enough to do anything about it now.

"Yeah. Come on, Hollander," Rozanov growled. Rozanov, who did not care at all about the poor hotel maids.

"Fuck," Shane gritted out. And he came so hard that most of it shot up and hit him in the chest. He was so dazed by his own orgasm that he almost didn't register when Rozanov tensed and stilled behind him. Rozanov grunted and came *inside of Shane's body.* Into a condom, but still. Shane's body had made that happen, and he couldn't quite wrap his brain around that fact.

Then, to Shane's dismay, Rozanov collapsed on top of him, crushing Shane and the mess all over his chest into the mostly clean bedding.

"Now the bed's all dirty," Shane complained before he could stop himself.

"What?" Rozanov said sleepily. "Shut up."

Shane closed his eyes and enjoyed the weight of Rozanov on top of him.

Eventually, Rozanov rolled off and went to the bathroom to clean up. Shane shifted carefully to his back, already feeling the pain that was going to make it hard to sit down tomorrow.

With Rozanov safely out of the room, Shane grinned stupidly at the ceiling. He was maybe happier than he should be that his most successful sexual experience to date was with Ilya Rozanov.

The smile faded as he wondered how in hell he was

ever going to experience this again. Because he couldn't keep letting Rozanov fuck him. Obviously. And he wasn't sure how to safely find other men to do it.

"Hit the showers, Hollander," Rozanov said as he left the bathroom. "I will get dressed and leave."

"Oh," Shane said. Of *course* he was going to leave. What the fuck had Shane been expecting? He stood up. "Yeah. Okay. Well…"

Rozanov put one hand on Shane's shoulder in a fairly condescending way. His lips were twitched up in an irritating little smile. "Was fun," he said.

"Yeah, um. Thanks, I guess."

Rozanov nodded, then turned to pick up his scattered clothing. Shane went to the bathroom, closing the door behind him.

When Shane left the bathroom, freshly showered and wearing a towel, Rozanov was gone. There was no trace of the man, other than the messed up bedsheets. Shane grimaced at them, then pulled off the top sheet and dropped it on the floor. He imagined that hotel maids probably dealt with worse shit than this all the time.

He'd leave a big tip.

He dropped the damp towel beside the soiled bedding and got himself dressed. He wasn't going to spend the night here. He made sure he had removed everything he had brought into the room, then dropped a fifty-dollar bill on the dresser for the maid and left to go back to his apartment. Alone.

Chapter Eight

It couldn't have been a closer race.

It was the night of the NHL Awards in Las Vegas, and all anyone had been talking about leading into it was who would win the Rookie of the Year award. Both Shane Hollander and Ilya Rozanov had scored over fifty goals. In fact, they had each scored exactly sixty-seven goals. Both men had helped their teams reach the play-offs for the first time in years, though both had been eliminated in the first round. The two men had been the most talked-about players in the league all season, sparking fierce debate among fans and the press about which of them was the better player.

Shane knew that it was impossible to definitively answer that question, but being named Rookie of the Year would certainly feel good.

Rozanov brought something out in him. Shane wasn't the type of guy who needed to be the best player on the team—he just always *was*. And maybe that was it. Maybe Shane had been a little bit bored before Ilya Rozanov came along.

Rozanov was a lot of things, but he wasn't boring. He

frustrated Shane on the ice, and flustered him off the ice. Shane wanted to crosscheck him in the mouth, and then kiss it better. He wanted to forget about him, and he wanted to play every game against him. He wanted…

He wanted to win this fucking Rookie of the Year award.

He wanted to rub it in Rozanov's face.

He wanted to rub himself *on* Rozanov's face.

The Canadian rock band on stage finally finished their song and a B-list celebrity walked out on stage, holding an envelope.

This was it.

Shane's mother put her hand on his arm. She was as nervous as he was. Maybe more.

Shane gave her a weak smile, and waited.

The reception afterward was as raucous as anyone would expect a Vegas hotel banquet hall packed with professional hockey players to be. Most of the guys were pretty drunk, but Shane couldn't have gotten drunk even if he *had* been legally old enough to order a drink in Nevada because he was faced with an unending parade of people slapping him on the back and congratulating him. Some even tousled his hair.

The only person Shane hadn't seen that night was Ilya Rozanov.

Secretly, Shane had been searching for him all night. Half the times he'd been talking to someone, he'd been looking over their shoulder. He never caught even a glimpse of golden-brown curls, which should have been easy to spot, given Rozanov's height.

He wondered if Rozanov had just gone back to his room.

The thought made Shane angry. What a fucking

baby. If Rozanov had won, Shane would be here, in this room, ready to congratulate him. If Rozanov wanted to spend his first NHL Awards sulking in his hotel room, that wasn't Shane's problem.

Or maybe he just wanted to stealthily get drunk in his hotel room, and then come to the party. Rozanov wasn't old enough to order a drink here either.

"You seen Roz anywhere?" someone asked him suddenly.

Shane flinched. He felt like his mind had been read.

"No!" he said, way too quickly. And with more blushing than was necessary. He took a breath. "Why would I know where Rozanov is?"

The guy—a forward for Toronto—shrugged. "Thought you guys might be at the kiddie table together or something."

"No," Shane said. "I haven't seen him. At all."

"Okay, well. Congratulations, kid." He squeezed Shane's shoulder and walked past him.

It was hot in the room. Too many people. Quite a few of the guys had removed their jackets and ties. It was getting harder to tolerate the atmosphere of the place without the help of alcohol.

Shane scanned the room for his parents. He spotted his father slumped in a chair, drinking what Shane was sure was a Sprite. Shane's mother seemed to be talking a star goaltender's ear off.

"I'm just gonna step out for some air," Shane told his father. "Just for a minute. I'll be back."

"Sure," Dad said. He looked exhausted. "I'm going to try to convince your mother it's bedtime in a minute anyway."

"Good luck." Shane smiled.

As soon as he left the room, Shane felt the relief of the

air-conditioning that flowed, unencumbered, through the mostly empty hallway. He leaned against the wall for a minute and exhaled.

He wondered what room Rozanov was in.

No, he thought. *He's a fucking baby and he doesn't deserve...anything.*

Was Rozanov really that upset, though? He was normally so cool and collected. If anything, Shane would have expected him to show up at the party just to show everyone how unbothered he was about losing.

He knew where Rozanov couldn't be right now: the casinos. The bars. He could be in his room. Or...someone else's room. Or in his own room with someone else.

Shane frowned. He pulled his phone from the pocket of his tuxedo jacket so he could check the time. Almost two in the morning. Not that time meant anything in Las Vegas.

Shane had never been to Las Vegas before. He had just flown in the night before, and hadn't really done any sightseeing yet. He probably wouldn't get a chance, because he was flying out tomorrow afternoon. He had been told, when he had checked in, that the hotel offered a spectacular rooftop view of the city. Feeling restless, and not wanting to rejoin the party, he decided he may as well check it out.

He took the elevator to the top. There was a trio of loud, drunk girls in the elevator with him. He pressed himself into the back corner and fixed his eyes on the glowing floor numbers as the elevator ascended.

"Oh my god! Is it your wedding day?" one of the girls asked him suddenly.

"Pardon?"

"The tuxedo," she said. "Did you get married today?"

"Oh. No."

"He doesn't have a *ring*," one of her friends hissed.

They all erupted into giggles.

Shane turned his eyes back to the numbers above the doors. They weren't moving fast enough.

"Are you going to Strat-speeeer?" the first girl asked.

"To where?"

"Strat-o-sphere," she said again, more slowly.

"Um."

"Stratosphere," one of her friends explained. "The bar on the roof."

"There's a bar on the roof?"

They all laughed again. "You are so cute," the friend said. They nodded and giggled some more. "Come to the bar with us!"

"I can't. Sorry." Jesus, this was a long elevator ride.

By the time they finally reached the top, the girls had forgotten about him. They stumbled out of the elevator and turned right, presumably in the direction of the rooftop bar. Shane turned left.

There was a lot of noise coming from the bar. Pulsing music and loud, drunken voices. On the other side of the roof, there was a quiet corner that looked out over the city. It was a place that Shane guessed was normally used for weddings. It was empty now.

Almost empty.

Shane didn't see him, at first. All black in his tuxedo, with his head bent down over the railing, Rozanov blended right into the darkness. Then he raised his head and let out a white cloud of smoke.

"It's not worth jumping over," Shane said, moving to stand just behind him.

Rozanov turned. He didn't even seem surprised to see

Shane. He took another long drag of his cigarette then said in a tight voice, "Is the party over, then?"

"No. I just needed some air."

Rozanov exhaled. The smoke swirled around his face and then floated up into the desert sky. "Such an exciting night for you."

"I guess."

Rozanov rolled his eyes. *I guess.*

"It could have gone to either one of us."

"It went to you."

"Yeah, well, you know. Who knows how they decide these things?" Shane wasn't sure why he was even saying this stuff. He didn't need to apologize for anything. He'd earned that fucking trophy. "So you're just sulking up here all night, then? It bothers you that much that I won?"

Rozanov took another drag and turned back to the view. He said something that Shane couldn't hear.

"What was that?" Shane asked, moving to stand beside him against the rail.

"Not everything is about you, Hollander." He didn't look at Shane at all when he said it. His voice hadn't been angry. He just sounded…tired. And sad.

Shane studied his profile. His own anger left him, and he found himself *caring* about Ilya Rozanov, which was an odd sensation. "So what is it then?"

Rozanov dropped the butt of his cigarette on the ground and stamped it out. He laughed a little, without any humor at all. "What do you want, Hollander?"

"Nothing. I just wanted some air. To see the view."

"Well," Rozanov said, sweeping a hand through the air in front of them, "here is view."

Shane's eyes turned toward the blanket of city lights

that sprawled beneath them, but they quickly found their way back to Rozanov's face. He saw the clench in Rozanov's jaw, and the hardness of his eyes.

"I go back to Russia. In three days."

"Oh."

They were both silent for a long time. Shane wasn't sure if Rozanov had more to tell him or not. He decided not to push. It wasn't like they were friends.

"I should get back," Shane said, after several minutes of gazing down at the city. "My parents might still be at the party."

"Your parents," Rozanov said. "Right."

"I guess... I guess I'll see you next season."

Shane stuck out his hand. Rozanov looked at it. Then he turned his head left and right, looking all around them.

A split second later, Shane found himself pushed back from the railing, against a wall. Rozanov's mouth was pressed hard against his, and his hands gripped his arms roughly, fingers digging into his biceps.

Shane felt panicked. This was super fucking dangerous. And stupid. And confusing. And...

Shane kissed him back, just as angrily. Because fuck this guy for doing shit like this. Hiding away all night on a fucking rooftop, smoking a goddamned cigarette in the dark like the worst cliché of a brooding heartthrob. Making Shane feel bad for winning an award that he completely fucking deserved. And then, on a whim, pressing Shane against a wall and kissing him like he would die without Shane's mouth on his. Kissing him until Shane's senses were full of hard muscle pressed against him and the taste of cigarette and the slick heat of Rozanov's tongue in his mouth.

What the fuck.

Shane grabbed Rozanov's lapels and shoved him back. They couldn't do this here. At all.

Shane looked frantically around them. There was no one. But, Jesus, there *could have been*.

Rozanov leaned in to kiss Shane again, and Shane dodged him.

"No," he said. "No way. Not here. What's *wrong* with you?"

Rozanov gave him that crooked grin that did absurd things to Shane's stomach.

"We can't," Shane said. He meant it, but it hurt to say. "I have to go. You should go to bed, Rozanov."

The smile disappeared.

"See you next season," Rozanov said. Then he turned and walked toward the elevators.

Shane waited a few minutes so they wouldn't have to ride down together.

Next season. Next season would be different. He was going to end this stupid thing between them and focus on his game.

Part Two

Chapter Nine

December 2013—36,000 feet over Pennsylvania

Tap. Tap. Tap. Tap.

Ilya could hear Ryan Price's foot drumming against the floor, even with an empty seat between them. Even though Ilya was wearing headphones, and watching a very loud *Fast and Furious* movie.

Ilya glanced over. Price's knee was bouncing, jostling the paperback novel he was balancing, open and upside down, on his thigh. Price was gripping both armrests and his eyes were closed. He looked bad.

And he was definitely going to drop that book on the floor. And then he would lose his place.

Ilya sighed, hit pause on the movie, and removed his headphones. He didn't know Price very well. No one did; he had only joined the team at the start of this season. He was a gigantic defenseman, but his real position on the ice was enforcer. His job was to make sure no one interfered with the more talented players. Ilya could take care of himself, but playing with guys like Price meant he didn't have to.

Ilya talked shit on the ice, got under other guys' skin,

and then Ryan Price had to take their punches. Pretty sweet deal for Ilya.

"Price," he said. "Your book."

No response.

"Price," Ilya said again. Still nothing, so Ilya reached out and poked his arm. "You okay?"

Price's eyes flew open and he jumped a little, causing his book to tumble to the floor. Ilya watched it fall in dismay. He had failed.

"Sorry," Price said. "Was I tapping my foot?"

"Yes."

"Sorry," Price said again. "Just, um, nervous flier. Sometimes."

"Ah." Ilya bent and retrieved the book. He glanced at the cover before handing it back. *Anne of Green Gables.* Wasn't that a children's book for girls or something? "You lost your place."

Price gave a thin smile. "It's okay. I've read it before. It's kind of just… I bring it on planes as kind of a comfort thing."

Ilya could not figure this guy out. He was even taller than Ilya, and much bulkier, with shoulder-length red hair and a beard that made him look like a biker gang member. He could knock a guy out with one punch. Some of the toughest opponents in the league were scared to face Price in a fight.

"Is it the red hair?" Ilya asked. He didn't understand Price, but he could at least try to help him calm down. *"Anne of Green Gables?"*

Price stared at him like he had no idea what he was talking about, and then he laughed. It was quiet and uneasy, but it was still a laugh. "Yeah, maybe."

This was, Ilya was pretty sure, Price's fourth NHL

season, but he had played for three different teams already. He was quiet in the dressing room, scary on the ice, and clearly a nervous wreck on planes, so Ilya imagined he didn't make friends easily.

"Are you like this every flight?" Ilya asked. He couldn't imagine what that would be like. Price was definitely in the wrong line of work if he hated flying.

Price shook his head. "Not every flight. I mean, yes, I'm always nervous, but not always this bad." His cheeks flushed, as if he hadn't meant to even admit that he was more terrified than usual. They were en route to Montreal from Raleigh, North Carolina, which wasn't a particularly long flight, but it had been a turbulent takeoff. Maybe that had been the difference. Ilya didn't really want to talk about it, and he figured Price didn't want to either.

So he gestured toward his iPad. "*Fast Five*. Have you seen it?"

"Yeah. I think so. Is that the one with the bank safe chase scene?"

"Yes. Is the best one." Ilya flipped down the table for the unoccupied seat between them, and moved his iPad onto it. He only had the one set of headphones, but he always had subtitles on. It helped to improve his English.

He handed Price the headphones, figuring he could use a fully immersive distraction.

"Oh, uh…" Price ran a hand through his bushy hair.

"Is okay. I will tell you if pilot says we are crashing."

The joke was a risk, but it paid off. Price snorted and took the headphones. "Thanks."

They watched the movie, Price listening and Ilya reading, and Price's leg remained still for the rest of the flight. He even asked the flight attendant for a Coke, which had to be a good sign.

When Ilya got tired of reading movie dialogue, he stared out the window into blackness. He had, in truth, been trying to distract *himself* with the movie, because heading to Montreal always put him on edge. It wasn't nerves, it was…something else. Anticipation, maybe. He didn't want to say excitement.

They would play tomorrow night, their second matchup of the season. Montreal had been in Boston for their season opener in October. Boston had won in overtime, and Hollander had been in a terrible mood when he'd shown up at the room Ilya had booked in the hotel down the street from where Montreal was staying.

Ilya liked it when Hollander was angry. He liked it when Hollander took out his frustrations on Ilya's body. He liked him cursing him as he fucked Ilya's mouth.

These were the kinds of thoughts that Ilya had been trying to distract himself from with the *Fast and the Furious* movie. Because thinking about this fucked-up thing with Hollander made him feel pretty disgusted with himself. It also made him uncomfortably aroused, which only made him feel *more* disgusted with himself.

Yeah. Super fucking healthy.

"Roz, you awake?"

Ilya glanced up so see Cliff Marlow's face peeking over the seat in front of him. Cliff was a year younger than him, a bit of an idiot, and probably Ilya's best friend.

"No," Ilya deadpanned.

"I've been talking to this chick in Montreal. We've been sending each other messages on Instagram for a couple of weeks. She's hot as fuck. Check it out." He thrust his phone into Ilya's face. There was, indeed, a hot woman on the screen.

"Good job," Ilya said.

"So she wants to meet up after the game tomorrow night. She's hot for hockey players, and she said she could bring her friend. You want in?"

Oh, no thanks. I will be busy fucking Shane Hollander in a hotel room.

"We have a curfew tomorrow night. Early flight the next morning, yes?" Ilya reminded him.

"Yeah, I know, but…" Cliff looked wistfully at his phone. "I gotta see her. Maybe I can just…no. You know what, Ilya? I'm gonna be completely honest here: I'm probably going to break curfew. It's not like I'll miss the bus to the airport."

"I am assistant captain, shithead. Do not tell me about your plan to break curfew."

"I thought that 'A' was for asshole."

"Funny."

"So, no to going out with me tomorrow night?"

"No. But have fun."

"I remember when you used to be fun, Roz."

"I *am* fucking fun." *Gonna have a solid hour of fun before I'm back in time for curfew.*

Cliff nodded at Price, who was watching the movie intently and didn't seem to notice him at all. Cliff's face was a question mark, and Ilya had no idea what the question was. So Cliff, being an asshole, held a hand to the side of his face to block it from Price's view, and mouthed *Weird guy, right?*

Ilya shrugged. Maybe Ryan Price was weird, or maybe he just wasn't exactly what people were expecting him to be. Ilya was certainly in no position to fault someone for that.

The following evening—Montreal

"I'm telling you right now," J.J. said, "if fucking Rozanov starts shit with you tonight, I'm taking him out."

Shane pulled his shoulder pads over his head and began securing them in place. "If you go for Rozanov, Ryan Price is gonna go after *you*."

"Fuck Price. I'll send that dumb motherfucker crying back to wherever the fuck he's from."

"Nova Scotia, I think."

"I'm just saying—" J.J. pointed his shin guard at Shane, for emphasis "—Rozanov gives you trouble, I'm ending him. Price or no Price."

Shane politely ignored the fear that J.J. was trying not to show. J.J. was one of the biggest players in the league and could handle himself in a fight, but Ryan Price was a fucking terror.

Price was just one of the things that made these games against Boston extra tense. Montreal was a city that buzzed with excitement about their hockey team all winter—you could *feel* the electricity in the air every home game day. And whenever Boston was in town, Shane felt like the city was pulled as tight as he was. Every cell in his body sparked with the need to get on the ice and face Rozanov. And when the games were over, he pulsed with a different kind of need.

A loud bark of laughter interrupted Shane's thoughts. Hayden thrust his phone in his face. "Hey, look at what the fans are doing outside."

It was a video, posted to Twitter, of a group of people outside the arena burning what appeared to be an effigy of Ilya Rozanov.

"Well, that's a bit much," Shane said.

J.J. grabbed the phone. "Ha! This is happening now?"

"A few minutes ago," Hayden said.

"Beautiful. Love it."

Hayden took his phone back and studied the screen. "They didn't make the dummy ugly enough."

Sure, Hayden. "They've probably burned effigies of me in Boston," Shane said.

"Oh yeah! They totally have. Here, let me go to You-Tube..."

"Yeah, no. I actually am trying to focus on winning a hockey game right now. No YouTube, please."

The team's PR manager, Marcel, came into the dressing room, and Shane sighed.

"Shane," Marcel said. "NBC wants to talk to you. You good?"

"Sure. I'll be out in a sec."

The broadcasters always wanted to talk to Shane before the games, especially before games against Boston. He tried to think of a new and exciting way of answering the question, "What does Montreal have to do to win tonight?" as he made his way to the hallway outside the dressing room.

"Last question, Shane: What does Montreal have to do to win tonight?"

Shane put on his best "thinking" face, to give the impression that he certainly hadn't expected this question. "Get the puck to the net, take shots, stay out of the penalty box..." *Score more goals than the other team before the game ends.* "We're in good shape tonight, everyone is healthy, so I think we're definitely going to make it tough for Boston."

"Thank you, Shane, and good luck tonight."

"Thanks, Chris."

Shane tried not to begrudge these interviews. Whenever he had to do one, which was often, he would think of the kids who were watching. He used to love seeing his favorite stars interviewed on television before and after the games.

Back in the dressing room, he picked up his phone to send a quick text to his parents. He messaged them before every game.

He saw that he had a message waiting for him, and it wasn't from his parents.

Lily: How many times can you come in one hour?

What. The. Fuck.

This was dirty fucking pool, even for Rozanov. They didn't text each other *before* the games. Especially not about shit like that.

He definitely wasn't going to write back. And he definitely wasn't getting hard in his jock strap.

Fuck. He *was* hard. And now he was writing back.

Ilya nearly choked when he saw Hollander's reply.

Jane: I dunno. Twice, maybe?

So fucking pure! So honest and sweet.

Ilya: You are very bad at sexting.

Jane: Who taught you that word?

Ilya: Your mom.

Okay, that was pretty stupid. But Hollander loved his mom and that probably *would* bother him.

Jane: Stop. I'll text you after the game.

A few seconds went by.

Jane: If you're lucky.

Ilya snorted. Hollander was probably so proud of himself for that dig.

Ilya: Are you hard right now?

No answer. Ah well. Ilya knew he was crossing a line with these texts, but it was just so damn fun to tease Hollander. He could just picture him now, in the Montreal dressing room, blushing as he shoved his phone into a bag or something so no one would see it.

He hoped Hollander was still mad about it later, when they met in a hotel room.

Ilya frowned at the abandoned-looking three-story building the cabdriver had delivered him to. He checked the address again, and confirmed that it was the same as what Hollander had texted him. *The fuck?*

Hollander's only instruction had been for Ilya to go around the back of the building, text him, and wait at the door. So Ilya did that, trying not to think about being murdered in a dark empty lot behind a creepy building.

If he believed Hollander had a diabolical bone in his body, Ilya would suspect he was about to be pranked.

The back door opened a minute after Ilya sent the text, and all it revealed was Hollander, who glanced nervously around as if he was expecting a S.W.A.T. team to descend on them.

"Get in here," he said. Ilya stepped past him, into a dimly lit stairwell, and Hollander locked the door behind them.

"What is this place?" Ilya asked.

Instead of answering, Hollander pushed him hard with both hands. "Fuck you for texting me before the game, you asshole!"

Ilya grinned. "You *were* hard, weren't you? For how long? The whole game?"

Hollander glared at him, then said, "Follow me."

He led them up way too many stairs, to the top floor, and then used a key to unlock another door. It opened to reveal a large loft apartment, only partially finished, from the looks of it. The walls looked like they had been freshly plastered, and hadn't been painted yet. There was a ladder leaning against one wall, and an open box of tools beside it. The kitchen area had a brand-new countertop and cupboards, but no appliances.

"Is this your place?" Ilya had never been to Hollander's home. It had always been hotel rooms before. The idea excited him.

"No. I mean, I don't live here. But, yes, I own it."

"You will move here?"

"No. It's just an investment, or whatever. And I thought it could be a safe place to…meet."

Hollander was damn cute when he was embarrassed.

"Did you buy a building so we would have somewhere to fuck, Hollander?"

Ilya assumed he was trying to look stern, but the flush of his cheeks was ruining the effect. "*No*. It's an *investment*. I'm having it renovated and then I'll sell the condos. And I already have a tenant lined up for the commercial space on the main floor."

"Wow. Businessman."

Hollander folded his arms. It did not make him look any more intimidating. "Enough questions. We're not here to talk."

"Yes. Where do you want me? On that ladder? On the pile of wood over there?"

"In here, idiot."

Hollander crossed the room and opened yet another door. This one led to…

…a fully finished bedroom. Like, a really nice one.

"I, uh, I kinda made the bedroom the priority. And the bathroom. So we could—"

But Ilya didn't let Hollander finish his sentence. He gripped Hollander's arms and pushed him back against the closest wall and kissed him. Hollander had bought them a fucking *building*.

Ilya had been sure, all summer, that this would be the year Hollander would call it off. But he had thought the same thing last summer too, after their rookie seasons had ended with Hollander shoving Ilya away after they'd kissed on a Las Vegas rooftop. But when their teams had met for the first time that second season, Ilya had texted him a hotel room number and Hollander showed up twenty minutes later.

"You were smoking," Hollander complained now, as he broke away from their kiss.

"Only one."

"You aren't supposed to be smoking."

"You aren't supposed to be talking." Ilya pushed Hol-

lander's chest and knocked him flat onto his back on
the bed. Ilya took a moment to gaze down at him—at
his flushed cheeks and mussed hair, and at the strip of
exposed skin where his T-shirt had ridden up. Then
Ilya pounced.

They kissed in their usual combative style for a
while—Hollander rolling them to pin Ilya down and
attack his mouth, before Ilya would flip them and re-
gain control. Shirts came off, then pants, then socks and
underwear.

"An hour," Ilya murmured. He was on top now, biting and licking his way along Hollander's collarbone.
"Then I have to go."

"Then hurry the fuck up."

Ilya smiled against Hollander's skin. He was such a
little brat. Ilya raised himself up and straddled Shane's
waist, making sure to squeeze just a little too hard with
his thighs. He took his own dick in his hand and stroked
it slowly, thoughtfully. "You want this, Hollander?"

And, oh god, Ilya could *see* the war going on in Hollander's head. He could see how much he wanted to tell
Ilya to fuck off and die, but more than that, he could
see the way Hollander's tongue poked out to moisten
his lower lip.

"Starving for it, yes, Hollander?" Ilya slid forward,
positioning his body closer to Hollander's face. To his
mouth. Hollander's chest was heaving beneath him, and
he glared up at Ilya with dark, intense eyes. "Is okay,"
Ilya said soothingly. He tapped the head of his cock
against Hollander's lips. "You can. Take it."

"I hate you."

"Yes. I know. Show me."

"Fuck," Hollander whispered, seemingly to him-

self. Then he parted his lips, and licked the moisture off Ilya's slit.

Ilya's hand shot out and gripped the headboard. It seemed like a nice headboard, sturdy. He expected he'd find out exactly how sturdy soon enough.

Hollander teased the head of Ilya's dick for a maddeningly long time, but, damn, what a show. Ilya watched Hollander's eyes flutter closed as he sucked the head into his mouth. His tongue rolled around it, flicking the underside of Ilya's dick and then dipping into the slit. It was so fucking good, and not nearly enough.

Hollander growled, seemingly as frustrated with the angle as Ilya was, and pushed him down to the mattress before taking Ilya's cock into his mouth again. This time Hollander made a meal of Ilya's dick, his head bobbing in a quick rhythm that Ilya was *not* going to be able to endure for very long. Not if he also wanted to fuck Hollander in their allotted hour of time.

But Hollander wasn't letting up. He tugged at Ilya's balls with just the right amount of pressure, and Ilya could feel Hollander's erection sliding along his thigh.

"Hollander…" he warned. He was flying way too high, too fast.

Hollander moaned, or maybe he'd tried to form a word around Ilya's dick, but all it did was cause vibrations that Ilya really *didn't* need right now.

"Fuck. *Fuck.* You have to stop. If you want me to fuck you…"

Hollander ripped his mouth away from Ilya's cock, but then he went very still. "Shit. Oh god. Fuck."

Ilya felt wetness splash against his thigh. Hollander's body jerked a couple of times, and then he buried his face in Ilya's shoulder. *"Fuck."*

"Hollander?"

"I'm sorry," he groaned. "I can't believe I just…you didn't even *touch* me!"

And Ilya just…laughed. Because it was fucking funny.

"Don't fucking laugh at me."

"Been a while?" Ilya teased.

Hollander kept his forehead planted on Ilya's shoulder, hiding his face completely. "Shut up."

But Ilya laughed harder. He laughed until Hollander joined in, and then they were both holding each other and laughing until they were wiping tears from their eyes.

"You could win the fastest shot competition."

Hollander punched him lightly in the chest. Ilya rolled to his side, dumping Hollander on the mattress beside him. "Is too bad. I wanted to fuck you. Do you still want?"

"I don't think I can. I think I'm too fucking embarrassed to get it up again."

"Is that a challenge?"

"No. But can I…finish what I was doing?"

Ilya flopped onto his back again and folded his arms behind his head. "Go for it."

And Hollander did, but this time he was far less frantic and took his time. Ilya enjoyed every second of it.

Ilya would be lying if he said Hollander had the most talented mouth that had ever been wrapped around his dick. But he was so…eager to please. So determined to be good at this. For Ilya.

There was something very sweet about the way Hollander was sucking him off right now—like he wasn't trying to just get it over with, even though Hollander had already had his own orgasm. He seemed to legitimately enjoy making Ilya feel good.

Ilya always did feel good with Hollander. He didn't want to say it was better than it was with anyone else, but it was…different. And not only because Hollander was a man. Ilya hadn't been with a man who wasn't Hollander in…huh. Over a year. Almost two, maybe? But that wasn't it.

Hollander glanced up at him, and Ilya smiled and stroked his hair. The clock was ticking, and Ilya really did need to leave, so he gently held Hollander's head and guided him so he'd hit the rhythm Ilya needed and… there. Yes. Oh fuck…

"That's good, Hollander. Just like that. Make me come."

Hollander moaned and dug his fingers into Ilya's thighs, keeping the pace with his mouth that Ilya had set. The familiar, exhilarating pressure of impending release gripped Ilya's body—the high that he couldn't stop chasing—and he squeezed his eyes shut.

"I'm going to come. Oh, fuck, Hollander."

Hollander pulled off, replacing his mouth with his hand. "I want to see it."

Seconds later, Ilya erupted. He cried out, much louder than usual, as a white-hot orgasm rocketed through his body.

"Holy shit, Hollander," Ilya gasped when he was able to speak again. "I'm dead. You killed me."

Hollander was sitting up now, and staring at the mess on Ilya's stomach. "That was really hot."

"Yes."

"I'm glad we were in an empty building where no one could hear you."

And then Ilya felt the rare and unwelcome sensation of his cheeks heating in embarrassment. He didn't usually yell like that when he was coming.

He didn't want to think about it, so he said, "I have to go."

"All right."

Fifteen minutes later, they were waiting at the bottom of the stairs for Ilya's taxi to arrive.

"Is a nice building," Ilya said, because he hated the silence. "You don't want to live here?"

"No. But renovations might take a while, so I'll probably be able to use it for…this. For a bit." More silence, and then Hollander said, "You must be excited for the Olympics. In Russia."

"Yes." Ilya *was* excited. But thinking about the expectations of his home country, of his father, made his stomach hurt. And made him want a cigarette.

"Been dreaming of the Olympics my whole life," Hollander said. "I can't wait."

"For what? A bronze medal?"

"Fuck you."

Ilya laughed. "Hey, remember when you shot your load for like no reason at all?"

Hollander glared at him, but Ilya could tell he was trying not to laugh. "Oh my god. Go to hell."

"Amazing trick."

"Your cab must be out there, right?"

Ilya put his hand on the door, but before he pushed it open, he leaned down and kissed Hollander quickly on the mouth.

"Good night, Hollander."

"Good night."

Ilya was grinning like an idiot for the entire cab ride back to his hotel.

Chapter Ten

February 2014—Sochi, Russia

"Shane Hollanderrrrrrrr!"

Shane nearly jumped at the sound of his name being bellowed behind him. He spun around, and spotted two familiar faces approaching him: Carter Vaughan (yelling) and Scott Hunter (not yelling). Scott was the captain of Team USA's men's hockey team, and Carter was his teammate both here and in New York, where they played for the Admirals.

Shane had been walking, alone, on the beach in Sochi. He had the rest of the day and night off, and had been at a bit of a loss of what to do. His parents had considered traveling to Russia but had ultimately decided against it. For one thing, the travel arrangements and accommodations were a nightmare. Shane had convinced them that it really wasn't worth the hassle, and pointed out that they'd watched him compete in international tournaments since he was a teenager. And maybe he was being overly cautious, but there had been a lot of articles leading up to these Games about possible security concerns, and he wanted to keep his parents safe.

Shane had had no idea what to expect before he'd

arrived in Sochi. He'd never been to Russia before, and he wasn't sure this over-the-top spectacle was the best representation of Rozanov's homeland. He found himself wondering, often, about the pressure Rozanov was feeling. Being in the Olympics at all was thrilling and stressful enough for Shane without it being in his country.

"What's up, guys?" he said as Carter and Scott caught up with him. "Did you know there was going to be a beach here? What the fuck is this place, right?"

Carter laughed. "No! There are fucking palm trees here! I thought Russia in the winter would be, like, cold."

"Congrats on your win last night," Scott said. Scott was a super nice guy. Carter was nice too, but Scott was, like, an angel who was really good at playing hockey. He *looked* like an angel: blond hair and blue eyes and built like a Navy SEAL who was also a model and maybe also a firefighter.

"Thanks. It was a pretty easy win, but I'll take it."

"These early games are all easy. Who are we playing next, Scotty? Fiji?"

Scott frowned at him. "Denmark. And I don't want anyone being cocky about it."

"Yes, sir," Carter teased.

Carter looked nothing like Scott, with his dark skin and brown eyes, but he was just as attractive. The difference was that Carter *knew* he was attractive. He was the kind of guy who took over a room, but in a good way. Everyone liked him.

"How are you finding the accommodations?" Shane asked.

"Are you kidding?" Carter asked. "I'm sleeping on a *cot*—"

"It's a twin bed," Scott corrected him.

"Whatever. A fucking twin bed, wedged between two other twin beds. One of them has this fucking oaf snoring away on it."

"I don't snore."

"And the other has Sully—Eric Sullivan—and I don't even know that kid, but he's even bigger than Scott. I would like to find the Sochi Four Seasons."

Shane laughed. "I'm rooming with J.J., and your teammate, Greg Huff."

"Well, Huff doesn't take up much space," Carter said, "but J.J. is a giant."

"He's not a fan of the beds either."

"What are your plans for tonight?" Scott asked.

"I thought I'd watch some of the speed skating."

Scott's face lit up. "Yeah? That would be cool. I saw the men's figure skating short program is tonight too."

"Oh, right. That's probably going to be packed."

"Those fucking guys are brave to be here, you know?"

"Brave?" Scott asked.

Carter lowered his voice and glanced around the beach. "Yeah, like…because of the gay thing, right? Some of those guys are risking their lives for real here. Brave as hell."

"Right," Scott said. He turned his gaze to the ocean. Shane knew about Russia's laws against homosexuality, but he'd been trying not to think too much about stuff like that. He just wanted to enjoy the Olympics, win the gold medal, and go home. But now he was thinking about Dev, a guy he'd trained with a bit from

Ottawa who was on the men's speed skating team, and who Shane knew was gay. He was here. Was he terrified? He must be.

"They should have beach volleyball at these games!" Carter said cheerfully. "Women's beach volleyball. That's exactly what the Winter Olympics needs, right?"

Shane nodded, but he was still thinking about Dev. And about Rozanov.

Rozanov could take care of himself. This was his home turf. He would know how to keep safe.

"You still with us, Hollander?"

Shane blinked and looked at Carter and Scott. "Sorry. What did you say?"

"We were going to check out the McDonald's in the athlete's village. Thought it might be fun. Want to join us?"

"Um, I think I'm going to…" Text Rozanov? Try to lay eyes on him? Make sure he'd not been arrested for blowing a ski jumper or something? "Relax a bit in my room. Still jet lagged, y'know?"

"You can relax in that room?" Carter laughed. "Good luck, then. You have my number?"

"Yeah, I have it. I'll see you guys later."

Shane tried not to walk too quickly as he left, but he was suddenly desperate to make contact with Rozanov. The only problem was he had no idea where to find him.

He sent a text. Having a good time?

There. That was cool and casual. Just a friendly "Hey, we're both at the Olympics! Fun, right? Also, are you in jail?"

He waited all night for a reply, but none came.

The Olympics were bullshit.

Ilya had been on edge all week. It had been days of

smiling for the Russian media and mingling with government officials who made his skin crawl. Men and women who supported their country's leader without question, and who expected Ilya to do the same. Ilya hadn't had any time to enjoy himself; he'd barely had time to focus on his game.

And it showed.

The Russian men's hockey team was a mess. These sorts of international tournaments were always awkward, with players being tossed together to form a "dream team" of superstars who had no idea how to play with each other, but this team was especially hopeless. Too many egos. Too much pressure, here in their home country, making tempers run high in the dressing room and on the ice. Too many stupid penalties being taken, too few goals being scored.

They were already out of the running for a medal, and that was beyond humiliating. Ilya just wanted it all to be over so he could go…home.

When had he started thinking of Boston as home?

Tonight Ilya's attendance was requested (required) at a ridiculous gala, which was just a chance for the government to show off to foreign dignitaries. It was exactly the sort of event he couldn't stand.

And making it worse was the fact that his father would be there. His father, who had only spoken to him this week to let him know how badly he had let Russia down, would be parading his famous son around the ballroom as if he was proud of him.

But first, Ilya was expected to go to his father's hotel room. He wished he was strong enough to refuse.

He wasn't. So he knocked on the hotel room door five minutes before six o'clock, because anything past five minutes early was late, in his father's eyes.

The door opened, and there was Grigori Rozanov, in all his intimidating glory. He was wearing his full dress police uniform, and Ilya could see his stern frown even through the gray beard that covered his face. He was almost fifty years older than Ilya.

He stepped aside to let Ilya into the room. He waited for Ilya to remove his wool overcoat, and then the inspection began. His father's eyes raked over him while Ilya stood there, like a trembling child who was awaiting punishment. There was nothing—*nothing*—wrong with Ilya's tuxedo. It was classic black, perfectly tailored, and his bowtie was impeccable. He had even given himself the closest shave he'd had in years. But his father would find something.

"You need a haircut," was what Grigori finally settled on. Ilya had let his hair grow out this past season, but he'd slicked it back tonight.

"Yes, sir."

His father frowned at his hair for another minute, as if he could scare it back into Ilya's scalp, before he crossed the room to the bar. He poured vodka into two tumblers, and handed one to his son.

"The Minister wants to meet you tonight."

The Minister of Internal Affairs was who he meant. His boss.

"I will be honored," Ilya lied. He wanted to toss back the vodka and pour himself four or five more.

"You *should* be honored that he would want to meet you. After last night."

Ilya bit down on the inside of his cheek.

"To lose to Latvia," his father continued. "How could you have allowed that to happen? How are you not ashamed?"

"I *am* ashamed, Father."

His father waved a hand. "Not nearly enough. They don't teach you discipline in the American league. You are sloppy now. It's a shame because you had such promise when you were young."

I am only twenty-two. I am one of the best hockey players in the world.

"I am a better player now than I have ever been. The team just hasn't been working well together."

Wrong thing to say.

"You are the captain, are you not? Whose fault is it if the team isn't working together?"

The coach?

Instead of saying anything, Ilya looked at the floor and waited for his father to change the subject.

Grigori stepped closer, setting his vodka on a table, and began to needlessly adjust Ilya's bowtie. "Aagh. Who tied this for you? Your mother? She doesn't know how to do this properly."

Ilya froze. His breath caught in his throat, and he swallowed hard before saying, as evenly as possible, "No, Father. Mom is dead. Remember?"

And then Grigori froze, and Ilya could see the confusion in his eyes before he blinked and shook his head. "Yes, of course. I know that. I was thinking of your stepmother."

"And where is Polina tonight?" Ilya asked, ignoring his father's obvious lie.

"Home." No further explanation. Fine. Ilya didn't care anyway.

His father released Ilya's bowtie and smoothed a hand over his lapels.

"We should go," Ilya said.

Grigori's brow furrowed. "Yes…"

"To the gala," Ilya supplied. "For the Olympics. You are going to introduce me to the Minister."

Grigori's head snapped up, eyes blazing. "I know that!" He turned away from his son and threw open the closet door. He pulled his overcoat off the hanger and put it on.

Ilya didn't like his father, but he hated watching him deteriorate. He wondered if it would be easier when Grigori's brain was fully gone and he no longer had to suffer the embarrassment of drifting in and out of himself.

"With me, Ilya. And behave tonight. Try to make up for the shame you have already brought your country."

He made it hard to feel sorry for him.

"Of course. I will."

As Ilya followed his father down the hallway to the elevators, he felt his phone buzz in his pocket. He quickly glanced at the screen.

Jane: Having a good time?

He really did not need Shane stupid Hollander to be trying to make contact. Not here. Not now.

He ignored the message, and stuffed his phone back into his pocket.

Shane saw Rozanov standing at the top of the lower bowl of seating during the Sweden versus Finland game. He was alone, wearing a long, black wool coat instead of his team jacket. His collar was turned up. His hands were in his pockets.

Shane was wearing his Team Canada jacket and knit

hat. At the next break in play, he left his seat and walked around the perimeter of the seating until he was standing next to Rozanov.

"Hey," Shane said.

Rozanov looked at him and shook his head. "Not here," he said tightly.

"No, I'm not... I just wanted to see...how you're doing."

"Fine. Go. Sit down."

Shane frowned. Rozanov looked exhausted. He had dark rings under his eyes, and his face was very pale. But the most noticeable—and alarming—change was in his eyes. The playful spark that always made Rozanov's hazel eyes dance was just...gone. Extinguished.

"I—"

"We are not...anything. Not here, Hollander." Rozanov's eyes darted around them, as if searching for threats. It was the first time that Shane had ever seen Rozanov look uncomfortable.

"Are you okay?" Shane asked. He spoke as quietly as he could over the noise of the arena.

"Please go."

"You didn't answer my text and I thought..." Suddenly all the ways Shane might finish that sentence seemed stupid. *I thought you were in danger. I thought you were in jail. I thought you were...sad.*

"No, I didn't answer your boring text. Now will you go?"

Rozanov was being an asshole, which was nothing new, but he didn't seem to mean it. In fact, Shane would bet that Rozanov would actually really like him to stay. He looked like he could use a hug.

But obviously Shane wasn't going to hug him here,

so he just nodded and walked away. He didn't really have time to think about Rozanov anyway; Canada was going to be playing in the quarter-finals the following evening against either America or, if Finland lost this game, Sweden.

Rozanov, and his team, was done. And Shane knew that had to feel awful. Team Russia had just been... terrible. It wasn't Rozanov's fault, but Shane knew he would be beating himself up about it. Hell, Shane would be beating himself up, if it were his team.

By the time Shane returned to his seat, Rozanov was gone.

Chapter Eleven

June 2014—Las Vegas

At the end of the season, the league asked Rozanov and Hollander to present together at the NHL Awards. Because the league was cute, they asked them to present the award for Most Sportsmanlike.

Shane was waiting backstage in his tuxedo. Alone. No one knew where Rozanov was. They were supposed to walk out on stage together in three minutes.

"Where the hell is Rozanov?" a panicked director asked.

"I don't know," Shane said. "We, uh, don't exactly talk much."

The director stormed away, swearing.

Shane hadn't been lying. He hadn't spoken to Rozanov, off the ice, since the brief words they had shared at the Olympics. The humiliation of not even making it to the bronze medal game had seemingly been enough to cause Rozanov to not even want to look at Shane anymore, let alone talk to him. Touch him. Kiss him.

Shane had felt sorry for him, but then Rozanov turned the shame of losing so horribly in the Olympics into fuel that propelled him, and the Bears, all the way to the Stanley Cup.

Shane had watched that final game with Hayden and some of the other guys who had stuck around Montreal after their team had been eliminated in the third round. Shane had been sick with jealousy, but had also been undeniably proud when he'd watched Ilya Rozanov lift the cup over his head and *roar*. There had been tears streaming down Rozanov's face as he'd hollered and hollered, and Shane had seen that this was more than the pride of being the best player on the best team in the NHL that year. Rozanov had proved something to somebody.

Shane had been shocked to find tears in his own eyes as he'd watched the raw emotion explode out of Rozanov. It was as if, with every heave of the cup over his head, Rozanov was saying "Fuck you, fuck you. I did it. Fuck you," To someone.

Maybe to Shane. But he didn't think so. He hoped not.

The last time they had *really* spoken had been almost six months ago, before the Olympics, and Shane hadn't actually done all that much talking. What he *had* done was let Rozanov push him to his knees in the middle of his hotel room and fuck his mouth until Shane's eyes watered.

Shane tugged at his shirt collar, now, and tried to will his blush away.

"Looking for me?" a familiar voice drawled behind him.

Shane whipped around and was faced with Ilya Rozanov looking *so fucking good* in his tux. He'd grown his hair out over the past season, and that night he'd been wearing it slicked back and tied in a little bun. He looked like a European fashion model.

"Fuck, Rozanov. What the fuck? We're on in like five seconds!"

"Fifty seconds. We are fine."

"Does it matter to you that everyone backstage has been having a heart attack looking for you?"

"Not really."

Shane's hands rolled into fists at his sides. "Where were you, anyway?"

"Busy."

"Oh yeah? With who?"

Rozanov just smirked. "We're on."

He strode out onto the stage, leaving Shane to stupidly scramble to catch up with him. *Fuck him. Not even a text for five months and now he's going to be all sexy and annoying like nothing's changed?*

They went to the podium and recited their dumb banter about the importance of having respect for your fellow players. Shane did not have to pretend *at all* to hate Rozanov in that moment.

They got a lot of laughs. The fact that Shane was practically speaking through clenched teeth probably only enhanced the comedy.

"Hey," Rozanov said, "before we give out the award, can I get a selfie?"

"What?" Shane asked. It was all part of the script.

"Just a quick one. I mean, when will this happen again, right?"

"Fine, but hurry up."

Rozanov wrapped an arm around Shane's shoulders and pulled him tight against him. Everyone laughed. Rozanov held his phone out and snapped, Shane noticed, at least six quick photos.

"Give me your number. I'll send it to you."

"No chance," Shane deadpanned.

Laughter.

Rozanov was slow to move his arm from Shane's shoulders. When he finally did, he let his fingers brush the back of Shane's neck, making every hair stand up.

Shane felt his cock swell a bit, and silently cursed him.

They read the nominees, gave the winner his trophy, and then Shane left the stage as quickly as possible. He kept walking until he found a small bathroom backstage. He entered, and left the door unlocked.

Less than thirty seconds later, Rozanov slipped inside and locked the door. He crowded Shane up against the wall. Shane was *seething*; he stared Rozanov right in the eye and waited for him to make the first move.

"Well?" Rozanov said.

"Well what?"

He gestured to the floor. "Are you not going to suck my dick?"

Shane's eyes narrowed. "Fuck you! Why don't *you* suck *mine*?"

"Hmm." He traced a finger over Shane's clenched jaw—so gently it made Shane close his eyes and part his lips involuntarily. "Maybe ask nice."

Shane wanted to tell him to go fuck himself. But instead, to his mortification, he heard himself say, "Please."

Rozanov raised an eyebrow. "You want me to kneel on this dirty bathroom floor? You have to ask nicer than that, Hollander."

"Please," Shane gritted out. "Get on your knees and suck my dick. Please."

Rozanov pressed his palm where Shane's erection strained against his tuxedo pants, making Shane gasp and tilt his head back against the wall. Rozanov leaned in and brushed his lips over Shane's ear.

"No."

He let go of Shane, and stepped back.

"What?" Shane sputtered.

"No. I will not do anything to you in here. We will go back out there, and sit in our seats, and then go to the party. And *then*, when you have been waiting all night for it, you will come to my hotel room. And I will maybe do more than suck your dick."

Shane felt dizzy. And angry. And kind of impressed by Rozanov's English. It had really come a long way.

"You're really going to leave me like this?"

"Yes. For now."

"Fine," Shane grumbled.

"Aw," Rozanov cooed with mock sympathy. "I will make a deal: if you win MVP tonight, I will blow you, fuck you…whatever you want."

Shane swallowed. "And if *you* win?"

A wicked smile unfurled across Rozanov's face.

"I will let you know."

He put his hand on the door handle and was about to leave when he quickly turned and grabbed the front of Shane's jacket. He kissed him roughly, then let him go.

"Good luck tonight," he said.

And then he was gone.

Shane left the party as early as he could. He wished he had the willpower to stay later, to make Rozanov wait. He wished he had the strength to stand Rozanov up.

He'd been on edge for hours, half hard and buzzing with need. He'd had a few beers, which was a few more than he usually had, and his brain was only able to focus on his desire to get off as soon as possible.

He had a text with Rozanov's room number, and he'd seen him slip out of the party a few minutes ago. They hadn't spoken since the bathroom backstage.

Rozanov had won. Of course he had won. And now Shane had to find out what exactly he wanted from him.

They had done…everything? Shane was pretty sure they'd done everything at this point. Blow jobs: check. Hand jobs: of course. Fucking: yes, but only with Shane bottoming. Shane couldn't see Rozanov wanting to change that up. He hoped not, anyway.

Shane sent Rozanov a text as he approached the door, and he heard it click open just before he arrived. He entered quickly.

Rozanov had an enormous suite booked at the Las Vegas casino where the award ceremony was held. He stood in the middle of it now, most of his tuxedo already removed. He was down to just the sleek, black pants, with his dress shirt half unbuttoned. His feet were bare. Shane had removed his bowtie and stuffed it in his pocket when he had unfastened a couple of his own shirt buttons earlier, but he had some catching up to do.

"Here to congratulate me?" Rozanov said.

"I guess."

Rozanov spread his arms out, as if to say *Well?*

"Congratulations," Shane said flatly.

"Thank you. Now take off your clothes."

Shane had been kind of hoping Rozanov would help him with that, but he obeyed, draping each discarded piece of his suit carefully over the back of the sofa.

Rozanov didn't remove any of his own clothing. He just leaned against a glass table and crossed his arms, watching Shane.

"Shouldn't we—I mean. There are windows." There were *a lot* of windows.

"We are on the sixteenth floor."

"Yeah, but..."

Rozanov pushed himself off the table and flicked his hand in the air, gesturing for Shane to follow him to the bedroom.

Shane was down to his briefs. When he reached the bedroom, Rozanov was already drawing the curtains across the windows.

"On the bed," he instructed, without looking at Shane.

Shane did his best to appear comfortable and relaxed on the giant bed, as if he wasn't nervous as hell about whatever Rozanov had planned. He expected Rozanov to join him on the bed, but instead, Rozanov left the room.

He was gone for an obnoxiously long time. When he returned, he was holding a glass of clear liquid. He sat himself in a chair against the wall at the end of the bed, and took a sip.

"Mm. I am impressed with this hotel. This vodka is not so easy to find."

"Okay," Shane said impatiently.

"Touch yourself."

"What?"

"Show off for me. Let me watch you."

"You—*what?*"

"Is my special night, Hollander. I want to watch you." Every inch of Shane flushed red. "I—I've never..."

Rozanov grinned. "I thought maybe not. So—" he gestured with the hand that wasn't holding the drink "—show me. How do you touch yourself, Shane Hollander?"

Fuck.

Shane wanted to protest, but since his briefs were not at *all* concealing how excited his dick had gotten in the past minute or so, he felt his argument would be weak.

"Give me some of that vodka, then," he said. "I'm too sober for this."

Rozanov shook his head. "No. The vodka you can have after. As reward."

"Fuck. You."

Rozanov laughed. "Is good vodka! Come on. Look at your poor dick, Hollander. Give him some attention, yes?"

Shane glared at him, but Rozanov only crossed his long legs and leaned back in his chair, comfortable as anything.

"Close your eyes," he suggested. "Pretend you are alone. How do you start?"

Shane exhaled and closed his eyes. He tried to ignore the smirking Russian in the corner as he placed a nervous hand on his own stomach. He rubbed slow patterns over his skin, letting his nerves wake up.

He heard Rozanov shifting in his chair. Shane's lips curled up a bit; maybe he still had some power here.

His palm flat, he rubbed his hand over the bulge in his shorts, slow and deliberate. He let out a low, shameless moan, and slid his hand lower to cup his balls.

If Rozanov wanted a show, he was going to get a fucking show.

He rubbed himself through the fabric of his briefs for a few minutes, making sure to emphasize the outline of his erection. He already found himself enjoying this; his fear was forgotten.

He opened his eyes and looked directly at Rozanov, whose gaze was locked on Shane's crotch, his lips parted.

"Come on, Hollander," he said in a low rumble. "Show me."

Shane lifted his hips, hooked his thumbs into his waistband, and tugged the underwear down to his thighs. His cock sprang free, hard and glistening.

"Stroke it," Rozanov instructed. "Make yourself come for me."

Shane wrapped his fingers around himself, but instead of stroking, just slid his thumb over his slit a couple of times.

"There is lube in the drawer," Rozanov said. "Beside the bed."

"Mm. Get it for me." *There. Fuck you, Rozanov.*

Rozanov stood without protest and retrieved the bottle of lube. He held it out to Shane, but when Shane reached for it, Rozanov pulled it away. He laughed at Shane's glare, and tossed the bottle onto the bed.

"Would you like to know," Rozanov asked as he settled himself back into his chair, "how it feels?"

"How what feels?"

He leaned forward, grinning like a shark. "The Cup. Do you want to know what it feels like to hold the Stanley Cup?"

"Oh *fuck you.*"

Rozanov laughed. "I cannot describe it anyway. Impossible."

"I'll find out for myself soon enough," Shane grumbled.

"Of course. Now, show me how you like it, Hollander."

That request, Shane thought, was almost sweet. Considerate. He removed his briefs completely and picked up the bottle. He made a show of drizzling the lube directly on his cock.

If Rozanov thought Shane was going to be chatty during this thing, he didn't know Shane very well. Shane would be surprised if he uttered two words.

He stroked himself with slow, lazy movements. He closed his eyes again and let pleasure light up every part of him. With his other hand he reached down and played with his balls. He arched off the bed a bit, gasping and moaning.

He wondered if Rozanov was going to start touching himself too. He cracked an eye open and it seemed that Rozanov was happy to just watch. But he was leaning forward now, and he looked a little flushed.

Shane opened both eyes. He wanted to get off the bed and crawl on his fucking knees to where Rozanov was sitting. He wanted to nuzzle his cock through his pants. He wanted to press his open mouth to that bulge he could see from here.

The thoughts made Shane's hand speed up. He let out a broken "ah" sound and planted his feet flat on the bed, legs splayed, knees bent.

"Open yourself up," Rozanov said. "Use your fingers."

Oh fuck. Shane felt simultaneously mortified and excited. He reached for the lube.

"Yes. Let me see you open yourself for me."

"You gonna fuck me?" Shane managed to get out.

"We'll see."

Shane got to work.

It was undeniably humiliating to be splayed out on the bed like this, Shane's fingers two knuckles deep in his own ass while Ilya Rozanov calmly sipped his vodka and watched everything like he was going to be tested on it later.

The only thing that could make the situation more embarrassing would be...

"Please," Shane gasped. *Begged.*

"Please what?"

"I—I need..."

He could tell that Rozanov was starting to lose his composure. He could see how his Adam's apple bobbed sharply as he swallowed, the way he ran his teeth over his bottom lip.

"What do you need, Hollander?"

"*You.* Fuck me. Please."

Rozanov sucked in a breath, and then he stood and placed his glass on the side table. He slowly undid the last of his buttons and let the shirt fall to the floor behind him. He walked to the end of the bed, and Shane crawled to him, just like he'd imagined doing. He crawled along the mattress until his face met the bulge in Rozanov's tuxedo pants. He nuzzled and mouthed at it, and Rozanov buried his fingers in Shane's hair and murmured something in Russian.

Shane didn't know if Rozanov was saying something encouraging, or reverent. Or maybe he was calling

Shane a slut. Shane felt a little slutty, in that moment. He felt *wild*. He wanted Rozanov's cock in every part of him at once. He wanted to come right away or not for hours. He wanted to kiss Rozanov and maybe also punch him for being such an arrogant fucking prick.

And he hated himself for wanting any of this. But not enough to stop. Never enough to stop.

He opened Rozanov's pants and pushed them down to his ankles, along with his underwear. He wrapped his mouth around Rozanov's cock and moaned with relief.

"So good for me. Look at you."

Shane let out another mortifying moan, hating himself for loving this so much.

Rozanov let him suck for a few blissful minutes before he shoved Shane down onto the bed. He twirled his hand in the air.

"Turn over," he said.

Shane did as he was told, and raised his ass in the air far too eagerly. He heard a rustle of a condom being opened, and then saw the empty wrapper hit the floor when Rozanov tossed it aside. Rozanov was breathing heavily as he slicked himself with lube, and, *damn*, Shane loved it when Rozanov lost his ability to stay cool and collected.

Rozanov fucked him hard with one strong hand between Shane's shoulder blades—pressing him down to the mattress. Shane was louder than he wanted to be, begging for more even though that was probably an impossible thing to ask for. Even though it was embarrassing to be this desperate for Ilya Rozanov.

He came so hard that he actually *yelled*. There was no other word for it. And, once again, he had made a mess of some hotel bedsheets.

His ears were still ringing with his own orgasm when he felt Rozanov freeze behind him and cry out. And then Rozanov's forehead was pressed against Shane's back as both men struggled to catch their breath.

"Jesus, Hollander," Rozanov panted as he flopped to his back beside him. His hair had fallen out of its little ponytail and was clinging to his forehead in a damp swoop.

Shane carefully flipped to his back, leaving the wet spot on the bedsheets between them. "How about that vodka?"

Rozanov laughed. "Yes. Give me a minute."

Shane grinned. He knew he'd be at least a little mortified and ashamed later when he thought about this night, but at that moment, he was giddy.

Rozanov did eventually leave the bed and, after cleaning himself in the bathroom, brought Shane a damp washcloth and an ice-cold glass of vodka. He brought himself a cigarette and a lighter.

He sat with his back against the headboard, one leg bent and the other outstretched. Still naked, but for his gold chain and crucifix. He lit his cigarette and Shane didn't even have the energy to lecture him about it. Especially since he looked so goddamned sexy.

Instead, Shane sipped his vodka, which was gross. He really didn't drink anything beyond beer very often. At least it was cold against his tongue.

"Are you heading back soon?" Shane asked, just to make conversation.

"Back?"

"To Russia. For the summer."

Rozanov exhaled a long stream of smoke. "Yes."

"Oh."

They were silent a moment, then Shane couldn't help but ask, "Why?"

Rozanov shrugged. "It is home."

"But…do you *like* going there?"

Rozanov didn't answer. He took another drag of his cigarette and closed his eyes.

"I should sleep," he said finally.

"Oh. Yeah. I should… I need to get going, anyway."

"Yes."

Ah. There was that shame Shane had been expecting. He got cleaned up in the bathroom, then went to the main room to retrieve his clothes. He put on the pants and the shirt and carried the rest of the tuxedo. Rozanov didn't leave the bedroom.

"See you," Shane called out.

"Goodbye, Hollander," Rozanov replied from the other room.

And Shane left. He realized, when he was back in his room, that they hadn't even kissed. He also realized, with horror, that he regretted that.

Part Three

Chapter Twelve

Ilya had a man pinned under the weight of his body.

The man was big, almost as tall as Ilya, and pressing back against him aggressively. Ilya wedged a knee between the man's thighs, holding him firmly in place.

"Fuck off, asshole," the man growled.

Ilya leaned on him harder.

"All right, let him go, Rozanov," the referee said. "I'll call holding if you don't back off right now."

Ilya released the other man's jersey, raising his hands innocently.

"Fucker," the other man growled. He shoved Ilya before he skated away from the boards where Ilya had trapped him.

"That wasn't nice," Ilya called after him.

Ilya could hear the boos and taunts from the crowd as he skated to the bench.

Fuck you, Rozanov!

You're a fucking pussy, Rozanov!

Go back to Russia, you piece of shit!

Et cetera.

Ilya smiled to himself. He actually loved this. He

loved being on the road, and disappointing home crowds
across North America. He loved the insults, the booing, and, most of all, the sound of a crowd so gutted by
his team's performance that they couldn't even bother
to boo. A winded, humiliated crowd. That was Ilya's
favorite sound.

The crowd was still loud in Philadelphia. This was
not an easy city to silence. He would have to work extra
hard tonight to get that glorious, devastated quiet he
craved.

He sat on the bench next to Brad Hammersmith.
Brad was a veteran forward. He was also about a hundred years old.

"Making friends?" Hammersmith asked.

"I'm playing hockey."

Hammersmith snorted.

A Philadelphia defenseman skated by the bench
when the play had stopped. "Keep it up and see what
happens, Rozanov," he threatened.

"I know what will happen. My team will win."

"Suck my dick, Rozanov."

Be the best blow job of your life, sweetheart. Ilya
winked at him.

"Faggot," the other player grumbled.

Ilya shrugged. It was half true.

Maybe, like, thirty percent true.

At that moment, the scoreboard screens showed a
highlight from the Montreal vs. Ottawa game that was
also happening that night. Hollander had just scored a
goal. Of course.

Ilya watched the footage of Hollander taking a quick
pass and scoring with the impossible accuracy that he
was known for. Ilya watched him hug his teammates,

and the way his face lit up with a wide, jubilant smile. Ilya found himself smiling a bit too, on his bench in Philadelphia.

Well, now he was going to have to score *two* goals tonight.

October 2016—Montreal

"Jackie is pregnant."

Shane stopped dead in his tracks in the middle of the Gulf of Saint Lawrence ecosystem at the Montreal Biodome. "*Again?*" he said.

Hayden laughed. "Jesus, thanks."

"Sorry! I mean, congratulations."

Hayden shot him an amused look. "Yeah, you sound super happy for me."

Shane gestured to the stroller Hayden was pushing his one-year-old son in, and then toward the twin three-year-old girls who were peering into a touch tank. "Well, I mean…"

"Yeah," Hayden sighed. "I know. But Jackie's happy. I mean…she's fucking bored, right?"

The nearby parent of a wobbly toddler glared at them.

"Sorry," Hayden said quickly to the offended party. Then, to Shane, he said, "I gotta watch my language. Jackie always says so."

"Hazard of our occupation," Shane said.

"I know I—hey! Jade, sweetie, don't splash your sister!—I need a swear jar or something at home."

"I don't think you can afford that."

As a man without children, or a wife, Shane was in the minority among his teammates. Most of the guys were married well before the age of twenty-five. Hayden had married Jackie at twenty-one, after only dating her for a year. Shane had been there the night they'd met. Hayden had dragged Shane and a couple of other guys out to a club, where Hayden had met his future wife, and Shane had left to have one of the most embarrassing sexual encounters of his life with a very patient woman named… Olivia? Ophelia?

But Jackie was great. Hayden had done well marrying her. And their kids were adorable, even if naming the twins Jade and Ruby was a *choice*.

"Thanks for coming with us," Hayden said, stooping to pick up the pacifier that his son, Arthur, had dropped on the ground. Hayden gave it a quick wipe on his shirt and plunged it back into Arthur's mouth. Shane made a disgusted face that Hayden didn't see. "Jackie's sister is visiting and they wanted to go shopping and shit."

"Swear jar," Shane said.

"Right. Shopping and *stuff*. Anyway, it's hard going anywhere with these three monsters, so I appreciate the help."

"My pleasure, man."

Shane was sincerely enjoying himself. The Biodome was a good place for him to go without getting mobbed. People were so distracted by the animals, and by trying to wrangle their own children, that they weren't bothering to look at the other adults in the room. Shane was also wearing a ball cap and a simple black jacket to try to blend in even better. So far it was working.

"Oh shit—I mean, shoot—looks like Ruby is trying to steal a starfish." Hayden nudged the stroller handles toward Shane. "Here, you watch Arthur for a second, okay?"

He was darting toward the touch tank and the twins before Shane could reply.

Shane knelt in front of the stroller and smiled at the sleepy-eyed little boy. "Hey, buddy," he said. "You having a good time?"

Arthur reached out and grabbed the front of Shane's ball cap.

"Let's go see some penguins!" Hayden said. He had returned carrying one twin under each arm.

"Penguins!" both girls squealed at once.

"Penguins!" Shane said, clapping his hands and trying to mimic the girls' excitement.

Hayden huffed. "All right, children. Follow your big brother Shane."

He set the girls down, and they each took one of Shane's hands. Shane's heart clenched. Their hands were so *tiny*.

In the Antarctic room, Hayden and Shane were able to sit on a bench with the stroller parked next to them while the twins ran up to the glass to look at the penguins.

"So Jackie has this friend..." Hayden said.

Oh, Jesus. Here we go again.

"No," Shane said.

"I know, but listen. She's gorgeous, and she's cool. She's a yoga instructor. You like yoga, right?"

"I'm sure she's great, but I'm really not interested in dating anyone right now."

"Why the f—I mean, why on earth not? You're young, you're rich, you're famous, you...look like you."

Shane gave him a flirty look. "Hayden, do you find me attractive?"

"Look, pal. If I was a woman, I'd be all over you."

Shane laughed. In truth, he could think of worse scenarios than having Hayden Pike all over him. But he wasn't going to tell *him* that. Besides, Hayden was his best friend. He'd never had anything but platonic feelings for him, blond hair, green eyes, and cleft chin aside.

"So this friend," Hayden tried again. "Samantha is her name. I think you would really like her."

Shane buried his face in his hands, almost knocking his own ball cap off. "Please stop trying to set me up on dates, Hayd."

"I just want to see you happy! And I want you to have a hundred kids so you can know my pain!"

Shane scrubbed his hands over his face and looked up to see Jade and Ruby shoving each other in front of the glass.

"Fuck it. I gotta break this up," Hayden grumbled, already walking toward them.

Shane sighed. "Tell your dad to lay off my love life, all right, Arthur?"

But Arthur had fallen asleep.

Shane imagined telling Hayden that he was into men. He knew Hayden wouldn't shun him or anything. He maybe wasn't the most *worldly* guy, but he wasn't a bigot either. At worst it would probably make things awkward between them. Maybe it wouldn't, but Shane didn't want to risk finding out. There really wasn't any reason to, anyway. Shane probably *would* meet a nice girl someday and settle down and then his occasional attraction to men would be moot.

His imagination continued to wander, conjuring a scenario where he told Hayden that he'd been hooking up with Ilya Rozanov since their rookie season. The hypothetical look on Hayden's face made Shane snort out loud. He quickly covered his mouth and turned to look at Arthur, as if to suggest that the sleeping toddler had made the weird noise.

"Excuse me, are you Shane Hollander?"

Shane looked up and saw two teen girls gawking at him.

"Erm…" he said smoothly.

"Oh my god! You *are*! Can I get a selfie with you?"

"It's pretty, um, dark in here," Shane said. He tried to catch Hayden's eye. If he started taking selfies with fans here, it would never end.

"Please?" The girls were both pouting now.

Shane kept himself from sighing. It wasn't like he was doing anything else at the moment. "Sure. What's your name?"

The girls lit up. "Oh my god, thank you! I love you so much! I'm Emma."

"I'm Jessica."

"Nice to meet you, Emma and Jessica."

They arranged themselves so they would all fit in the frame of Emma's iPhone screen. As she was snapping pictures, Hayden returned. "Uh-oh," he said.

It only took a second for Shane to realize that Hayden was referring to the dozens of heads that were now turned in the direction of his little photo shoot.

Sure enough, as soon as the girls thanked him and walked away, a man and his son approached Shane. He ended up being stuck in the Antarctic room for twenty minutes taking photos with fans and signing whatever objects they happened to have on them. When Shane made his apologetic excuse to leave, he found Hayden by the exit.

"Those assholes," Hayden grumbled.

"They're *fans*, Hayden."

"They didn't even recognize *me*!"

Shane laughed and slapped him on the back. "I'll take a selfie with you, if you want."

"I never should have become friends with you."

Shane smiled and held the door for him so he could push the stroller through.

"Seriously!" Hayden continued. "My ego can't take it, man! It's like being friends with the damn sun or something. Wait—do I have all of the kids? How many kids are here?"

"Three. Ruby is hiding behind you."

"Okay." Hayden exhaled. "I can't believe we're having another one."

"You sure it's just one?"

Hayden's eyes were pure terror. "Don't even joke, Hollander."

October 2016—Washington

Ilya stretched out on his hotel bed and amused himself by tapping on the various customization options for the 2017 Audi Spyder. He had a 2015 Spyder already, so it wasn't like he *needed* a new one.

But he didn't have one in Vegas Yellow…

The television was turned to ESPN, but he wasn't paying much attention to it. At least, not until he heard the name *Shane Hollander*.

It was just one of these dumb fluff pieces that the twenty-four-hour sports networks relied on to fill air time, a little glimpse at Hollander's life away from the rink for the fans.

On the television, Hollander was standing on some

sort of dock surrounded by the calm blue waters of an enormous lake. Thick green forest lined the banks.

"When the demands of the season are over, this is where Shane Hollander comes to relax and recuperate: his five-thousand-square-foot lakefront cottage."

Ilya sat up. He had never seen any place that Hollander called home.

"This is my favorite place on earth," the Hollander on the television said. "I just finished building this one a couple of years ago. My family's cottage, the one I spent summers at growing up, is just over there." He pointed off-camera to his right. "I was still spending my summers there until this one was finished."

"Awww, so fucking sweet, Hollander," Ilya said, rolling his eyes.

There was some footage of Hollander kayaking alone on the lake, looking serene and stupid as he gazed around at nature. His voice played over the footage, talking about the place healing his soul or some dumb shit.

There were sweeping shots of some of the rooms of the cottage. A spacious, high-ceilinged living area with a leather sectional sofa and some very Canadian-looking plaid throw pillows and blankets; a modern, high-end kitchen with a large island in the middle; a pool table and a bar; a gym that had a wall of floor-to-ceiling windows that overlooked the lake.

Then, without warning, they cut to a shot of Hollander doing fucking yoga on the dock.

"I got into yoga last year and I think it's really helped me focus, and it's definitely increased my flexibility." Hollander's voice played over a lingering shot of him holding some ridiculous pose.

"Jesus Christ, you are so fucking boring," Ilya muttered.

Hollander *did* look flexible, though.

The segment went on a little longer. Hollander talked about how important it was for him to have a place close to his parents. How he had offered to build them a new cottage too, but they'd refused. He laughed when he said that. When he laughed his nose crinkled, and Ilya's stomach flipped.

Ilya wondered if Hollander had ever fucked anyone in that cottage. Probably. Probably some nice, wholesome girl that he had met while…canoeing. Or whatever.

Ilya had filmed one of these dumb things too. He had taken the camera crew to the garage where he stored his collection of European sports cars. The segment had had a decidedly different vibe from this Hollander one.

But that's the way it had been for over six seasons: Shane Hollander was the wholesome, heroic sweetheart, and Ilya Rozanov was the obnoxious rock star. They were polar opposites, according to any NHL analyst, and therefore destined to clash forever—neatly dividing hockey fans in the process.

It's the way it *should* have been. Shane and Ilya *were* opposites in almost every way imaginable, but it was getting harder for Ilya to deny that there was something in his *core* that was drawn to Hollander. Instead of getting him out of his system with their hookups, each one just made him want *more*.

It was dangerous fucking stuff.

Chapter Thirteen

"Heading out?" Hayden asked from where he was watching television on the hotel bed.

"Yeah. Just for a bit. Meeting a friend."

"If you say so." Hayden grinned. Shane swallowed and tried not to let anything show on his face. His insides roiled with shame and fear and anticipation.

"Just a friend," Shane said.

"I won't wait up."

"It's not—" Shane closed his eyes and calmed himself down. "It's not that type of friend. I'll be back soon."

Hayden studied him a moment. "Well, that's too bad. You need to get laid."

"I'm fine." Shane tugged his jacket on and checked himself quickly in the mirror before leaving the room.

He shouldn't be doing this.

They had arrived in Boston that morning and had a short practice that afternoon. The game was tomorrow afternoon, which meant he had the whole evening free.

Rozanov lived in a building that was a short cab ride from the hotel. They had moved their Boston hookups from hotel rooms to Rozanov's penthouse last season.

Shane had been against the idea at the time, arguing that he didn't want to risk being spotted entering Rozanov's building. He had legitimately been concerned about that, and still was, but his real objection—the one that he didn't voice—was that he didn't want to make what they were doing seem more...personal. Meeting in hotel rooms or at Shane's investment property was one thing, but every time Shane went to Rozanov's actual *home*, he felt his world tilt a bit. It was an extra layer of wrongness thrown on top of the mountain of bad ideas they had been scaling for six years.

When he was on the steps in front of the building, he sent the text. I'm here.

The door clicked and he let himself in, taking the elevator all the way to the top. He told himself that he would talk to Rozanov tonight. That he would end this thing, and then he would go back to the hotel. He had lost count long ago of how many times he had broken this promise to himself over the years.

Rozanov answered the door wearing low-slung sweatpants and no shirt. Shane swore under his breath. All thoughts of just talking to Rozanov left his mind.

As soon as Shane entered the penthouse, Rozanov turned and walked toward the bedroom. He didn't say a word to him. Shane removed his shoes, dropped his coat on the floor, and followed him.

"The fuck is this?" Shane asked as he entered the bedroom. "You're not speaking to me anymore? Just expect me to follow you like a dog?"

"Shh," Rozanov said. He tilted Shane's head up and kissed him hungrily. Shane surrendered immediately, pushing his tongue into the other man's mouth and slipping his hands into the back of his sweatpants.

Shane couldn't think of a single reason why they needed to talk to each other anyway. Not anymore. Not when Rozanov was sucking on his tongue and sliding Shane's shirt up his chest.

The shirt came off and Shane shoved Rozanov down to the bed so he was sitting at the end of it. Shane fell to his knees and hauled Rozanov's sweatpants down. He didn't feel like wasting any time.

Rozanov wasn't wearing underwear, and his cock was half hard already. Shane took it into his mouth.

"Jesus, Hollander," Rozanov said. He placed a hand on the side of Shane's face. "Couldn't wait, could you?"

Shane closed his eyes. He should have felt embarrassed, but he loved the feeling of Rozanov growing harder against his tongue. He never felt submissive, doing this. He loved reducing Rozanov to whimpers and Russian profanity. And, god help him, he especially loved doing it here, in Rozanov's home. In his *bedroom*.

Their relationship was weird. Obviously. Shane knew that nothing about this was normal.

The facts were these: they were two of the biggest hockey stars in the world, and for whatever reason, they both enjoyed fucking each other. The other thing they were in total agreement on is that no one could *ever* know that they enjoyed fucking each other. It would be best if no one knew that they liked to fuck men at all, but it definitely couldn't get out that the superstar rivals were very familiar with each other's dicks.

Rozanov brushed a thumb over the freckles on Shane's cheek, just under his eye.

"Stop," Rozanov said in a low voice. "Enough. Stop."

Shane pulled off and waited.

"I'd like to look at you tonight, I think. You on top?" Rozanov asked.

"Okay," Shane said, but the request made him nervous. Usually Rozanov just took him from behind, on a bed or against a wall. Shane could pretend (or pretend he was pretending) that Rozanov was someone else that way.

Shane quickly pulled off the rest of his clothing. Rozanov took a moment to raise an eyebrow at Shane's rigid, untouched cock. Shane blushed. "Shut up," he muttered.

Rozanov grinned and scooted back on the bed, naked and sprawled out with his hands behind his head. Shane couldn't help but grin back. This was so fucking weird, but maybe they could just pretend it wasn't, for an hour or so. Maybe they could just be two guys who wanted to have sex.

Rozanov slapped his own thighs, an invitation, and Shane went to him.

Later, when they were fucking, Shane braced himself with a hand flat on Rozanov's chest. Rozanov covered that hand with his own, which surprised Shane. Rozanov never took his eyes off his face, except to watch when Shane started stroking himself.

Shane saw the glazed look in his eyes, and the way his mouth was hanging open, and he rode him harder.

"Fuck," Rozanov grunted, and, without warning, he flipped them both over so he was on top, staring down at Shane as he held his legs and thrust into him wildly. His crucifix chain dangled between them, scraping Shane's chest.

When Shane's orgasm hit him, it was hard and sudden. His release seemed endless, splashing his chest and even up to his throat.

"Yes, sweetheart," Rozanov panted, and Shane didn't even have a chance to be shocked by the pet name before Rozanov was coming too. When it was over, he dropped to his elbows over Shane and kissed him messily.

They took turns getting cleaned up in the bathroom. When Shane walked back into the bedroom, he stood stupidly in the middle of the room, near his pile of clothes on the floor. He should probably go.

But Rozanov was lounging on his bed and he patted the mattress next to him, so Shane went. He lay on his back beside Rozanov, not touching him, and stared at the ceiling until Rozanov rolled to his side, propped on an elbow, and gazed down at him.

Shane felt the same anxiety that had flooded him the last time they had been together. There was something a little too…tender…in the way Rozanov was looking at him. And there was something that was far too soothing about the way Rozanov's fingers combed through Shane's short hair, and curved down to trace the bridge of freckles that stretched across his face.

Shane had always hated his freckles. He had been surprised to learn, when he had become famous, that a lot of women seemed to find them very sexy. Or at least they found them adorable. He was even more surprised that Rozanov seemed to hold some sort of fascination with them.

Rozanov leaned in and pressed kisses to Shane's hair and face and down to his throat. The kisses weren't seductive or heated. They were light and sort of…adoring. Shane's eyes fluttered closed, suddenly very sleepy, and he heard Rozanov murmur something to himself in Russian, and felt the words tickle the skin under his jaw.

"Hm?" Shane asked distantly.

"You could stay," Rozanov said.

"Stay?"

"Stay here. Tonight."

Shane's eyes opened. Rozanov was looking at him seriously again.

"You want me to stay here?"

Rozanov seemed to realize what he had just asked, because his face changed and he shrugged, forcing a half grin. "I'm not done with you yet."

"Oh." That was more familiar. "I can't stay. You know that."

"You could. The game is tomorrow afternoon. No morning practice."

"I told Hayden—"

Rozanov rolled his eyes. "Is Hayden your mother?"

"No. But he's…expecting me. I told him I was meeting a friend."

Rozanov snorted. "That was a lie."

Shane laughed at that. "Yeah. Well."

Rozanov lowered himself until his nose was inches from Shane's face. "Stay."

Shane couldn't stay. There were probably a million reasons why he couldn't stay.

"Okay," he said.

Rozanov smiled and kissed him. They stayed in the bed for a long time just…making out. Not really escalating things. And that was new. Shane really did like kissing Rozanov, but this seemed indulgent. And dangerous.

"Are you hungry?" Rozanov asked.

"For?"

"Food."

Shane looked at him, and Rozanov laughed. He hopped off the bed and onto his feet. "Let's eat something."

Rozanov put his sweatpants back on, and this time grabbed a T-shirt from his dresser to throw on with them. Shane retrieved his own jeans and T-shirt from the floor and followed him into the kitchen.

"I got, um, ginger ale. You like that shit, right?"

"Yeah. I do." Shane looked at him oddly. Shane didn't often drink because he didn't want to do anything that might compromise his performance on the ice. Over the years he had developed an affinity for ginger ale as a substitute for beer. But it wasn't like he'd ever talked about that to Rozanov.

Instead of asking Rozanov how the hell he knew that he liked ginger ale, or why he cared enough to buy some, he asked, "You want to order takeout, or—"

"Do you like tuna melts?"

"You want to make me a tuna melt?"

Rozanov shrugged. "I'm making one for me. I can make two. Ginger ale is in fridge."

He seemed to really want Shane to drink the ginger ale. As Shane took one from the fridge, he wondered if it might be poisoned.

Rozanov was setting canned tuna, a baguette, and cheese slices on the counter, so Shane leaned back against the fridge and watched his fellow NHL superstar make him a sandwich.

"You head down to Florida after this game?" Rozanov asked, as if he didn't know the answer.

"Yeah. Couple games down there. Then over to Dallas and up to St. Louis."

Rozanov nodded. "We are in town here for this week. Then out west for a while. Ginger ale good? Cold enough?"

"Yeah, it's great. Thanks."

He looked pleased. Shane watched him carefully distribute the mixture of tuna and mayonnaise and lemon juice on some baguette slices. It was weird, this domestic scene. It wasn't anything that they had done before.

The melts went into the oven and Rozanov grabbed himself a bottle of Coke out of the fridge. Shane realized that he knew that Coke was Rozanov's beverage of choice. So maybe they *had* picked up things about each other over the years, without really trying.

"Ready in ten minutes," Rozanov said. He left the kitchen and went to sit on the couch in the living room. He turned on the television, which was showing the Buffalo vs. Chicago game.

Shane sat at the opposite end of the couch. He'd first considered the leather recliner that was next to the couch. Whatever they were to each other, they weren't *boyfriends*. He knew how to behave around him when they were naked and pressed against each other, and he knew how to play against him on the ice, but just hanging out with their clothes on was uncharted territory.

"Jesus," Rozanov said as they watched a Buffalo player get hauled to the penalty box. "You know that guy? Ryan Price?"

"I mean, just from playing against him. And, you know, not wanting to fight him." Price was huge, and tough as hell. "You played with him, right?"

"Yes. For one season only. He was…not what you would think."

"What do you mean?"

"Like…quiet. Doesn't make friends, really. But not a bad guy. Just…weird. Sort of."

"Well, he does seem to get traded every season. It would be hard to make friends that way."

"He is probably hoping he gets traded again. Buffalo is terrible."

"They definitely are."

They watched in silence for another minute and then Shane asked, "What's your favorite city to play in? On the road?"

Rozanov considered it. "I like New York. Because it's New York. They fucking hate me there."

"They hate you everywhere."

"They like me in Florida. Is all Boston fans down there. You?"

"I like Ottawa, because it's my hometown. Toronto, because of the history between our teams. And, you know, anywhere warm, I guess."

"L.A. is good. Beautiful women." Shane noticed Rozanov stealing a glance at him as he said this.

"Sure. Yeah," Shane said. "There's beautiful women everywhere, really."

"When you are rich and famous, yes."

They were silent a moment. The game went to commercial.

"There was a girl," Rozanov said. "In New York. I used to see her when I was in town."

"Used to?"

"She is getting married."

"Oh." Shane looked into his ginger ale bottle. "Are you…upset about that?"

"What? No." Rozanov seemed genuinely surprised, and maybe amused, by his question. "Was not like that.

Just…convenient to have a reliable woman to sleep with in New York. With three teams to play against there, we are there a lot."

"You think she's the only woman in New York that would be willing to sleep with you?" Shane teased.

Rozanov smirked. "I think I will find someone."

Another silence fell. Shane wondered if Rozanov was expecting him to share a piece of similar information. He couldn't, really, so he said, "I find it hard, being so… high profile, you know? It's hard to just…sleep with someone. Sometimes."

"Yes. It is good to have reliable person."

Shane offered him a small smile. "It is."

Rozanov nodded and got up to go to the kitchen. "Stay," he said. "I bring it here."

Shane focused on the television and not on what they had just been talking about. Rozanov returned with two plates that he seemed to put some care into arranging tuna melts, potato chips, and dill pickles on.

"Another drink?" he asked.

"No. I'm good." Shane kind of couldn't believe that Rozanov had made them both dinner. He found it, he realized with some horror, adorable.

"Do you like them?" Rozanov asked after a minute of silent eating.

"What? The tuna melts?"

"No. Girls."

Shane was caught off guard. "Oh. Sure. Yeah. I like them. Of course." This bit of stammering did not match the answer that first popped into Shane's head, which was: *not really*.

"Never hear about you with girls," Rozanov said plainly.

"Well. It's private."

"Right. Private."

"I keep a lot of things private!" Shane said. He waved a hand between the two of them and added, "Obviously."

Rozanov didn't reply for a moment. Then he turned back to the television and said, "I like girls."

"Yeah, no shit."

"But I also like you."

"Well, lucky me," Shane grumbled.

"Not as a person, of course," Rozanov teased. "But you have a good mouth." He took a suggestive bite of his dill pickle.

At that moment, Rozanov's phone rang. He looked at the screen and muttered something in Russian. "I have to take this. Sorry."

"It's fine," Shane said, because of course it was.

Rozanov stood and walked out of the room, speaking to whoever was calling in Russian. Shane was left alone on the couch with his mind reeling.

The truth was that he hadn't ever had what he would consider to be a successful relationship with a woman. He'd had a decent amount of experience with them, but he couldn't think of any sexual encounters with women that had actually been great. He wasn't sure how any of the girls felt about it. Maybe they had just been excited to get into bed with a hockey star, and that was enough to distract them from how halfhearted his efforts had been.

He didn't like being the one doing the fucking all that much; he *loved* being fucked. Shane had always been too embarrassed to ask the women he'd been with to use a dildo on him, so he more or less forced himself to *endure* the act of fucking women. Once he was aroused enough he could kind of get into it. It was a means to an end—the same end he was seeking no matter who he was with or what they were doing with him. He was obviously very athletic, which the women seemed to appreciate, and that probably covered the fact that he wanted it to be over as quickly as possible. At least, he hoped so; he would hate for a woman to feel unappreciated. If he didn't think they were getting something pleasurable out of being with him, he would stop altogether.

He preferred blow jobs. When a woman was sucking his dick it was easy enough to close his eyes and imagine…anyone…with their lips wrapped around him. The problem was that he wasn't so keen on reciprocating. He *would*, because he wasn't an asshole, but he had to really psych himself up for it, and he was almost certainly terrible at it. He'd heard teammates talk about eating pussy like it was the closest thing to heaven on earth. Shane had never gotten it.

But maybe he hadn't met the right girl yet. That was what he kept telling himself. It made complete sense to him; just because he hadn't really had his mind blown in the bedroom by a woman yet didn't mean it was impossible. There must be a girl out there somewhere who could make him feel like he did when he was with—

"Sorry," Rozanov said again when he sat back on the couch. "My father."

"Oh." And Shane knew he should ask whether or not everything was okay at home or something, but he was now consumed by one thought:

No one makes me feel like Ilya Rozanov does.

And because the terror Shane was feeling was probably all over his face, Rozanov was the one who asked, "Is everything okay?"

"What? Yeah. Of course. Um…is your dad all right?"

"Yes," Rozanov said, a little too quickly and dismissively. "Fine."

"Is he—?"

"You're not eating," Rozanov said, gesturing toward the mostly untouched plate of food on the coffee table in front of Shane.

"Sorry. It's good. I was just, um…distracted by the game."

Rozanov nodded. They went back to watching the game and this time Shane made sure to eat his food. He kept stealing glances at Rozanov while he ate, as if seeing him for the first time.

Oh god. What the fuck?

The game ended, and the feed switched to a Western Conference game that was in progress. Rozanov cleared their dishes away and, when he came back, wedged himself between Shane and the arm of the couch. He turned slightly and wrapped an arm around Shane, guiding him back to rest against his own chest. Shane was surprised, but he went willingly. Very willingly.

Resting against Rozanov like this, in his home, watching hockey, full of the food he had just made him…this was exactly what they *weren't* supposed to be doing. This was what *couples* did.

But Rozanov's chest was so warm and solid, and Shane could hear his heart beating where his ear was pressed against it. Rozanov's fingers were idly playing with his hair, making Shane sleepy and unreasonably happy.

Eventually, Rozanov moved his other hand to slide

up Shane's thigh and cup him through his jeans. He massaged him with one big, skilled hand, and Shane's cock quickly responded. When the bulge threatened to rip through the denim, Rozanov flicked open the button on his fly and carefully pulled down the zipper. Shane hadn't bothered putting his briefs on again, so his cock popped out, and Rozanov started lazily stroking it at a frustrating pace.

Shane squirmed against Rozanov, even thrusting his hips a bit to try to get him to pick up the pace. He rubbed his back against the bulge he could feel in Rozanov's sweatpants, hoping it would inspire a little more urgency in the other man. Rozanov didn't take the bait. He was maddeningly gentle and patient, and had even started to press light kisses to Shane's hair.

Shane wasn't sure why he was letting Rozanov drive anyway. He flipped himself around and kissed Rozanov hard. At this angle, Shane was taller than him, and he could thread his fingers through Rozanov's hair, tug his head back, and attack his mouth with as much force as he wanted. His sudden aggression drew a satisfying moan out of Rozanov, and Shane wanted more; he wanted to see how many moans and hisses he could wring from him.

He wedged his knee into the tight space between the back of the couch and Rozanov's hip, and pressed himself down onto Rozanov's lap. He squeezed him with his thighs, holding Rozanov in place as he ground his cock against Rozanov's stomach.

"Why do I need this so much?" Shane muttered the words against Rozanov's lips, and hoped the other man hadn't heard them.

"Need what?" Rozanov asked, as if he didn't know.

Shane didn't answer. Instead, he raised his hips so he could haul down Rozanov's waistband and pull his cock out.

"Fuck, Hollander."

Rozanov's head fell back on the arm of the couch, and Shane took the opportunity to kiss and lick and bite his neck. Then he took both of their cocks in his hand and started stroking them.

"Yes. Do that," Rozanov moaned.

It was dry, and a little rough, but it was exactly what Shane wanted. Rozanov bucked up into his hand, and Shane knew it was what he wanted too. He brought their mouths back together and kissed Rozanov wildly.

"Wait." Rozanov grabbed Shane's wrist and stopped his furious stroking. He pulled Shane's hand to his face and spit in his hand. Which was gross. But instead of making a face or bitching at him about it, Shane found it absurdly arousing.

The saliva didn't add a ton of lubrication, but by then Shane's cock was leaking enough to make up for it. He stroked faster, with his forehead resting on Rozanov's shoulder. Shane was very close, and judging by the way Rozanov was thrusting his hips and babbling in Russian, he wasn't far behind.

"You like that?" he growled. "You gonna come for me, Rozanov?"

"Fucking make me, Hollander."

Shane gasped, and his stroking became frantic and sloppy and he was so close…

"Come on," he gritted out.

Then Rozanov went very still and said, "Oh god. Shane…" and he came in hot bursts, coating Shane's hand and allowing Shane to use the slickness to bring himself off almost immediately, with the sound of his first name being spoken in a breathless Russian accent still ringing in his ears.

They held each other, both breathing heavily as they waited for their hearts to stop racing. But Shane didn't think his heart would ever stop racing.

Shane. He called me Shane.

He pulled back so he could see Rozanov's face, and was shocked to see him staring at him with the same wide-eyed terror that Shane felt.

"Ilya," he said, barely more than a whisper.

Ilya didn't answer. Instead, he crushed their mouths together and kissed Shane in a raw, uncontrolled way that felt like an apology.

Oh no. Oh fuck. Oh no.

When they broke apart, Ilya rested his forehead against Shane's and they just breathed together. Shane held Ilya's face in his hands, and Ilya was stroking his back.

Was Shane supposed to say something? Nothing had actually been admitted here. No grand declarations. No questions asked.

Shane untangled himself from Ilya and stood. "I should go."

It was an understatement. Shane *needed* to get the fuck out of there. Immediately. He clumsily tucked himself back into his jeans as he staggered backward, away from Ilya. *Shit, where did I leave my underwear?*

"Go?"

"Yeah... I...uh, I shouldn't stay. I can't. We can't. This is..."

Ilya shifted on the couch, stretching one arm across

the back and resting his ankle on his knee, casual as anything. "This is nothing, Hollander."

Hollander. You called me Shane. "I know. I just… team meeting in the morning. I forgot."

That made Ilya laugh. It wasn't warm. "*You* forgot about a team meeting? Sure."

Shane was already at the door, shoving his feet into his sneakers. Fuck the underwear; he needed to leave. "Thanks for the tuna melt. Um…"

Ilya sighed loudly and raised himself off the couch. Shane was frozen in place, staring in terror as Ilya slowly walked toward him. When he reached him, he tugged down on the hem of Shane's T-shirt, straightening it for him. "Good night, then."

Shane met Ilya's intense gaze. His eyes were *daring* him to stay, and, god, Shane wanted to take that dare.

"Good night," Shane said, barely above a whisper. He bent and grabbed his coat from where it was still lying on the floor, then stood and put his hand on the doorknob. He turned to look at Ilya one last time.

Ilya's eyes lost their heat, and his brow furrowed, as if he'd just realized that Shane was really leaving. Then, just as quickly, he schooled his face to its default expression of cool indifference.

Shane wanted to kiss him, but he opened the door instead, and darted into the hallway. He strode past the elevators, straight to the stairwell, not wanting to linger outside Ilya's door. He jogged down the sixteen flights of stairs, trying to put as much distance between himself and temptation as possible. When he reached the bottom, he leaned back against the wall of the stairwell for a moment.

What is happening?

This was bad. This was really fucking bad. Shane's heart was racing, and it wasn't from taking the stairs. Every fiber of him wanted to run right back up those stairs and into Ilya's arms. To wrap himself around him and go to bed with him and *wake up with him*.

And that was why Shane marched straight out of Ilya's building, and didn't stop walking until he was safely back in his hotel room.

In his panic, he wasn't careful enough about not waking Hayden. He wasn't in the room for ten seconds before the bedside lamp was turned on.

"How'd it go?" Hayden asked, grinning sleepily. "You in love?"

"No!" *No! Jesus.* "I'm gonna take a shower."

"Why? To wash off the sex you weren't having?"

"Go fuck yourself, Hayden."

"Oh, I did. Couple of times. Thanks for the empty room."

Gross.

Shane went into the bathroom to take a shower and freak the hell out in private.

Chapter Fourteen

November 2016—Montreal

"Hollander. What the fuck are you doing right now?"

Shane frowned into his phone. It was his teammate, J.J. Boiziau, calling. J.J. who *always* called and *never* texted.

"Nothing. Why?"

"Fuck that. Get your ass downtown. My buddy Francois, you know, the chef? He's having a little after hours party at his restaurant, and get this, the cast of the fucking *X-Squad* movie they're filming here is gonna be there!"

"All of them?"

"I don't fucking know! Enough of them! There are some fucking *hot* chicks in that movie, man! Get the fuck in your car. You know the restaurant, right? Djon-Djon?"

"Uh. Sure. You took me there once, right?"

Shane's first instinct was to thank J.J. for the invitation, but to tell him that he was going to stay in. But he knew from past experience that saying no to J.J. would result in hourly calls for the rest of the evening to let him know what he was missing.

Besides. It wasn't like Shane had anything better to do. Nothing besides watching the end of a Boston hockey game on television and quietly panicking about the freshly unearthed feelings he was harboring for Ilya Rozanov. He could definitely use a distraction.

He put on some nicer clothes and drove himself to Mile End. It was late on a Tuesday night, and the streets were quiet. He found a parking spot near the restaurant and stepped out of his SUV into the cold.

Most things on the street were closed or closing, but he could see the lights on in the hip, Haitian-inspired restaurant on the corner. The sign on the door said the restaurant was closed, but the door opened for him before Shane even reached it.

Inside there was music and laughter and warmth. The small space was crowded, and something smelled delicious.

"Hollander! Yes, bitch! Get over here!"

J.J. towered over everyone in the room. He was six feet, seven inches and over two hundred and fifty pounds of pure muscle. He had very dark skin and a thick French accent. The contrast between J.J. and Shane, physically, was almost comical. Shane stood a full ten inches shorter than him, and weighed about seventy pounds less.

J.J. was also *loud*. And he loved to talk. He held court no matter what room he was in. He was French and fashionable and loved food and wine—the perfect Montreal celebrity. Everyone loved him.

Aside from a couple of his teammates, Shane didn't *know* anyone at the party, but he certainly recognized a few movie stars in the crowd. Shane was pretty famous—extremely so, on the hockey scale—but even he was a little star struck in this company.

He made his way to the bar, where the bartender seemed to have no problem serving people well after closing. The slim, attractive, dark-skinned man was making elaborate cocktails for the all-star guests.

"Can I get a beer?" Shane asked him, in French. "Whatever you have on tap is fine."

"Shane Hollander can have whatever he wants here," the man said with a sexy little smile. He poured Shane a beer and rested it on a coaster in front of him.

"Thanks," Shane said. He slid a ten-dollar bill across the bar.

The bartender held up his hands and said, "On the house."

"Oh. Well, you keep it then."

The man shook his head, smiling. "It's an honor."

Shane smiled back and stuck out his hand. "Shane," he said. "Please."

"Maxime," the man said, shaking his hand.

"Nice to meet you, Maxime. Are you having a good night?"

"This crowd? Are you kidding? Rose Landry is here, man!"

"Seriously?" Shane asked. He looked over his shoulder, almost involuntarily, searching the crowd for the famous actress. He quickly turned back to Maxime when he realized what he was doing.

Maxime was grinning. Shane shrugged and grinned back. He'd love to catch a glimpse of Rose Landry, but he was sort of enjoying looking at Maxime. He decided to put some space between them before that fact became obvious.

He spent the night mingling, letting J.J. pull him around the room. He stood in small circles of people and laughed at their jokes; he didn't make many of his own. He avoided the bar and eventually found an empty table in one corner. He was ready to leave, but he just wanted to sit for a moment.

"Please tell me you're hungry," a woman's voice said. Shane looked up and saw a slim woman with dark, glossy hair and a very expensive-looking top draped over equally expensive-looking jeans.

Rose Landry.

"The chef just handed me these fritters and they look delicious, but I can't possibly eat them all," she said, sliding into the booth next to Shane. She set a plate on the table that was piled high with Haitian salt cod fritters. She smiled at him, took one, and popped it into her mouth. Her eyes went wide with surprise.

"Oh my *god*! These are so good! You have to eat some." She belatedly raised her hand to cover her mouth as she spoke. Then she laughed at herself.

"Sorry," she said, after she swallowed. "I'm a pig. I'm Rose, by the way," she said, holding out her perfectly manicured hand.

Shane smiled and shook it. "Shane," he said. "Nice to meet you. I'm a fan."

"Well," she said, leaning in a bit, "would you be surprised to know I'm a big fan of *yours*?"

"You like hockey?" Shane asked.

"I was born and raised in Michigan," she said. "Damn right I like hockey!"

"Oh! Well…thanks."

"You're welcome. Eat a fritter, Shane Hollander."

Shane lost track of time as they sat in the booth and talked over (delicious) cod fritters. Rose was easy to talk to. Surprisingly so. They bonded over descriptions of the lakeside cottages where they had each spent childhood summers. She had an older brother who had played hockey in college, and then he became an engineer. Her parents, like Shane's, worked in government.

"Have you been to Montreal before?" Shane asked.

"Once. I was shooting a role in a super terrible FBI versus terrorist whatever movie. I can't even remember what it was called."

"Under Dark."

"Oh my god. Shut up. You *saw* it?"

Shane shrugged, and grinned. It really had been terrible. "I fly a lot. Watch a lot of movies."

"Thankfully it was only a small role. But I was only in Montreal for a week that time. And it was summer."

"It's a little different here in the winter."

She leaned it and said, in a hushed tone that was playfully conspiratorial, "Michigan, remember? Winter can't scare me."

Something fluttery happened in his stomach. He felt his cheeks heat a bit, and then he asked, as smoothly as possible, "So, you gonna be in town for a while this time?"

Her smile let him know she knew exactly what he was really asking.

At the end of the night, they exchanged contact info, and made loose plans to meet for dinner whenever both of their schedules permitted. Shane left the restaurant with a little spring in his step. It had easily been the best connection he had made with a woman…ever. He liked Rose. He wanted to get to know her better. He was excited by the idea of spending more time with her.

And she was very pretty. Obviously.

But mostly Shane just loved talking to her. She was

funny and she asked a lot of questions, but none of them had made Shane uncomfortable.

Shane liked a girl!

In the car, driving home, he laughed at how ridiculously high his standards were.

December 2016—Detroit

Ilya woke alone in his hotel room in... Detroit? Yes. He was in Detroit.

He glanced over at his roommate's abandoned bed, and then at the clock. Eight thirty.

He exhaled and scrubbed his eyes before he sat up. It was no surprise that Carmichael was already up and out of the room. That guy was such a morning person, it was gross.

Ilya threw on some sweats and made his way to the Starbucks in the hotel lobby for some coffee and a breakfast sandwich. Two of his teammates, Cliff Marlow and Victor St-Simon, were sitting at a table.

"Roz! You gotta see this. You'll shit, man!" Cliff called out.

Ilya couldn't imagine what the hell would be that interesting to him. He made his way over to the table and Victor held out his phone for him to see. There was a headline that read, *Is Rose Landry dating NHL star Shane Hollander?*

"No," was Ilya's immediate reaction. He hoped it sounded more dismissive to his teammates than shocked.

"Right?" Cliff laughed. "She's, like, a super-giant movie star! How the fuck did he even meet her during the hockey season?"

"She's been filming a movie in Montreal," Victor

read. "They met at a mutual friend's party…according to unnamed sources."

Ilya snorted.

"There are pictures," Victor said. "Look."

He held his phone out again, and Ilya grabbed it. He scrolled through four paparazzi photos of Shane having dinner with the gorgeous, dark-haired movie star. In one of them Shane was laughing.

Ilya scowled and handed the phone back to Victor.

"Probably nothing," he said.

January 2017—Boston

It wasn't nothing. As the weeks went on, more and more paparazzi photos of Shane and Rose Landry together were hitting the internet. Photos of the two of them walking together, smiling at each other, leaving restaurants together, *kissing* each other.

On the cheek. Just on the cheek. It could still be nothing.

Ilya turned up the resistance on his stationary bike. What did he care, anyway? Why shouldn't Hollander be dating a beautiful woman? Rozanov had slept with a beautiful woman two nights ago. And another one the night before that.

The thing was… Hollander didn't *do* that. Ilya assumed Hollander *must* have sex with people who weren't him, but there was no evidence of it. He didn't want to think about it too much either way.

He had definitely never known Hollander to go on consecutive dates with a woman. To be seen with a woman often enough for the press to notice.

Hollander had a girlfriend.

Maybe Hollander was in *love*.

Ilya pushed himself on the bike until his thighs screamed in protest. He stopped, and took a long haul from his water bottle.

He knew this ridiculous thing between them wasn't going to last forever. It was just…convenient. So maybe it was over now. So what?

Boston was playing in Montreal next week. The week after that was the All-Star Game. Would Hollander just…ignore him?

As Ilya was exiting the team gym, he stubbed his toe on one of the other bikes. He bellowed a string of Russian profanity and hurled his water bottle at the wall. He tried to control his breathing as he watched the water seep into the black and gold carpet.

"Jesus," Cliff said as he stepped off his treadmill. "What the fuck's wrong with you?"

"Nothing," Ilya growled. "Stubbed my toe." He left the room in a hurry, not bothering to pick up the water bottle.

Hayley, he thought to himself. He would text Hayley and see if she was doing anything tonight. He liked Hayley. She was fun, and she had dark hair.

And freckles.

One week later—Montreal

When Shane's phone buzzed, an hour after the game against Boston ended, he had expected it to be Ilya.

It was Rose.

Come out with us tonight. We'll be at Ultraviolet.

Shane felt a confusing mixture of anxiety and relief

sweep over him. He hadn't been sure what to say to Ilya, if he had texted him. If he had wanted to…see him.

Because Shane had a girlfriend now. Sort of.

And his girlfriend wanted him to come to a club with her and her friends. Shane hated nightclubs. He never allowed himself to have more than a couple of drinks, which was not nearly enough for him to be comfortable on a dance floor.

But his girlfriend—his gorgeous, movie star girlfriend—wanted him to go out dancing with her. And that was a thing that boyfriends did. Right?

And if he had to endure his teammates teasing him about dating her—last week Shane had found a giant bouquet of about sixty roses in his locker room stall, which was a very expensive and stupid prank—then he should at least try to enjoy himself.

OK, he texted back. What time?

Ilya was absolutely *not* going to text Hollander. Not a chance.

What he was going to do instead, apparently, was sulk around his hotel room and snap at his roommate for no reason at all.

"Hey!" Ryan Carmichael said, after the umpteenth undeserved bitchy comment from Ilya. "Fuck you! What's your problem, anyway?"

Ilya sighed, and sat himself on the end of his bed. "Nothing. Fuck this. I need to get laid. Let's go out."

"Out where?"

Ilya swept his hand in the direction of the large window. "We're in fucking Montreal! We find a club! Come on."

Carmichael blinked at him, then smiled. "Fucking right, man! I'm gonna text Victor and Cliff."

* * *

After six very successful NHL seasons, Shane had gained a reputation for two things:

1. Being a natural leader and an outstanding playmaker, and;

2. Being absolutely no fun at all.

Shane felt this second accusation was unfair. He was plenty fun. He could relax with a beer and joke around. He was social. He…

He hated clubs. That was something he couldn't deny. He didn't dance, he didn't like crowds, and he didn't like the pressure to pick up women. At least tonight he didn't have to worry about that last thing.

He found Rose and her friends in a VIP area at the club. She stood up and kissed him quickly in greeting. He recognized most of the people there. Two of them were her costars from the *X-Squad* movie: Miles and Jiya. Miles was a young actor with a massive fan base, due to his work as a teenager on a popular television drama. He was extremely attractive, with light brown skin, perfectly groomed stubble, and the most incredible eyes Shane had ever seen. They were gray—so pale they were almost silver. He was looking effortlessly gorgeous in a long-sleeve black top, slim-fitting dark gray pants, and a black knit hat.

Shane nodded at him awkwardly and received a slow, absurdly sexy smile in return. Shane looked away quickly and moved to sit next to Rose.

"Good game tonight," Rose said.

"Oh, thanks. You watched?"

She smiled apologetically. "I wish. We just finished filming for the day a couple of hours ago. I was checking the score on my phone, though!"

She took his hand and squeezed it, then pulled it over to rest on her knee. It was probably as natural as anything for her, but Shane felt like everyone was just staring at their joined hands.

What is wrong with me?

A server appeared and Shane ordered a beer. Everyone else seemed to be drinking vodka. He was definitely *not* going to get into *that* shit tonight.

They sat and drank and talked for over an hour as the club filled up. Rose's voice was noticeably hoarse from shouting over the music. Shane had barely said ten words; he just enjoyed listening to everyone else and laughing when someone made a joke. When he couldn't follow the conversation, he sipped his second beer, watched the dance floor, and stole a few glances at Miles.

Which was dumb because Shane was here with *Rose Landry*.

"Come dance with me!" Rose exclaimed suddenly. She stood up and tried to pull Shane with her.

"Oh," Shane said. "No... I, uh..."

"Come *on*. I never get to dance!"

"That is a lie," Miles laughed.

"Well, I want to dance with Shane."

Shane heard Miles say something that sounded a lot like "That makes two of us," but he couldn't be sure over the music.

Shane surrendered and put his beer bottle on the table. He stood and allowed Rose to lead him to the dance floor.

Shane really, really needed to up his fashion game. Hanging out with Rose and her friends made him feel like a slob, and being on the dance floor only empha-

sized how uninspired his wardrobe was. He had made
an effort tonight, but his deep plum polo and dark blue
pants seemed kind of basic. His sneakers were nice,
though.

Rose put her arms around his neck and they danced.
Or, at least, *she* danced. She was stunning, and she
moved to the music with so much carefree joy. Shane
was mesmerized.

Most of the girls on the dance floor seemed more
like… Rozanov's type. Or, at least, what he was pretty
sure Rozanov was into, based on photos that Shane had
seen on the internet completely by accident and not because he sometimes did image searches for Ilya Rozanov. He could easily imagine Ilya flirting with any one
(or two) of the array of blonde, tanned girls with dark
eyelashes and shimmery lips.

He wondered what Ilya was doing tonight. Had he
been…disappointed…that they hadn't hooked up?

Was *Shane* disappointed?

Rose flicked her dark hair around and laughed. "I
love this song!" she yelled.

Shane smiled back. He had no idea what song it was.
He kept his fingers on Rose's waist—barely touching—
as she closed her eyes and slid a hand down his chest.

Shane understood what was supposed to be happening here. He was supposed to be…escalating things.
Touching her, teasing her. Making her want him. And
then they would kiss and press closer together and…

So why wasn't he?

Ilya headed straight for the dance floor as soon as they
entered the club. It was late and the place was packed. A
quick scan of the place told him that there were plenty

of good options. Plenty of gorgeous girls who could take his mind off Shane stupid Hollander.

Wait.

It was impossible not to spot Rose Landry on the dance floor. Even in this crowd, she stood out.

And it only took him a second longer to realize the man she had her arms around—who had his *hands* on her *waist*—was Shane Hollander.

Fuck it.

Ilya moved purposefully to the other side of the dance floor. He found a girl inside a minute who was happy to press her body against his. By the next song, she had her tongue in his mouth.

He wondered if Hollander saw him.

Miles joined them on the dance floor, and Shane dropped his hands from Rose's waist. Rose turned and smiled at Miles, and danced with him for a while. Miles kept looking over her shoulder at Shane. There almost seemed to be a hint of invitation in his eyes.

Shane looked away uncomfortably. He stood on the dance floor, just barely swaying, with his arms hanging limp at his sides. Now that Miles was here, he could probably slip away. Go back to the VIP area. Maybe even go home.

His eyes landed on a man he was sure was Victor St-Simon, a player for Boston. He was smiling at a girl he was dancing with. Shane frowned and glanced around. He spotted Ryan Carmichael. And Cliff Marlow.

And Ilya Rozanov.

Ilya was dancing with a girl. His head and shoulders towered over most of the crowd. Shane moved through the sea of dancers toward him without even realizing he was doing it.

He got close enough to see the way the heat of the room was causing Ilya's damp hair to curl even tighter than usual, and the way his skin glistened the same way it had during the game. But the games didn't have lighting like this; at the games, the music wasn't pounding and Ilya's body wasn't writhing and the whole room didn't scream *sex*.

Ilya had on a V-neck T-shirt that was almost transparent, despite being a dark color. Sometimes a light would hit him just right and Shane could see the outline of his bear tattoo, and the glint of his gold chain. The girl he was dancing with had her back to him, and she seemed to be grinding her ass into his crotch. Ilya was watching her, eyes hooded, lips parted. Shane watched as he bit down on his lower lip and closed his eyes before bending his head to kiss her neck. She turned and leaned up and kissed him. It was a wild, filthy kiss. She had her hands up the front of his shirt.

And Shane felt sick. He needed to leave.

He realized, suddenly, as if waking from a dream, that he was standing alone in the middle of a dance floor…not dancing. Just…staring. At Ilya.

He couldn't let Ilya notice him.

Ilya pulled away from the kiss and smiled at his very willing partner. She was a good kisser. She had a tongue piercing. He liked that.

He glanced around the club, wondering where the best dark corner was to—

Holy fuck.

When his gaze landed on Shane Hollander, Shane's eyes went wide.

Had Shane just been…*watching him*?

Ilya couldn't resist pushing it. He gave him what he believed to be his sexiest smile, and bent down to whisper in the girl's ear. "Should we take this somewhere else?"

He never took his eyes off Shane.

"Sorry," she said, surprising him. "Not tonight, babe. I'm here with my boyfriend. He likes to watch me. It turns him on. But I'm leaving with him."

The fuck? "Your…boyfriend?" He looked around nervously.

She laughed. "Relax. He's not gonna hit you. He likes it, like I said." She kissed his cheek, turned, and left him.

And Shane was gone.

Furious, and now even more desperately in need of release than he had been before he'd left the hotel, Ilya stormed off the dance floor and grabbed Victor by the arm. "I'm leaving."

"With that girl? Right on, man."

Ilya didn't answer him.

Back at the hotel, Ilya jerked off in the shower before throwing himself angrily onto his bed.

He couldn't sleep. He curled on his side and watched the minutes tick by on the alarm clock beside the bed.

Stupid fucking Shane Hollander. Stupid Rose Landry.

Oh god, what was wrong with him? Why did he care? Ilya had been ready to let that weird girl with the kinky boyfriend do whatever she wanted to with him.

What did it matter what Shane was doing when Ilya didn't require him?

Except Shane had been *watching him* make out with that girl. And Shane had looked so fucking good. Not, like, clothes-wise; Shane's wardrobe was as boring as he was. But something about seeing Shane Hollander in that environment had been...exhilarating.

What if Ilya had been able to get closer to him? Would Shane have danced with him, right there in that packed Montreal nightclub? Would he have let Ilya push that stupid polo up and run his hands over the hard lines of his abs? Would he have tilted his head back and sucked in a breath when Ilya kissed his neck?

No. It would never have happened. Shane was with Rose now. And he and Ilya couldn't even appear to be friendly with each other, let alone be spotted grinding against each other in a club.

He pinched the cross that hung around his neck and rubbed it with his thumb as he scowled into the dark room. He had never in his life been angry about someone sleeping with someone else. He was largely indifferent to most things.

Was it just that Ilya liked his sex with a generous helping of danger, and Shane provided both? Or was he just being childish about having to share his favorite toy with a gorgeous movie star?

Somewhere, buried deep in his brain, there was a third reason that was screaming for attention.

Ilya ignored it.

Chapter Fifteen

One week later—Montreal

Shane liked Rose Landry. He did.

She was easy to talk to, and she had a warmth about her that drew people in. She was a bigger celebrity than he was, but she handled it so easily. She laughed a lot, and when she asked people questions—which was often—she genuinely seemed to care about their answers. Maybe it was because she was an actress, but she always seemed very interested in people. Always observing. And she remembered every detail.

They had slept together a couple of times. It had been...fine. Better than usual, really. Except Shane knew she wouldn't be so dazzled by his stardom that she would be able to overlook his performance, and that had made him nervous. Which had made it more difficult for him to...perform.

But she had been patient and helpful, and he'd completed the task both times. He may have noticed some surprise on her part that it seemed to be such a chore for him—especially the second time. He was sure she wasn't used to that.

Tonight, Shane was alone with her at a private table

in a wine bar in Old Montreal. He had actually been surprised when he'd arrived and found her alone there. He'd been expecting the usual crowd of Rose's friends and coworkers.

"I thought it would be nice to have some time to… talk," she'd explained. "Just the two of us."

"Sure." Shane had nodded. "Yeah. You're right. It's nice."

They talked for a long time, over wine and charcuterie. At one point Rose laughed at some dumb joke Shane made. "You're so cute," she said. "Have I told you how cute you are?"

"No," Shane said, blushing a little.

"You are. I'll tell you," she said, leaning in, "Miles is *extremely* jealous."

"Of me?"

She laughed. "No, silly! Of *me*!"

"Oh." Shane let that sink in. *"Oh!"*

Rose's eyes bugged out a bit. "Wait…did you not notice that Miles is gay?"

"Um… I guess I hadn't really thought about it," Shane lied.

"Well, he is. And he's low-key in love with you."

"Oh." Shane knew he was blushing. He hoped the dim lighting hid it.

"Are you…surprised that a young actor is gay, Shane?"

"No—I mean…no."

She leaned back in her chair. "Are there, like, gay hockey players?" she asked. "I mean, obviously, yes, there are, right? But are there any *openly* gay hockey players?"

"No," Shane said. "I mean, yes. There are gay players. Bi players. Whatever. I'm sure there must be, yeah.

But no one has ever…come out. Publicly." *Why is she asking me about this?*

"Hm," she said.

"What?"

She gave him a small smile. He wasn't sure what it meant. "I'm sorry. I'm going about this the wrong way."

"Going about what?" And suddenly Shane felt like he was staring down a slap shot. He braced himself for impact.

She reached out and put her hand on his. "Shane. I really like you. But… I'm getting the vibe that maybe I'm not…doing it for you."

"You are! You do! I like you a lot too!"

"You like talking to me."

"Yeah…"

"Do you like…*kissing* me?"

"Sure."

She laughed. "Wow."

Oh god. Shane was fucking this up. "I mean…yes, of course I do!"

"It's okay, Shane. I just…get the impression…that maybe you would rather be kissing, just for example… Miles?"

Shane didn't know what to say. He had never encountered a direct accusation like this before.

Except it wasn't really an accusation. Rose wasn't judging him. She was just trying to understand him.

He stared into his wineglass. He knew he had taken too long to reply already. The jig was up.

"It's okay," she said again, her voice soft and warm. Her fingers brushed over his hand reassuringly.

"I like you," Shane said quietly. "I like being with you. I like talking to you. But the sex part… I know it's…a problem."

"It's not a problem," she said. "A problem is something you can solve. We're like…a square peg and a round hole." She scrunched her nose. "Ew. No. Gross. Forget I said that."

Shane laughed. "I get it."

"We just…aren't supposed to fit together. And that's fine. But we can't keep trying."

Shane nodded. "For the record, I'm not sure that I'm…like Miles, exactly."

When he met her eyes, she smiled. "Well, it's nothing that you need to figure out today." She took a sip of her wine, possibly for courage, because the next words out of her mouth were, "Have you ever been with a man?"

For whatever reason, Shane didn't feel like lying. He'd made it this far.

"Yes."

"And? Was it different?"

"Of course."

"I mean…was it better?"

Shane's memory supplied him with flashes of golden brown curls and sparkling hazel eyes and a playful smile and hard muscles and of strong hands holding him down as he was entered and filled and…

"Yeah," Shane said softly. "Yeah. It was better." He cleared his throat. "The thing is… I kind of prefer to be the hole. Than the peg."

"Ha!" Rose threw her head back in delight. Shane laughed too. He felt lighter, suddenly.

Later, before they left the bar, Rose gave him a mischievous look over the rim of her wineglass and said, "So…should I give Miles your number?"

"No. Thank you, but no. I need to…figure some stuff out."

"I know. I was just joking. Mostly."

They waited outside for her driver and she said, "Let's be friends. And I don't mean in an 'I hope we can still be friends' bullshit way. I mean it. Let's be friends. Let's be *best* friends. Because I really do care about you a lot, Shane. And I feel like you might not have anyone else to talk to about…certain things."

"I'd like that. You're right. I don't. And I care about you too. We'll be friends. You have my number. Text me. Text me all the time. Please."

"Whenever we're in the same city, we'll hang out. I promise."

She hugged him as her driver pulled up. He hugged her back and kissed the top of her head. He was surprised to feel tears in his eyes.

The same night—Boston

Svetlana was his favorite.

Ilya watched her now, perched on the end of his bed, naked, flipping through channels searching for the Vancouver vs. Colorado hockey game. When she found it, she slapped the remote down on the mattress and shimmied back until she was beside Ilya, against the headboard. She pulled the cigarette from between his lips and took a drag.

"I thought you quit," she teased.

She had vivid blue eyes, and long, straight hair that was so blonde it almost had no color at all. She couldn't have looked less like…

"Why is Matheson still on the power play line?" she complained at the television, in Russian. "It's bullshit. He's been horrible all season. They should put Bogrov in."

"Why don't you coach Colorado, then?" Ilya asked, snatching back his cigarette.

"They would be lucky to have me."

Ilya laughed. He had first met Svetlana three years ago, when she'd worked for the Lamborghini dealership in Boston. He had been surprised to learn, after he had slept with her the first time, that she was the daughter of a retired Russian Boston Bears star player. She possibly knew more about hockey than Ilya did.

"What was *that* shot?" she asked the television. "He should have gone high!"

"Mm. It is a little harder when you are the one who is actually doing it."

She waved her hand dismissively. "What would you know?" she said. Then she smiled, and they both laughed.

Despite her fierce love of hockey, she never treated Ilya with any reverence. Maybe it was being the daughter of a former superstar that made her unable to put Ilya on a pedestal. She seemed to want exactly what Ilya wanted: a no-expectations hookup from time to time. They had fun together, and she was incredibly beautiful. The fact that Ilya could speak to her in Russian was a bonus.

"Ugh. Matheson again. He's terrible!"

"Why do you even care about Colorado?"

"I care about all teams. I don't like good Russian players being put on the second line so a no-talent Canadian can hog the spotlight."

"No talent?"

"No talent! None! You can tell him, next time you see him."

"I will."

"Good. You tell him Svetlana Vetrova says he is terrible."

"I'll see him next week at the All-Star Game."

"I can't believe Matheson is an all-star. It makes no sense."

"He is beloved."

"He is terrible."

Ilya rolled his eyes and smiled.

"You are playing with Shane Hollander this year, right? In the All-Star Game?" Svetlana asked, as if she didn't know the answer.

"Yes. Is he also terrible?"

"No! No, Hollander is amazing. I *love* Shane Hollander." She sort of purred the last few words.

"Traitor."

"He's a beautiful skater. Such talented hands. And so cute."

"Now you are trying to make me angry."

"You can't argue those facts, Ilya."

"No," Ilya said, grinding the butt of his cigarette into a small plate he was using as a makeshift ashtray. "I can't argue them. He is very good."

"And cute."

"If you say so."

She pulled her knees to her chest. "Are we going to fuck again, or should I get dressed? I'm cold."

Ilya considered her question, then shrugged. "I'm hungry. You should get dressed."

She looked momentarily surprised, then her features changed to match his own cool indifference. "All right."

She stood up and began retrieving her clothes from the floor. Ilya watched her, but his mind wasn't on her slim, perfect body.

Would he have shrugged if Shane had asked him if they were going to fuck again? Would he have turned down his chance to enjoy his body as many times as he possibly could? *Don't you dare put your clothes on, Hollander. I'm not done with you yet.*

The truth—the truth that he tried so very hard to ignore—was that *no one* set him on fire like Shane Hollander. All of these women…they were gorgeous. Fun. Very sexy. But he didn't think about them after they were gone. He didn't long for them. With them, he could be sated.

He grimaced at himself as Svetlana pulled her shirt back on. Shane Hollander was not an option. He wasn't ever an option, not really. This thing between them needed to stop. It was bad for both of them, and Ilya knew they should end it.

What scared Ilya was how desperately he wanted it to *continue*.

But not enough to embarrass himself. Which was why he hadn't even bothered texting Shane when their teams had played against each other in Montreal last week. He had no interest in being rejected by Shane Hollander.

He'd also had no interest in seeing Shane Hollander with his hands all over Rose fucking Landry in a night-club, but fate seemed determined to rub Hollander in his face. A fucking *nightclub*! If he couldn't be safe from Hollander there, then where?

Ilya wondered if Rose Landry would be joining Shane in Florida for the All-Star Game. He wondered if Rose Landry would be accompanying Shane to everything from now on. Maybe they would get married.

For the first time ever, Ilya was not looking forward to the All-Star Game.

Chapter Sixteen

January 2017—Tampa Bay

Shane was nervous. After six and a half seasons, he was used to his fucked-up arrangement with Rozanov, but something felt different now. Maybe it was because he had finally spoken aloud to someone about his…possible preference. Or maybe it was because of the weird way things were left the last time he and Rozanov had been together, in Ilya's apartment. Or maybe Shane just felt surer of what he wanted now, after walking away from a relationship that had been almost perfect.

Almost.

He *wanted* to see Rozanov this weekend. He wanted to be with him, alone, behind closed doors; he was tired of lying to himself about it.

This year, finally, Shane would know what it felt like to play *with* Ilya Rozanov. Six All-Star Games and this was the first time they had been placed on the same team. Injuries and weird, gimmicky team arrangements that the league kept coming up with had prevented it from happening before.

He wasn't the only one who was excited about him being Ilya's teammate. The press was having a field day

writing about this monumental event where Shane and
Ilya would have to put aside their supposed animosity
and learn to work together. Was it even *possible*, they
wondered?

Shane smiled to himself as he hung up his suit in the
hotel room closet. *If they only knew.*

But, truthfully, if *he* only knew what Ilya was thinking these days. He wasn't sure if Ilya wanted to end
things, or if he wanted to push things further. He really
had no idea what to expect from his temporary teammate this weekend.

He glanced at his watch. The team meet-up down-
stairs was starting in a few minutes.

Shane blew out a breath, then checked himself in
the mirror.

Let's do this.

Ilya hadn't texted Hollander in over two months.

Not that they had ever regularly contacted each other
before, but this silence had been particularly deafening.
The past few weeks had been the first time that Ilya felt
sure that, if he texted him, Shane wouldn't reply.

Shane would probably show the text to his movie
star girlfriend, and they would laugh at how pathetic
Ilya was.

No. That wouldn't happen. Of course Shane wouldn't
do that.

Maybe.

Ilya fumbled his package of nicotine gum out of his
pocket and popped a piece in his mouth. Had Shane
brought his girlfriend to All-Star weekend? Would he
introduce her to Ilya?

God.

Ilya ran out of time to fret, because at that moment, Hollander walked into the bar. Every head turned. Some guys actually stood up, for fuck's sake.

Ilya leaned against the bar and watched Shane shake hands and clap guys on the back. He watched him smile and laugh with everyone. He looked relaxed and confident, like a man who had gotten his life together. Like a man who didn't question himself anymore. He looked...

Christ, he looks so fucking good.

Maybe Rose had taken him shopping or something. Suddenly he was dressing like the millionaire he was. He had on a white, button-up linen shirt, open at the collar, with the sleeves rolled up. They *were* in Florida, after all. It was tucked into slate blue pants that fit him perfectly. The outfit was finished with a woven belt and some stylish gray sneakers with no socks.

Ilya was wearing shorts, and a shirt that was covered in palm trees because he'd thought it would be funny. Now he felt like a fucking idiot.

He ordered another drink just so he'd stop staring at Shane.

He cursed himself for feeling so gloomy. It should be a fun weekend; the hotel was a fucking beach resort.

Someone moved into the space next to him at the bar. Without looking, Ilya knew it was Hollander.

"Hey, teammate," Shane said.

"Hello, *Captain*," Ilya said, because Shane *had* been selected as the captain of their All-Star team. Of course.

Shane flagged the bartender down and Ilya noticed the expensive watch on his wrist. A gift from Rose, maybe?

"So this should be fun, huh?" Shane said. "Always

wondered what it would be like to play on the same team."

"Have you?"

"Nice that it's in Florida this year, eh?"

"Mm."

Shane's beer arrived and Ilya watched him take a long haul off the bottle. He watched his throat work as he swallowed.

He couldn't take it anymore.

"Did you...bring anyone? With you?" Ilya asked.

Shane shook his head. "No. I mean...my parents thought about it, but they've been to so many of these things and they're already going to Mexico next month, so..."

"Ah." Rose Landry must be busy filming somewhere.

Shane's tongue darted out to lick his upper lip. Ilya could have sworn it happened in slow motion.

"Nice shirt," Shane said with a grin.

"Thought I'd get in the spirit. You know."

"You can pull it off." He raked his eyes over Ilya's body, and Ilya's heart sped up. "Looks good."

Ilya probably could have said something similar in return, but he was too busy staring at the hollow of Shane's throat.

"Jesus, look at this! Fucking beautiful!" A pair of giant arms landed heavily across the shoulders of Ilya and Shane. The intruder, Mike Brophy—a huge defenseman for New Jersey—pulled Ilya's and Shane's heads together. "This is what it's all about! Fucking Hollander and Rozanov working together! Love it!"

Shane had managed to pull his head from Brophy's bicep, and gave the big man a wary smile. "Should be fun, yeah," he said.

"Don't listen to a word this fucker says, though," Brophy said, elbowing Ilya roughly. "Can't trust this asshole. Whatever he tells you, he's probably fucking with you."

"I'll keep that in mind," Shane said.

Brophy left, with departing arm punches to both of them.

"I think we can expect a lot of that kind of thing this weekend," Shane said. He turned so he was leaning back against the bar on his elbows.

"They should give us a chance to get to know each other," Ilya said. He leaned in and dropped his voice. "We might even have something in common."

Shane smiled at the floor, the color rising in his cheeks.

"You look good too," Ilya said. "Someone take you shopping?"

Shane looked at him. "If I tell you something, do you promise not to tell anyone? Or make fun of me?"

Ilya felt an icy stab of dread in his stomach. He braced himself, and said, "Sure."

"I, uh…" Ilya waited for the words. *I'm seeing someone. I'm engaged. I don't need you anymore.* "I hired a personal stylist."

For a moment, there was silence. Then Ilya burst out laughing. "Fuck off!" he said, delighted.

"I shouldn't have told you."

"No! I love it! Got tired of looking like shit?"

"I didn't—" Shane was trying to look angry, but Ilya could tell he was fighting a smile. "I just mostly wore, you know, athletic stuff. I guess. Track pants and T-shirts and stuff. Some guys in the league are so fashionable and I just thought… I could use some help."

"This has nothing to do with Rose Landry?"

"What? No. I mean…yeah, her friends were all really well dressed all the time. I guess maybe I felt like a slob when we went out together. I've never really cared about clothes and I thought… I don't know. I just want to present myself better. Not always dress like I'm heading to the gym."

Ilya didn't miss the past tense of what Shane was saying about going out with Rose, even with his imperfect English. "Are you and her not…"

Shane shook his head. "We're not. No. It was just a short thing. She's great. We just weren't, um…compatible."

He looked seriously at Ilya then. Ilya wanted to kiss him.

"Anyway," Shane said, gesturing toward the room with his beer bottle, "I should say hi to everyone." He stepped away from the bar.

"Right."

Ilya put his hand over his mouth to hide his ridiculous smile.

It was a fun weekend. Everyone had a lot of free time on Saturday, before the Skills Competition that night. A lot of the guys lounged around the pool, soaking up the Florida sun, or headed to the beach. Shane spent some of the afternoon by the pool.

The league had asked the fans to vote for the All-Star team captains this year, and they had chosen him. Shane felt a little embarrassed about it because, even though he had been the captain of the Voyageurs for two and a half seasons now and this was his sixth All-Star Game, the honor of being named All-Star team captain normally went to one of the most senior players on the team. Shane was only twenty-five.

But being named captain over Rozanov had felt pretty sweet.

Rozanov was in the pool with a couple of other players and their kids, being loud and goofing around. Shane was sitting on a deck chair with a bottle of water, shaking his head and smiling as he watched him challenge the kids to a swimming race. He would "lose" every time, and then he would act outraged and accuse the kids of cheating. The kids were laughing so hard Shane was worried they might drown.

"Last race!" Ilya announced. "Championship match. Winner takes all! No other races count!"

"No way!" one of the kids yelled at him.

"Come on. One more race. If I lose… I will buy you candy bars from the machine."

That was enough to get the kids to line up across one end of the pool.

"Hey! Hollander!" Ilya called suddenly. Shane nodded at him.

"You gotta watch, okay?" Ilya said. "Make sure none of these cheaters cheats."

"Okay."

"You kids know who that guy is?" Ilya asked.

"Shane Hollander!" most of them said at once.

"Really?" Ilya said, feigning shock. "You've heard of that guy?"

They laughed. One of the braver ones said, "He's the best player in the league!"

"Okay, you're out of the race. Out of the pool. Out of Florida. Goodbye. Where's your dad?"

The kids laughed more. Shane laughed too. He wondered if Ilya ever thought about having kids. He was good with them.

Finally the race began. Ilya took an early lead, then pretended to have been attacked by a shark.

"You gotta buy us candy bars!" one of the kids said.

"Aw, damn. Hey, Hollander! I need, like, ten bucks!"

Shane almost flipped him off, but then remembered the kids. "Did Boston stop paying you or something?" He grinned.

"I forgot my wallet!"

"Of course you did."

Ilya hoisted himself out of the pool. Shane's breath caught a little as he watched him make his way over to his chair. His wet swimsuit clung to his thighs and his crotch, and water ran in little rivulets down his chest. When he reached Shane's chair, he shook his head violently so water flew all over Shane's dry clothing.

"Ah! Fu—" Shane stopped himself. "Knock it off!"

Instead, Ilya swooped down and wrapped his arms around him. Shane's eyes went wide.

"Get off! What the—" He was shocked that Ilya would do something this…*public*. Shocked and a little thrilled.

But to everyone watching, this was just typical Rozanov being a playful asshole. Everyone was laughing as Shane squirmed in a halfhearted attempt to free himself.

When he finally let go, Shane shoved him and tried to look annoyed, but he knew his face was flushed and he couldn't help grinning. Ilya straightened up to full height, looming over Shane with the sun behind him. Every inch of him was glistening gold.

It took every ounce of Shane's willpower to stop himself from reaching out for him. He looked magnificent.

He was looking right back at Shane with his wet hair falling into his eyes, and Shane followed his gaze down to his own chest. His shirt was wet and clinging to him. It was a white and blue gingham checked shirt, and parts of it were transparent now.

"You wrecked my shirt," Shane said.

"Sorry," Ilya said. He didn't sound sorry.

Shane licked his bottom lip.

Ilya quickly turned away from him. "Hey! Brophy! I need ten bucks! Hollander's a cheapskate."

Ilya moved from center to right wing for the All-Star Game so he could play on a line with Hollander. He was happy to do it; he'd been waiting a long time for an opportunity to play with Shane.

And playing with him was everything he had imagined it would be.

He actually felt bad for their left wing linemate, Carson, because as far as Ilya was concerned there was no one else on the ice. Hollander could actually *keep up* with Ilya, and it was like they were reading each other's minds when they passed the puck. They had barely had any time to practice together; they just clicked in a way Ilya never had with any other player. It was exhilarating.

Ilya took a pass from one of the defensemen and he took off. When he glanced to his left, he saw that Shane was right there with him. He crossed the blue line, fired the puck over to Shane, Shane knocked it back to him, and Ilya returned it at the last second. Shane shot it cleanly into the top corner of the net for his fourth goal of the game.

Shane raised his arms in celebration and he just looked so *happy*. He was beaming and his eyes were crinkled and his cheeks were flushed. Ilya embraced him, and Shane wrapped both of his arms tight around him. Ilya felt a puff of Shane's hot breath on his neck, and he could see the glisten of sweat on his skin and Ilya kissed him, hard, on the cheek. He was sure, to the crowd, that it looked like Ilya's usual obnoxious shenanigans, that the kiss was just another way of annoying Hollander. But the truth was he simply couldn't help himself. He had seen an opportunity, and he had taken it.

"What the fuck?" Shane laughed.

Ilya felt his own cheeks flush, which was a rare and uncomfortable feeling.

"Nice goal," he said.

"Nice assist," Shane said, shooting him a weird look.

Ilya grinned and shrugged. He thumped Shane on the back in an overly macho way and skated toward the bench.

On Sunday night, after the game, a bunch of the guys went to a Mexican restaurant that one of the Tampa Bay players claimed had the best food in town. A few others just drank at the hotel bar. There were several room parties happening too.

Shane was sitting on the beach, alone. It was dark, but there were still quite a few people out walking in the moonlight. He supposed that was exactly what you came to Florida for.

He just needed an hour or so to himself. The weekend had been challenging for a lot of reasons. He had tried to keep some distance between himself and Ilya, both because he couldn't trust himself not to touch him in some telling way, and also because the media was so obsessed with the two of them playing together despite "hating" each other that he didn't want to give them any fuel. And, he supposed, he didn't want to change the narrative either. The rivalry was good for the league, good for their careers, and, most importantly, it was a very good cover for the truth.

He dug his toes into the cool sand. He listened to the waves that he could just barely see in the darkness. This was nice. So much of his life was spent indoors. Arenas and gyms and hotel rooms and airports and planes.

Someone sat beside him, a few inches away. He didn't even need to look.

"Found you," said Ilya.

"You were looking for me?"

"Of course not."

They sat in silence for a while. Ilya planted his hands behind him, next to Shane's in the sand, and stretched his long legs out. His feet were bare, like Shane's. "I looked up the word," Ilya said. *"Compatible."*

"What?"

"I thought I knew what it meant. But I wanted to check."

Shane thought for a moment, then realized what Ilya was referring to. "Oh."

"You and Rose Landry…"

"Yeah. Not compatible. Not in that way, anyway."

Ilya was quiet. Shane looked around to see if anyone was close enough to hear them. They seemed to be alone.

It was very dark.

"When do you fly out?"

"Early," Ilya said.

"Me too. Columbus."

"Toronto." When Ilya said it, he rolled the "r" slightly and pronounced the second "t." Shane smiled.

Without warning, Ilya moved his hand until it was right next to Shane's, and then he hooked their thumbs together. Shane's first instinct was to pull away, but he resisted. Instead he closed his eyes, and tried not to hope for impossible things. He also resisted the urge to rest his head on Ilya's shoulder.

"What room are you in?" Shane whispered.

"Twelve seventeen."

"I'd like to talk. Somewhere private."

Ilya pulled his thumb away. Shane wanted to grab it back.

Ilya stood and said, "See you soon," before walking back toward the hotel.

Chapter Seventeen

Ilya stood in the middle of his hotel room. Did Shane actually want to talk to him? Was "talking" code for something else, like it always had been before? Had Shane felt the shift in their relationship that Ilya had, the last time they were together? If so, was he looking to break things off and run away…or lean into it? Or maybe he didn't know what he wanted, because Ilya sure as fuck didn't.

He also knew that what they both wanted probably didn't matter anyway.

Ilya wished they could go for a walk or something—a moonlit stroll on the beach. He was tired of hotel rooms.

His phone buzzed. *I'm here.*

He opened the door immediately.

Shane slipped in. His clothes were rumpled and a little sandy from the beach. His hair had been tousled by the ocean breeze.

He crossed the room without speaking and sat on the end of the bed. He clasped his hands together and looked at the floor.

"Whoa," Ilya said. "This looks serious."

"It's not… I mean…sort of. Just…shut up a second, all right?"

Ilya sat himself on the dresser, directly across from the end of the bed, and waited.

"It's…" Shane grimaced. "It's not just me, right?"

"Not just you?"

"I mean…you feel it too, don't you?"

"Feel what?"

"God, fuck you. You know what I mean! The last time we were…together…it was…different."

Ilya shrugged and looked away. He knew it was the wrong reaction, but he felt a horrifying swell of emotion that he couldn't let Shane see.

"Don't act like you don't know what I'm talking about," Shane said angrily. "This is hard enough without you being an asshole."

Ilya turned back to him, his face carefully hiding everything he was feeling. "What do you want, Hollander?"

"I—" Shane didn't seem to have any idea of what to say next.

"We get together, and we fuck. Is simple," Ilya said.

"Simple," Shane grumbled. "Right."

Ilya shrugged again. "Is simple for me."

"Bullshit."

Ilya rolled his eyes. Why was Hollander saying any of this? Why now?

"I think I'm gay," Shane blurted out.

Ilya looked at him, startled, for a moment. Then he laughed. "Oh yeah? What gives you that idea?"

Shane glared at him, which made Ilya laugh more.

"The last time my dick was in your mouth, I thought you might be a little gay," Ilya teased.

"Fuck off. *You're* not gay."

"No," Ilya said, serious again. "Not completely."

"Well… I think I might be. Completely."

Ilya studied him a moment, then said, "Okay. So you are gay. So what?"

"Well, it's sort of a big deal! To me, at least. Sorry if I'm boring you!"

Ilya slid off the dresser and went to the mini fridge. He pulled out a can of Coke and a can of ginger ale. He handed the ginger ale to Shane as he sat beside him on the bed.

"Why are you telling me that you are gay?" Ilya asked quietly.

Shane laughed humorlessly. "Who else am I gonna tell?"

Ilya took a sip of his Coke. "You are not the only gay NHL player. Probably."

"I know."

"So?"

Shane sighed. "It's not just…being gay," he said, awkwardly, as if he was still getting used to the word. "It's *you*. You and me. Being gay is one thing. Hooking up with your arch fucking rival is another."

"That is why it is a secret."

"I know that, but…" Shane ran a hand through his own hair in exasperation. "Last time we were together it was…nice," he said quietly.

Ilya was silent a moment, then admitted, "It was."

"It felt like we were…more."

"We can't be more, Hollander."

Shane turned his head sharply to look at Ilya. "Would you want to be? If we could?"

"We can't."

"That's not what I asked."

Ilya stood up and set his Coke can down hard on the dresser. "It doesn't fucking *matter*!"

Shane flinched and fiddled with the can of ginger

ale that he hadn't even opened. "I can't keep pretend-ing I don't like you," he said finally.

"You *don't* like me," Ilya argued.

"I do. I… I maybe like you too much."

Ilya's heart clenched. "Don't," he groaned. "Don't fucking do this, Hollander. I'm not…"

"Worth it?"

Ilya glared at him. "*Gay.* I'm not gay. And I can't be…anything close to it, okay?"

Shane laughed. "Well, you're doing a shitty job of that!"

"Not in public. I can't… I would not be able to go home."

"Your family?"

"*Russia.* I could not go home to Russia."

Shane looked horrified. "What would happen to you?"

"I do not want to find out."

He seemed to consider this. "Would your parents… help?"

Ilya shook his head and sat himself on the floor against the wall. "My father is a cop."

"Oh," said Shane. "Jesus."

"My *brother* is a cop."

"What about your mother?"

"Dead."

"I'm sorry."

"I was young," Ilya said, waving a hand as if his mother's death was of no consequence to him, which was far from the truth. "I have a stepmother. She is… very young for my father." He snorted. "My *mother* was very young for my father."

"Oh."

Ilya exhaled slowly. "My father was not ever an easy man to live with. He is very…set in old ways. Very strict. My brother, Andrei, is much like him. But now… my father is sick."

"Sick? Like…cancer?"

Ilya shook his head. "No. Alzheimer's."

"Oh. Shit. I'm sorry."

Ilya nodded. There. Now someone knew.

"He must be proud of you, though? You're a super-star!"

Ilya almost laughed at that. "He did not want me to leave. Wanted me to stay in Russia."

Neither man said anything for a while.

"I love my country," Ilya said. "But I could not stay there."

"Would have made *my* life a lot easier," Shane joked.

They both laughed. Shane shook his head and looked at the ceiling. And Ilya just…stared at him. At this oddly insecure superstar who was so beautiful and sweet and *here*.

"You look really fucking good," Ilya said.

Shane stood and placed his ginger ale on the dresser next to Ilya's abandoned Coke. He sank to the floor, straddling Ilya's outstretched legs.

"Hey," Shane said softly.

Ilya gave in and reached for him. As soon as he had Shane in his arms, he was done for. He leaned forward and took his mouth. It felt different this time, as he wrapped his arms around Shane's back and pulled him close against his body. Shane's hands cradled Ilya's face as he kissed him with the force of everything they had almost said out loud.

It was late and Shane knew he needed to go back to his own room, but he was in bed with Ilya. Not just in bed, but *cuddled together*, with Ilya gently stroking his hair.

Shane was rolling Ilya's crucifix between his thumb and his finger.

"Are you religious?" Shane asked. "Or do you just wear this?"

"I don't go to church anymore."

"But you believe in God?"

"Yes. I think so."

Shane didn't reply. He just considered this information.

"You think that is silly?" Ilya asked.

"No! No, I'm just surprised, I guess."

Ilya laughed softly.

"What?" Shane asked.

"You don't believe in God, but you believe if you put right skate on before left you will play a terrible game."

Shane shook his head and smiled. "That's different. That's science."

Ilya snorted and kissed the top of his head. "It was my mother's."

"Oh." He stopped twirling the cross and rested it gently against Ilya's chest. "Do you want to talk about… anything? Your family?"

"No," Ilya said. "Not tonight."

"You can, though, you know. Talk to me."

For a moment, Ilya was very still. "Thank you," he said.

Shane wondered if Ilya felt it too. The heaviness of the aftermath of their encounters. The impossibility of everything. Shane felt it every time. The whole point of their hookups was to provide release, but Shane only felt more tangled up each time.

"I should probably go," Shane said.

Ilya didn't reply, so Shane moved to get out of the bed. Ilya pulled him back, and Shane found himself on top of him, and then being kissed by him, and then he was under him.

"Stay," Ilya said.

"Can't." But he loved that Ilya was asking.

"No one will even fucking notice. This weekend is chaos."

"Too risky."

Ilya shook his head. "When will I have you for as long as I want?"

Shane's heart leapt. "I don't know. As soon as possible?"

"Yes." Ilya leaned in and kissed him. "After I win the Stanley Cup this year, we should go somewhere."

Shane huffed. "You're not winning that cup. And where on earth would we go?"

"I don't know. Somewhere no one knows us."

"What, like the moon?"

"No, like… Fiji."

"Nope. All it takes is one Canadian tourist with an iPhone."

"We'll climb a mountain. Find a cave."

Shane smiled sadly. They weren't going anywhere together and they both knew it. "You're going back to Russia this summer?"

"Yes."

"Well then."

"Where will you go?"

"To my cottage, mostly," Shane said.

"Sounds nice."

"It is. It's my favorite place on earth." Although this bed was providing some strong competition. He indulged in one last kiss, shifting so he covered Ilya's body with his own as he drank him in.

"I have to go." He brushed curls out of Ilya's eyes

and Ilya grabbed his wrist, then pulled Shane's hand to his lips. He lightly kissed the tips of Shane's fingers, and Shane's breath caught.

"Do you?" Ilya asked. God, his voice was sexy when he was sleepy, all frayed and throaty. He pressed a kiss to Shane's palm.

Shane closed his eyes, just to relieve one of his over-stimulated senses. It would be so easy just to give in…

"Yeah," he said. "I do." With a lot of effort, he left the bed and gathered his clothing from the floor. Sand spilled out of the cuffs of his pants, on the hotel carpet, as he dressed. Ilya stayed on the bed, possibly watching him. Shane couldn't bring himself to look at him, afraid that he'd end up back in his arms if he so much as glanced in his direction.

When he was at the door, he finally allowed himself to look back at Ilya. He was sitting up, the white bedsheet covering his bent knees. He was chewing his lip, as if considering whether or not to say something. There was a long, tense silence between them, and then Ilya said, "Good night, Shane."

A jolt of pleasure zipped through Shane's body every time Ilya called him by his first name. "Good night, Ilya."

He checked to make sure the hallway was empty, then slipped out of Ilya's room. Because the hall was empty, no one saw the smile that nearly split Shane's face in half.

Chapter Eighteen

February 2017—Montreal

Two weeks after All-Star weekend, Shane received a text from "Lily."

Can you believe that shit with Zullo?

Frank Zullo was a defenseman for the New York Admirals who was known to be a hot mess. He had gotten arrested the previous night for bar fighting or something, and now he was off the team.

Shane: Yeah. It's wild. I can't believe they put him on waivers.

Lily: I fucking hate that guy.

Shane: Always seemed like an asshole, yeah.

He could recall a few times when Zullo had hurled a homophobic slur at himself or his teammates.

Lily: Fuck him. Scott Hunter must be happy.

Shane: Oh yeah. You could tell he always hated him.

Lily: One less homophobe in league.

Shane: Yeah, like one million to go, though.

He was in the middle of making his post-run smoothie. He turned on the blender and watched his phone for the next text.

This was new. He wondered why they hadn't thought to do this before: talk to each other about hockey, even if it was mostly gossip. In the past they had only texted each other to discreetly arrange their hookups.

He wondered what had inspired Ilya to engage him this time.

Lily: Where are you? Home?

Shane: Yeah. Just got back from a run.

Lily: Nice. All sweaty? :p

Shane laughed. About to take a shower.

Lily: We should Skype while you do that. Video phone.

Shane: My phone would get wet.

Lily: Why have we never Skyped before?

Shane was surprised by this. You'd want to?

Lily: Maybe. Would you?

He assumed Ilya was talking about, like, phone sex. Or video sex. Or whatever. Shane had never done anything like that with anyone before. But it *was* a possibility for them. If neither of them saved the call, it would be safe, right?

Shane changed the subject. Nice goal last night.

Lily: Yeah, well. You know.

Then,

Lily: I have to tell you this story Hammersmith told us last night...

They texted back and forth for most of an hour. By the end of it, Shane was stretched out on his couch, his thumbs flying over his phone's keyboard, and frequently laughing into the empty room. He eventually reminded Ilya that he really did need to take a shower. He was surprised at how hard it was to end their conversation.

He had the embarrassing urge to write *Wish you were here* or something. He resisted. Instead he wrote, Later, and punctuated it with the emoji of a smiley face wearing sunglasses. Ilya signed off with the emoji of a kissy face.

Boston

Ilya had been texting Shane one-handed.

He hadn't told Shane that he had fucked up his elbow during the game last night. It had just got caught a weird way against the boards, and now it hurt to straighten it.

He had been ordered to rest, and he was bored. He

told himself boredom was the *only* reason he had texted Shane.

Because of his injury, and the fact that it was, like, nine in the morning, he had been mostly kidding when he had suggested phone sex. But he wondered if Shane would actually do it someday. He couldn't imagine…

Or, maybe he *could* imagine. Because suddenly he was. Quite vividly.

He could just see it. Shane with his determined little face, pretending not to be terrified. Where would he be? On his bed? On his *actual* bed? The one that Ilya had never shared because he had never been to Shane's real home?

Ilya closed his eyes and sank into the pillows on his own bed.

What was Shane's room like? Boring, probably. White walls. Probably a framed photo of his parents on his nightstand. Ilya quickly changed it to a framed photo of himself. An autographed one.

Shane probably had houseplants. His bedroom probably had a lot of natural light. There was probably a small bookshelf with some dull motivational books and some sports biographies. His bedsheets were probably blue.

He probably wore, like, full pajamas to bed. The kind with buttons.

But maybe he didn't always button them up. Maybe he just lounged in bed with his pajama shirt open and the pants riding a little low. His bedside lamp would be on so he could read his boring book.

And then, when he got tired of reading, he would put the book down neatly on his nightstand, then yawn and stretch himself out. The shirt would fall open a little more.

And maybe Shane's eyes would close, and he would let his hand travel lazily down his chest and over his abs. He'd brush it over his thighs and sigh as the bulge in his pajama pants grew.

Ilya was not doing a good job of resting.

Stupid elbow injury. Why did it have to be his right one?

This Skype thing *needed* to happen. He would coax some dirty talk out of that pretty little mouth of Shane's. He would force Shane out of his comfort zone. He could make it a challenge. Shane couldn't resist a challenge.

He gripped himself awkwardly with his left hand and gave himself a slow stroke.

He wanted a whole day with Shane. A weekend. A week. He wanted to be somewhere that no one could possibly interrupt them. Maybe that would be all he would need. Just the opportunity to get Shane Hollander out of his system. He needed to drink his fill and walk away.

Because he *would* have to walk away. This thing was already getting too complicated.

March 2017—Boston

It was full speed ahead now.

Boston and Montreal were neck and neck for the top spot in their division, and the playoffs were only a month away.

Shane wanted a third championship ring as much as Ilya wanted a second one. Winning the Stanley Cup the past two seasons hadn't lessened his drive at all. There was always a bigger goal to reach for.

The record for most Stanley Cup wins by a single

player was eleven. Shane knew that number might be a little lofty, since that record came from a time when there were far fewer teams in the league. But winning six would put him with some of the repeat champions of the '90s, so that was his secret goal.

No. His actual secret goal was seven.

Shane was focused. He had been playing very well all season and was leading the league in scoring by a narrow margin over Rozanov. He knew that must be bothering the shit out of Ilya.

Shane had been trying not to think about Rozanov too much. Usually that was their unspoken agreement this late into a season. They would fool around whenever they were in the same city up until March or so, then they both focused on hating each other until next season.

Which was why Shane had been surprised to get a text from Ilya that morning.

Lily: What time do you fly out tomorrow?

Shane stared at his phone, dumbfounded. He certainly hadn't expected to be seeing Ilya before or after the game tonight.

Shane: Early. Why?

No reply. Shane felt kind of bad about the "why." That was needlessly bitchy. He knew why.

A few minutes later, Ilya wrote back. What are you doing now?

Now? Now was one o'clock in the afternoon on a game day. Against *Boston*.

Shane: Nothing. I'm in my hotel room.

He stopped himself from writing "why" again.

Lily: Come over?

Shane's heart stopped. Come over? *Come over?* Now?

Shane: I can't! Don't be stupid.

Lily: Come over. Not for long. An hour?

Shane actually let out a surprised laugh.

Shane: No. Come on. We both know that's a bad idea.

Lily: Everything we do is a bad idea. Come over.

When Shane didn't reply, Ilya added, It will be worth it. I promise. ;)

Shane shook his head. There was no way he was going to go over there. He could list a million reasons why he couldn't go over there, and he ran them through his head as he grabbed his jacket and left the hotel room.

"I thought you were not coming," Ilya said with an annoying little smirk.

"Yeah, well…"

Ilya's smirk grew into a genuine, warm smile. Shane's heart lurched. And then they were kissing and pulling at clothing and stumbling toward the bedroom, not breaking contact.

They had to be quick. Shane not only needed to leave

soon, he shouldn't even have been there in the first place. Ilya pushed him down on the bed and went to work on him with his mouth.

Shane watched him as he licked and sucked his cock, and allowed himself a moment to wonder at Ilya's desperate need for this *before a game*. Why was he so hungry for Shane that he had broken their sacred rule?

God, he was good with his mouth.

Something is wrong with Ilya. The thought hit Shane suddenly.

He should ask him about it.

After.

For now, Shane reached a hand down and caressed Ilya's face. He let his fingers drift into his soft hair. He played with it, gently, and Ilya looked up at him. His eyes were dark, but there was more than lust there. Shane nodded at him, and Ilya turned his gaze down and focused on getting Shane off.

Shane came quickly, and Ilya swallowed it all with an encouraging hum. When he was done, he kissed his way up Shane's body until he reached his mouth. Shane kissed him hungrily, and then he flipped them both over and slid down to return the favor.

In the wake of his own release, Shane could feel himself starting to panic. This was weird and bad and *weird*. They should a thousand percent *not* be doing this.

Which was, like, one percent more than the usual amount that they should *not be fucking doing this!*

Except Ilya was breathing Shane's name—his *first* name—like a prayer and gazing at him like he was just as close as Shane was to saying something truly embarrassing and stupid and definite.

Shane dug his fingers into the hard muscle of Ilya's thighs as he took his cock deeper into his mouth. If he kept his mouth busy, he wouldn't be able to use it to ruin everything.

Ilya warned him, because he knew Shane didn't always like to take it in his mouth. But this time Shane did want it, and he sucked harder until Ilya cried out in a mixture of Russian and English and came down Shane's throat.

Shane flopped beside Ilya on the bed. Ilya started laughing.

"What?" Shane asked.

"Fuck."

Shane didn't reply, but he felt the same way.

"I have to go," he said, after a quiet minute.

"Yes."

Shane sat up, and moved to leave the bed, when he remembered. "Hey, um. Are you...all right?"

"Hm?"

"Are you okay? I mean... I know we don't really... talk. But if you need to—"

"I'm fine," Ilya said. He said it calmly and easily. Shane didn't buy it.

"Is it...is your dad..."

Ilya sighed heavily and scrubbed a hand over his face. "My father is dying. But that is not the problem."

"Oh."

"It is Polina. My stepmother. She is..." He twisted his hand around in the air, searching for the word.

"Sad?" Shane guessed.

Ilya laughed darkly. "No. She is...planning. For her future. My father does not have any money left."

"Oh."

"She has been calling me."

"Ah." Shane understood now.

"She wants money. They all want money. My brother. My father before he…"

Shane reached over and took Ilya's hand. "Will you give them any?"

"I already have. Plenty of it. They want more." He laughed again. "They don't give a shit about me or my career. They just know I make a lot of money."

"I'm sorry." Shane brushed a thumb over Ilya's knuckles.

"The last time I talked to my father on the phone was a couple of weeks ago. He asked if I could pick up some bread on the way home."

Shane didn't know what to say. It was truly heartbreaking.

"The worst part is…" Ilya said quietly, "I like talking to him better. Like this. He was a real fucking asshole when he was…himself."

"Are you going back to Russia this summer?"

Ilya shrugged. "Yes."

"Do you…have to?"

"You should leave," Ilya said abruptly. He didn't sound annoyed or angry. Just tired, and maybe a little sad. He pulled his fingers away from Shane's.

"I know. But…"

"Go. I didn't ask you to come over to talk."

"Well…you can. If you ever want to. I mean, you can just call me. Or text. Or if we're in the same city and you want to just talk instead of…"

Ilya cracked a crooked grin at that. "Instead of?"

"As well as?"

"I like that better."

He leaned forward and kissed Shane. It was as soft and sweet a kiss as Shane had ever received from anyone.

"I apologize in advance for tonight," Shane murmured. "We're gonna destroy you guys."

"Dream on, Hollander."

Ilya made sure that Boston won the game. Not a trouncing, but a respectable two-goal lead when the final siren rang to end the game. Ilya scored twice, Shane had scored once. Ilya's favorite kind of game.

He had every intention of meeting up with Hollander tonight, even though they'd already stolen an hour together that afternoon. He still knew, in the back of his mind, that this thing with Shane needed to end. That it couldn't be more than sex. But somehow it had just evolved on its own, and suddenly he no longer worried about looking too eager. He could admit to himself that he wanted to see Shane as much as possible, and he found that he wasn't worried about letting Shane know it anymore. For now, at least. The day would come when they would have to end it, but for now Ilya was happy to steal as many moments as possible.

He said good-night to his remaining teammates, and left the arena. He was looking at his phone as he walked out of the players' entrance, trying to decide what obnoxious jab he should text to Hollander, when the phone started ringing.

It was his brother.

Ilya almost didn't answer, but he could think of one reason why his brother might be calling that had nothing to do with money.

He answered.

Shane had been expecting a text from Ilya. He was sitting alone in his hotel room—Hayden had left to call his wife—trying not to let the mistakes of that night's game haunt him.

He's not going to text, he told himself. *You already saw him today. Why would you see him again?*

But he thought maybe Ilya felt the same way about their...well, not *relationship*, but...arrangement? That maybe Ilya *liked* spending time with Shane. That they weren't just doing this because it was, in its own complicated way, convenient. Or dirty, or wrong, or irresistibly hot. That maybe Ilya's stomach fluttered with excitement too, every time their teams were scheduled to meet. That maybe Ilya was also sometimes randomly struck by a memory of a teasing remark, or a smile, or of gentle fingers stroking his hair, and would have to hide his giddy little smile.

That maybe he watched Shane's games and was secretly proud when Shane did well. Because that's how Shane felt when Ilya had a good night. Which was ridiculous.

Shane waited until midnight and Ilya still didn't text him. He thought about being the one to make contact, but decided against it. Wanting to hook up with Ilya twice in one day was nuts. And it was way too late at night now anyway. They were flying to Detroit in the morning.

Shane lay awake for a while, staring into the darkness, wondering if it was that Ilya hadn't wanted to see him again, or if maybe something had happened that had kept Ilya from texting.

He decided that he was making a big deal out of nothing, and eventually fell asleep.

Chapter Nineteen

The next day—Detroit

"Did you hear about Rozanov?"

Shane stopped tying his skate and looked at the bench across from him, where Gilbert Comeau and J.J. were chatting in French.

"What about Rozanov?" Shane asked, also in French.

They both looked at him, surprised, no doubt, by the slight panic in his voice. Comeau shrugged. "He didn't fly to Nashville with the rest of his team today."

"He flew separately?" Shane asked stupidly.

"No," Comeau said, looking at Shane like he was a little bit dumb. "He isn't in Nashville."

"He didn't get hurt last night," J.J. said. "Not that anyone noticed, right?"

"I don't think so," Shane said, quickly replaying the last few minutes of the game. Ilya had seemed fine. He hadn't left the ice in pain at any point during the game.

"Maybe he's sick," Comeau said. "I'm sure we'll find out. Right now ESPN is just saying that he didn't go to Nashville."

"Right," Shane said quietly.

He ran through a number of alarming scenarios in his

head before he finally stood up and grabbed his phone off the shelf above his head.

Are you ok? he texted.

He didn't get a reply. There was still no reply by the time the team left the dressing room to go warm up. When he returned to the dressing room afterward, he quickly checked his phone. Still nothing.

Forget about it, he ordered himself. *It's game time.*

He'd probably learn what had happened after the game. He was sure it would be mentioned during the broadcast of the Boston vs. Nashville game.

Shane did not play the best game of his life. Probably one of the worst games of the season for him, but his team managed to win anyway. Shane couldn't remember ever being so eager for a game to be over. When they got back to the dressing room, he shucked his gloves off and immediately checked his phone.

Nothing.

Shane sat down hard on the bench, staring at his phone. He opened his web browser and searched "Ilya Rozanov Nashville" to see if any more information had been released. He found fans speculating on social media, and he saw an official ESPN story that just said "undisclosed reasons" and that there was no word whether Rozanov would be joining his team in Tampa Bay for their game in two days' time.

This whole thing was very strange. Shane couldn't *sneeze* in public without the hockey sites reporting that he was deathly ill and how that should affect your sports betting. Ilya Rozanov, one of the biggest stars in the league, just disappeared with no explanation and no reporters seemed to be digging very hard. Or offering possible reasons.

Which meant…they must *know* the reason. And they were respecting Boston's likely request for discretion.

Which meant…absolutely nothing good that Shane could think of.

Shane got showered and changed faster than he ever had in his life. He found a private corner of the hallway outside the dressing room and did something he'd never done before: he called Ilya Rozanov.

He wasn't expecting him to answer, but he wanted the missed call to at least be recorded on Ilya's phone. He wanted Ilya to know he was concerned.

But Ilya did answer.

"Hollander?"

"Yeah. Hi."

There was a long silence.

"Are you okay?" Shane asked finally.

He heard Ilya huff out a humorless laugh. "I don't know."

"Where are you?"

"Home."

"In Boston? Are you sick?"

"No. Home. In Moscow."

Shane wasn't expecting *that*.

"*Moscow?* Did something happen? Oh, shit. Your father?"

"Yes. Dead."

"Ilya, I—"

"What are people saying about me?"

"Nothing! The media has been very secretive about it. The Bears must have—"

"Good. I will be back by end of week," he said stiffly.

"You should take more time."

Ilya snorted. "You'd like that, wouldn't you?"

"Stop. I'm being serious."

More silence.

"I'm so sorry, Ilya." He didn't know what else to say.

Ilya didn't reply, but Shane could hear a sharp sniff, and then a tight, throaty noise.

"Ilya—"

"I will be back in a few days. I should go."

"All right."

"Goodbye, Hollander."

"Wait," Shane said, way too loudly.

Ilya waited.

"Just…call me, all right? If you need to talk. Or text me. Whatever. But… I'll listen. I want to help, if I can."

Ilya was silent for a moment. "You did. Thank you."

He ended the call.

Shane leaned back against the wall and blew out a breath.

Two days later—Buffalo

Shane hadn't really been expecting to hear from Ilya again. He was surprised when, after his game in Buffalo, he received a text.

Lily: Are you alone?

Shane stood up, mumbled a hasty reason for leaving to Hayden, and went out to the stairwell.

Shane: Yes.

Lily: Can I call you?

Shane: Yes.

His phone rang and Shane answered it immediately. The stairwell was silent and empty. He leaned against the wall of the landing below his floor.

"How are you doing?" he asked, not even bothering with hello.

"I feel like… I don't know. Bad."

"How's your family treating you?"

Ilya gave a dark laugh. "Like I should not be here."

"That's ridiculous. He was your father."

"Yes, well." There was a pause and Shane waited. "I am paying for everything, so that makes me…of use."

"How's your—I mean, how's his wife?"

"Upset. But not about my father. Everybody thinks so, but no. She is scared for herself."

"Because there's no money?"

"Yes. That."

"What about you? Are you…upset?"

Ilya sighed. "I don't know. Maybe about the wrong thing."

"You wish things could have been different?" Shane guessed.

"I wish… I wanted him to… I don't know." He sighed again. "English is too hard today."

"I'm sorry. I wish I spoke Russian."

"You could probably learn it in a week," Ilya grumbled. "Perfect. No accent."

Shane laughed. "I don't think so." He was about to ask if Ilya had anyone there in Moscow that he could talk to, but it was pretty obvious that he didn't. Why else would he be calling Shane?

"Where are you right now?" he asked instead.

"Walking. A park. I needed to get out."

"Cold?"

"Fucking freezing."

Shane was suddenly struck by a ridiculous idea. Or maybe it was a brilliant idea. He decided to share it before his brain had a chance to figure out which.

"Tell me everything you want to say," he said. "In Russian. I won't understand but…maybe it will help?"

There was a silence that was long enough for Shane to physically cringe at himself. He was about to take it back, when he heard Ilya quietly say, "Okay."

The next several minutes were filled with Ilya's voice, sounding more animated and flustered than Shane had ever heard him. He was used to Ilya saying more with a teasing smile or a calculating look than with actual words. But now it was like a dam had burst, and Shane sat himself on the stairs and let it wash over him.

Without the ability to translate any of it, Shane could just enjoy the sound of Ilya's voice, which he barely recognized now. The words were so quick and confident, unrestricted by Ilya having to carefully piece together his sentences like when he spoke English. It felt intimate—like they were somehow sharing a bigger secret now than when they slept together.

And there was something undeniably sexy about hearing Ilya speak so fluidly in his mother tongue.

When he was finished, Ilya gave an embarrassed-sounding little laugh and said, "I am done."

It was jarring to hear him switch suddenly back to English. Shane felt his head clear like he was waking from a dream.

"Feel better?" he asked.

"Yes. Thank you."

Shane lowered his voice and said, "Maybe you could teach me Russian someday."

"Only useful phrases," Ilya said. Shane could practically *hear* his crooked smile. Then Ilya purred something in Russian.

"What does that mean?" Shane asked.

"Get on your knees."

"Oh." Shane quickly scanned the stairwell again to make sure he was still alone. He was already more aroused than he should be after listening to Ilya pour his heart out. "And what other useful phrases could you teach me?"

Ilya laughed. "I can think of many, Hollander."

Shane shifted on the stairs. "I wish you were here now."

Shane couldn't believe he had actually allowed himself to say that out loud. They didn't *wish* to be together. They reluctantly hooked up when they were in the same city because it was something to do.

He felt his mortification melt away when Ilya said, in a low voice, "Me too."

Moscow

Something occurred to Ilya after he ended the call with Shane: maybe Shane had recorded that call and was going to run it through some sort of translating app later.

But Shane wouldn't do that, would he?

Ilya stopped into a coffee shop and ordered a cappuccino. While he waited for it, he tried not to imagine scenarios where Shane would somehow translate every word that Ilya had just said.

Mostly he had just been ranting about his family, but he had included an admission that he wished things could have been different with his father. That he had stupidly always hoped that his father might tell him that he was proud of him.

That admission would have been embarrassing enough, but Ilya had also slipped in an *"and on top of everything, I'm pretty sure I'm in love with you and I don't know what to do about it."*

It was saying those words out loud, even more than venting his frustrations about his family, that had truly made Ilya feel lighter. It was a secret he had been carrying for far too long, locked away so deep inside that he had even been keeping it from himself. But as soon as he let himself acknowledge it, and now say it, he felt relieved. Not because he could do anything about these feelings, but at least he had allowed himself to accept them. And he had, in the most cowardly way possible, said them aloud to Shane.

Shane wouldn't translate anything. That wasn't why he had asked Ilya to unload on him in Russian. He was being a friend.

A friend?

Sure, Ilya could admit that he and Shane were friends now. He had certainly been the only person Ilya could think of when he'd decided he needed to talk to someone today.

He walked out of the shop with his cappuccino and reluctantly headed in the direction of his father's house. The funeral was the next morning. After that, he could leave what was left of his goddamn family behind.

The next day—Montreal

Shane had barely gotten in the door of his apartment before he texted Ilya. He had been thinking about him all day.

Shane: How are you doing?

He wasn't sure if Ilya would reply or not. He might be busy. His father's funeral had been that morning. It was late in Moscow now, after ten o'clock at night.

Lily: Fantastic.

Shane waited.

Lily: A little bit drunk, actually.

Shane: Can I call you?

Lily: Yes.

When Shane heard Ilya's voice, he sounded more exhausted than drunk. "Hollander."

"How are you holding up, Ilya?"

"Great. Wonderful." Shane heard him sigh. "Is quiet here."

"Are you alone? Where are you?"

"My condo. I have one here. In Moscow. For the summers, you know."

"Right." Shane didn't like the idea of Ilya being alone right now.

"If you are wondering if I will be back in time for our game in Montreal—"

"I don't give a shit about that, Ilya. You know that's not why I'm calling."

Another sigh.

"Should you really be alone right now?" Shane asked.

"I am not alone," Ilya said. "You are here now, yes?"

Shane's hand flew to his chest to make sure his heart

was still beating; he could have sworn it had just melted into a gooey puddle. He wished he could warp to Moscow. Just instantly appear in Ilya's apartment and hold him and tell him it was all right to be conflicted about his father's death. That he didn't owe his family anything. That he should leave them all behind because they made him miserable and he doesn't need them anyway.

Instead he said, "Yeah. I'm here."

"And where else are you?" Ilya asked.

"I'm home now. Montreal."

Shane heard mattress springs squeak as Ilya presumably settled himself on his bed. "Tell me about your home, Hollander," he said in a tired voice. "What does it look like? I try to imagine it…"

"You do?"

"You will not let me see it."

"That's not…" Shane grimaced. "It's not because I don't want you here. You know that."

"I know nothing. What does it look like?"

"It's, I don't know…it has big windows."

"What can you see out of them?"

"Buildings, mostly. A bit of the water."

"Fancy kitchen?"

Shane laughed. "Yeah. Too fancy, probably. I barely use it. I could probably get by with a toaster and a blender."

"What is your favorite thing about your home?"

"I dunno. It's close to the practice rink?"

Ilya snorted. "Figures."

"It's private. Good security. Hey, I made a donation to the Alzheimer's Society of Canada. For your father."

Ilya was quiet a moment. "That is nice of you. Might be good for me. Can be…what is the word…passed on?"

"Hereditary?"

"Yes. Hereditary."

Neither man said anything for a moment.

"Listen, Ilya—"

"What about your bedroom? What is it like?"

Shane didn't want to talk about his stupid bedroom, but he understood what Ilya was doing. He left his living room and headed for the bedroom.

"It's nice. Pretty basic. I mean, it's enormous. Big windows. But not much in it."

"What color is your bed? The blanket?"

"Blue. Like, navy blue."

"I knew it."

Shane smiled and sat on the bed.

"Do you have books? In your room?"

"A few."

"What are you reading? What one is beside your bed?"

"A book about the 1972 Canada/Russia series, actually."

Ilya laughed. "Do you read books that are not about hockey?"

"Sometimes," Shane said. "I mean, no. Not very often."

"You are obsessed."

"Of course I am. Aren't you?"

"Maybe. In a different way."

Shane picked up the book and flicked the end of the bookmark with his finger. It had been nestled between pages forty-one and forty-two for over a month. "Hockey has always been everything to me. For as long as I can remember."

"It has been for me as well. But…more as like…an

escape. Is that right to say? My brain is not good right now."

"Yes," Shane said quietly. "An escape. That's right. It was never an escape for me. It was just what I loved to do."

"I love it also," Ilya said. "Hockey is…fun. And I am very good at it."

Shane laughed. And Ilya laughed.

"Is wild how much money they pay me to play this game," Ilya said.

"Tell me about it," Shane agreed.

"I don't want to come back here."

Shane was confused by the sudden topic change. "To Russia, you mean?"

"*Da.* I want to become American. Or Canadian. But I am in America, so…"

In that moment, Shane wished like hell that Ilya played for a Canadian team.

"You should," Shane said. "Have you looked into—?"

"We should get married," Ilya said.

"What?" Shane flushed right down to his toes.

"Not to each other," Ilya said. Then he started laughing and couldn't stop.

"I *knew* you didn't mean to each other," Shane lied.

When Ilya finally stopped laughing, he said, "I can marry an American girl. You should get married, Hollander. You want children, yes?"

"I've already told you… I don't want to marry… anyone."

"There is a nice Russian girl in Boston. American, I mean. But from Russia. Svetlana. I like her. I could marry her, I think."

"Oh."

"She is…what is word?…sensible. Marriage would be like business deal, yes? Just until I am citizen."

"You don't love her, then?"

"No," Ilya said quietly. He sounded like he was falling asleep. "Not her. No."

Shane knew he should end the call, let Ilya get some sleep. But instead he blurted out, "You should come to the cottage this summer."

"Cottage? What are you talking about, Hollander?"

"My cottage. In Ontario. You're not going back to Russia, so…come to my cottage with me. It's quiet, and beautiful and…private."

For a moment, Ilya didn't say anything, and Shane thought he really had fallen asleep.

"I will think about it," Ilya said finally.

"Okay."

"I am tired."

"Yeah, I can tell. Get some sleep, all right?"

"Yes. Good night, Hollander."

They ended the call and Shane sat on his bed for a while after, not moving. It occurred to him that they'd just had an entire conversation that hadn't been about sex at all, and was barely about hockey.

It also occurred to him that his heart was beating like he was in the middle of a run, and his mouth was dry. He had *actually* just invited Ilya to his cottage! The fact that he had even done that was absurd, but what if Ilya actually accepted?

What if he had Ilya all to himself at Shane's favorite place in the world? If there was no one to interrupt them, no one to hide from, no one to remind them of all the reasons they shouldn't want each other…

It would be too much. Shane would never be able to hold back everything he had been trying to pretend he didn't feel. He would blurt something out that he would never, ever be able to take back.

He's never going to be your boyfriend, Shane.

Oh god. That *was* what Shane wanted, wasn't it? He didn't just want to be Ilya's dirty secret. He didn't want their relationship to be nothing but sex. He wanted to comfort Ilya when he was sad, and talk to him on the phone, and snuggle together on the couch and watch movies. He would take the short phone call they had just shared over any of their sexual encounters.

Well, *almost* any of their sexual encounters.

Shane groaned and fell back on his bed, covering his face with his hands. He was *super* fucked.

Chapter Twenty

The next day—Moscow

Ilya would fly back to Boston tomorrow.

Andrei was the executor of their father's estate, what little of it there was, and Ilya had fulfilled his duties as a son. He was done.

He'd realized, over the past few days, that he truly had no reason to return to Russia. He probably would, someday, but he couldn't see spending another summer here. Any obligation he had felt had died with his father.

He had made an impulsive decision to give his Moscow condo to his brother. Andrei could sell it, or meet his mistresses there. Ilya couldn't care less; he just didn't want to deal with selling it. There wasn't even anything in it that he wanted.

He sat on his bed in that condo. It would be his last night sleeping there.

He could think of one thing he would like to do to commemorate the occasion.

Ilya: Are you home?

The reply was immediate.

Jane: Yes.

Ilya smiled and wrote, Skype?

He waited, and wondered if Shane understood what Ilya was suggesting.

OK, Shane texted back. Just a sec.

Ilya decided to make things a little clearer for Shane, just in case he didn't get it. He pulled his T-shirt off and dropped it on the floor, then stacked some pillows in front of the headboard and settled himself on the mattress. He sent Shane a video call request.

Shane accepted, and then there he was, filling the screen of Ilya's iPad. He was wearing a hoodie and... *glasses?*

"Holy shit, Hollander! Do you wear glasses?"

"Oh!" Shane reached up and touched the frames of his glasses, as if he didn't believe Ilya. "Just when I read. It's, um...new." He pulled them off.

"No!" Ilya said, grinning. "I like them."

"Well..." Shane said, and damn if he wasn't blushing already. "I *can* see you a lot better if I leave them on." He slid the thick black frames back into place. "What?" he asked, because Ilya couldn't stop smiling.

"What were you reading? Your boring hockey book?"

Shane's eyes narrowed behind the glasses. "Are you just calling to make fun of me?"

"No. Not only that."

He watched Shane bite his bottom lip. *God, he's cute.*

"Were you thinking we could, y'know...do stuff?" Shane asked nervously.

"Yes. But first, show me your bedroom. I am dying to see it."

"Really? All right." Shane tapped on the screen and

flipped the camera. Suddenly, Ilya was looking at a king-size bed with a navy blue comforter.

"That's the bed," he heard Shane say off camera.

"Oh, is it?"

"Fuck you. You asked for this. Here's the dresser. And the bathroom is over there. And the closet. And here's the view…"

Ilya decided he didn't care about the view or the bedroom anymore. It was as boring as he had been expecting. It could have been a hotel room.

"Why don't you get on the bed?" he suggested.

"So much for small talk, I guess."

"And take your shirt off."

"Bossy."

Ilya waited as Shane put his tablet or whatever down, causing the screen to go black. He heard rustling noises, and then Ilya was looking at the end of Shane's bed.

"Better?" Shane asked.

"No. Turn the camera around."

"Oh, shit. Here." And now a shirtless Shane Hollander's face and shoulders (and glasses) filled the screen.

"Better."

"How are you? I've been…thinking about you."

Ilya's heart flipped. He hoped it didn't show on his face. "I am okay. I might not come back here, after today."

"Is that scary?"

Ilya shrugged. "Right now it feels…good. Like, um…"

"A weight has been lifted?"

"Yes. Maybe like that. Is there a way I can see more of you?"

"Oh. Yeah…maybe I can…just a sec."

Ilya propped his own iPad up on his nightstand and stretched out with his hands behind his head. When Shane reappeared on the screen, it seemed he had done something similar because now Ilya could see from the top of his head to the waistband of his sweatpants.

Ilya wanted, more than anything, to be able to cover Shane's body with his own. To kiss his way down his chest and stomach.

Shane smiled. "It's good to see you again."

"I'd like to see you wearing nothing but those glasses," Ilya said.

"I don't think my camera can show that much at once."

"Next time we are together, then."

"Yeah. Next time."

Ilya let his head sink into the pillows. He kept it turned, facing the camera. "Do you remember, after the NHL Awards in…what year was it?"

"Two thousand fourteen," Shane said quickly. "Yeah. I do. I… I think about that night a lot."

"Do you?"

"It was memorable."

"It was," Ilya agreed. "You put on a show for me."

"I can't believe you talked me into that."

"I think you like to be told what to do, Hollander."

Shane sucked in a breath. "Maybe. A little."

"And you're a little show-off."

"I am not."

"You are. You love praise. You want everyone to see how good you are."

"Yeah, well. So do you."

"No. I know I am good. I don't care what people say."

Shane leaned forward and pointed an accusing finger at the camera. "Bullshit. You love the awards. The good press. The fans. You love beating me."

"I love beating everyone, but yes. You the most."

"Why?"

Ilya shrugged. "Because you are the best."

"I'm not. What about Scott Hunter? You like to beat him too. You're always talking shit about that guy."

Ilya waved a hand dismissively. "Hunter is a million years old and he's terrible this year."

"He's like three years older than us, and he's been on fire lately."

"Whatever. I don't want to talk about Scott Hunter."

"I think you just have a fetish for good boys."

Ilya laughed. "Is that what you are?"

"That's what *you* say," Shane said. "What everyone says."

"Mm. But I know the truth about you. I was the one in that hotel room in Vegas with you, yes? No one else."

"Yeah," Shane breathed. "Just you."

"Are you hard right now, Hollander?"

"What do you think?"

Ilya smirked. "Show me. Get on your knees. Face the camera. Show me."

Shane obeyed immediately, which Ilya found incredibly hot. His head went out of the frame, but Ilya could see his abs, and the way his sweatpants pulled tight against his obvious bulge when Shane spread his knees wide on the mattress.

"You too," Shane said, off-camera. "I want to see."

Ilya copied Shane's position, showing Shane exactly how aroused he was already. Fuck, he wished they were together somewhere.

"I wish you were here," Shane said, before Ilya could.

"Yes. What would you do?"

"I'd take those pants off."

Ilya smiled, though Shane couldn't see it now. He tucked his thumbs into the waistband of his track pants and slid them down off his hips. When he looked up, he saw Shane stroking himself through the fabric of his sweatpants.

"No underwear," Shane observed. "You were planning for this?"

"Maybe." He wrapped his hand around his cock and stroked it slowly. "My pants are off. What would you do now?"

Shane dipped down into the frame. His head was cocked and his hair flopped to the side. It was fucking adorable. He smiled at Ilya. "I think you know exactly what I'd do, after all these years."

"Still want to hear it."

Shane's face left the screen. He gripped himself harder through his sweatpants and moaned. "I'd take you in my mouth. I'd suck you all the way down. Fuck, I… I wish I could. Right now."

"Mm. Me too. Love your mouth, Hollander."

He loved a lot of things about him.

"Would you want me to fuck your mouth? Or just keep still and let you do the work?"

"Keep still. I'd do it. Make you feel so good."

And now Ilya moaned.

Shane yanked his pants and briefs down so they were stretched wide across his spread thighs. He stroked himself, sliding his thumb over his slit. Ilya knew it must be wet; Shane always leaked like a fountain.

They both stroked themselves without talking for a

minute or two, and then Ilya saw Shane's hand pause and drop to his side.

"Hey, um, Ilya?"

"Yes."

He watched Shane's hand lift out of the frame, probably so Shane could run it nervously through his hair. Ilya stilled his own hand.

"Something wrong?" he asked.

"No. But… I think I'd rather see your face."

Ilya was grateful that Shane couldn't see his face at that exact moment, because he was pretty sure it had the world's sappiest expression.

"Sure, Hollander," he said gently.

Shane laid himself back down on the bed with his head nestled on one of his pillows. He reached and pulled his tablet closer to his face and smiled shyly. Ilya melted a little more, and positioned himself the same way on his bed, pulling his own iPad close.

"I forgot about the glasses," Ilya said. "Already."

"You really like them, huh?"

"I do."

Shane beamed at him. Ilya couldn't stop himself from smiling back. It felt like they were really in bed together, facing each other. Talking at the end of a long day.

Shane's eyes fluttered closed and Ilya knew he was touching himself again. And Shane had been right— this was better. Watching Shane's face so closely as he pleasured himself was far more intimate than if Ilya had been watching his hand on his cock. Not being able to see what Shane was doing to make himself sigh and moan was intensely arousing.

"You are very beautiful," Ilya said.

Shane smiled without opening his eyes. "Come on."

"Is the truth. Your freckles." Ilya grazed a fingertip over his own cheek. "I am nuts about them."

"I have no idea why. I hate them."

"Noooo…" Ilya moaned. "Hollander. They are stunning."

"Stunning?"

"Yes. Am I not using that word right? Very beautiful. Um…take my breath?"

"Wow. All right." The skin under Shane's freckles turned very, very pink.

"The first time I met you. Those freckles…"

"The first time? You mean at the World Juniors? In Saskatchewan?"

"Yes."

Shane huffed out a surprised laugh. "You were such a dick to me."

"Mm. I did not like you. Just your freckles."

Shane shook his head a little on the pillow. "Thanks, I guess."

"I told you…" Ilya grinned. "You love praise."

When Shane didn't reply, Ilya said, "And you like to hog it all for yourself. You asshole."

Shane laughed, and his nose crinkled. The freckles got all bunched up under his glasses, and Ilya nearly died.

"You're *very attractive*, Ilya," Shane said, in an exaggerated, placating tone.

"Not good enough. I want details."

Shane opened his eyes, and rolled them. But he said, "That crooked fucking smile of yours. I can't even tell you…that smile haunts me."

"Haunts you? Like a ghost? That doesn't sound like a good thing."

"It is. And your eyes. I love your eyes."

"So romantic, Hollander."

"Fuck you. You asked for compliments. Are you even doing anything down there or am I the only one doing any work?"

Ilya laughed. "You're not the only one."

"Good."

Off camera, Ilya hauled his pants the rest of the way down and off.

"Hold on," Shane said. "I need to grab the lube."

Ilya took the opportunity to do the same. "Surprised you even need it," he said. "You get so wet."

Shane snorted. "As if."

They were quiet for a minute, just gazing at each other as they stroked themselves with slicked fingers.

"Do you ever think of me?" Shane asked. "When you're doing this? Alone?" He blushed furiously as soon as he said it. Cute as hell.

"Yes."

"I do too. A lot. All the time. Maybe…every time, honestly."

Ilya raised an eyebrow. "Every time?"

He saw Shane's shoulder lift in a tiny shrug. "I've never…had anything. Like this. With anyone else."

"You have not been with another man?" Ilya may have held his breath as he waited for the answer.

"I have."

Ilya exhaled. Of course he had.

"Who?" He hadn't meant to blurt that out, but it was too late to take it back.

Shane pressed his lips together. "No one. Stop distracting me."

But now Ilya was curious. Shane was so careful. Who would he risk having sex with?

"Tell me. Was it another player?"

"No."

Ilya decided the only way to get this information out of Shane was to make it sexy.

"Did you go to a bar? Did you see someone you could not resist?"

"I went—*fuck*—I went to Mexico with Hayden and a couple of the other guys. A few—*ah, god*—years ago. We went out one night and, yeah, I was terrified but… fuck, it had been so long."

"You don't let yourself have release enough, Hollander. I don't know how you do it."

Shane laughed, a little darkly. "I haven't come since I saw you last, you know that?"

Ilya inhaled sharply and sped up his hand. It occurred to him that he hadn't had an orgasm in a couple of days himself, which was an epic drought for him.

"Tell me about this man in Mexico."

"There's not much to tell. He was big. He looked like he was, y'know, what I was looking for."

"A big, strong top?" Shane looked so embarrassed, Ilya took pity. "Was he? What you needed?"

"No. I mean, sort of. But…"

"Did he hurt you?"

"No. He just wasn't…"

Ilya needed to hear it. "Wasn't what?"

Shane clenched his eyes shut and said, "You. He wasn't you."

Ilya damn near lost it. Shane was going to ruin him, saying things like that.

"Was he the only one?" Ilya couldn't stop the questions from falling out of his mouth now.

"There was a guy in L.A., at a club. I went out by myself. I was desperate."

"And?"

"We sucked each other off. I was nervous the whole time."

"Aw."

"And that was it. Two guys. And you."

God. "Mexico top. Hollywood blow job guy. And me."

Shane laughed. "Yeah. And a bunch of disappointed women."

"A bunch?"

"A few. *Anyway*, I'm trying to jerk off here, so…"

Ilya laughed. They both went back to the task at hand.

"Hey," Ilya said. He waggled his eyebrows playfully. "Do you think you can beat me?"

It took Shane a second. Then he laughed. "You want to *race*?"

"Come on, Hollander. Let's see what you got."

Shane shook his head, but he was grinning. "You're an idiot," he said affectionately. "Fine. Bring it."

And those words of challenge caused a bolt of desire to rocket through Ilya. He should have no problem winning this battle.

"I think…" Shane said, his voice strained already, "I think the winner should be whoever holds out the longest. More impressive."

"No way. You would cheat."

"I would *not*! Cheat how?"

"I can't see your hand. You could just stop."

"I won't."

Ilya shrugged. "Fine. You always shoot off so fast anyway. Will be an easy win for me."

Shane scowled at him, but then something caused his eyes to squeeze shut and he let out a quiet little gasp.

Ilya chuckled. "Fucking hopeless," he said.

Then Shane opened his eyes and there was definitely something dangerous in them. "You know the night of the draft, in that hotel gym?"

Ilya groaned. *Fuck.* "I wanted to pin you to the floor," he confessed. "I could not stop staring at your mouth. I thought you would notice."

"I didn't. I was too busy trying to stop myself from straddling you. Kissing you."

"Fuck, Shane."

"I couldn't believe how much I wanted to. It terrified me. I had never…"

"Never wanted a man?" Ilya huffed.

"No. At least, I didn't think I did. But you…god, Ilya. I went right back to my room and jerked off thinking about you."

Now Ilya squeezed his eyes shut. He stroked himself harder, faster. He suddenly couldn't care less about winning this dumb contest. He gasped out, "Me too."

Shane groaned, and they both worked themselves roughly as the room filled with the sounds of their breathing.

"I can't wait to touch you again," Shane murmured. Then he sucked in a breath and let out a high, manic sound, and Ilya knew if he just held on for another minute he would win because Shane was definitely about to come.

"Ah, fuck. Dammit. I'm so close," Shane gasped.

Ilya couldn't even respond. He forced his eyes open so he could lock his gaze with Shane's.

"Oh fuck," Shane said quietly. "I'm coming."

And normally Ilya would want to see it, but in that moment he couldn't imagine anything sexier than Shane Hollander's face as he came. Ilya felt pleasure flood every part of him as he climaxed hard, covering his fist and his stomach with his release.

"Holy fuck," Shane panted. "That was huge. I'm a mess over here."

Ilya flopped onto his back and stared up at the ceiling.

"I'm fucked," he murmured in Russian. "I am so fucking in love and it's horrible."

When he looked back at the screen, he could see Shane's sex-drunk eyes gazing longingly at him from behind his glasses. "It's sexy when you speak Russian. You know that?"

"Because I don't sound ridiculous? Like with my accent?"

"Tell you a secret? Your accent doesn't sound ridiculous. At all."

"No? You like it?"

"I do. And I want to learn Russian. I wasn't kidding about that."

"I'll teach you."

Shane smiled so wide and bright, Ilya almost had to look away.

"I should let you sleep," Shane said.

"*Da.* Yes. Okay."

And then…

Shane kissed the tips of two fingers and reached out and touched them to the screen.

And Ilya's heart fucking *stopped*.

"Good night, Ilya."

Ilya felt an awful lump in his throat. He had buried

his father yesterday, but he hadn't cried. He hadn't cried in over ten years. But he knew, in that moment, that he *had* to end this thing with Shane. It was never supposed to have gotten to this point. He was never supposed to have *fallen in love* with Shane Hollander. He should have ended it long before because now it was going to hurt so fucking much.

What on earth else could they do? If they kept this up it was only a matter of time before they got caught, and that would be a fucking disaster. Ilya didn't think the NHL had an official rule about being romantically involved with a rival player, but only because the league couldn't possibly imagine one being necessary. That's how shocking a revelation this would be if Ilya and Shane were found out. Ilya's deepest fear was that he would be kicked out of the NHL—or at least not be offered a spot on any team—and then he might have to go back to Russia, and he didn't want to think about what would happen to him then.

Ilya's stakes were higher, but he knew their relationship would only negatively impact Shane's career too. And, despite what the hockey world believed, Ilya didn't want that.

"Good night, Shane," he said, keeping his voice as steady as possible. As soon as he closed the window, he covered his face in his hands and released all of his anguish and frustration and fear into the lonely apartment.

Chapter Twenty-One

April 2017—Montreal

Shane could see Ilya standing near the centerline as their two teams warmed up before their final match of the season. He was talking to one of his teammates, helmet off, his hair still soft and dry around his face.

Shane hadn't seen him, hadn't talked to him, since Ilya's team had arrived in Montreal. They had texted a few times after Ilya had returned from Moscow, but he hadn't seen him face-to-face after their memorable Skype call, if that counted.

He was on the ice now, standing on the edge of the centerline that served as a barrier between the teams during warm-ups. Shane watched the toe of Ilya's skate swivel onto the wide, red line on the ice. It looked like a dare—or an invitation.

Shane skated the perimeter of Montreal's half of the ice and came to a slow stop in front of Ilya. "Hi."

Ilya glanced at him and nodded. "Hollander."

Shane flipped his stick around so he could pretend to be inspecting the tape on his blade. "We still on for tonight? After?"

Ilya nodded again, his gaze fixed on the corner of the arena. "Same place?"

"Yeah."

Shane could see a tightening in Ilya's jaw. "Hey," he said, as quietly as possible. "You all right?"

Ilya turned and met Shane's eyes, and Shane felt a stab of longing in his heart. They were so close, but they couldn't be more under the microscope than they were right now.

"We'll talk later," Shane promised.

"Yes. Later."

Ilya skated away. Shane watched after him, and then he felt Hayden's elbow bumping his arm. "What did Rozanov want?"

"Nothing," Shane said, blinking and turning to face Hayden. "I was just…offering my condolences. You know."

The news had gotten around that Rozanov's father had died. Shane hoped the press wouldn't ask Ilya too many questions about it.

"Oh. Yeah. That's nice of you," Hayden said. "I should have thought to do that. It's just… Rozanov, y'know?"

"He's not a bad guy," Shane said, a little daringly. "It's mostly an act."

"Pretty convincing one."

"Yeah, well…" Shane almost said *we all have secrets*, but he stopped himself. Instead, he said, "Let's just make sure we win this one, all right?"

"Fucking right."

Ilya loved playing against Hollander almost as much as he loved fucking him.

He was in the corner with him now, battling for the puck, and this was his favorite part of any game.

Hollander won, and skated away with his prize. Ilya

smiled to himself and raced off after him. Shane was a better stick handler, but Ilya was a faster skater, and he caught up with him and poked the puck off his blade from behind.

Ilya had the puck for all of three seconds before Shane forced him into the boards and stole it back. Then he took off again, with a challenging (and somewhat flirty) glance back at Ilya. Ilya grinned and launched himself after him, but this time Shane was *flying* and Ilya was struggling to close the gap and then...

Oh god. No.

It happened so fast, Ilya could barely process it. One second, Shane was racing down the ice, and the next he was slamming against the boards after colliding hard with Cliff Marlow.

And then he was crumpled and motionless, on the ice, and Ilya didn't know what to do.

"Shane?"

Blurry, bright shapes and screeching noise.

"Don't move, all right? Just stay still. We're going to take you off the ice."

Ice?

"Hollander?"

A different voice.

"Ilya?" *Did I say that?* Shane heard his own voice, but had he moved his lips? He blinked, trying to get his eyes to focus.

"Is he all right?" That was Ilya's voice for sure. It sounded different, though. It was...unsteady. Panicked.

"Mmokay," Shane murmured. He had no idea if it was true, but he didn't want to hear the worry in Ilya's voice anymore.

"We're going to move you onto the spinal board, Shane. Keep your head still, please."

Spinal board?

"Ilya, please stand back," the authoritative voice said. And the dark blur that had been looming over Shane disappeared.

"We're not alone," Shane slurred. "Ilya. They can see us."

He felt hands on his arms and legs. He felt straps securing him to a board.

"Is he all right?" Ilya's voice again.

No one answered him.

"Tell him," Shane said. "Tell him I'm fine."

He wanted to turn his head to look at Ilya, but he couldn't now.

Suddenly, he was in the air. He watched the lights and the rafters and the banners that hung from them pass in front of his eyes as he was carried off the ice. He heard applause.

Oh god. What if I'm not okay?

What if I never walk again?

"What happened?" he gritted out.

"You took a blow to the head. You went into the boards."

Fuck.

"There's an ambulance waiting."

Shane pressed his lips together. His eyes were stinging. He was *scared*.

"My parents," he said. "They're at the game."

He watched the paramedics share a look, then one of them nodded. "We'll make sure they know where we're taking you."

Shane closed his eyes because keeping them open was too difficult.

"We need you to stay awake, Shane. All right?"

"Yeah. Sure," Shane said. As the confusion started to clear, he was able to focus on the pain that shot through him.

He felt cool air on his feet as someone removed his skates. "Can you move your toes?"

Fuck. He really, really hoped so. Feeling the cold air had to be a good sign, right?

"Good," the paramedic said, because apparently Shane had successfully wiggled his toes.

Thank god. Thank god. Thank god.

The paramedics did things around him and talked to each other and reminded Shane to stay awake every time his eyelids closed.

Shane thought of his parents. *They must be so worried.*

He thought of Ilya. He wished he could text him. He wished he could tell him he wiggled his toes.

He wondered who had hit him. He had no memory of it.

They must be showing the footage of the hit over and over again on television.

This had never happened to Shane before. Somehow, in all his years of playing, he'd never been laid out cold.

It only takes one time.

His vision was blurry again, but this time it was because of the tears that had formed in his eyes.

The game had been almost over, right? Shane couldn't remember, but he was sure it had been the third period. Montreal had been winning.

What if I can't play in the playoffs?

He was two goals ahead of Ilya in the scoring race with one week left of the regular season. He could kiss that lead goodbye.

"Shane? We need you to keep your eyes open, okay?"

"Sorry."

Ilya had to wait until morning before he could go to the hospital. His team was leaving for the airport in two hours.

He was the team captain. It wasn't unheard of for the opposing team captain to check to make sure the player his teammate had taken out was all right.

Fucking Marlow. He knew Cliff felt bad. He hadn't mean to hit Shane so hard, or at such an awkward angle. But Ilya still wanted to kill him.

He was given Shane's room number by an overly interested woman working behind a desk at the hospital. She seemed to be impressed at Ilya's display of sportsmanship.

The door was open a crack, so Ilya gently pushed it open. Hollander was elevated a bit by the hospital bed into an almost-sitting position. The room was, to Ilya's relief, otherwise empty.

"Ilya!" Shane exclaimed. He had his left arm in a sling.

"Hi," Ilya said awkwardly. "I just needed—are you—?"

"I'm okay," Shane said. He smiled shyly, and Ilya knew he was happy to see him. "I mean, I have a concussion, and a fractured collarbone. I'm out for the playoffs. But…"

"Could have been worse."

"Yeah."

"Marlow is…he feels bad," Ilya said stupidly. "He

was very…angry at himself. And I am mad at him as well."

Shane snorted. "It's part of the game. I know he's not a vicious player. We all get our bell rung eventually, right?"

Shane must have been on some *good* drugs. He was actually grinning.

"He probably doesn't want to meet my mom in a dark alley, though," he joked. "She's out for blood."

"I will warn him."

Ilya wanted to touch him and know that he was really, *really* okay. He had barely slept last night. He'd spent the whole night sick with worry and refreshing sports sites looking for news of Shane's injuries. He couldn't close his eyes without seeing Shane's unmoving body on the ice.

It must have shown in Ilya's eyes, because Shane extended his good hand and said, in a soft voice, "Hey."

Ilya nudged the door closed and crossed the room until he was right next to Shane's bed. He gently brushed his fingers over Shane's face as Shane gazed up at him and smiled.

"You scared me," Ilya admitted.

"Scared myself."

"But you will be okay?"

"Yeah, I'll be okay. I wanted to tell you last night. I wish I could have texted you. I was—"

"Shhh."

Shane's eyes fluttered closed as Ilya's fingers trailed into his hair. "I had been looking forward to last night," Shane murmured.

"Yes."

"I'm mostly mad at Marlow for fucking *that* up."

Ilya laughed.

"When will we get a chance again?" Shane asked.

And, so help him, in that moment Ilya wanted to tell him he would stay with him. That he would move into his apartment and help him with his recovery and make him sandwiches and watch the playoffs with him and read him his boring hockey book.

But, of course, he couldn't.

"I will be busy. Winning the Stanley Cup," Ilya said with a forced smirk.

Shane grimaced.

"I'm sorry," Ilya said, and he meant it.

Shane closed his eyes again. "It sucks."

"I know."

"I wanted to talk to you last night, before this happened."

Ilya had wanted to talk too. But he was sure Shane wouldn't have liked what he had planned to say. He had convinced himself that the only sensible thing to do was to end this thing between them entirely. No good could possibly come of it. Ilya's heart had entered into it, and that changed everything. It wasn't thrilling or fun anymore—it was torture. He was going to tell Shane as much last night, but now...

"Shane," he sighed.

Shane reached his hand up and took Ilya's, tangling their fingers together and holding tight. "Will you come to the cottage?"

"I—I don't know." No. No, there was no way Ilya could do that. He couldn't possibly spend that much time alone with Shane. Not if he ever wanted to be free of this.

"We can have a week or two, Ilya," Shane said. "Haven't you ever wanted more time?"

Ilya's stomach clenched. He should just say no. Let Shane believe that he didn't want any more from him than the hour or two they stole a few times each season.

But instead he brushed his thumb over the back of Shane's hand and said, "Of course."

"Then come to the cottage. Please. It will just be the two of us, completely alone for as long as you want to stay."

And, god, that sounded so perfect. And Shane was looking at him like his heart would shatter if Ilya said no.

So Ilya took the coward's way out.

"Maybe."

Shane beamed at him like he wasn't a man who was in a hospital bed with serious injuries.

The door handle turned and Shane quickly released his hand. Ilya jumped back and turned to face the nurse who entered the room.

"Uh-oh," she said with a smile. "You're not trying to smother him with a pillow, are you, Mr. Rozanov?"

"No," Ilya said, giving her a shaky smile in return. "I was just…leaving, actually."

"Thank you for coming," Shane said, all business. "I appreciate it."

Ilya nodded. "Get well soon, Hollander."

He quickly left the hospital room of the man he loved, and forced himself to focus on winning the Stanley Cup.

Chapter Twenty-Two

May 2017—Ottawa

"Rozanov is hurt."

Shane turned his head from where he was lying on the couch to look at his mother. "What makes you say that?" he asked.

"He's protecting his ribs. You can tell by the way he was angled. Look," she said, pointing at a slo-mo replay on their television. "Right there. He turns away from the hit. He could have taken Hunter off the puck there, but he chickened out."

Mom was right, of course. Shane already knew that Ilya was secretly playing the second round of the play-offs with bruised ribs.

Montreal had been knocked out in the first round by Detroit, and Shane felt terrible about that. Detroit had just squeaked into the playoffs, and it should have been an easy round for Montreal. But Shane hadn't been able to play, and their goaltender had gotten some sort of flu, so the team had struggled and, ultimately, lost.

Shane *should* have been there, helping his team, but instead he was recovering at his parents' house in Ottawa. His headaches were getting better, but he was still very tired. His collarbone was mostly healed.

He hadn't heard from Ilya as often as he would have liked, but he knew he was busy. Focused.

"I think New York is going to win the Cup," his mother said.

"New York, eh?"

"Yes. Scott Hunter is determined. You can see it. Nine seasons without a cup! He'll make sure he gets this one." Yuna Hollander was rarely wrong about these things.

"Well," his father said cheerfully, "at least we won't have to watch Rozanov lift the cup."

Shane grimaced. In truth he would love to see Rozanov lift the cup.

"It was nice of him to visit Shane in the hospital, though," Mom pointed out. "He gets points for that." Dad made a noise of agreement.

Shane wished he could remember the details of that hospital visit. His brain had been muddled by the injury, and more muddled by the drugs. He could remember Ilya's gentle fingers on his face and in his hair. He remembered being so happy to see him. Even now, just knowing that Ilya had made the trip to the hospital filled Shane with a tingly warmth.

Shane was so completely in love with him. He would hit his head all over again just to be alone in that quiet hospital room with those careful fingers and those concerned eyes.

He was in love with him and he could never, ever tell him that.

But maybe…maybe he could at least tell his parents… part of the truth?

Jesus, but how? Just...blurt it out? How did people do this?

Not while watching hockey together, surely.

"Have you heard from Rose Landry lately?" his mother asked, completely out of nowhere. And wasn't that a fucking sign?

"Yeah, she texted me when I was in the hospital. She saw that I got hurt."

His mother looked pleased by that.

Well, no time like the present. "We're not...we're just friends, Mom."

"I know. Your schedules would make a relationship very difficult. But other players do it. Look at Carter Vaughan and that Gloria what's-her-name from TV."

"No, it's..." Shane sat up a little, and winced at the pain in his head. "It's not our schedules. I mean, yeah, that would make it hard, but that's not the reason."

His mother looked at him sympathetically. "When the right one comes along, you'll know," she said.

And Shane chickened out. Because he couldn't tell them that the right one *had* come along, and it was the pissed-off Russian man who was currently heading to the penalty box on their television.

"Yeah," he said, "I know."

He had the most ridiculous urge to send Ilya a text that just said *I love you*. He had those words trapped inside of him, filling every part of him, and, the strain of keeping them from slipping out was getting harder to endure.

Instead, he texted Rose.

Shane: My mom is wondering when we're getting back together.

She replied a few minutes later. Ha!
Then,

Rose: Sorry. It's not really funny. How are you? How's your head?

Shane: Getting better. I can watch tv without sunglasses now.

Rose: But watching tv with sunglasses on is COOL!

Shane replied with the sunglasses face emoji.

Rose: Do you have a hot male nurse taking care of you?

Shane laughed, which caused both of his parents to look at him.

Shane: No. I'm at my parents' house.

Rose: That's a shame.

Shane: Maybe I could ask them to hire me a hot male nurse? Is that a good way to come out?

Rose: I legit LOL'd, Shane.

Shane laughed too.
"Who are you texting?" his mother asked.
"No one," Shane said quickly. "Hayden." *Lies upon lies.*
"How's the baby?"
Baby? Oh! "Great! You know. Hayden and Jackie are totally in love with her." *Probably.*

"You shouldn't be looking at your phone so much. It's not good for your concussion."

"I *know*, Mom!" Shane snapped.

She threw her hands up dramatically. "Sorry for caring about the health of your brain!"

He rolled his eyes. "Trust me. *Plenty* of people are concerned about the health of my brain."

He'd been staying with his parents since leaving the hospital, and it was starting to wear on him. He was lucky to have them, and he couldn't imagine having to suffer through this recovery on his own, but he was craving his independence.

Although, there was *one* person he wouldn't mind having around. But that person was looking frustrated as hell on his television.

Sexy too, though. Ilya had a thick playoff beard—the kind that Shane had always been envious of. Even when Shane had played all the way to the Stanley Cup finals, the best he'd been able to manage was a few pathetic tufts of hair, spaced out like islands on his face. Ilya had a full, dark beard that framed his plush lips, and oh god. Now all Shane could think about was wanting to feel that beard rub against his thighs.

The thing that he had been trying not to worry about too much—because his situation was depressing enough—was that he wasn't entirely confident that he would feel *any* part of Ilya rubbing against him ever again. And wouldn't that be the world's saddest joke? As soon as Shane finally admitted to himself that he *wanted* to be with Ilya, their weird arrangement might be permanently off the table.

Not that either of them had said anything specific about ending things. They hadn't said much of anything to each other since the day Ilya had left Shane's hospital room. Shane just had a sense that maybe this whole thing had become too much. It had become more difficult to contain, or to pretend it didn't mean anything. The only safe option was to walk away.

Shane was expecting Ilya to tell him as much as soon as the playoffs were over. And it was looking, as the final minutes of the game ticked away, like the playoffs would be over for Ilya tonight.

The stupid part of Shane wanted to fight for Ilya. For *them*. The sensible part—the part that was in control of most things in Shane's life—knew there couldn't possibly be a future with Ilya. There couldn't be a *present* with Ilya. They needed to end things quickly, and cleanly, and never look back. The other path led to nothing but heartache and scandal and misery and…soft Russian words being breathed against Shane's skin. It led to falling asleep with strong arms wrapped around him, and waking up to a lazy, crooked smile and playful kisses. It led to homemade tuna melts and the precious times when Ilya would offer Shane the tiny pieces of himself that he usually kept so carefully guarded.

The game ended. Ilya's season was over. It was only a matter of time before everything would be over. And Shane didn't know what he could do to prevent it.

But he knew he wanted to.

June 2017—Boston

Jane: I can't believe New York is finally going to win the cup.

Ilya couldn't believe it either. Scott fucking Hunter was going to be a Stanley Cup champion in about forty seconds.

Ilya: I hate Hunter.

Jane: No you don't.

Ilya: I do.

Jane: Stop. I'll get jealous if you keep talking like that.

Ilya laughed. Alone, in his penthouse in Boston, he laughed.

The final seconds of the final game of the final series of the playoffs ticked down, and then the game was over. The ice filled with excited men in blue jerseys, and Ilya turned his full attention to his phone so he wouldn't feel the sting of envy too sharply.

He was *bored.* The playoffs had ended for him weeks ago. At a loss for what to do or where to go, he'd holed up in Boston. It was his only home now, though he had no real friends in the city. There were teammates who stayed for the summers, but none he was close to.

But his car collection was here, and that wasn't nothing.

Though the last time he had visited his garage, three days ago, it had kind of felt like nothing.

He wasn't inviting Svetlana over anymore because… just because.

So he was watching hockey, alone, and texting the man he desperately wished he could be sharing his summer with.

Ilya: Do you think Hunter is going to drink tea out of the cup?

Jane: Caffeine? No way. Hunter isn't that hard-core.

Ilya laughed again.

Ilya: Milk then.

Jane: Warm milk. And then straight to bed!

Ilya glanced up at the television and saw the Stanley Cup being handed to a beaming Scott Hunter.

Jane: I'm happy for him.

Ilya: Of course you are.

He'd had every intention of ending things with Shane. He hadn't been able to do that. Not yet. For now they could text each other and tease each other and pretend they were just friends or whatever.

Shane's invitation for Ilya to come to his cottage still existed. Shane wasn't pushing it, and Ilya wasn't acknowledging it, but it was there. If it weren't the worst idea in the world, Ilya would be on his way to Wherever-the-Fuck, Ontario, already.

Players on the television were kissing their wives and holding their children. It would be nice, Ilya thought, to have someone to kiss after winning the Cup.

Maybe that should be his goal for next year: forget about Shane, and find himself a woman he could like enough to keep around until the end of the playoffs.

Ilya reached for the remote, and was about to turn off the television when...

Holy shit.

Holy. Shit.

Scott fucking Hunter was *kissing* a *man*. Not, like, one of his teammates on the cheek in an "I love you, bro" kind of way. Scott Hunter was kissing a man wearing street clothes *full on the fucking mouth*. It looked like tongues were involved.

Ilya's phone buzzed.

Jane: Holy shit.

Jane: Are you seeing this?

Jane: What the fuck?!!!? Is that his boyfriend???!!!!!

Ilya just stared at the television, at Scott Hunter and his probable boyfriend. Or Scott Hunter and the random cute man he had pulled out of the crowd. Ilya couldn't process what he was seeing. How could it possibly be real?

But there Hunter was, smiling at this mystery man like he was the only thing that mattered in the world. And holding his face as he leaned in to kiss him again. Ilya felt like he was watching all the worst things about his life getting sucked up by a tornado.

Then the cameras cut away, and Ilya looked at his phone.

Jane: What is happening??!!! Did he really just do that???!!!

Ilya stabbed the call button.

There was only one ring before, "Holy shit, Ilya! Can you belie—"

"I'm coming to the cottage."

Part Four

Chapter Twenty-Three

Shane drummed his fingers anxiously on the steering wheel.

He wished he could have gone into the airport to greet Ilya properly, but *one* of them alone in the airport would turn enough heads; the two of them together would be pandemonium.

He pulled his ball cap down lower and watched the rearview mirror.

He was still in shock that Ilya had accepted his invitation, though he supposed he had Scott Hunter to thank for that. Hunter had come out, *very* publicly, the night he had won the Stanley Cup. He had also spoken about it openly in interviews that night, and even more openly in his speech at the NHL Awards last week. Shane had watched that speech…a few times. He wished he could have been at the awards to see it in person, but it seemed like an unnecessary burden on his freshly healed body to fly to Las Vegas.

But still, he would have liked to have shaken Hunter's hand.

Instead, he had sent him an email. He had written

several drafts of the email before sending one that simply acknowledged Hunter's bravery. He had chosen his words carefully, because he didn't have Hunter's courage. Not yet, anyway.

But maybe Hunter would figure out what Shane was actually trying to say anyway.

Having an NHL player come out as gay for the first time was exciting, but a player on every team in the league could come out and it still wouldn't help Shane's situation. Being gay—or whatever—was not really the thing that would create a scandal. Fucking your biggest rival over the course of your *entire NHL career* was something that no one would understand. Not one person. Shane felt that even Scott Hunter, the NHL's new poster boy for acceptance and tolerance, would be alarmed if he knew what he'd been up to with Ilya.

They would be a joke. If the world found out about them, that was all they would be: the depraved hockey players who secretly fucked each other. And Shane didn't want to be that. At all. He wanted to be the best hockey player in the world, and he wanted to be in a relationship with the man he could finally admit he was in love with, without shame or fear.

But he couldn't. All he could have were these two weeks alone with Ilya, hiding where no one would find them.

He heard the wheels of the rolling duffel bag before he saw Ilya in the mirror, crossing the parking garage.

Shane considered getting out of the car, but decided to stay where he was. Once they were at the cottage they would be safe, but there was no point in blowing it now. He just needed to make it out of Ottawa without anyone noticing that Shane Hollander and Ilya Rozanov were hanging out together in July.

As Ilya got closer, Shane saw that he too had his ball cap pulled low, and was wearing large aviator sunglasses. Shane wondered if anyone had recognized him inside the airport.

He popped the back of the SUV so Ilya could load his bag in. They didn't say a word to each other until Ilya slid into the passenger seat. "What the fuck are you driving, Hollander?"

"A Jeep Cherokee."

Ilya snorted.

"What? It's practical!"

"You're a millionaire."

"What's wrong with a Cherokee?" Shane asked, starting the engine. "It's good in the snow. It holds lots of stuff. It's a good car."

"Is good if you are a dad in the suburbs."

"Better than a stupid sports car where my knees are over my damn head."

"Hm."

They didn't talk again until Shane had exited the parking garage. "Good flight?" he asked.

"Sure."

"It takes about two hours to get to the cottage."

"Okay."

"Are you hungry or anything? We could stop and one of us could…"

Ilya shrugged.

"I think you'll like the cottage," Shane said. "It's really relaxing."

"Is that what we are going to do?" Ilya asked. "Relax?"

Shane swallowed. He turned onto the on-ramp for the highway.

"I hope so," he said finally. "I would like to relax with you. For once."

He glanced over for a second. Ilya was looking out the passenger-side window.

"I stocked up on groceries yesterday," Shane said. "We shouldn't need to…leave. Very often."

They drove in silence for a few minutes. Shane wondered if Ilya was as panicked as he suddenly was. Two weeks. Alone together. Possibly constantly alone together.

What the hell had he been thinking when he'd suggested this?

"Thank you," Ilya said suddenly. "For inviting me."

Shane felt his panic subside. "I'm glad you're here."

"I am also glad. But…terrified, right?"

Shane laughed, relieved. "Yeah. Me too."

They both knew this was a point of no return. More so even than the first time they had kissed, or fucked. This was a new frontier, a new level of intimacy.

"Did anyone recognize you in the airport?"

"No, I don't think so."

Shane nodded. "The cottage is way down a private road. We'll be totally alone there."

"No family coming to visit?"

"No, I, uh, I told them I need a couple of weeks of solitude. I told them it was a, I don't know, psychological thing. Like a mental training meditation thing."

"So sneaky."

"We won't be bothered."

He noticed Ilya chewing on his thumbnail.

"I've, uh, I've been looking forward to this," Shane said.

"Yes. Me too."

Shane smiled and took one hand off the steering wheel. He reached over and Ilya quickly tangled their fingers together and squeezed.

Two weeks. For two weeks they could pretend that their situation wasn't impossible.

Ilya was hit with a sudden wave of "holy shit, this is really happening" when Shane parked the car in front of the large lake house that Ilya had seen profiled on television.

Ilya was pretty sure a cottage was usually a lot smaller than this giant, stone-front house, but it was certainly, as Shane had promised, remote. He didn't think he had ever been anywhere quite like this before; somewhere that he could truly let his guard down and not worry about being recognized.

No wonder Hollander loved it.

Hollander, he realized, had removed Ilya's bag from the trunk and was carrying it toward the house, as if Ilya was his visiting aunt or something.

"I can carry my own bag."

Shane just kept walking. "How are your ribs?" he asked.

"My ribs are fine. I can carry the bag."

"I can't believe you played with those bruised ribs."

"You can't?"

Shane shot him a grin over his shoulder. "I guess I can."

He opened the door and they stepped inside. It truly was a spectacular house. It was all wide open and spacious, with high ceilings and exposed beams. The opposite wall was floor-to-ceiling windows overlooking the lake. Ilya could see an enormous deck with a pool and a hot tub. Beyond that there was a dock and a boathouse.

"Make yourself at home," Shane said.

Ilya sauntered into the living room. He removed his sunglasses and hooked them on the front of his T-shirt. And here was everything he had seen on that television show: the leather sectional sofa, the spectacular view, and the ridiculously Canadian-looking plaid throw pillows and blankets.

Jesus Christ. He was in Shane Hollander's *home*.

"So, I could give you a tour, if you like," Shane said. "Or, if you're hungry…like I said, I stocked up on groceries. There's a beer fridge in the games room next to the pool table…"

Shane was standing a good six feet behind Ilya. Ilya turned away from the view of the lake to face him.

"The tap water here is actually excellent," Shane continued. He was so obviously nervous. "There's a natural spring nearby and…"

Ilya closed the distance between them in slow, deliberate steps. Shane tilted his head up to face him, and Ilya could see him swallow.

They stood for a moment, silently staring at each other, waiting for whatever was going to happen next. Finally, Ilya reached a hand up and brushed the backs of his fingers against Shane's cheek. Shane unconsciously licked his lip and Ilya moved in to kiss him.

The moment Shane's mouth opened under his, everything made sense. All of Ilya's nerves left him, and he grabbed at Shane's T-shirt and pulled him closer. Shane made a little moaning sound and plunged his fingers under Ilya's ball cap, knocking it to the floor. He tangled his fingers in Ilya's hair and began walking him backward to the leather sofa.

They hadn't been together for months. The ridiculous thing was, Ilya hadn't been with *anyone* in all that time. For the first time in his life, he hadn't *wanted* to be with anyone else.

But now he felt like he was going to burst if Shane didn't touch him the way he'd not been able to stop thinking about.

He went willingly down to the sofa when Shane shoved him. He kept a firm grip on Shane's T-shirt so the other man immediately tumbled on top of him. Ilya winced as his sunglasses were pressed into his chest, then he pulled them off and threw them, clattering, to the floor.

Ilya kissed Shane wildly, jerking his hips up to get more friction on his cock, and was delighted to feel that Shane was as hard as he was.

He pulled Shane's shirt off over his head and slid his hands down to open Shane's fly.

"Fuck," Shane panted. "I'm...it's been kind of a while... I might not last long."

"Yes. Same. But we have two weeks, right?"

Shane laughed. "Right." Then, "Wait...same?"

"Hm?"

"You said 'same.' You haven't...been with anyone? Lately?"

Ilya grimaced. He probably shouldn't have admitted that. But...

"No."

"Like, not since—?"

"No. Not since. Can we please get back to—?"

"Really?" Shane pulled back so he could look Ilya directly in the eyes. He looked stunned and way, way too happy.

"Is not a big deal, Hollander. Relax."

"It's been, like—"

"Months. Yes. Which is why I would really like to—"

"I haven't either," Shane said quickly. "Not since the last time we were together. In Boston."

"Well then…" Ilya said, moving his hand to continue to work his way into Shane's pants. But Shane didn't go back to grinding his hips or attacking Ilya's mouth with filthy desperate kisses. Instead, he reached up and gently brushed a lock of hair out of Ilya's face. Ilya could only stare, mesmerized, at Shane's face as he looked down at him with so much…tenderness.

"I have an idea," Shane said. He was brushing his thumb over Ilya's bottom lip as he said it.

"What?" Ilya asked, with more bravery than he felt.

"Let's be honest with each other. For these two weeks, let's just…say what we're actually thinking. Maybe…say how we really feel."

I can't, Ilya wanted to say. *I can't because if I do you'll think I'm pathetic, or, worse, you'll say it back and then what the fuck are we supposed to do?*

"I will try," he said instead.

"Will you?" Shane asked skeptically.

"Yes! I will do anything if it will make you touch my dick right now!"

Shane laughed and shook his head. But then he slid down Ilya's body and hauled down Ilya's shorts, and *thank Christ.*

Shane took him into his mouth and everything was simple again. Ilya felt a wave of pleasure mingle with a wave of relief, and he was able to relax and enjoy the determined way Shane always approached sucking him off.

Ilya cheated and murmured, "I would stay here forever if I could" in Russian. He felt Shane sigh around him, but it sounded more dreamy than exasperated. Maybe he understood what he meant. Maybe some feelings couldn't be hidden behind foreign words.

As expected, Ilya didn't last long. Neither did Shane, when Ilya immediately returned the favor. But the surprising thing was that the blow jobs were not the best part of the afternoon. Afterward, now that they had taken the edge off, they just relaxed against each other on the sofa. The clothing that had stayed on their bodies was rumpled and unfastened; their hair was messy. They talked quietly to each other as they—there was no other word for it—*cuddled* for over an hour. Shane was twisting strands of Ilya's hair around his fingers and gently releasing them; Ilya was tracing his fingertips over Shane's freckles. Every now and again, Ilya would kiss Shane's jaw, or his throat, or, one time, the tip of his nose.

Ilya couldn't believe what he had been reduced to. He was…*infatuated*. It was disgusting.

But it was hard to care when Shane was lying on top of him, his smooth chest and stomach touching every inch of Ilya's own. His bangs hanging down to brush Ilya's nose. His dark eyes, and his freckles, and his *smile*. Shane looked so happy. Somehow, Ilya made him happy.

Ilya wanted to always make him happy.

Ilya wasn't at all surprised to learn that Shane had a complete indoor hockey training facility at his cottage.

Shane had excitedly led him to the one-story building beside the main cottage and opened the door to reveal a large synthetic plastic rink, a net with shooting targets, passing targets, and a whole bunch of exercise equipment. The wall facing the lake was all windows.

So now they were on the "ice" in sneakers, passing a puck back and forth.

"I didn't tell you," Ilya said, "about after the NHL Awards."

"After?"

"Yes. I went out. With Scott Hunter."

Shane missed the next pass. "What do you mean?"

"There was a club having a Scott Hunter night, whatever the fuck that means."

"A club? Like…"

"A gay club. Yes. So I thought I would go."

"I'm sorry. You went to a *gay club* in *Las Vegas* with *Scott Hunter*?"

"And his boyfriend. Yes. Nice guy."

Shane's brow pinched. "Why didn't you tell me this before?"

Ilya shrugged. "I forgot." Which wasn't true at all. He just wanted to see *this* exact expression on Shane's face. Ilya privately thought of it as his "scrunched confusion" face.

"Was it…what was it like?"

"Was fine. A little boring but, you know, Scott Hunter. What can you expect?" Ilya snatched a new puck from the pile beside him with his stick blade and sent it over to Shane. This time Shane caught it on his stick easily.

"So, does Hunter know you're—?"

"I did not say anything. He may have guessed something." He grinned. "There were some very hot men there."

And now Shane's face changed to the expression Ilya called "clenched disapproval."

"I'm glad you had a nice time," Shane said tersely.

"Point is, I went to a gay bar with NHL players and it was…exciting, you know?"

Shane nodded, and returned the puck to Ilya. "I'll bet."

"I give Hunter shit, but what he did was brave. Kissing his boyfriend on TV like that. And the speech at the awards."

"It was. It really…made me hopeful. That things might be changing."

Ilya shot the puck back to Shane. "It made me jealous," he admitted.

Shane laughed. "You wanna kiss me on television?"

"Yes. After I win the Stanley Cup."

Shane spread his arms out. "Oh, so in this romantic scenario, you've just defeated me?"

"Yes. Sorry."

"I'm not going to be in the mood to kiss you if I've just lost the Stanley Cup, Rozanov."

"But you would be so proud of me!"

Shane rolled his eyes. "You are the most obnoxious person on earth. I have no idea why I—" He stopped himself just in time. "—why I put up with you."

Ilya pushed against the ice with his sneakers and slid over to Shane. When he reached him, he kissed him loudly on the cheek.

"I'm hungry," Shane grumbled. "Come on. Let's see what's in the fridge."

"Are you going to show me to my room, or…?"

Ilya was leaning against a pillar in the middle of the living room, wearing that fucking crooked smile that always made Shane lose his mind.

"Well, I have four guest rooms," Shane said, playing along. "Would you like one with a view?"

"I need one with a king-size bed."

Shane walked toward Ilya and grinned. "They all have king-size beds."

"And an en suite bathroom."

"Oh," Shane said, with mock concern. "I'm afraid there's only one room with an en suite bathroom."

"I have very specific needs."

"I'll try to be accommodating."

He breathed the last words against Ilya's lips and then kissed him. It was slow and wonderful.

"I want to sleep in your bed, Shane Hollander," Ilya murmured.

"I want to do lots of things in my bed."

"Show me. Take me to bed."

Shane led him to the room that took up half of the second floor. The sun had set, but in the morning they would see the view of the lake through the windows that wrapped around two of the walls.

He watched Ilya take the room in; he watched him examine the pictures on the walls and the items on his dresser.

"This is your room," Ilya said, more to himself maybe than to Shane.

"Yeah. Probably even more so than my room back in Montreal. This place is…home."

"This is your parents," Ilya said, pointing to a framed photo sitting on the dresser.

"Yep."

With a playful little grin, Ilya flipped the photo so it lay facedown. "Do not want to shock them," he said. Shane laughed.

Ilya moved to the bed and sat on the end of it. Shane sat beside him. "It's kind of surreal. Having you here."

"Yes. Bad or good?"

"Good," Shane said quickly. He took Ilya's hand and squeezed. "Really good."

"Good." Then, without warning, Ilya turned and pounced on him, pushing him down on his back on the mattress. Shane didn't have time to be surprised before Ilya's mouth was on his.

Shane moaned helplessly and arched his body against Ilya's. He wrapped a leg around Ilya's thighs and pulled him closer.

The kiss felt weird, and Shane realized it was because neither of them could stop smiling.

"You're here," he murmured.

"Yes. Now take off your clothes."

Shane laughed and quickly removed his clothing. He fired each garment in the general direction of his laundry hamper, then sprawled out on his back and watched Ilya peel his own shirt off.

Ilya slid a hand down his own bare chest, like a stripper. He paused at the button on his shorts, and raised an eyebrow at Shane.

"What's this Magic Mike shit?" Shane asked, grinning.

Ilya responded by pushing both hands into his own hair and tilting his head back dramatically. He thrust his crotch out, and Shane cracked up.

"Here, let me help you." He crawled on his knees on the bed until he could press his mouth against Ilya's stomach. He licked along the lines of Ilya's muscles, and he heard Ilya let out a shaky breath.

"Don't tease me," Ilya said. "I have waited too long for this."

"Mm." Shane opened the front of Ilya's shorts and playfully nipped at his chest. "Months."

"Years," Ilya sighed. "Years I have wanted to have you in your real bed."

Shane froze. "Years?"

Ilya wrapped long fingers around Shane's jaw, and tilted his head up to meet his gaze.

"Yes."

Shane swallowed. "Get those shorts off," he managed to scrape out.

Ilya had barely slipped the last of his clothing off before Shane reached for him. He needed to feel his weight on him. He needed to kiss him and touch him and feel him grow hard against him (although it looked like he was a little late for that).

Ilya was here, and Shane would finally know what it was like to be with him when they had all the time they wanted. Ilya had promised him two weeks, and Shane was giddy with the vastness of time that was spread before him.

Ilya kissed him, slowly and greedily. His erection brushed against Shane's belly, and Shane wriggled against it to give Ilya as much friction as possible. Ilya responded by gripping both of Shane's wrists and pinning them to the mattress.

"Oh," Shane gasped. He shamelessly tipped his head back to give Ilya better access to his throat. Ilya took advantage of his generous offer by sucking the sensitive spot just under the hinge of Shane's jaw.

Ilya was going to leave a mark—a *hickey*—if he kept sucking at Shane's neck, but Shane realized that it didn't matter. For the first time ever, they didn't have to worry about evidence. About anything. No one would ever know what happened here.

"Harder," Shane said. "I want to see it later."

Ilya growled and pressed his mouth harder to Shane's skin. He sucked hard enough that, for a hysterical second, Shane wondered if he might actually be a vampire.

Are there Russian vampires?

No, dummy. Vampires aren't real.

Just as the pain was crossing over to uncomfortable, Ilya pulled away. Shane was flooded with relief and the delicious burn that pulsed from the spot where Ilya had marked him.

Ilya gently licked the spot, and Shane squirmed happily.

"Mine." Ilya's breath tickled Shane's skin when he spoke the single word.

"Yours," Shane said dreamily.

"All of this. For two weeks. Is mine."

Forever, Shane wanted to say. *Forever if you ask.*

He knew it was impossible, but in that moment he would do anything to make it work. There *had* to be a solution to their problem.

But, for now, he just said, "Fuck me. Please."

Ilya sat up, and then flipped Shane to his stomach. He laid a light kiss between Shane's shoulder blades.

Oh god, Shane wanted this. He wanted to thrust his ass into the air and to command Ilya to hurry the fuck up, but Ilya was making a slow journey down Shane's body, placing a soft kiss on each notch of his spine. He was in no hurry at all.

"Gorgeous," Ilya sighed between kisses. The word, in his accent, was dark and lush. It slid over Shane's skin, and in that moment he *felt* gorgeous.

Ilya reached the base of Shane's spine, and Shane expected him to pull away, maybe grab the lube. But instead, Ilya did something he had never done before: he kept going.

His tongue slipped into the crease of Shane's ass as his big hands pulled his cheeks apart. Shane held his breath. He couldn't believe Ilya was actually going to—

"Oh, god. *Ilya.*"

Shane felt the wet heat of Ilya's tongue lapping at his hole and he had *never* experienced anything like it. It was impossibly intimate. It was so bold and fearless and so...*Ilya.*

His tongue paused a moment, and Ilya said, "Good?"

"Fucking *great.*"

He heard Ilya chuckle behind him, and then the lapping continued. Shane's eyes rolled back and he groaned. How could something be so relaxing and so exciting at the same time? He was almost angry that Ilya had been holding out on him all this time. But that wouldn't be fair; Shane appreciated this for the gift it was.

He was wild with need. His cock was rigid against the mattress, and it took all of his willpower not to start humping the bed. He didn't want to move at all because that might make Ilya stop. And Shane wasn't sure how much longer Ilya could keep doing this but...

Oh.

Ilya's tongue was *inside him.*

Warm and slippery and intrusive. It was somewhere it definitely was *not* supposed to be. But it felt so, so, so, so good.

"Fuck. *Fuck.* Ilya...holy god. That's amazing. Thank you. Fuck."

The *thank you* was embarrassing, but Shane didn't dwell on it. Just like he refused to be embarrassed by the desperate noises Ilya was drawing out of him by *fucking his ass with his tongue.*

Shane was going to come. The realization hit him suddenly, and, in a panic, he jerked his hips off the bed to remove any friction against his aching cock. Unfortunately, the move also caused him to smash Ilya in the face with his ass.

"Aah! What the fuck, Hollander?"

"Sorry!"

He turned to look over his shoulder, and Ilya was rubbing his jaw and scowling.

"I'm sorry!" Shane said again. "I was just... I didn't want to come yet."

Ilya rolled his eyes, but his lips twitched. "I guess that is a compliment."

"It is," Shane agreed quickly. He flipped over to his back. "That felt incredible."

"Good."

"Did, um...did you like doing that?"

Ilya nodded. "I did. Yes. Until you bashed me in the face."

Shane bit his lip to keep from grinning, but Ilya noticed. With a snort that didn't really sound angry, Ilya bent down until their faces were inches apart.

Shane tilted his chin up for a kiss before he remembered where Ilya's mouth had just been. Did he care?

No.

He leaned up and kissed him, and he didn't really taste much of anything. It was just the familiar heat of Ilya's mouth on his. He felt the press of Ilya's hard cock against his hip, and the need to have it inside of him flared right back up in Shane.

"Please."

Ilya looked around and Shane pointed to the nightstand to the right of the bed. Ilya opened the drawer and pulled out a bottle of lube and a condom, but he didn't close the drawer right away.

"What?" Shane asked.

"I was hoping there would be toys."

"I don't keep any here."

"You have a big stash in Montreal?"

Shane blushed. "No!"

"No? Still just one lonely dildo?"

Yes.

Shane slammed his head back on the pillow. He was not above whining at this point. "Please shut up and fuck me."

Ilya wasted no time positioning himself between Shane's legs and driving into him. Shane wasn't sure if he was trying to say *be careful what you wish for*, but Shane wasn't feeling sorry at all.

Shane cried out into the room. He let himself be as loud as he'd always wanted to be, because he *could*.

"Oh, Shane. Yes. I want to hear it."

Ilya slammed into him over and over, making the headboard bang against the wall. Shane reached a hand up to steady it, but Ilya just covered his hand with his own, bracing himself against the wall and fucking him even harder.

Shane lifted his legs and rested his ankles on Ilya's shoulders. Ilya growled and lunged forward, folding Shane in half and sinking deeper inside him.

Ilya's face was slick with sweat, and his eyes were

wild. "Shane. Fuck—I—holy shit. You're amazing, Shane. So fucking good."

Shane could only make high, whimpery noises in response. He was going to come. There was nothing touching his dick, but it was going to happen. Any second now.

"You look like—are you going to come, Hollander?"

"Yeah," Shane gasped.

"Oh fuck. Yes. Come on."

Ilya thrust faster, keeping his eyes on Shane's dick, and then Shane erupted. He screamed and arched and watched with Ilya as his dick coated his stomach and chest.

"Shane…" It was the only word Ilya managed to grit out before he stilled and came inside him.

For long moments, neither of them moved. They both panted and gazed at each other, and there were words that Shane was dangerously close to saying. He could feel them, thrashing around inside him, desperate to get out, but he forced them down.

And then Ilya placed a palm on the side of Shane's face and just *looked* at him, and for a wild second Shane thought *Ilya* was going to be the one to say those forbidden words.

But he didn't. Instead, he pulled out of him and fell on the mattress beside him. Shane rolled to his side, and Ilya did the same, facing him. Shane smiled because the last time he'd had this view of him, Ilya had been in Moscow, and Shane had been in Montreal.

"We could stay in this bed for two weeks," Shane suggested.

Ilya shook his head. "No. I want to fuck you in every room of this house."

Shane squirmed and blushed. "I have a hot tub, you know."

Ilya made a face. "Hot tubs are terrible for sex. Have you tried it?"

"No."

"Is horrible. Too hot. Uncomfortable."

"Well, I also have a pool."

Ilya leaned in and nuzzled under Shane's chin. Shane tipped his head back so Ilya could trail kisses over his flushed skin.

"And a pool *table*," Ilya murmured.

Oh god.

"The felt is very delicate," Shane squeaked.

Ilya snorted. "Do you ever relax?"

Shane pulled away so he could glare at him. "You're really going to make fun of me now? While you're a guest in my home? In my *bed*?"

Shane was assaulted by a lazy, crooked smile.

"No," Ilya said. "I like you, Hollander."

It wasn't an earth-shattering confession, but the words still moved Shane enormously.

"I like you too, Rozanov."

Chapter Twenty-Four

The following evening, Ilya leaned against the rail of the deck and watched Shane flip burgers on the barbecue. Shane seemed very excited about the burgers. He had followed a recipe online.

Ilya took a sip of his beer. "Why the fuck are you making eight burgers?" he asked.

"That's how many the recipe was for!"

"You can't do math? Cut it in half?"

"Leave me alone."

Instead, Ilya stood directly behind Shane and draped an arm across his chest. He kissed him behind the ear. "No," he murmured.

Shane tipped his head back, and Ilya could see the color that had flooded to his cheeks.

It was exhilarating, to be outdoors like this and to be able to touch each other the way they wanted to.

Christ. He hadn't even been here for two days yet and already he had no idea how he was going to be able to go back to the real world.

"I would bring some of the burgers over to my parents' cottage, but that would ruin the whole I-can't-be-disturbed-I'm-meditating lie I told them."

Ilya kissed his neck. "Have you ever lied to your parents before?"

Shane shuddered. "Probably. I mean… I must have. But not often, no."

"You love your parents. You are a good son."

"I try to be."

"They don't know how bad you can be."

"Stop it."

"What is your mother's name?"

Shane pulled away, and turned to face him. "What are you doing? Why all the questions?" He was frowning, as if he suspected Ilya was making fun of him.

"What? I want to know about your family! All I know is your mother is Japanese or something. Probably where you get your looks."

"Half of them, yes."

"And your dad is…boring? Is that where you get your boring from?"

Shane shook his head, but he was smiling a bit. "My dad is *not* boring."

"He is exciting?"

"He's…normal. He works for the Treasury Board of Canada."

"Super exciting."

"He played hockey for McGill."

"Wow. Is McGill a town? What the fuck is McGill?"

"It's a school! A university in Montreal! A very famous one."

Ilya shrugged and took a sip of his beer.

"My parents are awesome," Shane said, turning his attention back to the grill. "Seriously, they're the best."

"Maybe I will meet them someday."

Shane froze. Ilya saw the tension grip his back and shoulders.

"Relax," Ilya said. "Was a joke. I know I won't—"

"I'd like you to," Shane said quietly. "I mean… I wish you could. You know. If things were…different."

Ilya reached out and tapped Shane's elbow. Shane turned to face him.

"Do they know?"

"About you?"

"No," Ilya said. "About *you*."

Shane looked down and shook his head. "No."

"They would not be…good? If you told them?"

"I don't know."

"You said they are the best."

Shane looked up. "They are. I mean… I think they would be fine with it. I know they would be, really. They love me. They've always supported me. They aren't homophobic at all, I don't think. It's just not something we've ever really talked about."

"Maybe you should."

Shane turned and picked up a plate that he started piling burger patties on. "Sometimes I think I would have told them by now. If it wasn't for…"

Ilya raised an eyebrow that Shane couldn't see. "This is my fault?"

"No. Yes. Sort of. I just think…if I had a *normal* dating life or whatever. I mean, still dating men, but not… doing whatever we're doing. With, you know, *you*."

"You don't want to tell your parents that you are fucking Ilya Rozanov?"

Shane sputtered out a laugh. "No. I definitely do not want to have to explain *that* to them."

"Why would you, though?"

"What do you mean?"

"You can tell your parents that you are gay, I think,

without telling them the names of men you are fucking. I am pretty sure about this."

"I know! I know. But…" Shane sighed. "Forget it. It doesn't matter. Let's eat these burgers before they get cold."

Ilya wanted to push him to say more, but instead he just followed Shane to the table.

The truth was that Shane thought about Ilya meeting his parents a *lot*.

He was kind of obsessed with the idea.

He couldn't even form a clear thought about why it was so important to him. For one thing, it was an absurd, terrible idea and there was absolutely no reason why he should want it to happen.

He had even imagined benign scenarios where they are at a function—maybe the NHL Awards—and Shane just casually says, "Mom. Dad. Have you met Ilya Rozanov?" And they would meet. And they would shake his hand and Ilya would nod politely at them and tell them it was nice to meet them. Then it would be over, and his parents would shake the hand of the next person who approached them and they would have no idea— *no idea*—how much of a relief it would be for Shane to have witnessed just that simple contact. To know that the two people he loved the most had touched the skin of Ilya Rozanov, and had looked into his eyes, even for a second, and that Shane now had concrete proof that all three of them existed in the same world.

These were the thoughts that kept Shane awake at night. Total and complete madness. His deepest, most closely guarded desire was to just have his parents make contact with the man he'd been secretly fucking for seven years. Part of him felt that, if it happened, *some-*

thing would become clear. *Something* would finally make sense.

The *real actual truth*—the truth that Shane mentally stomped on every time it dared try to get his attention—was that he wanted Ilya to meet his parents for the same reason anyone wanted their boyfriend to meet their parents: he loved him, and he wanted them to love him too.

Except Ilya was *not* Shane's boyfriend. And, even if he was, if Shane introduced Ilya as his boyfriend they would be beyond confused. For one thing, he supposedly hated Ilya Rozanov. And *they* hated Ilya Rozanov. And everyone in the whole goddamned world of hockey knew that Shane Hollander hated Ilya Rozanov. So even introducing them formally at the NHL Awards would be weird.

His biggest nightmare was that he and Ilya would be caught together somehow. Paparazzi or whatever. And then the world would know, but more importantly, his *parents* would know. They would find out that their son was gay and their son was *being gay* with Ilya Rozanov.

Ilya Rozanov, who, at that moment, was sitting across from Shane at the table on his patio, eating the food Shane had prepared for him. He had mustard on the corner of his lips.

If Shane removed all of the complications of their relationship—the rivalry, the expectations for both of them, the fact that Ilya was kind of a dick—he could just be proud of the fact that the man was *really* hot. Like, Shane had definitely snagged himself a ten.

That morning, Shane had woken up early because he hadn't closed the blinds the night before. Sunshine had streamed into the room, reflecting off the white bedsheets, and off the beautiful man who had been wrapped up in them.

Shane had taken advantage of the moment, while Ilya had still been asleep, as an opportunity to drink his fill of him. Ilya had been on his back, his arm draped over his forehead, his long fingers curled against the pillow. Shane had traced a fingertip down that arm, over the swell of Ilya's bicep, because he couldn't help it. The morning light was making everything beautiful, and Shane was in love, so he had leaned in and lightly kissed Ilya's wrist.

When Ilya's eyes had fluttered open, Shane's face had been inches away from them. He had seen the initial confusion in Ilya's expression before it softened into a shy smile.

It had been a perfect morning.

A perfect day, really. They had worked out *very* competitively in Shane's gym, then lounged by the pool, and eventually headed down to the boathouse. Shane had suggested they take the kayaks out, but that got dropped as soon as Ilya spotted the Jet Skis. The rest of the afternoon had been spent racing around the lake, laughing and soaking each other. Ilya was never happier than when he was in control of a high-speed vehicle.

Although, he had been pretty happy later on, when Shane had pinned him to the wall inside the boathouse and they'd stripped off their bathing suits and taken each other in hand...

It had been a really good day.

And now they were eating burgers that Shane had totally aced, and drinking beer on the deck as the sun set, and it was everything he had ever wanted. He imagined a life of spending summers together at the cottage. It was his intention to make this his permanent home after he retired. He wondered if Ilya would be into living here when—

What the hell, Hollander? Getting a little ahead of yourself, aren't you?

But these were the thoughts that consumed him these days: Ilya meeting his parents, Ilya spending the summers with him, Ilya making a home with him.

He'd give anything to go back to the simplicity of the early days, when all that consumed him was the confusing desire to have Ilya's dick in his mouth.

For seven years, they'd been getting away with this thing. Their luck had to run out sometime, right?

Ilya stared at the fire because he wasn't sure what else he was supposed to do, exactly. This seemed to be the extent of the entertainment a bonfire provided: it burned, and you looked at it.

The bonfire had been Shane's idea, of course. Ilya could think of better things to do with their evening alone together than watch logs turn into ash, but Shane had been so damn excited about it.

But it was a beautiful night—the air was a bit chilly, and the fire was warm, and Ilya was pressed against Shane on a little bench made out of a chunk of tree.

It wasn't terrible.

"How is your head?" Ilya asked. Shane had complained of a headache that afternoon. He'd said they had been common since his injury.

"Oh, better now. Thanks."

That was good news, because Ilya very much wanted to do sex stuff later.

Shane's phone suddenly lit up, the screen startlingly bright in the dark that surrounded them. When Shane glanced at the screen, his face lit up almost as brightly.

"What?" Ilya asked. He couldn't help it.

"Oh," Shane said absently as he typed something. "Nothing. Just a message from Rose."

Ilya snorted. *Rose.* "What does *Rose* want?"

"She's just checking in. She—hey. You're not *jealous*, are you?"

"No." It was the least convincing lie ever.

"Ilya. I'm *gay*."

"Not too gay to fuck Rose Landry."

Shane put the phone down and glared at him. "Oh my god. I only *slept with her* a couple of times, and they were both disasters. Believe me, she is *not* looking for a repeat performance."

Ilya suppressed a grin. "Disasters?"

"I'm not giving you the details, so shut it," Shane grumbled. He poked at the fire for the hundredth time. Ilya wasn't sure it actually did anything useful, but Shane seemed to enjoy doing it.

There was something a little creepy about sitting in this small pool of light in the middle of total darkness. It was so eerily quiet—just the crackling of the fire, the occasional lap of water from the lake, and—

A fucking wolf. That was a fucking wolf howl.

"What the fuck was that?" Ilya said. He couldn't conceal the terror in his voice. But who the fuck cared, because they were surrounded by hungry wolves!

Shane laughed. "It's a loon."

"A what?"

"A loon!" Shane was really laughing now. "It's a bird. Like a duck, kind of. Oh my god, you thought it was a wolf!"

"What the fuck bird makes a noise like that?"

"A loon!" Shane said again. Then he doubled over in hysterics. Ilya wanted to push him into the fire.

"Fuck you and your loon!" Ilya said. "Stupid Canadian wolf bird."

Shane looked up at him, still laughing. His whole face was crinkled up: eyes, nose, freckles. Ilya wanted to grab embers from the fire and smash them into his own eyes because he could not bear to look at this adorable, crinkled, happy face.

"Look," Shane said. He made a tunnel out of his hands, brought them to his mouth and…

Made the wolf bird noise.

No human should be able to make that noise.

"You speak bird now too?" Ilya asked flatly.

Shane cracked up again, and shoved him. Ilya fought like hell not to, but he started laughing too.

"I speak fluent bird. No accent!" Shane gasped.

"I fucking hate you."

Shane leaned against him. "No you don't."

Ilya sighed. No. He didn't.

He picked up his can of Coke that was resting on a chunk-of-tree table next to the bench and took a sip. He handed Shane his ginger ale.

They sat in comfortable silence for a long time.

"Have you talked to your family in Russia at all?"

The question came out of nowhere, which meant it was something that had been on Shane's mind for a while. Also, it probably wasn't the *real* question that Shane wanted to ask.

"No. Is just my brother there now. And he sucks."

"Oh. Right."

A much less comfortable silence fell between them.

"I'm sorry," Shane said, for no reason at all.

"Why?"

"Your family. My parents are so great. I just…wish you had that too."

Ilya shrugged. "My mother was great."

He knew he shouldn't have said that, because it was only going to lead to—

"How did she die?"

It had been fourteen years, almost, but a lump formed in Ilya's throat anyway.

"An accident," he said sardonically. He said it because that was what his father had told everyone. It was what Ilya had been told, very sternly, even though he had known it wasn't true even at the age of twelve. *She had an accident, Ilya. You understand, yes?*

"An accident?" Shane asked. His hand was on Ilya's arm now, squeezing him through the sleeve of his hooded sweatshirt.

"Yes," Ilya said, with a tight, humorless smile. "She accidentally swallowed a whole bottle of pills. Oops."

He felt Shane's body tense. He was sure Shane couldn't even imagine such a thing. Not in his perfect little family.

"Ilya," he said softly. "I'm so sorry."

Ilya pursed his lips and shook his head. The fire was looking very blurry now.

"How old were you?" Shane asked.

"Twelve." And then, somehow, words scraped their way out of Ilya's throat that he had never shared with anyone before. "I found her."

His voice broke on the last word, and Shane was on his feet, hauling Ilya up with him. Shane engulfed him in his arms and held him tight, letting Ilya bury his face on his shoulder.

"I don't want you to think she was weak," Ilya said. "She wasn't. She was…amazing. But she was so sad. And my father was so hard on her and…"

Ilya didn't cry. Not really. He wiped quickly at his

eyes to remove the moisture and just breathed Shane in. He smelled like wood smoke because everything around them smelled like wood smoke, and it made Ilya want a cigarette.

But mostly he just wanted to hold Shane close to him in this place where no one would ever find them. He wanted to stand in the spotlight of the campfire under the endless stars and feel Shane's fingers stroking his hair and not think about his horrible father or his wonderful, desperately sad mother. He didn't want to think about hockey, or rivalries, or what was going to happen when these two weeks were over.

"You're so strong," Shane murmured in his ear. He kissed his temple. "You're incredible. I—"

Ilya held his breath.

And then another fucking loon screamed over their heads. And both men completely lost it. They held each other as they shook with laughter. It was a wonderful relief to laugh after all that.

They sat back down, but this time Shane tucked himself into Ilya with his legs pulled up on the bench. Ilya wrapped an arm around him and kissed the top of his head.

"Is there more wood for the fire?" Ilya asked.

"Yeah. There's lots."

"Good."

Chapter Twenty-Five

"What the fuck? You can't pick Montreal!"

"I just did," Ilya pointed out, gesturing his PlayStation controller at the television.

"Well then… I'm picking Boston."

"Good choice."

"I'm going to fucking destroy you."

"I *am* you."

"You aren't anything," Shane grumbled.

Ilya laughed and nudged him hard. "I'm on the cover of the game."

Shane shoved him against the arm of the couch. "Big deal."

They had barely gotten past the first puck drop when Shane's phone rang.

Shane glanced at it and frowned. "It's Hayden. I should get it."

Ilya rolled his eyes and hit pause.

Hayden.

He didn't actually know Hayden Pike at all. He knew he was an average forward, extremely unremarkable in the looks department, and Shane's best friend.

Shane walked a few steps behind the couch, standing between the living room and the kitchen. "Hey, Hayden. How's, um…how's the baby?"

Ilya smirked to himself. Shane had forgotten Hayden's baby's name.

"Amber. Right. Is she…good?"

Hayden must have had a very long answer to that question, because Shane went silent for a while. Ilya endured about five minutes of Shane saying nothing but "Oh yeah?" and "That's cool" and "Right" before he stood and gave Shane a *look*.

Shane shrugged at him. *What do you want me to do?*

Ilya had an idea.

He crossed the room until he was standing right in front of Shane. He gave him a little smile, and Shane furrowed his brow at him.

Ilya's gaze darted down to Shane's crotch, then back up again. Shane shook his head silently.

"So how's Jackie doing?" Shane asked the phone. "Tired?"

Ilya unfastened the button on Shane's shorts. Shane shook his head again, more forcefully this time.

But he wasn't, like, *stopping him*.

Ilya slowly pulled down the zipper, and was rewarded with a sharp inhale from Shane.

Shane's shorts dropped to the floor, and Ilya sank to his knees.

He glanced up and saw Shane mouthing *Don't*, eyes bugged wide.

Ilya pulled an exaggerated confused face. *Don't what?*

He carefully peeled Shane's briefs off and slid them down to join his shorts on the floor.

To be fair, Shane's dick was soft, so maybe he really *didn't* want Ilya to be doing this. Ilya sat back on his

heels and glanced up at Shane's face, trying to gauge
whether or not he was into this game.

Shane bit his bottom lip as he gazed back at him,
and Ilya knew it was game on.

"Uh, just one second, Hayden. My mom is calling.
One sec."

He hit the mute button on his phone and snarled at
Ilya, "What the *fuck*? Knock it off!"

"I think you want it."

"I... I mean..."

"No?"

"It's fucking creepy."

"Is hot, though, yes?"

Shane huffed. "Later, okay?"

"I might not want to later."

"Ilya..."

"I won't touch you. If you don't get hard, I won't do
anything. Deal?"

Shane's mouth fell open. "I *won't* get hard."

"Okay. Then no problem."

Shane scowled at him, then went back to the call.
"Sorry about that, Hayden. My *mom* can be really *annoying* sometimes."

Ilya grinned up at him. He made a show of putting
his hands behind his back. Shane's eyes shot daggers
at him, then they turned up to the ceiling. "My head's
a lot better. Totally recovered, I think. Still get headaches sometimes but...yeah, exactly... I've been working out, yeah."

Ilya watched Shane's cock intently. He knew Shane.
Frankly, this was one of the only times he'd seen his
poor undersexed dick soft. Usually it was as straight as
a fucking rod whenever Ilya was in its vicinity.

Shane's dick was exactly like the rest of Shane: tidy and smooth. And eager. His balls were almost hairless, and Ilya was sure that, like Shane's chest, was natural. His seemingly disinterested cock slumped over them, nestled in a neat patch of dark hair.

He wanted to take it all in his mouth. He wanted to feel Shane grow hard against his tongue.

But he'd made a promise, and he could wait.

He turned his eyes up to Shane's face, and caught him looking down at him. Ilya licked his lips.

"Uh...oh, really? That's cool. When did that happen?" Shane pressed his lips together, and his cheeks flushed.

Ilya smiled, because, sure enough, Shane's cock had twitched and was starting to plump up.

Ilya watched it for a minute, enjoying the rare intimate spectacle. Shane's hand curled into a fist at his side. His eyes were squeezed shut, like he was trying to stop his erection from happening through concentration.

It wasn't working. At all.

Shane was fully hard in under a minute, the head of his cock bobbing excitedly in front of Ilya's lips.

"Wow," Shane said, his voice straining. "So do you think she's going to...oh. Right. Yeah."

Ilya ignored the head of Shane's cock and dipped his head lower. He cupped Shane's balls gently in his hand, and pressed his lips to them. Shane's body jerked, but he didn't move away.

"Sorry," Shane said to Hayden, his voice remarkably even, "is Mark your sister's husband? Oh. Okay. Got it."

Ilya sucked one of Shane's balls into his mouth, enjoying the heavy weight of it. Shane made the tiniest little moan.

This was great. Ilya loved playing like this. He wasn't even sure what the goal was of this game, but the fact that Shane hadn't ended the call led Ilya to believe that he was enjoying the challenge of staying quiet. To his credit, Shane's whimper was barely audible when Ilya started stroking a finger behind his balls.

Ilya was proud of him. But he still wasn't going to make this easy for him.

Starting at the base, Ilya licked a wide stripe up the shaft of Shane's cock, finishing by lapping the glistening precome at the tip.

"Hurnnhh," Shane said, then grimaced.

Ilya put his considerable blow job skills to work, taking Shane deep and bobbing his head as he sank his fingers into the muscles of Shane's thighs.

"Oh…oh yeah? That—that's cool," Shane stammered into his phone.

Ilya glanced up at him. Shane stared right back, cheeks flushed and eyes challenging. Ilya couldn't believe Shane hadn't hung up yet. Did he really want Ilya to make him come while he was still on the phone?

Ilya kept going, and Shane's voice got more and more strained, and how on earth was Hayden not noticing this?

Shane's thighs trembled under Ilya's hands, the muscles in his stomach flexing, and Ilya was fascinated to see how Shane was going to handle this, because he was definitely about to come.

Shane pulled the phone away from his ear and frantically hit the mute button. "Aaagh. Fuck!" His free hand grabbed Ilya's shoulder, fingers tightening almost painfully as he spasmed and emptied himself into Ilya's mouth.

Shane took a deep breath, in and out, once his orgasm had finished, and hit the mute button again. "You there? Sorry. Bad connection out here sometimes."

Ilya scrambled to the couch so he could smother his laughter with a pillow.

Shane must have ended the call, because suddenly he was on top of Ilya, on the couch, hitting him with another pillow. "Fuck you, you asshole! That was the worst!"

Ilya pulled the pillow he was holding to his face away. "It was not."

"God, fuck you. Why was that so hot?"

"Because you like to be bad, Shane Hollander."

And, whoa. Saying those exact words twisted something inside of Ilya. He was just teasing Shane, but he wondered how true those words were. Was that, perhaps, all this was to Shane: rebellion? Was that all *he* was to Shane?

His worry must have shown on his face, because Shane stopped hitting him with the pillow. He pulled Ilya's hand to his mouth, and kissed his palm.

"That's not why I do this. With you. Maybe it was when we started, I don't know, but it isn't now and it hasn't been for a long time."

Ilya moved the hand Shane was holding to brush the hair out of Shane's eyes. "Okay."

Why do you do it now? He wanted to ask, but he was scared of the answer. So instead he pulled Shane down for a kiss.

"So," Ilya said casually, when they broke apart, "how's Hayden?"

Shane collapsed against his chest, and Ilya held him as they both shook with laughter.

* * *

Ilya had been formulating a plan.

It was early stages, and probably bad, but he couldn't stop his brain from working on it.

He couldn't see a realistic scenario where he and Shane were anything more than what they were now. He wasn't even sure what he wanted them to be. When his imagination was reckless enough to conjure images of the two of them together, as a couple—living together? *Married?*—fuck, it was ridiculous.

"You all right?"

Ilya jerked to attention to find Shane—wearing only a bathing suit—standing in front of the Adirondack chair Ilya was sitting in. He had a book in his hand and glasses on his face, and he was frowning down at Ilya like a concerned lifeguard/librarian.

"Yes," Ilya said, waving a hand. "Is nice view. The lake."

"You looked like you were thinking about something heavy."

Ilya shrugged. Shane sat himself in the chair next to him and waited.

"I wish I had been drafted by a Canadian team," Ilya said.

"What? Why?"

"It would make things easier."

"Things? What, like—do you mean…what do you mean?"

Ilya sighed heavily. What exactly did he want to say here? "I mean… America is not so good for Russians now. And Russia is not so good for… Russians like me."

Shane was silent a moment. "Are you in any danger?"

"No. I don't think so. But I am very careful. I would like to…not have to be."

Shane nodded. "I think things will get better in America, right? And maybe in Russia too?"

"Maybe."

"Do you still want to become an American citizen?"

"I don't know. I am thinking…maybe somewhere else."

"Oh."

"I have been thinking…" Ilya said. He'd never said any of this out loud before. He maybe hadn't even formed it altogether in his head before. "I am a free agent, after next season."

He definitely had Shane's full attention now. "You'd leave Boston?"

"I have just been thinking. Maybe…a Canadian team."

"Holy shit, really?"

"Yes."

"Like where?" Ilya could see the thoughts play out on Shane's face like a movie: *What if we played together in Montreal? No. Montreal couldn't afford both of us.*

"Not Montreal," Ilya said gently.

"No. I know."

But good god, now Ilya was imagining that. Playing together, living together, *being* together.

It was never going to happen.

But it was a nice thought.

"I could marry Svetlana," Ilya said, out of nowhere. It was the following night, and they were playing pool.

Shane frowned at the three ball that just missed the side pocket. He would have made that shot if Ilya hadn't *just casually dropped his worst nightmare on him.*

"Oh?" Shane asked calmly.

"She is American, so it would mean American citizenship, but she would do it."

"Would she?"

"I think so. Yes. She is Sergei Vetrov's daughter. Did you know?"

"What? Really?"

"Yes. She would help me."

Shane watched Ilya sink the twelve ball. And then the fourteen ball. He felt like snapping his own cue over his knee.

"Do you—I mean—is she someone that you would… want to marry?"

Ilya straightened his posture and looked at him. "I like Svetlana, yes. But it would be for citizenship."

"But," Shane said. He had to say this next part. It had been eating away at him for too long. "You want to get married, right? To a woman, I mean. You're not…like me. You like women. And I'm sure… *Svetlana* is gorgeous and fun and…all that stuff. Right?"

"Yes," Ilya said. "I do. She is. But."

"But?"

Ilya shrugged, and he looked like he was possibly *blushing*. "I have this problem," he mumbled.

Shane waited.

"I like women. I always was thinking that to get married would be nice. Kids. All of that. Someday. But… this problem will not go away."

Shane bit his lip. "Tell me about this problem."

"Is so annoying." Ilya sighed, and Shane could see him fighting a grin. "Always I am with beautiful women. Wonderful women. Everywhere."

"Sounds rough."

"Yes. Listen. These women, they are so sexy and fun, but is no matter. I cannot stop thinking about this short fucking hockey player with these stupid freckles and a weak backhand."

"A weak backhand?" Shane couldn't stop smiling.

"Yes. And he is just so boring and he drives a terrible car and...that is my problem. All of these beautiful women and I am always wishing they were him."

Ilya bent to take his third shot. "Is terrible problem."

Fuck. Shane was going start crying right here in his games room. He swallowed and steadied himself. "Do you want the problem to go away?"

"No," Ilya said seriously, looking Shane dead in the eye. "I do not want the problem to ever go away."

"Don't marry Svetlana," Shane blurted out.

Ilya raised an eyebrow.

"Just...don't. I know it wouldn't be...for love or whatever. But don't. I couldn't—we can figure something else out, okay?"

Ilya looked surprised, but he nodded.

"Okay."

"I was thinking," Ilya said. It was late morning the next day, and they were sitting on the deck with coffee. "If I played for a team that was not Boston. Maybe in the west. The rivalry would not be such a big deal."

Shane seemed to consider this. "That's true. We'd only play against each other twice a year."

He frowned and Ilya knew he didn't like that idea any more than he did. *We'd only* see *each other twice a year.*

"Is...like, sacrifice. For future gain, yes?"

Shane brightened. "Future gain?"

"Yes. Our rivalry has been huge. But maybe we can help it to…fade away? A little?"

"Yeah…" Shane said. He was getting excited. "Yeah! I don't like the idea of you being so far, but we could make people forget all about us as rivals and maybe no one would care about us at all one day."

"One day. Yes."

Shane smiled shyly at him, and Ilya grinned back, and they both sat there, smiling stupidly at each other while they thought about the possibility of *one day*.

"I have another idea," Shane said. He'd been thinking about what Ilya had proposed all day and he had come up with a plan of his own. He propped himself up on an elbow and poked the sleepy Russian in the shoulder.

Ilya rolled over. "What idea? About what?"

"What if you played for Ottawa?"

"Ottawa? Is almost as bad as playing for Boston. We would be rivals just the same."

"Yes, but listen. First of all, Ottawa desperately needs a star center, so there's an opening there. But what if you played there and we…changed the narrative a bit?"

"The what? What the fuck with these words, Hollander? I'm tired."

"Sorry. I just mean…we would still be rivals on the ice, but we wouldn't have to pretend to be enemies. I mean, lots of guys have friends all over the league. But we're, like, the only guys who have this whole story built around them where we can't stand each other and love nothing more than destroying each other every time our teams meet."

"That story was kind of true, for a long time, Hollander."

Shane smiled a little. "Yeah, well. It's not true now. I think it's safe to say that, right?"

"Sure."

"There are going to be new players—younger players—and new rivalries will form. Do we really need to keep this dance up until we both retire?"

Ilya's brow furrowed. "Is very late, Hollander. This is a lot of English. What is your idea?"

"You play for Ottawa, I play for Montreal. Those cities are two hours apart. We start a charity together, you and me. Something that benefits both cities. So now people see us working together on something. We make up some story about how I approached you with this idea, and—"

"Or I approached you."

"Whatever. The point is, we tell the press, the fans, everyone, that by working together on the cause that means so much to both of us, we have developed a mutual respect for each other…"

"Yes. And also we are fucking each other. Any questions?"

"Fuck *off*! This is a great idea, Rozanov!"

Ilya laughed. Shane hit him with a pillow.

"Is not bad," Ilya finally conceded. "So we start this charity…"

"And it wouldn't be bullshit either. I've been wanting to start one anyway. We'll do something that means a lot to both of us."

"Yes. Okay."

"We still play hard against each other on the ice,

obviously. I mean, I am never going to stop enjoying beating your ass."

Ilya snorted. "Sure."

"And…like I said. We're two hours away from each other. All year."

He wanted Ilya to see this vision as clearly as he could. It seemed tantalizingly possible. Easy, even.

"And you'd be in Canada. And you could apply for citizenship eventually."

"Yes. I understand that part."

"And maybe…someday. When we both retire. We can…be together. For real."

Ilya looked stunned by that part. "You really think that far ahead, Hollander?"

"I do about this."

"You want that? To be together?"

"I do. So much it terrifies me."

Ilya turned his face away from Shane, and was silent. Cold dread flooded Shane's stomach; he had admitted too much.

But Ilya turned back and quickly rolled on top of Shane and was kissing him and kissing him and kept murmuring the same thing in Russian over and over again until he pulled back and translated:

"I love you."

Shane froze. And then Ilya froze.

"Holy shit," Shane whispered. It wasn't how he had meant to respond.

"I…" Ilya's eyes were so wide and so scared.

"I love you too," Shane said.

Ilya gave a shaky smile and exhaled. "Thank Christ."

"Does it…does it feel like agony for you too?"

Ilya started to nod, then stopped. He shook his head slowly instead.

"Not anymore."

Ilya felt like his smile was going to split his face. He was overwhelmingly happy.

Shane was beaming up at him, eyes bright and freckles crinkled, and Ilya loved him. And Shane loved *him*.

Holy fucking shit.

Shane Hollander is in love with me.

He wanted to kiss him, but he couldn't stop looking at him.

"How could we let this happen?" Ilya asked, and his voice was shakier than he would have liked.

"I don't know. We are very stupid and irresponsible."

"Very dumb, yes. Oh god, Hollander." And then he did kiss him. How could he not?

Ilya got the urge to pin him down, as if he would disappear if Ilya didn't keep a tight grip on him. He wrapped his fingers around Shane's wrists and held them to the pillow on either side of Shane's head.

"This is real, yes?" Ilya asked. He just had to make sure.

"It's real," Shane said. His voice was low and adorably scratchy.

"I feel like… I am dreaming?"

"You're not. I love you."

Ilya wasn't sure his heart could take any more of this. It felt like it was pushing up against his lungs, making it hard to breathe. Hard to think. Hard to do anything except hold Shane down and kiss him over and over again.

Shane's back bowed against the mattress, and he

pressed his rigid cock against Ilya's thigh. "I want to be as close as possible to you," he said breathlessly.

"You are."

"No. I want…"

"Tell me."

"I want to be in your lap when you fuck me. Facing you. Holding you. I…ahh. Fuck, yes…"

He trailed off when Ilya wrapped his hand around both of their cocks.

"I want that too," Ilya said. "I love you."

They moved quickly, Ilya sitting with his back against the headboard and Shane straddling his lap. They kissed for a long time like that, as Ilya continued to stroke their cocks together.

"Oh god," Shane shuddered. "I have to—you have to stop. I need you inside me."

"Mm. Not yet. Stroke yourself for me."

"Can't. Ilya, I'll come. I swear—"

"Stroke yourself. A little. I think you can do it and not come."

Ilya had no idea why he got so much enjoyment from causing Shane distress, but he did. He loved to see him all agitated and struggling to keep control.

"If you love me…" Ilya added obnoxiously.

Shane's eyes narrowed. "I'm starting to question that."

Ilya shook his head, grinning. "You love me. Show me how much. Stroke yourself and maybe I will fuck you."

As if there was even a chance that Ilya wouldn't.

Shane wrapped trembling fingers around his cock and very carefully dragged them up the length of his shaft. Ilya gasped at this display of obedience. He knew

Shane wasn't lying about how dangerously close he was. His slit was dripping precome.

"I love how fucking wet you get, Shane."

"Sh-shut up." Shane's whole body was shaking. "I'm trying to concentrate."

Ilya chuckled. "Your dick wants you to go faster."

"Can't go faster," Shane gritted out.

Ilya lightly cupped Shane's balls, causing Shane to hiss out a breath and a string of profanity. "So tight, Hollander. Keep going."

Shane whimpered. "You bastard. You have to fuck me."

"Soon."

"Now."

A fresh bead of precome spurted out and Ilya caught it on his fingertip. Shane watched, wide-eyed, as Ilya sucked the finger into his mouth.

"God, Ilya. You are—*fuck*. Would you *please* fuck me?" Shane panted.

All right. Enough was enough. Ilya reached for the lube and a condom from the bedside table and got himself ready.

And, oh, god, when Shane sank down on him, his whole body trembling with need, it was the most incredible thing Ilya had ever felt. He rocked up into Shane's body as Shane held Ilya's face and kissed him.

He felt Shane *everywhere*.

Shane braced himself with a hand on the headboard, and the other on Ilya's shoulder, and used all of his considerable strength to ride the hell out of Ilya's cock. He trapped Ilya's hips between his solid thighs, and pounded that perfect ass down on Ilya's lap over and over and *fuck*.

Shane threw his head back, and Ilya watched his cock bounce in the space between them. Ilya wondered if Shane would shoot instantly if he touched it.

He wondered if Shane would shoot anyway, without any contact on his glistening cock.

"So good, Ilya. Holy shit. *Fuck.* I am so fucking close."

And suddenly Ilya realized that *he* was too. He had the endurance of a stallion with most partners, but he couldn't ever seem to control his body when he was with Shane.

"Do it, fuck. Give it to me, Hollander. I'm right there."

"I love you. I love you. Oh, shit. Here it comes—"

They both cried out as Shane's release splashed against Ilya's chest. His body spasmed around Ilya's cock and Ilya was hurled over the edge, coming hard with a garbled "I love you."

"Oh my god," Shane wheezed. His forehead landed on Ilya's shoulder. "That was perfect."

"Yes. Perfect." Ilya wrapped his arms around him and held him tight. *As close as possible.*

Eventually, Shane eased off him, and Ilya disposed of the condom. They cuddled together in bed, both men quiet and sleepy and deliriously happy.

"What was your mother's name?" Shane asked suddenly. His fingers were tracing the chain around Ilya's neck.

"Irina." Ilya hadn't said her name in so long, it felt strange in his mouth. "Why?"

"I was just thinking." He propped himself up on an elbow. "The charity we start, I think we should start a hockey school. Like, we could have summer hockey camps in Ottawa and Montreal."

"And we give the money away?"

"Yeah. I think we should give the money to mental health organizations. Maybe…suicide prevention?"

Shane was looking away, as if he were embarrassed, but Ilya held his chin and guided his face toward him.

"It was just an idea," Shane said quietly.

And Ilya was *not* going to cry right now.

"Shane," he said, "I love that idea."

"Yeah?" Shane smiled.

"Yes. It's very…" Fuck. What was the right word? *Was* there a right word for everything Ilya was feeling in that moment? He couldn't think of one, so instead he said, "She would have loved you."

"I wish I could have met her."

"Yes. Me too."

Shane yawned and snuggled against Ilya's chest. "Sorry. I'm exhausted."

"My fault, I suppose."

"Absolutely your fault. But I forgive you," Shane said with another yawn.

"Good night, Hollander."

"I love you."

"I love you too."

"Mm. Can you say it in Russian again?"

Ilya pulled Shane's hand to his lips and kissed his fingers. *"Ya lyublyu tebya."*

"Ya-loo-blue-tee-baa," Shane murmured back.

Ilya laughed, and turned off the lamp.

Chapter Twenty-Six

Ilya bounced on the balls of his feet and felt the dock bob in the water beneath him.

"Is this the dock that you do yoga on?" he asked.

"No, I don't do yoga on here. This was just where the camera crew asked me to…wait. Did you *watch* that thing?"

"Yes. Was great. I needed help sleeping."

"You're an asshole."

They watched in silence as a couple of ducks swam by. This was what passed as entertainment here in the middle of nowhere.

It was late morning and the day was already hot. Shane, like Ilya, was wearing only shorts. They had slept late after keeping each other up most of the night.

The sun shone on every inch of Shane: his skin, his hair, his *freckles*. He looked so achingly beautiful and happy.

It was a shame that Ilya was going to ruin it. A shame, but there was no choice about it: Shane Hollander was standing on the edge of a dock, and now his back was turned to Ilya. Like an idiot.

"How's the water?" Ilya asked.

"What?"

That was all the warning Shane got before Ilya pushed him off the dock with both hands. Shane let out most of a "motherfucker" before his head submerged beneath the dark water.

When he popped back up, he continued to splutter and swear as Ilya doubled over with laughter.

"Fuck. You!" Shane yelled, and he punctuated it with a mighty sweep of his arm that sent a wave of water at Ilya. It mostly hit Ilya's calves.

"Asshole!" Shane yelled.

Ilya ran off the end of the dock and plunged into the water in a perfect cannonball, right next to Shane. As soon as his head was above water again, he splashed Shane right in the face, just for good measure.

Shane tried to punch his shoulder, but Ilya grabbed his wrist and pulled him closer. He kissed him quickly, and Shane pushed him hard in the chest.

"What if my phone had been in my pocket?" Shane complained.

"It wasn't. You left it on the table. On the deck."

"Well…"

Ilya kissed him again. It was a little awkward to do when they were both treading water. Shane tasted like cool, fresh water.

As if to prove that it was still perfectly safe and functioning, Shane's phone started ringing in the distance.

"Uh-oh." Ilya smirked.

"It's fine. I don't need to answer it."

"No." He kissed Shane again, and this time he turned them so he had Shane's back pinned against the end of the dock. It was probably very uncomfortable for Shane, but he didn't seem to mind. They kissed enthusiastically, and Ilya planted his hands against the wood of the dock on either side of Shane's shoulders. Shane, to Ilya's surprise, wrapped his legs around Ilya's waist and pulled him tighter against him.

Ilya loved these rare moments that Shane was able to get out of his head and just let go. He loved that he could make Shane do that.

He loved Shane. God, he loved Shane.

They made out for a while like that before Shane reached back with both hands and hoisted himself up out of the water. Ilya quickly followed him. He pressed down on Shane, kissing him and forcing him to his back. He reached to grip Shane's erection through his wet shorts.

"Someone could see. By boat," Shane panted.

"Then keep a lookout." Ilya plunged his hand into the waistband of Shane's shorts and was rewarded with a delicious little whimper.

Shane's phone rang again.

Shane tilted his head back to look in the direction of the phone. "Fuck off," he yelled at it.

Ilya laughed and continued stroking Shane's cock. He was rutting a bit against Shane's thigh. The dock bounced vigorously in the water beneath them.

He nipped along Shane's jawline, and kissed his smile. He didn't think Shane was watching for boats at all.

"You like this, Hollander?"

"Yes. Yeah I… I've wanted this for so long."

"Wanted what? Tell me."

"You. Here. Outside like this."

Ilya sucked in a breath. "What do you want me to do to you?"

"Anything. I don't know. Everything."

"Tell me one thing." Ilya rocked harder and faster against the hard muscle of Shane's thigh.

"I...thought about you...fucking me. Outside. On the deck. Or...against a tree." His face flushed bright red, but Ilya smiled.

"Fuck, Hollander. You only had to ask."

Shane gasped and arched his back. Ilya stroked him faster.

"Maybe we could canoe or something. Out to one of these little islands," Ilya said, his lips brushing Shane's ear. "Totally alone, and I'll fuck you there, out in the open where no one will see."

"Oh fuck. Fuck. Ilya."

"Maybe someone will hear you. From their boat."

"Ahh."

The heat of Shane's release mingled with the cold, damp fabric of his shorts. Ilya thrust a few more times against Shane's leg and cried out as his own cock pulsed and spurted into his shorts.

He collapsed on top of Shane, panting.

Shane laughed breathlessly. "Wow. What the fuck?"

Ilya smiled and nuzzled Shane's neck. "I don't know. Couldn't help it."

"I can't even remember why we came down to the dock in the first place."

"Does it matter?"

Shane turned his head and kissed him quickly. "No."

After a minute, Ilya pulled himself up into a push-up position over Shane, then quickly kissed him before sliding back into the water. Shane followed him, figuring it would at least clean his shorts a little bit.

They swam for a while longer before they both decided they were hungry and headed up to the house. Shane was just about to step through the sliding glass doors when Ilya grabbed his wrist and tugged him back toward him.

"Is it okay if I tell you I love you again?" Ilya asked. His crooked smile was adorably shy.

Shane smiled back. Hell, he probably *beamed* back. "It's okay."

Instead of saying the words, Ilya kissed him. It was slow and deliberate, his tongue pressing against Shane's own, his fingers resting delicately on Shane's waist. Shane felt like his legs might give out on him. He made a contented little noise and stepped in even closer, so he could feel Ilya pressed against every inch of him. His hands slid over the lake-cooled skin on Ilya's back, eventually finding their way into his damp hair.

Ilya huffed and tilted Shane's head back, kissing him deeper and more possessively. Shane felt dizzy with happiness. To be held like this and kissed like this by the man he loved—the man who loved him back—here at the place he loved more than anywhere else in the world...

They both heard a noise.

They both whipped their heads around.

They both saw Shane's dad standing inside the house, staring, frozen, at where they were wrapped up in each other on the deck.

For a moment, no one moved. No one made a sound. Everyone. Just. Stared.

Then, very quickly, Shane's dad turned on his heel and walked toward the front door of the house. Shane let go of Ilya and said, "Shit!"

"Your father, yes?"

"Yes! Fuck. Shit. Okay…"

Shane held his head with both hands. *"Fuck!"*

"Should you—?"

"Yeah. Okay. I'll just…you wait here."

Shane walked quickly through the house to the front door. He opened it just in time to see his father's car disappear down the wooded road.

He stood there for a few minutes, wearing nothing but the wet shorts that he had very recently ejaculated into and a look of pure panic.

"Shane?"

He heard Ilya calling him, but he couldn't find his voice to respond.

"Hollander?" He felt a hand on his elbow. "He was already gone?"

"Yeah."

They both stood there in silence. Shane assumed that Ilya, too, was letting the enormity of this moment wash over him.

"This is bad," Shane finally said.

"You should go. Talk to him."

"Yeah. Shit. Yeah, I should. Probably best to do it now."

He heard Ilya snort behind him.

"It's *not* funny!" Shane snapped at him.

"A little funny."

Shane turned around, ready to glare at him, but when he saw Ilya's face he started laughing too.

"Jesus Christ," he said. "So much for easing them into it."

Ilya laughed harder. "Maybe he did not notice?"

They both cracked up. It was pure nerves, but Shane laughed until his eyes watered. His plan had been to tell his parents—soon—that he was gay. He had planned to give them time to digest that, and then he would tell them—eventually—that he was in a relationship. That he was *in love*.

And then, once all of that had settled with them, he would drop the real bombshell.

Now everything was happening in the exact opposite order.

"What the fuck am I going to tell them? *So, you're probably wondering why I was making out with Ilya Rozanov...*"

"Do you want me to come with you?"

Shane was surprised by this offer. *Did* he want that? Would that make things even more awkward? He certainly felt like he could use the support.

"I don't know. Would you really do that?"

Ilya took his hand and squeezed. "Yes. If it helps."

Shane nodded. "It might. It will be awkward as hell, but... I'd like you to be there, I think."

"Okay."

"We should probably get dressed first."

"Yes."

They got dressed quickly. Shane put on a T-shirt from a charity hockey camp he helped coach last summer, just to remind his parents that he was a good and normal person.

Ilya was wearing a Boston Bears T-shirt. Shane made a face. "*That's* not going to help."

"Oh, do they not know I play for Boston?"

Shane rolled his eyes. "Come on. Let's get this over with."

The drive to Shane's parents' cottage took about ten minutes, but it seemed way, way longer this time.

"Okay," Shane said as he parked behind his father's car. "Just…let me do the talking."

"No problem."

"Fuck, maybe you should wait in the car."

Ilya raised an eyebrow at him.

"No," Shane said. "No, never mind. Come on."

He exited the car and Ilya followed. Shane wondered if his parents were watching them through a window.

He didn't bother to knock. He never did, with them. He opened the door and said, as calmly as he could, "Hello? It's me. It's… Shane."

His parents stood from where they had both been sitting on the couch. It was clear that his dad had told his mom what he'd seen.

"Shane?" his mother said. She said it like she'd never heard the word before.

"Mom. Dad. I… I think we should talk."

"We forgot to buy dishwasher tablets," Dad said. He sounded shell shocked. "I just wanted to see if I could borrow some. I didn't know you had…company."

"Dad, it's okay. I'm sorry. You…shouldn't have found out that way."

"Found out what, exactly?" Mom asked. Her eyes were locked on Ilya, just over Shane's shoulder.

"Well, I… I'm gay. Which I was going to tell you. Soon. I just…sorry. I wish I'd told you."

His parents didn't say anything. They were both looking at Ilya like he was a mountain lion that was about to attack.

"Um, and this is… Ilya. Rozanov. You probably know that."

"Hi," Ilya said.

"And he's been…visiting. He's…we're, um…"

What *were* they, exactly? It occurred to Shane that he and Ilya hadn't even figured out what label they were comfortable with.

"Lovers," Ilya offered.

Fuck, way to choose the grossest possible word, Ilya.

Well, there was no going back from *that* word. Shane could only wait for the aftermath.

"But…you hate him," Mom said.

"No, I… I don't. I mean. Sometimes I do, kinda. But mostly I…love him. Actually."

"You…*what*?"

Shane's heart was racing. "Can we just…sit, maybe? I'm sorry. I know this is a lot at once. I didn't want this to be how I told you. At all."

No one said anything for a moment, then his father nodded and gestured to the living room furniture. His parents sat together on the couch. Shane and Ilya sat in separate chairs facing them.

"Shane…" Mom began. "I think we both…suspected… that you might be…gay."

"You did?" Shane had not been expecting that.

"Yes, well. We didn't know for certain, obviously. We just thought it might be a possibility."

"Geez. I had no idea you thought that."

"We know you pretty well," Mom said. She gave him a small smile, and that one tiny gesture made Shane want to weep with relief.

"What we did *not* suspect," Dad added, "was that you were…*friendly*…with Mr. Rozanov here."

"Ilya," said Ilya.

"Ilya, then."

"It's…a long story. And it doesn't even make sense to us," Shane said.

"None," Ilya agreed.

"When did this happen?" Mom asked. "Wait, was it the All-Star Game? You were on the same team—"

"No," Shane said. "It was…already going on then."

His father blew out a breath. "You sure fooled us. And…everyone else."

"So when?" Mom asked. She seemed desperate to figure out the timeline of this thing. Shane could see her mentally replaying the past several seasons in her head.

"Since, um, our rookie year," Shane mumbled.

He didn't think his parents could possibly look *more* shocked than they already had, but they definitely looked *more* shocked at this news.

"You can't have been…since your *rookie season*?" his mother gasped.

"No," Ilya said. "That's not right. Was before that." *Not helping, Ilya.*

"*Before* that?" Mom asked.

"A little before," Ilya clarified. "Summer before."

"You've been…in *love* this whole time?"

"No!" Shane said.

"God no," Ilya said at the same time.

"But then…" Mom started. "Oh," she said. And blushed. "I see."

"Anyway," Shane said. He was blushing even more than his mom. "The point is, we're…together. Sort of. Or we'd like to be. If it wasn't basically impossible."

For the first time, the looks of shock left his parents' faces and shifted to something like sympathy.

"I just don't understand," his mother said. "How could this have even happened between you? Weren't there any nice men in Montreal, Shane?"

"Probably," Shane muttered.

"Do your teammates know about…this?" Dad asked.

"No! No, no one does. *No one*. This is top secret, all right?"

His father stood up. "Would anyone like a beer? I could use a beer."

"Yes," said Ilya.

"Definitely," said Shane.

"Is that the strongest thing we have?" asked his mom.

Shane took the break in the conversation as an opportunity to look at Ilya. He seemed to sense Shane's eyes on him, and immediately turned to give him a questioning look.

How do you think this is going so far?

Not bad, right?

Not bad.

His father wordlessly handed each of them a can of Sleeman beer. He lingered in front of Ilya, but returned to his place on the couch without saying anything.

"I just…" Mom said. "I just can't believe any of this is real."

"I know," Shane said.

"All this time," Dad said quietly, almost to himself. "You've been holding this secret inside. The whole time."

"You didn't ever…" His mom sounded suddenly horrified. "You didn't ever *let* him *win*, did you, Shane?"

"God, Mom! No!"

Ilya laughed. "He does not need to *let* me win."

"I would never," Shane said quickly. "The team comes first. Always. And besides, I like beating him."

Mom was frowning at him, not quite believing his words.

"When you and Dad play Yahtzee, do you let *him* win?" Shane asked desperately.

"Never," Mom smiled, maybe understanding. She seemed to relax.

"Is your plan to just keep doing this? Keeping this a secret? Until you retire? Forever?" Dad asked.

"Maybe. I mean, yes. Probably."

"Oh, Shane." His mother looked so sad.

Dad shook his head. "Honestly? I don't see another way. I wish I did."

"I know," Shane said miserably. "*We* know. It's not something we can announce."

"I have to say," Dad said, "I'm surprised about you, Ilya. You've always had such a reputation as a, you know, a *ladies'* man."

"Is not untrue," Ilya said.

"Ilya likes both," Shane said.

"Oh," Mom said. His parents exchanged a concerned look. Shane was about to change the subject—because this was *way* too uncomfortable—when Ilya spoke.

"I have been with lots of women. That was not…fake. But…" He looked at Shane, and Shane held his breath. "I have only been in love with one person."

And suddenly Ilya looked very blurry through Shane's eyes. Shane swallowed down the urge to cry, and said, "Me too. Just one."

Shane's mother covered her mouth with her hand. She tapped her fingertips against her upper lip, and Shane knew she was about to go full Yuna Hollander on this situation.

Sure enough, a moment later she clapped her hands together and jumped up from her chair. "All right, so what's the plan?" she said. "We've got a problem, let's solve it."

Shane glanced at a bewildered-looking Ilya. He gave him a small smile. They had Yuna on their side now, and Shane couldn't imagine a better ally.

"First of all," Yuna said, "have you talked to Scott Hunter?" She said the name like it physically pained her to speak of the evil man who had stolen Olympic gold from her beloved son.

"I have," Ilya said. "But not about…us."

"I emailed him," Shane added. "I just, y'know, said I appreciated his bravery, or whatever. I didn't tell him about me. Or about Ilya."

Yuna was tapping her lip again. "He probably couldn't help. Not with this situation."

"He would probably be very confused about us," Ilya said.

"Confused is a word for it," Dad said. His shock seemed to have ebbed completely, replaced by something that looked a lot like amusement.

"I will say that, what Scott did, when he, um, kissed his boyfriend?" Shane couldn't believe he was saying this. He hadn't even told *Ilya* this. "That changed something inside me. It was…huge. It made me…want to try. Made me want to be braver, and to let myself try to be happy."

He looked at the floor until he couldn't bear it anymore, and then he glanced over at Ilya. Ilya's eyes were softer than he'd ever seen them.

"Yes," Ilya said. "Me too."

Shane cleared his throat. "We have one idea." He told his parents the Ottawa/Montreal plan he'd outlined for Ilya the night before.

"That," Dad said, considering, "isn't bad."

"You would leave Boston?" Mom asked, stunned. "For Shane?"

Ilya didn't hesitate. "Yes."

She frowned, as if she couldn't believe anything he was saying was real.

"Oh my god!" Shane exclaimed. "You're actually conflicted, aren't you, Mom?"

"What are you talking about?"

"You're bothered by his lack of loyalty to his team!"

"Well!" Mom said, as if that was a perfectly reasonable way to react to the fact that Ilya was so madly in love with her son that he was willing to throw his whole life into upheaval.

Shane turned to Ilya. "My mom, by the way, cares about hockey a *little too much*."

Ilya snorted. "Now I know where you get it."

Shane was about to flip him off, but remembered his parents. And then it all kind of hit him: his parents were here. With Ilya. The secret was out and they were all talking about Shane and Ilya as a *couple*.

And Shane suddenly felt a little light-headed.

It was all happening so fast: their confessions of love, being discovered by his parents, making plans for the future...

Oh god oh god oh god.

"Shane?" It was Ilya's voice, all concern. Shane felt a hand on his shoulder, and then he realized that he had his head between his knees. "Are you okay?"

Shane inhaled and exhaled slowly, keeping his head down.

Ilya's hand moved to Shane's knee as he crouched beside him, seeking his eyes. "Shane?"

"I'm okay," Shane said weakly. "I'm just…freaking out. Don't worry about me."

Ilya took his hands and rubbed his thumbs soothingly over the backs of them. "We are good here, yes?" he said. "Your family is here. And your boyfriend. And we are okay here."

Shane raised his head slightly. "Boyfriend?"

Such a ridiculous word. Such a ridiculous, wonderful word.

Ilya shrugged and grinned. "I think, yes?"

"Yes."

It was really too bad they were in his parents' living room, and that his parents were definitely staring at them, because Shane wanted to jump into Ilya's lap and kiss him into the floor.

"Since their rookie season," Shane heard his mother say. "I can't believe it."

"Looking at them now, I kind of can," his father said.

Chapter Twenty-Seven

They left Shane's parents' cottage with a promise to come for dinner the following evening.

Ilya wasn't sure how Shane felt about everything that had just happened, but *he* thought it had gone surprisingly well.

"Holy shit," Shane said. He hadn't even turned the engine on; he was just sitting in the driver's seat with his forehead on the steering wheel.

"It was okay, yes?" Ilya offered.

"I don't know. Do you think it was? Fuck. That was really weird."

"Well. Now they know."

Shane blew out a breath. "Yeah."

"We should go home."

Shane nodded against the steering wheel before sitting up and pressing the ignition button.

Ilya spent the entirety of the short drive back to Shane's cottage wondering if it was weird that he'd just called Shane's cottage *home*. He knew his grip on the English language was tenuous, but referring to a place he was staying for two weeks as "home" wasn't weird, was it?

If it *was* weird, Shane wasn't saying anything about it.

Shane actually didn't say anything at all during the drive back, other than a few muttered curse words. His hands were tight on the wheel. When they got back to the cottage, he dropped his keys into a bowl and strode into the living room with a hand in his hair.

"I need some air," he said, and he walked outside to the patio, leaving Ilya alone in the house.

Fortunately, Ilya had packed just the thing for this situation.

He went to the freezer and pulled out the bottle of vodka he had stashed there the day he'd arrived. It was the good shit, distilled in small batches and impossible to buy outside of Russia. He grabbed two glasses and carried them and the bottle outside.

"Is maybe a good time for this," he said, holding up the bottle.

Shane turned warily, and snorted when he saw the vodka. "The last time I drank that stuff was in Las Vegas. You remember?"

"Yes," Ilya said, carefully pouring a couple of inches into each glass. "But you did not ever drink *this* stuff. This vodka is special." He handed Shane one of the glasses.

Ilya closed his eyes as he took his first sip, enjoying the contrast of the frigid temperature of the liquid and the fire of the alcohol as it slid down his throat. Perfect.

He opened his eyes when he heard Shane sputtering and coughing.

"Oh, wow," Shane said. "That is *strong*. I might need some cranberry juice or something."

"If you mix that with cranberry juice I will drown you in the lake."

But Shane, seemingly unable to concentrate at all,

was already taking a second sip. "This has been the weirdest day of my life."

Ilya wanted to tell Shane that it had been one of the *best* days of *his* life. It had been awkward, sure, but Ilya felt that, if he hadn't quite been already, he *would* be welcomed into Shane's family, and that was no small thing. In fact, to Ilya, who had barely been welcome in his *own* family, it was huge.

He wanted to tell Shane that the closest he felt to home was when he was with him. It didn't matter if it was in a hotel room, or Ilya's apartment, or at that weird hideout building Shane bought in Montreal, or here at Shane's cottage; he was himself when he was with Shane. He'd left Russia, he was uneasy in America, and he'd spent his entire adult life drifting between continents and between lovers.

But now he had been reeled in by this annoying Canadian, and all that he knew was that he wanted to stay. He wanted to anchor himself to Shane and just…stay.

He couldn't *say* any of that—literally, he could not possibly come up with the English words to articulate any of the things he was feeling at that moment. So instead he plucked the vodka glass from Shane's hand and sat it on the table next to his own. Maybe alcohol *wasn't* the thing Shane needed right now.

He wrapped Shane in his arms, and held him. He nuzzled into Shane's hair and breathed him in.

"I love you," he murmured, because he *could* say *that*. After so fucking long he could finally say that.

Shane tilted his head up and studied Ilya's face with questioning eyes. "I love you too," he said. "Are you all right?"

Ilya nodded, and leaned in to kiss him.

It was exactly how Ilya had secretly always wanted to kiss Shane: a shameless display of adoration and care. Their tongues slowly caressing as Ilya held Shane's face in his hands and brushed his hair with his fingertips.

His heart flipped and tumbled helplessly around in his chest. There would be no going back from this. From any of this.

"I keep thinking about logistics," Shane said when they broke apart, as if Ilya hadn't just poured his heart into that kiss. "Like, the earliest you would be in Ottawa would be the season after next, when your contract is done with Boston, right?"

Ilya did *not* want to talk about any of this right now.

"Yes. Probably." He nibbled behind Shane's ear, hoping to distract him.

"So just over a year from now you're in Ottawa, and then we wait, what, another whole season until we announce the charity? It would have to be that long, right?"

"Mm," Ilya said. He really didn't care.

"So that's a year and a half or so until we can announce the charity. Which is the same as announcing our friendship," Shane said as Ilya slid his hands into the back of his shorts and pulled him closer.

"And then what?" Shane continued. "How many more years do you think you'll be playing?"

"Fuck, Hollander," Ilya groaned. "I don't fucking know."

"I'm just trying to get an idea of how long we'll be— what are you doing?"

Ilya had dropped to his knees, and he felt it was pretty obvious what he was doing.

"I am celebrating," Ilya said. He tugged Shane's

shorts down until they hit the wood of the deck. "You should join me."

"*Now?* My head is racing! How can you even be thinking about sex right now?"

"Because it is a beautiful day. And we are alone. And I met your parents. And I want you to calm the fuck down. And I love you."

"Oh."

Ilya leaned in and took all of him in his mouth, enjoying the novel sensation of the soft flesh resting on his tongue.

"Oh, fuck, Ilya," Shane gasped.

That's more like it.

He wanted to fuck Shane. Right here on the deck. But that would require stopping so he could go inside to grab lube and a condom. Stopping was unappealing.

For now, he put all of his efforts into taking Shane apart.

"You're way too good at that," Shane sighed.

Ilya hummed his agreement.

The thought hit him that this was it. This was going to be his sex life now. No more meaningless—but undeniably hot—one-night stands. No more booty calls while he was on the road. He was going to give it all up for this chance at something lasting. For the chance to hold the heart of the beautiful man who was exhaling Ilya's name like it was the most important word in the world.

Ilya had no problem giving it all up. He would give up so much more, if he needed to.

"Ilya. God, *Ilya.* So good. Don't stop. I love you."

In response, Ilya reached for his hand and tangled their fingers together. *I love you so much. Don't leave me.*

"Oh. *Yes*. Fuck, yes. I'm gonna—oh, holy shit, Ilya. Fuck, *fuck*…"

Ilya squeezed his hand as Shane pulsed and spurted into his mouth. Ilya swallowed and licked him clean with long, lazy strokes of his tongue.

"Fuck. Get up here," Shane panted.

Ilya rose to his feet, pulling Shane's shorts up with him, and Shane hauled him in for a very sloppy kiss.

When they broke apart, Shane gazed up at him with sex-drunk eyes.

"Wow," he said. "We're really going to do this, aren't we?"

The statement was vague, but Ilya understood. "Yes. If you want to try this, I will do what I need to do."

"I will too. Anything. I want this. I want *us*."

Ilya brushed Shane's hair out of his eyes. "Then I am moving to Ottawa, I think."

"And we're starting a charity."

"And we will become friends."

"And we'll see each other all the time. As much as possible. And spend the summers together. Here."

"Yes."

They kissed again. Ilya couldn't believe they had solved this impossible problem. Maybe it wouldn't go as smoothly as they imagined, but it was a plan.

"And when I retire," Ilya said, "after I have won twelve Stanley Cups and thirteen MVP awards—"

"The hell you will."

"And you have been retired for, like, eight years already because you got very bad at hockey…"

Shane laughed. "Okay."

"Then I will bring you to that dock out there. I will have hundreds of candles all over it…"

"That sounds like a fire hazard."

"Is on the water, Hollander. Fucking relax. Will be beautiful, you will love it. The candles. The lake. The full moon."

"Oh, is it a clear night?"

"Yes. Of course. And I will get on one knee—"

"Ilya—"

"And I will say, 'Shane Hollander, will you please marry me so I can become Canadian citizen faster?'"

Shane burst out laughing, and shoved him. "You're such an asshole."

"And you will say yes, because you are a nice, helpful guy."

"No," Shane said, taking his hands. "I will say yes because I will still be madly in love with you. And I'll want to spend the rest of my life with you."

And, oh god, Ilya didn't deserve him, but he didn't care. He was selfish like that.

"I mean it," Shane said softly. "I want to have a life with you. I know it will be awkward, and will still involve a lot of sneaking around for a while, but I'm playing the long game here. So, yeah. Whatever it takes, I'm in."

Ilya lifted their joined hands to his lips and kissed Shane's knuckles. "Does this mean I get to see your apartment in Montreal? Your real one?"

"You can even keep a toothbrush there. I'm going to sell that other place. I was being paranoid when I bought it. I'm sorry."

Ilya grinned. "Buying an entire building because you are nervous is very you."

Shane shook his head. "I really am sorry. I just wanted to protect what we had. I should have invited you to my real apartment sooner. I want you there. I want you in my life. All of it."

God, were they really going to be able to keep this a secret until they were retired? Now that they were both honest about what they were to each other, Ilya feared it might be impossible to hide their relationship from the world.

Especially when Shane looked at him like he was looking at him right now—like Ilya was *worth* all this trouble. Like he was worth loving.

"I want to tell everyone," Ilya said. "Right now."

Shane's eyes went wide with panic. "No! Don't. We have to stick to the plan."

Ilya sighed dramatically. "You and your plans. What if I just kissed you on the mouth at the next All-Star Game?"

"I'll punch you. I swear to god."

"You wouldn't. Not if I kissed you like this." Ilya cradled Shane's face in one hand, his thumb brushing Shane's cheekbone, and kissed him. He took his time, and finished with little nips to Shane's bottom lip. Shane, already boneless from the blow job, fell heavily against Ilya's chest.

"If you kissed me like that I would push you to the ice and start tearing your gear off," Shane murmured dreamily.

"That would be interesting." Ilya's cock was suddenly *very* interested in that imagined scenario.

"What if we just told our friends?" Shane suggested. "My family already knows. We could just...feel our way with the rest."

"Mm," Ilya said. "And what would your best friend Hayden Pike say?"

"He would probably think I was kidding."

"You *are* known for your pranks."

Shane laughed. "I want to tell him. I want him to know you like I do."

"Really?" Ilya made the word as suggestive as possible. "Do you think he'd like to join us? A night away from the kids, maybe?"

Shane buried his face against Ilya's shoulder, probably to hide his blush. "Stop it."

"Or maybe if Rose Landry wants a sexual experience with you that isn't a disaster..."

"No threesomes!" Shane said. "That's my hard rule."

"You've never tried it," Ilya scoffed. "You might love it."

"When have I ever loved something I thought I'd hate?" Shane said dryly.

Ilya chuckled and kissed the top of his head. "Let's go to bed."

"It's four in the afternoon."

"Yes, but when I am done with you it will be bedtime."

"Promises."

Ilya took his hand and pulled him toward the house. He picked up Shane's vodka glass with the other. No sense wasting it. "And tomorrow, I am going to keep you in bed all day."

"All day, huh?"

"Yes—bring the bottle in, yes?—and maybe the day after that also."

"For two weeks?"

Ilya shrugged. "I could maybe extend my stay."

Shane plunked the vodka bottle on the kitchen counter. "You can?"

"A little. Yes. If you will have me."

"I do have some other hot Russians coming to stay with me in a couple of weeks…"

Ilya gasped. "Shane Hollander! You have not ever told me that I am hot before."

Shane frowned. "I haven't?"

"No. I would remember."

"Well, I mean…obviously you're hot. Like, I-can't-believe-I-get-to-kiss-you hot."

"Come upstairs. You can kiss me and tell me about Ottawa. And maybe get me off because I am fucking dying."

Shane raced past him to the stairs. "Only if you beat me."

Ilya laughed. "Game fucking on, Hollander."

Epilogue

Sixteen months later—Montreal

"He tripped me! Hey, what the fuck, ref! That was tripping!"

Shane glared up at the ref, and then at Ilya, who was looming over him in his Ottawa jersey. "You fell," Ilya said.

"I didn't *fall*. It was *tripping*."

"Yes. Was you tripping over your own skates."

"Get fucked, Rozanov."

Ilya's lips quirked up. "Was planning on it."

And now Shane had to bite back a grin. He rose to his knees, then stood, still mad as hell. Ilya had totally tripped him.

The crowd was booing, cursing Ilya's name, and Shane got up in his face. "Stop being an asshole."

"Stop falling down."

Shane jabbed him in the chest with a gloved finger. He heard the crowd roar its approval. "You can't beat me without *cheating*."

Ilya raised an eyebrow. "You don't think?"

Someone grabbed Shane's arm and pulled him away. "All right, keep it in your pants, you two. Jesus."

"Hi, Hayden," Ilya said, grinning.

"I still don't like you, Rozanov," Hayden said.

"Oh no!" Ilya mocked him. "How can I impress Montreal's fifteenth best player?"

"Shane, I'm gonna punch him."

"Don't."

"I'm gonna punch him."

"No you're not," the ref barked. "Get back to your benches, all three of you. It's a commercial break. Go cool off."

Ilya winked at Shane and then skated to his bench. Shane could feel his cheeks burning.

"I still can't believe he's your...you know," Hayden grumbled as they headed for their own bench.

"Quiet."

"I know. I know. Just...it fucks me up, thinking about it."

"Then don't!"

"I mean, I could have found you a nice dude, if you had just—"

"Shut it."

They had reached the bench, and although Shane had come out to his teammates last season, he hadn't told any of them about Ilya. Hayden had done the math and figured it out after a Boston road trip a month ago.

"Hey, can I ask you something?" he had said as they'd walked to their cars after arriving home from a road trip. "You know how you used to go meet up with your mystery man every time we played in Boston? But now you don't?"

"Um. We, uh...broke up," Shane had said quickly. And unconvincingly.

"Uh-huh. But you've been driving to Ottawa a lot this month."

"Yeah, my parents live there. I've been, um, visiting."

"Your parents have always lived there, and they drive to Montreal even more than you drive to Ottawa. So I have another theory. I think your mystery man is Ilya Rozanov."

Shane had been flooded with a mixture of fear and shame, but also relief. He didn't say anything until they'd reached Hayden's car, and then he'd blown out a breath and nodded.

Hayden had blanched. "Holy fuck. I was sort of joking. Are you for real…doing stuff…with Rozanov?"

"Yes."

"Wait, *seriously*? Did he sign with Ottawa to be *closer to you*? What the fuck is happening?"

"It's one reason, yes."

Hayden had turned and placed both hands on the roof of his car, leaning forward like he was trying to breathe through a cramp. "Shane, this is not good, buddy."

"It's not ideal, no. But… I love him."

Hayden had looked at him, after he'd said that, like Shane had sprouted wings and a tail, and Shane had been sure he'd just lost his best friend. But, instead of yelling at him or getting in his car and speeding away, Hayden had just nodded and said, "I think I need to meet him properly, then."

They *had* met properly, once, since then, but it hadn't gone particularly well. Hayden couldn't think of Ilya as anything but the enemy, and Ilya had responded with relentless snark. So they weren't exactly friends.

"You sure you wanna do that press conference tomorrow?" Hayden asked. "I mean, no one knows that you guys are friends right now. You could keep it that way."

"I'm sure." Shane was definitely sure. He and Ilya had been planning for tomorrow for over a year.

He had sold the hookup building, and Ilya had sold (most of) his car collection. With the combined earnings, they'd started the Irina Foundation. Tomorrow, at a hotel conference room downtown, they would be announcing, and, more importantly, explaining the foundation they had created together.

"It's a good cause, I suppose," Hayden sighed. "I apologize in advance if Rozanov has a black eye for the press conference."

"Please don't punch him."

"I'll make a deal: if he stops being a fucking dick, I won't punch him."

Shane grimaced. Ilya was definitely going to have a black eye tomorrow.

Ilya found Shane in the bathroom down the hall from the conference room. He was gripping the counter and staring down into one of the sinks.

"Relax, Hollander," Ilya said. He was probably as nervous as Shane was, really, but Shane was much worse at hiding it. Ilya put his hands on Shane's shoulders and rubbed gently, careful not to wrinkle his light gray suit jacket.

"I'm nervous," Shane said unnecessarily.

"I know."

"We've been planning for this day for over a year and now it's here and I'm scared. I don't even know why!"

"Our plan has worked perfectly so far," Ilya said.

"Too perfectly. I keep waiting for something to go wrong."

It *had* seemed too easy, so far. When Ilya's contract had ended with Boston, Ottawa had been all too happy to sign him. Ilya had bought a large, private house on the edge of the Ottawa River with a four-car garage. The garage currently held two sports cars and a very sensible Mercedes SUV. ("Is good in snow," Ilya had explained sheepishly when he'd first shown it to Shane. "For driving between Ottawa and Montreal.")

They had agreed that it would be easier to continue in secret if they weren't both living in apartment buildings, so Shane had bought a house in Brossard that was still close to the team's practice facility.

Ilya wrapped his arms around his boyfriend now, to pull him back against his chest. Shane met his eyes in the mirror. "Your cheek looks better than I thought it would."

"Is still sore."

"Serves you right. You were an asshole to Hayden."

"Hayden is an asshole to *me*."

Shane sighed. "I have terrible taste in men. For friends *and* boyfriends." He closed his eyes and tilted his head back against Ilya's shoulder.

"Will be fine," Ilya said. He kissed Shane's temple and nuzzled his hair.

"Don't mess my hair up," Shane murmured, but he was smiling.

"Jesus." Ilya turned his head to see Hayden standing just inside the door with his hand over his eyes. "I'm still not used to that. You guys know this is, like, a *public* bathroom, right?"

Ilya dropped his arms, and Shane stepped away.

Hayden was right. Shane and Ilya weren't even out, publicly, as gay and bisexual, let alone as a couple. They'd agreed that they wanted their private lives to be their own, and they would only tell the people they wanted to include in that life. So far, it was a very small circle. A small circle that, much to Ilya's chagrin, included Hayden.

"Anyway," Hayden said, looking at the wall and not at them, "Shane, your mom asked me to look for you. They fixed the audio problem, so you can start any time."

"Okay, thanks. We'll be right out."

Hayden nodded. "I'll stand outside the door, but you have, like, two minutes, tops, all right? Don't, y'know, start anything."

Ilya knew Shane was rolling his eyes. "We won't. Geez, Hayd."

When the door was closed, Ilya laughed. "He thinks you can't come in two minutes?"

"Oh, shut up."

Ilya grabbed his hand and pulled him close. "I want to tell you, before we do this, that I am…very happy today. My mother would have really liked this. And I think she is with me today. And proud."

Oh, oops. Now Shane's eyes were glistening. "She has so many reasons to be proud of you, Ilya."

Ilya smiled at him. "I need to kiss you here, or else I will do it out there."

"Okay."

He held Shane's face in his hands and gazed at him for a few seconds before leaning in and kissing the hell out of him.

"I love you," Ilya said.

"I love you too."

Ilya nodded. "Remember that when I am being a dick to you out there."

Shane grinned and kissed him again. "Don't worry, I'm used to it."

The room was packed with people who were dying to see what announcement Shane Hollander and Ilya Rozanov would be making together. Shane wasn't sure what rumors had been stirred up by this press conference, but it was time to end the suspense.

They had agreed that Shane would do most of the talking. Ilya was by no means shy, but Shane knew he was uneasy making long speeches in English. Besides, Shane wanted to make sure everything was said in both English and French, since both Montreal and Ottawa were bilingual cities.

"Ilya and I have been competing against each other for over eight seasons. A lot has been said, and written, about our rivalry. About what makes us different as players, and as people. But I don't say enough how much I respect Ilya, not only as one of the best players in the NHL, but as a person. He is a great leader, a fierce competitor, and an amazing goal scorer. But over the years I have also gotten to know him off the ice, and I consider him a friend."

That statement alone created a swell of murmurs throughout the room.

Shane read through the words again, in French this time, and then continued. "When Ilya signed with Ottawa, we began talking about creating a charity together. Today that dream is a reality. The Irina Foundation will raise money and awareness for organizations that provide support, counseling, and assistance for people who are suffering from depression and other mental illnesses that can lead to suicide. It's a cause that is important to both of us, and I am very happy and proud to be working with Ilya to create something that can hopefully help a lot of people."

He translated in French, and as he finished, he heard Ilya clear his throat.

"Ah, I can only say my part in English." He smiled, which made the audience laugh. "This is not in the notes, but I want to say that the Irina Foundation is named for my mother. She battled depression without help for many years. She had no support, no medical treatment. When she…"

Shane didn't think. He just reached out a hand and placed it on Ilya's forearm, where it rested on the table. He hadn't expected Ilya to say any of this, but looking at Ilya now, Shane knew he *needed* to say it.

"My mother died when I was twelve years old. She lost her battle. This foundation is for her. It is to help people like her, so they do not have to fight alone."

Ilya looked down at the table and sniffed. Shane patted his arm, wishing he could hold his hand or kiss his hair. His chest felt tight, and his eyes burned.

After a long moment where you could have heard a pin drop in the crowded room, Shane spoke. "Thank you, Ilya."

He went on to explain the hockey camps they would be hosting in Montreal and in Ottawa that summer, with all proceeds going directly to the foundation. He named some of the organizations they planned to focus on when they made their first donations, and he announced his mother, Yuna, as the director and treasurer of the foundation. Neither he nor Ilya could imagine a better person for the job.

He ended by talking about their website, where people could make donations online, and then opened the floor to questions.

When it was over, Shane pulled Ilya out of the room. He texted Hayden. Need you to guard the door again.

Shane herded Ilya into the bathroom and pushed him back against the door as soon as it closed. He confirmed that the room was empty, and then said, "Oh my god. Come here." He stood on his tiptoes and kissed him. "I didn't think you'd say any of that."

"Neither did I."

They kissed again, completely unhurried, and Shane really hoped Hayden had gotten his text.

"I wanted to kiss you out there," Ilya said.

"I wanted to climb into your *lap* out there. I'm so fucking proud of you, Ilya. I'm…proud to be *with* you. I want you to know that, even if we keep it a secret, I'm proud to be with you."

"I know. Me too. When the time is right, we will stop being a secret."

Shane still wasn't sure when that would be. They had talked about waiting until one or both of them had retired, but that seemed like much too long a wait. Shane felt he could easily play for another ten years at least.

"Are you sure you need to go back to Ottawa today?"

"Yes. And you are flying to Chicago tonight."

"I know," Shane sighed.

"This is why I want my pilot license. Would be faster."

Shane groaned. "Please don't get your pilot license. I will be very mad if you fly into a mountain and die."

"Aw. Sweet."

There was a knock on the door, followed by Hayden's voice. "Hey, uh, could you guys wrap it up, maybe? I kinda need to get in there for legitimate bathroom reasons."

Ilya sighed and stepped aside, and Shane opened the door.

"Good press conference, guys," Hayden said as he strode past them toward the urinals. "Sorry about your mother, Ilya. That sucks."

Ilya gave Shane a look that said *this is your best friend?* Shane ignored him.

"You think it went okay?" Shane asked Hayden.

"For sure. It's like, powerful, right? Rivals coming together for a greater cause. I mean, no one in that room knows you guys are all in love and shit." He finished at the urinal and went to wash his hands. "But the way you were looking at Ilya, Shane, I thought people were gonna figure it out. Hell, I thought you were gonna start sucking face in front of the whole world. Like Hunter."

"No way," said Shane.

"We have better control than Scott Hunter."

Hayden flicked the water off his hands, then rubbed them on his pants. "Would have been memorable, though."

"Not really what we wanted the focus to be today," Shane said.

"Okay, well, I've gotta take the twins to a birthday party, so I have to split." Hayden stepped forward and hugged Shane. Then, with some hesitation, he extended his hand to Ilya.

Ilya shook it, then patted him on the back. "Thank you, Hayden."

"Yeah, well...sorry about your face, I guess. Not that you didn't deserve it."

"Is okay. My face can heal. *Your* face, however..."

"All right," Shane interrupted. "That's enough. Bye, Hayden." He shoved Hayden out the door and then turned to Ilya. "I'm gonna go find Mom. Come find me in a bit, okay?"

"Yes. I will."

Ilya found himself in the same position Shane had been in earlier: gripping the bathroom counter, staring into the sink, deep in thought.

His life was so close to perfect now, even with the secrets he was keeping. Secrets he was letting go of, like balloons, one at a time. Now the world knew he and Shane were friends. Now the world knew the truth about his mother's death. He imagined he would be hearing from Andrei about that, but he really didn't care. His brother had only called him a couple of times since their father's funeral, and only to ask for money, which Ilya had refused.

Fuck Andrei. Ilya had a better family now.

Shane's parents had come over for dinner last night at Shane's house, and there had been a moment— when Ilya had spilled some cooking wine and Shane had wordlessly handed him a cloth—that Ilya had been struck by how right it all felt. To be at home, with this man he loved, making food together for Shane's family. The family who had been so warm and welcoming to Ilya, once the initial shock had worn off.

Ilya hadn't been kidding about wanting to marry him. And not for citizenship, of course. He wanted to be Shane's husband, and to live together, and maybe even raise children together. Not as many children as Hayden had, but, like, a reasonable number.

Ilya had been snarky about Scott Hunter's lack of self-control, but sometimes he was dying to do the same thing. He would fantasize about grabbing Shane at the end of a game and kissing him, right there on the ice in front of everyone. Just get it over with and out there and anyone who had a problem with it could fuck off.

Baby steps, Ilya reminded himself.

The All-Star Game was coming up, though, and he and Shane would be on the same team again. Ilya was only about sixty percent sure he wouldn't kiss Shane against the boards if he scored a goal off of a pass from him.

Ilya smiled at his reflection in the mirror and smoothed his tie. He would have to warn Shane about the possibility of being kissed at the All-Star Game, just to stress him out.

He pulled out his phone to check the time, and a message popped up. Don't leave without saying goodbye.

Ilya wrote back right away. Never.

He had a surprise for Shane, actually. He had booked a room in this hotel. They had less than two hours before Ilya needed to hit the road, but after years of practice they were good at making the most of an hour or two of privacy.

1126, he texted, and waited for Shane's reply.

Shane: Seriously?! Best news ever. See you soon.

Ilya chuckled, set an alarm on his phone, and went to meet his boyfriend.

* * * * *

Acknowledgments

I would first of all like to thank my editor, Mackenzie Walton, who made this weird story so much better. I would also like to thank my husband, Matt, who listened to me nervously read this entire book out loud to him and responded with nothing but enthusiasm and support.

About the Author

Rachel Reid has always lived in Nova Scotia, Canada, and will likely continue to do so. She has two boring degrees and two interesting sons. She has been a hockey fan since childhood, but sadly never made it to the NHL herself. She enjoys books about hot men doing hot things, and cool ladies being awesome.

You can follow her on Instagram @RachelReidWrites. Her website is www.rachelreidwrites.com.

MY DINNER
WITH HAYDEN

This bonus story takes place three weeks before the epilogue in Heated Rivalry, *so it's an...epilogue pro-logue? Here is what happens when Ilya and Shane try to host a dinner party for Hayden and Jackie. Enjoy!*

November 2018—Montreal

Ilya opened the door of Shane's house to greet Hayden and his wife (Jessica?). He *could* have waited for Shane to finish washing his hands in the kitchen so he could join him at the door, but this was more fun.

"Oh god," Hayden said, as soon as he was faced with Ilya, "I don't think I can do this."

Ilya smiled, and stepped aside. "Please come in."

Hayden moved past him, his wife following closely behind. She, at least, offered Ilya a friendly, and possibly apologetic, smile as she handed him the bottle of wine they had brought.

"Shane!" Hayden called out. "Don't want to alarm you, but Ilya Rozanov is in your house."

Shane emerged from the kitchen, drying his hands with a dish towel. He was wearing dark pants and a blue button-up shirt that was open at the collar. Ilya was struck, not for the first time that night, by how good he looked, and by how right this all felt. Shane and Ilya, at home, having dinner with friends.

Even if the friends sucked a little.

"You promised you weren't going to be an asshole, Hayd," Shane complained.

"That's true," Hayden's wife confirmed. "You did promise that." She offered Ilya her hand. "I'm Jackie, by the way."

"Jackie," Ilya repeated. "Is nice to meet you. Your husband I am not sure about yet."

"He'll behave." Jackie was a beautiful woman with long, dark hair, sparkling green eyes, and an athletic body. She was much too good for Hayden.

Shane directed them all to the spacious living room. Ilya went to the kitchen to deposit the gifted wine and to get the (better) wine he had already opened. He definitely needed wine. When he entered the living room, things were already looking dire; Jackie was making small talk with Shane about his electric fireplace while Hayden was looking at the floor with his hands clasped between his knees.

Ilya set four wineglasses on the coffee table, then immediately plucked one and filled it generously. He handed it wordlessly to Hayden, because he looked like he could use it. Hayden accepted it with a wary nod and, because he had no class at all, took a giant gulp. After he'd swallowed, he wiped his mouth with the back of his hand, made a move to place the glass on the table, then seemed to think better of it and brought it back to his lips for another mouthful.

"I was just telling Shane how beautiful this house is," Jackie said.

Ilya handed her the next glass of wine, which she thanked him for before taking a small, sensible sip. "Yes," Ilya agreed. "We should give you a tour. The master bathroom has a very good shower." He looked directly at Hayden and winked. "Big enough for two."

Hayden's jaw clenched as he reached for the wineglass he'd only just set down.

"How are the kids?" Shane asked quickly. "How's Amber?"

"Great!" Jackie said brightly. "She's into everything, of course, now that she's walking."

Ilya considered his options for where to sit. Shane and Jackie were occupying the two armchairs closest to the fireplace. Hayden was sitting at one end of the sofa that faced them. Ilya could sit at the other end of the sofa, but he chose the more obnoxious option of perching on the arm of Shane's chair. Instead of handing Shane his wine, Ilya draped his arm around Shane's shoulders and hovered the glass in front of his lips. Shane tilted his head back to give him a look that was more annoyed than charmed, then took the wineglass.

"I would love to meet your kids," Ilya said. "Shane has told me lots of stories about them." It wasn't really true. Not the stories part, anyway. Ilya did legitimately like kids, though, and the Pikes had more than enough of them. He smiled warmly at Jackie, who beamed back at him.

"That's sweet," she said. "Maybe next time you're in town we can have you guys over in the afternoon. The kids love their uncle Shane."

Ilya nudged his boyfriend. *"Uncle Shane."*

"I haven't been a good uncle lately," Shane said. "I've been so busy."

"My fault," Ilya confessed.

"Jesus," Hayden muttered.

Jackie shot her husband a pointed look, and Shane stood. "Maybe we should eat."

Hayden stood just as quickly. "Yup. Definitely. Let's eat."

As Ilya made his way to the dining room, Shane tugged on his arm to hold him back. "Stop doing that," he hissed.

"Doing what?" Ilya asked innocently.

"You're intentionally bothering Hayden."

"Am not. I have not even asked his wife what she sees in him! I am being very good."

Shane's face got stern and adorable. "Behave," he warned.

In response, Ilya kissed his forehead. "Always, moy lyubovnik."

He took a moment to enjoy the flush that always appeared in Shane's cheeks when Ilya used Russian terms of endearment. He would definitely need to keep Shane's wineglass full tonight. He wanted him to loosen up and enjoy himself, and then get all snuggly in bed later.

Shane invited Hayden and Jackie to sit at the dining room table before rushing off into the kitchen. Ilya topped off their guests' wineglasses before saying, "Sorry to leave you alone, but I should help him."

"Of course," Jackie said. Hayden nodded through a mouthful of wine.

Ilya went to the kitchen, but paused a moment to lean against the entryway and watch as Shane dipped a spoon into the large pot on the stove and brought it to his lips to sample. He blew gently a couple of times before sinking the spoon into his mouth. His brow furrowed in concentration as he worked to determine if it was good enough to serve his best friends. It was cute, and Ilya loved him.

"How is it?" Ilya asked, moving away from the entrance to stand unnecessarily close to Shane in the spacious kitchen.

"I think it's good," Shane said, though he didn't sound sure. "Do you think it's too salty?"

Ilya kissed him, tasting only the barest remnants of the coq au vin on his tongue. "Tastes perfect," he said when he pulled away.

"Don't be stupid," Shane said unsteadily. He cleared his throat and said, "Taste it properly."

Ilya rolled his eyes and grabbed a fresh spoon. He dipped it into the pot, then made a show of dragging the sample into his mouth with his tongue. He slipped the spoon between his lips and hollowed his cheeks, moaning wantonly as he sucked and savored the rich flavor of the broth. The stew was fine. The plain arousal on Shane's face was delicious.

"Is good," Ilya said after he pulled the spoon from his mouth with a wet pop. "Where is the parsley I chopped?"

Cooking was something that he and Shane had gotten into together. It was enjoyable, finding recipes and learning new kitchen techniques. Working together on something, rather than competing (not that it was *never* competitive). Plus, there was delicious food to eat when they were done. And Ilya was pretty sure that the feeling of accomplishment made Shane horny. Win-win-win.

They ladled the stew into white bowls, Ilya wiping any stray drops from the rims with a towel. He artfully sprinkled the parsley on top of each one, then stole a

quick kiss before carrying the food out to their waiting guests.

"Wow!" Jackie enthused when Ilya placed one of the
bowls in front of her. "You guys made this?"

"We did," Ilya said. Looking at the food now, he felt a
little bit proud. Shane brought the remaining two bowls
out, then darted back to the kitchen to grab a basket full
of bread he had purchased at a bakery that morning.

"What is this?" Hayden poked at the stew with his
spoon like he suspected Ilya may have dropped some
razor blades in it.

"Coq au vin," Shane said proudly (and perfectly) as
he returned with the bread.

"That's French," Ilya added helpfully. Hayden glared
at him.

They all ate without speaking for a few spoonfuls.
Ilya wondered who would crack first. Not surprisingly,
it was Shane.

"Did you hear about that McFarland suspension?"

Hayden's eyes shot up, and Ilya could see the relief
in them. "Yeah! Holy shit, right?"

They gossiped with each other about the latest office conduct suspension, and Ilya took the opportunity
to offer Jackie a sympathetic smile. She smiled back,
and rolled her eyes. When Shane brought up the proposed new rules regarding defensive line changes, Ilya
decided to step up and be the hero.

"Let's not talk about hockey tonight," he suggested
mildly.

"Thank you," Jackie said.

Unfortunately, no one seemed to have an alternate
topic to discuss, so the four of them fell back into awkward silence.

"Well, we need to talk about *something*," Shane complained after a minute had passed.

"We could talk about how Hayden is eating around the mushrooms like a five-year-old," Ilya offered.

Hayden put his spoon down with a loud clank. "We could talk about what the fuck Shane sees in you."

"Hayden," Jackie scolded.

"Ah." Ilya nodded sagely. "You are jealous."

"What? No!" Hayden sputtered. "I'm not *jealous* of you. I'm not—Shane, I love you. You know that. But I'm not—" He turned to Ilya, who was now thoroughly enjoying himself. "Jesus, my wife is *right here*, you fucking asshole. And you know that's not what I meant."

Ilya just shrugged. He hadn't actually meant it, but now he was starting to wonder.

"The food is delicious," Jackie said, probably wanting to steer the conversation away from whether or not her husband had a giant crush on Shane. "I didn't even know you cooked, Shane."

"He's full of surprises," Hayden grumbled.

Ilya could see the tension in Shane's jaw and in his eyes.

"I got into cooking this past year," Shane said. He took a sip of water, and Ilya noticed a slight tremor in his fingers as he set the glass back down. "It's something we've been doing together, when we get the chance."

"That's sweet," she said, and sounded like she meant it. "We should cook together some time, Hayden."

"I suck at cooking."

"You suck at hockey," Ilya pointed out. "But you still play it."

Hayden looked pleadingly at Shane. "Seriously? *This* guy? I've got no problem with you being gay—"

"What a hero," Ilya said flatly.

Hayden turned to Ilya. "Shane can date all the men he wants! But *you* are a relentless douchebag and I've never liked you."

"Jesus, Hayden," Jackie mumbled.

Ilya raised an eyebrow. "You should save some of that for our wedding."

"Fuck, don't even—" Hayden shook his head, then went back to pushing mushrooms around his bowl.

There was a tense minute where no one said anything, and then Jackie asked, with a noticeable amount of forced cheerfulness, "So, Ilya. Did you get back to Russia over the summer at all?"

Jesus, this was a nightmare. "No," Ilya said. He couldn't think of anything to add, so he didn't.

"He was at my cottage, mostly," Shane explained. "And then dealing with moving to Ottawa."

"Right," Jackie said. "How are you liking Ottawa?"

"Fine," Ilya said. "Team sucks, but the city is not bad."

"I don't understand why you'd leave a contender like Boston to play for Ottawa," Hayden said.

"I am sure you don't understand a lot of things."

"Ilya," Shane said wearily.

"What happens when you guys break up, Rozanov?" Hayden continued, jabbing a fork between Shane and Ilya. "You gonna sign with Anaheim or something?"

Shane must have sensed Ilya was about to say something that almost certainly would have made Hayden smash the wine bottle on the table and come for Ilya's face with it, because he put a hand on Ilya's forearm and said, "Could you guys give it a rest? Please?"

"Yes, Hayden. Grow the hell up," Jackie said. "And

besides…" She leaned in, hands cupped around her wineglass and eyes glinting. "I want to hear how you two met."

Ilya snorted. He couldn't help it.

"I mean," Jackie said with a dismissive wave of her hand, "not how you *met*. We all know that, obviously. But when was the first time you…felt sparks?"

"I'll bet Shane was drunk as hell," Hayden grumbled.

"We don't all need alcohol to make people sleep with us," Ilya said. Hayden flushed, possibly realizing that Shane had told Ilya all about how he and Jackie had met at a nightclub years ago.

"I wasn't drunk," Shane said quietly. "I wasn't even old enough to drink legally."

"Wait," Hayden said. "Back the fuck up. You told me it had been going on for a while. I thought you meant a season or two. Not—how fucking young were you when you first—I mean. When you first…fuck, I can't. You know what I mean."

"Nineteen," Ilya said at the same time Shane said, "Eighteen."

Ilya shot him a curious look. "We were nineteen the first time we—"

"Oh," Shane said. "I thought the question was the first time we felt, um, sparks." His ears were bright red and Ilya wanted to bite them.

"Yes," Ilya said. His voice had gone soft, but he didn't care. "Eighteen, then. That's right."

The look that Shane gave him in response was so heated and adoring that Ilya wondered how rude it would be to shove Hayden and his lovely wife out the door right now.

"So, where were you?" Jackie asked, breaking the moment. "When you were both eighteen?"

"It was, um…" Shane started, but then appeared to be overcome with embarrassment at the memory.

"A hotel gym," Ilya finished for him. "The night we were both drafted."

"A *public* gym?" Hayden looked like he was going to faint. "Before you were even rookies? Are you fucking kidding me?"

"Nothing happened!" Shane explained quickly. "It wasn't like that. I just…felt something."

"Lust," Ilya supplied.

"*No*. Maybe. Shut up." Shane sighed. "Can we stop talking about this?"

"Absolutely," Hayden said.

The four of them stopped talking altogether. They ate in silence for another several uncomfortable minutes before Hayden rested his spoon beside his bowl of mushrooms and said, "You go back to Ottawa tomorrow, Rozanov?"

"Yes. But don't worry. I will be back in two weeks."

This visit, like he suspected most of them would be during this first season of living a couple of hours apart, was a short one. He'd had a day off, so he'd driven to Montreal immediately following his game in Ottawa last night. He'd arrived after midnight, and despite Shane having to get up early for practice, they'd kept each other awake for hours. Tomorrow afternoon Ilya was flying to Vancouver and wouldn't be back in Ottawa for a week. He had a day off when he got back, but unfortunately Shane would be on the road then.

It wasn't going to be easy, but it was definitely better than it had been before. Last season had been agony.

Ilya had still been playing for Boston, and knowing that Shane was *in love* with him had made keeping their secret so much harder. Before they'd admitted their feelings to one another, Ilya had always enjoyed the sneaking around. He'd liked Shane Hollander being his sexy secret. But the past fifteen months hadn't been much fun at all.

It was why Ilya had been unenthusiastic when Shane had suggested having Hayden and Jackie over for dinner. Their nights together were so few and far between that Ilya didn't want to share a single one with anyone else. Especially not Hayden stupid Pike.

Hayden had inadvertently stumbled on the truth a week ago by joking that Shane was secretly dating Ilya. Shane, who Ilya knew had been trying to figure out the right moment to tell his best friend that he was in love with Ilya Rozanov, had seized the opportunity and come clean. Hayden had been, understandably, dumbfounded.

This dinner was important to Shane, and Ilya knew the purpose of this evening was to make Jackie, and especially Hayden, understand what Shane saw in him. As far as Ilya was concerned, it wasn't anyone's business why Shane loved him. Ilya certainly didn't need to convince anyone that he was worth Shane's affection. Fuck them. It wasn't his job, or Shane's, to explain their relationship to anyone.

After dinner they retired to the living room. Other than the occasional comment on a piece of furniture or question about Shane's parents (both from Jackie), the room was silent. Ilya decided to put on some background music so it didn't feel like they were in a hospital waiting area. After another fifteen minutes of stiff conversation to a backdrop of Post Malone, he went to the kitchen to get more wine.

He briefly considered the vodka, but decided it would not be the best choice given his early morning the next day. Or the fact that he would prefer a cuddly Shane later to a horribly ill Shane.

When Ilya returned, Shane and Jackie were standing near the hallway that led to the stairs. "I'm going to show Jackie the house," Shane said. Ilya could very clearly read the unspoken message in Shane's words, *Stay here and bond with Hayden.*

Fuck. Ilya should have grabbed the vodka.

He refilled Hayden's wineglass, then his own, and then sat at the opposite end of the couch from Hayden.

"So," Ilya said.

"What are you doing with him?" Hayden asked abruptly. "What's your game here?"

"Game?"

Hayden stood up, and loomed over Ilya in what was probably supposed to be a threatening manner. "Is this a joke to you? Or do you just get off on fucking with him?"

"I do get off on fucking him. Yes."

Hayden's hands curled into fists. "That's not what I mean and you know it! Shane is, like, forbidden. Is that the appeal?"

Ilya's eyebrows shot up. "You do not think much of your best friend."

"I don't think much of *you.*"

Ilya sighed and nonchalantly crossed his legs. "And who *should* Shane be with?"

"A nice guy! Someone who… I don't know!" Hayden

threw up his hands. "Someone who fucking *cares* about him?"

All right. That was quite enough. Ilya stood, which gave him a good seven inches of height on Hayden. In the tight space between the sofa and the coffee table, Hayden had to look straight up at him. "You think you know what is best for him?"

"Yeah. I've known him since we were rookies."

Ilya's lips quirked up. "Maybe you were not listening at dinner, but so have I."

"Well, you wouldn't know it! He never fucking mentioned you."

"Funny. He didn't talk much about you either."

"I'm his best friend."

"I am his boyfriend."

"You've also slept with like a thousand women!"

Ilya scrunched his nose. "Is probably not a thousand."

He began doing some rough calculations in his head, but was interrupted when Hayden said, "Who do you think you are kidding here? You obviously aren't, y'know, *gay*."

"You have not heard of bisexuals?"

Hayden narrowed his eyes. "Bisexual, huh?"

Ilya switched to an overly animated, educational tone. "Some people like apples. Some people like oranges. *Some* people like apples *and* oran—"

"Oh fuck you. I know what it means."

"Then you know I can sleep with a million women and still fall in love with your best buddy Shane."

Hayden shook his head, looking more frustrated than ever. "Do you have *any* idea of what it will do to him if this secret gets out?"

Ilya huffed. "Yes. I have thought about it a bit."

"I won't let you hurt him."

"Okay."

"I'm serious." And then Hayden shoved Ilya's chest with both hands.

"Are you guys fucking kidding me?" Both men whipped their heads around to see Shane standing in the entrance-way. "Like, are you guys serious right now?"

"He started it," Ilya said. It sounded stupid even to his own ears.

Shane pointed at Ilya. "Do you know how long I have been wanting to do this? To introduce you to my friends as my boyfriend? Hayden and Jackie are my *best friends* and you are being an asshole."

"Fucking right," Hayden said smugly.

"And you!" Shane said, turning his fury on Hayden. "You're acting like I met Ilya yesterday or something. Just because you only found out about us recently doesn't mean our relationship is new. It's pretty fuck-ing solid, even if you don't want to believe it. Even if you don't want to consider the fact that we have been keeping this thing a secret for almost ten fucking years now!"

"Shane," Hayden sputtered. "I—"

"Do you know how *scared* I've been this whole time? Do you know how fucking terrifying it is to feel at-tracted to your archrival when you are *eighteen* and your rival also happens to be a *man*?"

Okay, maybe Ilya shouldn't have refilled Shane's wineglass as many times as he had.

"I have been so fucking scared and alone for so god-damned long and tonight was supposed to end some of that and you guys are acting like children. Fuck both of you."

There was a *loud* silence that hung in the room for what felt like an hour, and then Hayden said, very quietly, "You could've told me, Shane."

"What?"

This time, Hayden's voice was stronger. "You could've told me. I hate that you kept it from me all this time. That you thought you needed to."

Well, that was unexpectedly sweet.

"It hurts, y'know?" Hayden finished.

Shane's mouth was hanging open, and Ilya was torn between speaking on his behalf, and waiting to see what Shane would say. Curiosity won out.

"I couldn't," Shane said finally. "We hadn't even told *each other*. It took us years to figure out how we felt about each other. For me to figure out that I'm gay. But once we sorted it all out, I wanted to tell you. And I did. Eventually."

"And," Ilya added, because he couldn't help himself, "you've taken it super well."

Shane shot him a warning glance. Ilya looked away.

"I thought you hated him," Hayden said. "We talked about how much we hated him all the time. For years! And then I find out not only that you don't hate him, but you... I mean, you must love him so fucking much, right? Like, you'd have to, to go through all of this."

The unwavering way Shane met Hayden's eyes when he replied, simply, "Yes, I do," took Ilya's breath away.

"Wow," Jackie said, reminding Ilya that she was also in the room. That there were other people on earth besides him and Shane right now.

"Yes," Ilya murmured, unable to take his eyes off Shane's raised, determined chin.

"I'm sorry." Hayden sounded like all the fight had left him. "I'm making this about me, and it's not. This dinner was a big deal for you, and I fucked it up."

Shane didn't look like he'd been expecting that because he opened his mouth and closed it a few times before he finally nodded and said, "All right. Thank you."

"And," Hayden turned to Ilya, "if Shane loves you or whatever, then I guess you can't be such a bad guy."

"There are good things about me, I think."

Hayden scrubbed a hand over his face. "How the hell are you going to keep this a secret? Do you even have a plan?"

"Actually," Shane said, "we do. Go sit down and Ilya will get the cookies I bought for dessert." He fixed his gaze on Ilya, and Ilya nodded. "Then we'll tell you about the Irina Foundation."

Two hours later, Shane was closing the door behind Hayden and Jackie. Ilya placed a gentle hand on Shane's lower back, only to have him turn on his heel and march into the kitchen.

Uh-oh.

"Shane?" he called after him, but he knew Shane wouldn't turn back, or even acknowledge him. So he followed after his pissed-off boyfriend, and found him angrily loading the dishwasher.

"You are still mad," Ilya observed.

In response, Shane forcefully shoved the bottom rack of the dishwasher so it hit the back of the machine with a loud clatter of plates and cutlery.

"At me?" Ilya guessed.

"Yes," Shane ground out. "No. I don't know." He folded his arms across his chest and stared out the window. "I hate this."

"The window?"

"No. All of this." He gestured between himself and Ilya.

Ilya's heart dropped to the floor. "You hate…us?"

Shane squeezed his eyes shut. When he opened them again, his gaze was more miserable than angry. Ilya preferred angry. "I hate how we have to hide. I hate only getting these stolen moments with you. It's been so many fucking years of this, and I'm tired."

Ilya's heart returned to his chest. He took a step toward Shane, wanting to touch him but not wanting him to stomp away again. "I know."

"It's not fair! Hayden and Jackie get to just, y'know, *exist*. The night they first got together, I watched them make out on a dance floor."

"Pervert," Ilya teased.

"I mean I *saw* them. I wasn't watchi—shut up. The point is, they'd just met that night, and they were making out in front of the whole world without having to worry for one fucking second about anyone seeing them."

"Or their weird friend watching them."

Shane pressed his lips together, and Ilya knew he was trying not to smile. He counted that as a victory.

"They started dating, and then a few months later they were engaged and everyone on the team was congratulating Hayden. They had a big wedding and no one was, like, baffled and horrified that they were together." He exhaled. "What is that even like?"

"Probably like when you were dating Rose Landry."

Shane groaned. "Oh my god, Ilya. That was like two years ago. Let it go."

Ilya loved to tease him about Rose Landry, so, no. He would not be letting it go. Rose had since become one of Shane's closest friends, and was one of the few people who knew about Shane and Ilya. Ilya liked Rose a lot, actually.

"I wanted to feel *normal* tonight," Shane sighed.

"You want a normal relationship?" Ilya hoped not because that was something he could definitely never offer Shane, as much as he wished he could.

"It isn't fair. That's all. Hayden has been criticizing the hell out of you, and my relationship with you, as if it's all some ridiculous joke. And you don't do *anything* to help. I mean, I want people to understand why I love you, but you are so fucking terrible at showing them."

Oh.

"You want me to be different?" Ilya asked.

Shane let his arms fall to his sides. "I want you to not be a dick all the time."

"I'm sorry," Ilya said, and he hoped his words sounded as sincere as he meant them.

Shane snorted and turned toward the sink. He banged a couple of pots around, obviously pretending to be busy, until Ilya stilled him by resting a hand on his arm.

"Do you know what I was thinking all night?" Ilya asked gently. "When I was being a dick?"

Shane's shoulders tightened. "What?"

"I was thinking," Ilya moved closer, lining his body up with Shane's. Letting his chest brush against Shane's back. "About how much I loved this. Being at home with you. Even having friends over. Being a couple."

Shane's shoulders relaxed as he exhaled loudly. "I

love it too. I just wish we could have more of it." He turned to face Ilya, and his eyes were much too sad.

Ilya placed a hand on the side of Shane's face, brushing a thumb over his freckles. "Maybe I don't think about how it is unfair because…" He paused a moment, trying to choose his English words carefully. "I feel lucky. This is more than I have ever had."

Shane's face scrunched up in confusion. Definitely one of Ilya's top three Shane Hollander expressions. "More what?"

Ilya shrugged. "Love. Family. All that stuff."

Shane's face descrunched. For a moment, Ilya could swear he saw a tremor in his lip, but then Shane thunked his forehead against Ilya's chest.

"Why are you like this?" Shane moaned into Ilya's shirt. "Can't you let me be annoyed with you? Do you have to ruin it by saying romantic shit like that?"

"Romantic? I thought it was more pathetic."

Shane shook his head against Ilya's chest, and Ilya wrapped his arms around him.

"I love you," Shane murmured.

Ilya kissed the top of his head. It never got old, hearing Shane say that. Nothing had grown stale between them, even though it had been over a year since they had first said those life-changing words to each other. Maybe it was because their time together was always short, and precious. Maybe one day, when they were old and retired and making dinner together for the millionth time, Ilya's blood wouldn't heat at the sound of Shane's voice.

That day was not today, though.

Ilya tangled his fingers into Shane's hair and lightly

tugged, pulling his face away from Ilya's chest and tilting it up to meet his gaze.

"Don't you have something to say to me?" Shane asked wryly.

Ilya's lips quirked up, and instead of saying the words back, he leaned down and kissed him, slowly. Adoringly. The kind of unhurried, careful kiss that Ilya knew Shane wouldn't put up with for long. As expected, within a minute Shane let out a growl and took control. He kissed Ilya hungrily, wrapping one ankle around the back of Ilya's leg and pulling their bodies tight together.

This was the man that Ilya loved. Right here. Sexy and challenging and unabashedly on fire for Ilya. Without even looking at what might be in the way, Ilya hoisted Shane up and sat him on the counter. Something clattered into the sink, and something else fell to the floor, but neither man reacted. They kept kissing and yanking each other's shirts out of their pants. Shane shoved Ilya's shirt up, bunching it under his armpits, then slid his palms over Ilya's chest. Over the grizzly bear tattoo that covered most of Ilya's left pec. Ilya could admit to himself now that the tattoo was a bit much, but he'd been eighteen when he'd gotten it, and it gave Shane something to tease him about, so he couldn't hate it.

Ilya broke the kiss and pulled back a bit, smiling as Shane eagerly chased his mouth, leaning too far forward and nearly falling off the countertop. Ilya steadied him with one hand, but Shane wrapped his legs tight around Ilya's waist and yanked him back toward him, gripping the back of Ilya's head and locking their mouths together. Ilya responded by lifting Shane off the counter, placing his hands firmly under his ass. He spun them until Shane's back was pressed against the wall by the door, then kept kissing him.

Shane writhed against the wall as Ilya kissed his way down his neck. "Bedroom," Shane gasped. "I need you in me."

Ilya grinned against his neck. He loved it when Shane asked for what he wanted. "I can fuck you right here, *moy vozlyublenniy*."

"No. *Fuck*, maybe," Shane panted. "What does that one mean?"

"My horny animal," Ilya lied.

"Eat shit." Shane unwrapped his legs and lowered himself to the floor. "Bedroom. Come on."

He pushed past Ilya, darting toward the stairs. Ilya caught up with him on the landing, halfway up. He grabbed his arm and spun him, pinning him against the wall with hands on Shane's biceps. Ilya's lips hovered a breath away from Shane's.

"Whatever happens, I'm…" Ilya huffed in frustration, English escaping him again.

"What?" Shane's eyes were wide.

Ilya loosened his grip on his arms, sliding his hands down to grasp Shane's hands instead. "I will tell the whole world right now, if it is what you want."

Shane's brow pinched. "You would?"

"Yes."

Shane squeezed Ilya's hands. "I'm scared," he admitted. "I want to just…be with you. But I also don't want to deal with everything that we would have to deal with. And I don't want to lose you."

"You won't lose me."

"What if no one will sign us? What if you get *deported*?"

"Then I will fake my own death. We will move to a cabin in the mountains."

Shane shook his head. "I'm being serious."

"I am serious. If we hide forever, or tell the world right now, I am with you. I will quit hockey, or fight to stay. Whatever you want."

"It shouldn't be only my decision."

Ilya sighed. "I mean… I am yours, yes? To protect that, I will do anything."

Shane's eyes went gooey. "You're mine. Yes."

"Then…" Ilya brushed Shane's bangs aside. "Let me show you."

When they got to the bedroom, they stayed standing at the foot of the bed, kissing for long minutes. Eventually, Ilya began to slowly undress Shane. He carefully removed each item of clothing, covering the newly exposed skin with soft kisses and gentle bites while Shane shivered. In the morning, Ilya would be gone, and they wouldn't see each other again for weeks, but he would make damn sure Shane wouldn't doubt Ilya's devotion while they were apart. He would spend the rest of this night worshipping him. Ilya could sleep on the fucking plane.

"Yours," Ilya said again as he sank to his knees. He peppered light kisses around Shane's belly button and over the ridges of his abs. He flicked his gaze up to catch Shane's and found desire burning bright in his eyes. He was gorgeous, backlit by the soft light of the bedside lamp. Shadows dipped into the hard lines of this chest and stomach, accentuating his muscle definition.

"Yours," Shane whispered back.

Ilya nodded slowly, then slid Shane's pants down to the floor. Once the pants had been kicked into a corner of the room, Ilya pressed his mouth to the bulge in Shane's underwear. He breathed hot on Shane's cock through the black fabric of his boxer briefs. He traced the outline of Shane's erection with his tongue, then dipped his head to mouth at his balls.

"Holy fuck that feels good," Shane gasped. He curled his fingers into Ilya's hair, gripping but not controlling. Ilya was still in charge. Ilya would convince Shane with his body that everything would be all right. They were good. They would always be good.

When Shane's underwear was thoroughly damp and clinging to his erection, Ilya peeled them down and off, then reunited them with Shane's pants in the corner. Shane's cock bobbed eagerly in front of Ilya's face, but Ilya ignored it, returning his attention to his balls. He *loved* Shane's balls. They were naturally smooth and perfectly shaped. He loved the feel of them in his mouth, the weight of them, heavy with Shane's need for release.

"God, Ilya. One of these nights you're gonna make me come just from this, I swear."

Ilya waggled his eyebrows. "Could be tonight."

Shane groaned, but he was smiling. "No way. I need you to fuck me tonight. Please."

"Well…" Ilya ran his tongue up the length of Shane's cock. "You did say please."

"And could you take off your clothes? Pretty please?"

Ilya stood, then gave Shane a quick kiss before unbuttoning his own rumpled shirt just enough to pull it over his head. "On the bed," he instructed. "And take your fucking socks off."

In less than a minute, Shane was on his back, and Ilya was stretched over him, naked, and kissing him into the mattress.

There were a lot of reasons why it would be messed up if the world could see them right now, but *if* the world could see them right now, they'd have to get it, right? They'd have to see that what he and Shane had together was real and *good* and unstoppable. He knew it would be a shock to the hockey world when they finally held their planned press conference. They would only be announcing that they had started a charity together and that they were friends, but even those basic facts were going to blow some minds.

He could kiss Shane at that press conference. Just pull him in and kiss him in front of the cameras and reporters. Then it would be done.

Ilya grabbed the lube from the nightstand drawer. He sat up, straddling Shane's thighs, and drizzled the lube into his palm and over his fingers.

Ilya Rozanov and his boyfriend, Shane Hollander.

Ilya liked the sound of it. The idea of hockey commentators saying those words.

Ilya Rozanov and his husband, *Shane Hollander.*

Oooh. Better.

Hollander passes the puck to his sexy husband, Ilya Rozanov...

Okay. Maybe Ilya had gone a little heavy on the wine himself tonight.

Ilya took his time working Shane open, savoring every gasp and moan his gorgeous boyfriend gave him. Shane opened for him beautifully, welcoming Ilya's fingers inside. Ilya was always overwhelmed by how easily Shane gave himself to him; how much he trusted Ilya to give him exactly what he needed. Even when they had ostensibly been enemies, Shane had trusted Ilya not to hurt him.

"Please. Ilya." Shane's voice was stretched thin. Deciding that he had tortured Shane for long enough, Ilya reached again for the nightstand drawer.

Shane stopped him with a hand on his wrist. "Not tonight."

Ilya's breath caught. They had gone without condoms a few times over the past year, but Shane was fussy about mess, and often preferred using protection.

"Are you sure?" Ilya asked.

Shane's certainty was clear in his eyes, the same way it had been when he'd told Hayden that, yes, he did love Ilya so much. "I'm sure."

Well, Ilya certainly wasn't going to argue. He took his hand away from the drawer and placed it on Shane's cheek. Shane gave him a heartbreakingly adorable grin, and then Ilya kissed the hell out of him.

Entering Shane felt perfect. It always felt perfect, but doing it like this, with nothing between them, was exhilarating. Ilya had never had sex without protection before Shane, and the thrill of it nearly did Ilya in immediately every time they tried it.

Shane's face went slack and euphoric. "God, that's so fucking good," he murmured. He spread his legs wider, drew his knees in closer, begging Ilya with his body language to bury himself deeper. Ilya gripped Shane's thighs, pushing them back astonishingly far so he could slide in as deep as possible.

Jesus. Ilya needed to buy a thank-you gift for Shane's yoga instructor.

"Good?" Ilya asked, checking in.

"Amazing," Shane confirmed.

Ilya smiled. He still fondly remembered the first time Shane had sucked him—had sucked *anyone*—

back when they'd been nineteen and Shane had been terrified of his own desires. He'd been so unsure of what to do, but so determined to do it well.

The truth was that Ilya had probably been as terrified as Shane, back then. He'd just been better at hiding it.

The first time Ilya had fucked Shane had been a few months after that, and Ilya had been overly concerned with making it seem like it hadn't been a big deal. Like being inside Shane hadn't been a revelation. He'd left the hotel room as soon as possible after, afraid of what he may have said or done if he'd stayed even a minute longer.

He could say or do whatever he wanted now. There was no need to hide his heart now.

"I love this, Shane. I love you so much. You are beautiful. Perfect." He turned his head and kissed Shane's ankle. "Perfect," he repeated.

"I love you. Love you inside me. Fuck, it's so good. Always so good, Ilya. Want you to come in me."

Ilya grunted in response and sped up his thrusts, wanting to give Shane what he needed. Wanting to fill him up. Shane was stroking himself, which Ilya always enjoyed watching. His strong fingers flew over his cock as his back arched off the bed. Christ, he was spectacular.

He cried out as his release showered over his chest, his ass spasming around Ilya's cock. "Gonna come," Ilya warned, because holy fuck.

"Yeah," Shane rasped. "Give it to me. Come on."

Two more thrusts and Ilya was emptying himself into Shane. He tried to keep his gaze locked with Shane's as pleasure ripped through him, making it impossible to speak. When his orgasm finally subsided, he pulled Shane up and kissed him, holding him close.

"Fuck," Shane said breathlessly. "We're really good at that."

"The best," Ilya agreed.

Later, after they had cleaned themselves up and were snuggled together under the blankets, Shane said, "So. Two weeks?"

"Two weeks." Two weeks until their teams would meet for a Saturday night game. They had decided that they would hold their press conference the following morning.

A heavy silence stretched between them. How much would change for them? How much harder would it be to keep their true relationship a secret? Would it be easier to hide in plain sight as friends? Friends who spent their summers together? Who visited each other during the season, even? Who started a charity together?

Ilya supposed it didn't matter. They were doing it, and they would deal with the consequences when they happened.

"I'm ready," Shane said. His voice was clear and steady.

"Yes," Ilya said softly. "Me too."

* * * * *